Praise for Kathleen Grissom's bestselling novel
The Kitchen House

"I recommend *The Kitchen House*. This novel, like *The Help*, does important work."

—Alice Walker

"Forget *Gone with the Wind* . . . a story that grabs the reader and demands to be devoured. Wow."

—Minneapolis *Star-Tribune*

"A touching tale of oppressed women, black and white. . . . [This novel] about love, survival, friendship, and loss in the antebellum South should not be missed."

—*The Boston Globe*

"To say Kathleen Grissom's *The Kitchen House* is a page-turner wouldn't do it justice. . . . Grissom breaks away from the gate at a fast clip, the reader hanging on for the ride."

—Durham *Herald-Sun*

"Captivates with its message of right and wrong, family, and hope."
—*Sacramento/San Francisco Book Review*

"[Grissom's] . . . debut twists the conventions of the antebellum novel. . . . Provides a trove of tension and grit, while the many nefarious doings will keep readers hooked to the twisted, yet hopeful, conclusion."
—*Publishers Weekly*

"[A] pulse-quickening debut."

—*Kirkus Reviews*

"Difficult to put down."

—Bookreporter.com

"You will be thrilled by this intimate and surprising story."
—Robert Morgan, bestselling author of the
Oprah Book Club selection *Gap Creek*

ALSO BY KATHLEEN GRISSOM

The Kitchen House

Glory over Everything

KATHLEEN GRISSOM

TOUCHSTONE

New York London Toronto Sydney New Delhi

T

Touchstone
An Imprint of Simon & Schuster, Inc.
1230 Avenue of the Americas
New York, NY 10020

First Touchstone trade paperback edition February 2017

TOUCHSTONE and colophon are registered trademarks of Simon & Schuster, Inc.

For information about special discounts for bulk purchases, please contact Simon & Schuster Special Sales at 1-866-506-1949 or business@simonandschuster.com.

The Simon & Schuster Speakers Bureau can bring authors to your live event. For more information, or to book an event, contact the Simon & Schuster Speakers Bureau at 1-866-248-3049 or visit our website at www.simonspeakers.com.

Manufactured in the United States of America

1 3 5 7 9 10 8 6 4 2

The Library of Congress has cataloged the Simon & Schuster edition as follows:

Names: Grissom, Kathleen, author.
Title: Glory over everything : beyond the Kitchen house / Kathleen Grissom.
Description: First Simon & Schuster hardcover edition. | New York : Simon & Schuster, 2016.
Identifiers: LCCN 2016000133 (print) | LCCN 2016004254 (ebook) | ISBN 9781476748443 (hardcover) | ISBN 9781476748450 (softcover) | ISBN 9781476748467 (ebook) | ISBN 9781476748467 (eBook)
Subjects: LCSH: Fugitive slaves—United States—Fiction. | Underground Railroad—Fiction. | Plantation life—Southern States—Fiction. |BISAC: FICTION / Historical. | FICTION / Literary. | FICTION / General. | GSAFD: Historical fiction.
Classification: LCC PS3607.R57 G58 2016 (print) | LCC PS3607.R57 (ebook) | DDC 813/.6—dc23
LC record available at http://lccn.loc.gov/2016000133

ISBN 978-1-4767-4844-3
ISBN 978-1-4767-4845-0 (pbk)
ISBN 978-1-4767-4846-7 (ebook)

To my husband, Charles, for his unfailing support

I looked at my hands to see if I was the same person now I was free. There was such a glory over everything. The sun came up like gold through the trees, and I felt like I was in heaven.

—HARRIET TUBMAN

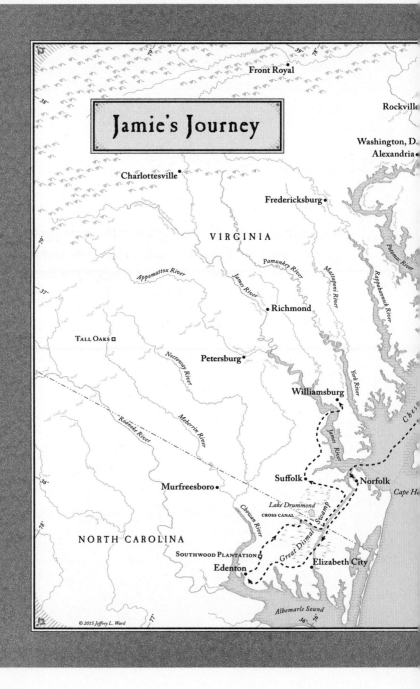

PART ONE

CHAPTER ONE

March 1830
Philadelphia

James

ROBERT'S FAMILIAR RAP on the door came as I was studying a miniature portrait of myself. The small painting, meant as a parting gift to my beloved, had just been delivered, and I was debating the artist's interpretation. I had to admit that Miss Peale's suggestion to paint my face in profile, and thus avoid the black patch covering my left eye, was a good idea. Too, she had captured my features well in this, my thirty-third year: the length of my oval face, my aquiline nose, and the cleft in my square-cut jaw. But I disliked the distinct set she had given my mouth.

Robert knocked again.

"Yes," I called, and my butler entered.

"A letter, sir," he announced, coming forward. I lifted the letter from the tray and noted the familiar script. Robert gave me a concerned glance, but a bell above the mantel clinked once, signaling that he was needed elsewhere. Fortunately, he made a quick exit.

Alone again, I slit the seal. Caroline's simple words were so potent that the paper vibrated in my hand.

> *Darling, I will see you this evening.*
> *Your C.*

I had avoided her for weeks, but my presence at the event tonight was mandatory, and now Caroline meant to attend.

Though I longed to see her, I was filled with dread. Time was running out, and I could no longer escape. Tonight I must tell her the truth, though in the telling I would almost certainly lose her. And to lose her was to lose my life.

Again Robert was at the door, but this time, after a sharp rap, he entered on his own. He looked about uneasily, as though unsure how to deliver his next message.

"What is it, Robert?" I finally asked.

"Sir, there is someone here to see you," he said, his eyes scanning my person and for only the briefest moment settling on the letter. "The caller is . . . at the back door," he added, indicating that my visitor was likely a man of color. Robert paused as though looking for words, an unusual thing for this sophisticated man who ran my household. "His name is Henry."

I stiffened. Surely it could not be Henry! We had an understanding.

"He said to tell you that he is Pan's father," Robert added carefully.

So it was Henry! I rose suddenly. Then, to cover my distress, I brushed at my jacket sleeves. "Have him wait in the kitchen," I ordered, until I remembered I would want complete privacy. "No. Take him to my study."

"Your study, sir?" Robert's eyes opened wide. My study, my private workroom, was seldom open to anyone but Robert, and that was only for cleaning. It had been that way for years.

"Yes, my study," I said with some irritation, and my butler quickly took his leave.

HENRY WAITED JUST inside the study. I closed the wide double doors firmly behind me and carefully made my way past both drawing tables to my desk. The three tall windows in this room shed enough of the darkening light for Henry to follow. I sat and nodded toward the chair across from me, but the visitor ignored my request as his dark fingers nervously circled the frayed brown hat that he held. I was momentarily startled to see his gray hair, then remembered that years had passed since I had seen him last.

He wasted no time with polite discussion and burst forth, "My boy gone! My Pan gone! They take him. I know they do. You got to help me!"

"Please, Henry! Slow down! What are you talking about? Where is Pan? What do you mean? He is missing?"

"This the third day. All along, I'm thinkin' he here working in the kitchen. When he don' come see me Sunday like always, I'm thinking he needed here, but then I hear that two more boys get took from the docks. Las' time I see him, I say again, 'You stay away from that shipyard, those men snap you up, put you on a boat, an' sell you down south.' That's why I come here to see him for myself, an' now Molly say she don' see Pan for two days an' was thinkin' he was with me."

My cook had said nothing. "Why didn't Molly come to me with her concern?"

"She say you got so much goin' on with sellin' your business and your trip comin' up that you don' need to be lookin' out for your help."

"Pan is more to me than help, you know this, Henry."

"I knows this, Mr. Burton. You treat him real good. He gettin' book-smart like you, and he learn how to work in the white man's house."

"He is a quick student," I said.

"My boy never go off like this on his own. He comes see me direct every Sunday, then goes back Monday mornin', jus' like always."

I tried to recall when I had last seen Pan. Wasn't it just yesterday that he had requested permission to take a book from my library? Or was that already two days ago? I had been so distracted with my own doings . . .

"He a good boy, he don' believe nobody mean him no harm. I tell him all the time, 'You got to be careful of those nigga traders.' At twelve years, he jus' the age they lookin' for. They get him on a boat, take him down the river, and sell him for a slave. You know what I's talkin' 'bout!" Henry's voice grew loud and I put my finger to my mouth. Henry leaned toward me and whispered loudly, "You know what I's talkin' 'bout!"

I did! I did know!

"There's word that two more boys is missin' from the South Ward, and they say that a schooner leave for the Carolinas this mornin'. I jus' know my boy's on it! You got to go get him! Pan's been tellin' me how you goin' down there on that 'scursion. You got to bring him back!"

I stopped him. "Henry! I don't leave for another month! If it is true that he was taken, how do you know that they would sell him in the Carolinas? In all likelihood, they would take him farther down." I spoke without thinking and, too late, saw the effect of my words. The man's shoulders dropped. It had grown dark in the room, but I could see well enough when he wiped his eyes on the sleeve of his coat. Then he fell to his one knee.

"Please, Masta James, please! I only ask for help one time, an' that's when I firs' bring my boy to you jus' after my Alice die. Our Pan come late to Alice and me, an' now he all I got left of her. I gets you the money, you go down, get him back." His voice caught as he choked back sobs. "I know what they do to him. I's been a slave. I'd soon see him dead before I see him sol' for a slave. Please, Masta James, he my only boy!"

"Stand up, Henry!" I said. "Get ahold of yourself!" How could he call me by that hated title? And to be subjugating himself on his knees! Had he no pride, no sense of having bettered himself? He was no longer a slave. And neither was I.

I HAD MET Henry twenty years earlier, when, at the age of thirteen, I arrived in Philadelphia, ill and terrified and fleeing for my life.

On the journey from my home in southern Virginia, I spoke to no one, mute from fear of discovery. I traveled with two secrets, one as damning as the other. The first was that, just weeks before, I had discovered that I was part Negro, a race I had been taught to loathe. The second was that I had killed my father, for though I was raised by his mother as one of her own, and was as white-skinned as my father, he denied me my birthright and was going to sell me for a slave. Because of his murder, patrollers were searching for me and would hang me if I was found.

I should have felt relief as I boarded each new passenger coach that took me away, but instead I became more fearful. The question of what I was going to do next loomed before me. Where would I go? How would I support myself? In my thirteen years, I had never been away from home. I had been raised as a privileged white child, cared for by servants on an isolated plantation. My doting grandmother, the woman who raised me as her son, had provided me with a fair education, but she had not taught me the fundamental skills of providing for myself. Now she was dead, my home was gone, and I was alone and in great danger.

When I arrived at the tavern outside of Philadelphia, I was so ill, frightened, and travel-worn that I scarcely knew to make my way inside. It wasn't until the coach horses were led back to the stables that I roused myself enough to walk into the noisy inn and ask for a bed. My head ached so that I was careless and withdrew my full purse. Then, before the transaction could take place, the smoke-filled room began to spin and my stomach heaved.

I just managed to stuff the purse back into my carrying case before I hastily made for the door; once outside, I ran for the back of the stables. There I leaned against the building as my stomach violently emptied. Then, before I could recover, I was struck from behind. I fell forward, though instinct had me clutch my traveling bag to me during the whaling that followed. In the end, the bag was wrestled from me, and with a last oath and some final kicks to my body, the thief was off. I tried to raise myself up to follow the man but, in the effort, lost consciousness.

When I awoke, I was looking into Henry's dark face. "You got to quiet down," he said. "You yellin' too loud."

Painfully, I raised myself on my elbow to look around. I was on a pallet on the dirt floor of what appeared to be a hut. I attempted to lift myself farther, but my head throbbed so that I lay back down. "How did I get here?" I asked.

"I find you out by the stables," he said. "Somebody work you over, but look to me like you sick before he got to you."

"Who are you?" I asked, squeezing my head to stop the throbbing.

"I's Henry. I work the stables back at the Inn. I's a runaway, like you." He stopped, then looked at me to see if I understood what he was trying to say. "I's a slave, like you," he said, as though to finalize a pact.

His words struck me like a blow. "I'm no slave!" I protested. "What makes you say that? I'm white!"

He looked at me sideways. "Maybe you is," he said, "but that not what you say when you outta your head."

"What did I say?" I struggled again to sit up. "Tell me! What did I say?"

"You say you is runnin', that somebody comin' after you."

Who was this man? Had he already alerted the patrollers? Suddenly I remembered my few belongings. "My traveling bag!" I said.

"'Fraid they got it," he said.

"Oh no!" I said, and defeated, I lay back down. There was nothing left! The money, the clothes, all were gone. Then another thought. "My jacket!" I cried out. "Where is my jacket?"

"You mean that coat you's wearin'?" Henry asked. "Even when that fever got you sweatin' it out, the one thing you don' let me take off a you is that coat a yours."

When Henry turned away, I reached down to feel the padded interior of my jacket where the jewelry had been sewn in. I sighed when I felt all the bumps and bulges, then I fingered the pockets, and when I felt my sketchpad and my small silver knife, I closed my eyes in relief.

"Here, it bes' you drink this down," he said, returning to me with a mug.

He was on his knees beside me, and when he handed me the drink, both he and the water smelled of the earth. I drank deeply.

"Why are you doing this?" I asked. "Why are you helping me?"

"Somebody help me out when I was runnin', like you," he said, while looking me over. "You got a bad eye, or do it come from the beatin' you took?"

I touched my useless left eye instinctively. "I was born with it."

Henry gave a nod.

"How long have I been here?" I asked.

"You bin here four nights," he said.

When he went for more water, I looked out on the dark night through the open door, then listened to the night sounds. They were not what I had imagined I would hear in a city. "Where are we?" I asked.

"We outside Phil'delphia," he said. "Far 'nough away that nobody comes out, but close 'nough that I get to my work."

What did this man intend for me? Had he already turned me in?

"What are you doing out here?" I asked. "Why don't you live in the city?"

"How 'bout you tell Henry more 'bout you?" he said, but I closed my eyes at the thought, and before long, I fell asleep.

THE NEXT EVENING I awoke to the aroma of a roasting fowl. Outdoors, I found Henry leaning over a fire and rotating our meal on a makeshift spit. When he glanced over and noticed me, he spoke. "You feelin' better?" he asked.

I nodded and tested myself by moving about. Though my arms and legs felt weak, my head did not throb as sharply as it had before.

Henry lifted a stick and poked it twice into the hot coals. When he raised it, the spear held two crusty roasted potatoes. He set each one in a wooden bowl, then removed the perfectly browned chicken from its spit onto a slab of wood.

"Sit," he said, waving me over with a dangerous-looking knife. Driven by my newly awakened hunger, I overcame my wariness and sat down across from him, watching as he used the knife to split the chicken in two. After he placed half a fowl in each bowl, he handed one to me, then set the large knife down on a flat rock between the two of us, putting it easily within my reach. The gesture gave me some relief, for I hoped it meant that he did not see me as a threat.

Then I could wait no longer. I used my teeth to tear the tender meat from the bone, slurping and sucking the juice off my fingers. The potato crunched, then steamed when I bit into it, and I sputtered an oath when I burnt my mouth, causing Henry to laugh, a solid sound that came from deep within.

"Boy, you somethin' to see when you eatin'," he said, shaking his head.

As my stomach filled, my worry about trusting this man was slowly replaced with curiosity. Although of average height, he was powerfully built across the shoulders. I guessed him to be close to thirty-five or forty years of age. His hair grew out wild from his head, and his skin color was of the darkest I had ever seen. He was a fierce-looking man, and under ordinary circumstances I would have given him a wide berth.

When he speared another potato and handed it to me, I noted he was missing a thumb. He saw me looking and held up both his opened hands, wiggling stubs where his two thumbs once were. "They take 'em before I run."

"Who did?" I asked, though I wasn't certain I wanted the answer.

"The masta, down Lou'siana," Henry said. He looked out into the dark, and speaking in a removed voice, he told me about himself.

Born into slavery, he had grown up with his mother and younger brother on a large cotton plantation. The master was brutal in his handling of his slaves, and when he learned that Henry was involved in planning a revolt, he punished Henry by cutting off his thumbs and forcing him to witness his mother's flogging. She died as result, and that was when Henry and his brother decided to make their escape. "We out by two days when he get shot down. Nothin' for me to do but run." He shook his head.

Somehow Henry eluded his pursuers, and after months of indescribable trials, he found himself in Philadelphia. Now, though free for two years, he remained on constant alert.

"If that masta get ahold a me, he finish me off. That's why I stay hid. Every day I's lookin' out. I ain't never goin' back to bein' a slave. They got to kill me first!" He sat quiet, as though exhausted from telling his story. Finally, he roused himself. "And what 'bout you?" he asked.

I was startled by his direct question. I had not expected to have him share his past so openly, and now he wanted the same from me. But how far could I trust him? Negroes were liars and thieves and always ready to take advantage of a white man. Yet so far, this one had only helped me. Dare I tell him how alone I was? Was it safe to tell him that when I fled my home, I left behind everyone and everything I cared about, knowing that I could never return?

"I knows you runnin' like me. Why you got to get away, it don' matter none to me."

"I shot my father," I said quietly, hoping that he heard me, for I did not want to repeat those words.

"We do what we got to do," he said.

"I hated him. His name was Marshall. I always thought he was my brother, but only a few months ago I found out that he was my father."

"Why you thinking he your brother?"

"My grandmother told me that I was her son and my dead grandfather was my father."

"And what 'bout your mama?"

"At the same time I found out Marshall was my father, I learned that my real mother was a Negro." It was difficult to believe my own words, for I still loved my grandmother as my true mother.

"So you take a gun to your daddy?"

"He was going to sell me for a slave," I said.

"You kill him dead?"

"Yes."

"And you a nigga?"

"My mother was a mulatto," I said. "Her name was Belle."

"Was she a light cullah?"

"Yes," I said.

"And your daddy was white?"

I nodded. "I look just like him. I'm as white as he was."

"That don' matter. You still a nigga. But you can pass. That's your bes' bet."

I had nothing to say.

"You got a family name?"

"Pyke," I said. "I'm Jamie Pyke."

"Not no more," he said. "You got to go by somethin' else."

I stared into the fire. How could this be? Until a few months ago, I had thought of myself as white, and now, unbelievably, I was a Negro without a name, running for my life.

As MY HEALTH returned, Henry's manner toward me remained genial, and because I felt no judgment of my character, I ceased judging him. In fact, I came to rely on him so much that I disliked it when he left for his work at the tavern. When I was alone, any unusual noise startled me, and I would leave at a run to hide in the trees. My heart pounded as I hid, watchful and terrified, until I would emerge, weak with relief to realize that the disturbance had come from deer passing through or squirrels chasing one another. Daily I feared that Rankin, the treacherous overseer from our plantation, and his son Jake, two of the most ruthless men I knew, would find me. It was almost certain that they were still searching for me, and though they were known for their dogged determination in locating runaway slaves, their notoriety came from their merciless treatment of their captives.

Then gradually, as I became familiar with the particular sounds that came from living in the woods, I adapted to Henry's primitive lifestyle. By the time we were well into the pleasant season of autumn, each morning after Henry set out for work, I quite happily spent the day in the outdoors. There, while gathering wood for our evening fire, I had the time to observe the wildlife around me. Birds were in abundance, and my childhood fascination with them grew.

My interest stemmed from a large book of bird illustrations that I had been given as a child. Kept indoors for most of my early years, when I was not reading the book, I used the images to teach myself to sketch and paint. When I grew older, I used a penknife to carve birds and woodland creatures out of wood. Now, alone in this forest, I often busied myself whittling and sketching, and for those hours I was free of worries.

I decided that I might remain with Henry indefinitely, but as colder weather approached, he began to suggest that it was time for me to consider my future. "You got to get into town, find some work an' someplace to stay," he said. "Snow comin'. It ain't nothin' like you see before. Snow here gets deep. Hard livin' out here."

"But what will I do? Where will I stay?" I argued, fear causing a high childish whine in my voice.

"You get a job easy enough if you go in passin' for white. Thing is, you do that, you got to be careful," he said.

I didn't tell him that I had never considered anything other than presenting myself as white. I had never and would never consider myself a Negro. In fact, the idea disgusted me.

Henry thought awhile before he continued. "You pass, you got to cut ties with any niggas that you know."

"I don't know any," I said.

"There's me," he replied, but it took a while before I caught his meaning.

* * *

AFTER I FOUND work in Philadelphia, I took Henry's advice, and we cut ties. My life progressed and I did well for myself, establishing a place in Philadelphia society.

I was alarmed, then, when Henry sought me out some fifteen years later; he was a link to my past that could ruin me if it were exposed. I was living as a white man, in white society, with no affiliation to any Negroes other than those of my household staff. Yet suddenly, he appeared with the request that I give employment to his seven-year-old son.

I might have refused him, but after I saw his desperation, and faced with the debt I owed him, I could not refuse. Thus I agreed to take in Henry's son, Pan, so he might be taught to perform the domestic duties in an established house.

On our first meeting, the young son struck me as rather delicate, with his slight build, dark skin, and ears that jutted out from his thin face. Pan's unflinching brown eyes met my own, an unusual habit for one of his race. And it was there, in the boy's eyes, that I recognized something of myself. For all of his bravery, they held something of the fear that I had felt when I first came to Philadelphia.

I agreed to provide for the boy, but I had no intention of becoming involved with him, and turned him over to Robert, my butler, and Molly, the cook, for use in the kitchen. A few weeks after his arrival, Molly reported back to me: "That boy, he's something! He work like I tell him to, but you never see nobody ask questions like he do. 'Why you do this? Why you do that?' He even ask if I show him how to write down his name."

Eventually, as Robert gave him more chores, I began to see Pan around the house more frequently. He was an uncommonly cheerful child, and when he saw me, he'd enthusiastically call out, "Hello, Mr. Burton!" And he didn't leave it at that. Almost always his greetings included other comments, such as "Did you see my new shoes?" or "I'm sure gettin' plenty to eat." His demeanor was so winning that in spite of myself, I began to take notice of him.

Then came the day he found me cleaning the cage of my much prized cockatoo, Malcolm. When Pan opened the door to my upstairs room, his eyes opened wide. "What you doin' with that bird?" he asked.

"I'm caring for him," I said.

"Ain't he supposed to be outside?" He looked back out the door. "Does Robert know you got him in here?"

Malcolm flew to Pan's shoulder, and though the boy stiffened, he stood his ground. When the bird began to nose Pan's ear, the boy did not move but rolled his eyes up at me. "He gon' hurt me?"

"No, I rather think he likes you," I said.

Malcolm leaped onto his favorite perch with a questioning squawk. Pan stared. "I sure never do see somethin' like him before."

"His name is Malcolm, and he is a salmon-crested cockatoo."

"Where did you get him?"

"He was my first friend when I came to this house," I said, surprising myself with my open answer.

"Your—"

"Naughty boy!" Malcolm interrupted, using his favorite phrase.

Pan gaped, then gave a nervous laugh. "That him talkin'?"

"It is," I said.

"That bird was talkin'?"

"Yes, he mimics very well."

The boy clapped his hands. "Make him talk again!"

His interest in the bird reminded me of myself as a child, and I decided to give him an opportunity. "I'll tell you what. You have Robert send you to me every day at this time, and I will teach you how to take care of him. Then you can hear him speak every day."

"You sayin' you let me help you out with this bird?"

"That's what I'm saying."

"Won't be no work for me!" he said. "But Robert don't want me foolin' 'round the house outside a the kitchen, 'less he say so."

"I'll speak with Robert," I promised.

It wasn't long before Pan was supplying Malcolm with the sycamore and dogwood branches that the bird loved to gnaw, and after the boy discovered how to keep Malcolm occupied, I often found the bird happily nipping at a swinging ear of corn or pecking at a carrot that hung above his perch.

Pan continued to surprise me with his quick mind, and because of his keen desire to learn, in time I began to teach him to read and write. One late afternoon, less than a year after his arrival, he stood beside my desk while once again I attempted to correct his use of the English language. As I was doing so, he leaned over to catch my eye. "Mr. Burton, why you doin' this for me?" he asked.

"Why *are* you doing this for me?" I corrected.

"Yes, Mr. Burton. You right. Why are you doing this for me?" he repeated my correction.

"You *are* right," I corrected again.

"I know I's right," he said. Then he repeated himself again: "I say, 'Why are you doing this for me?'"

"Can you be more explicit?" I asked. When I saw the confusion on his face, I worded the question another way. "What do you mean to ask when you say, 'Why are you doing this for me?' What do you think that I am doing for you?"

"You a white man helpin' out a nigga chil'. You teachin' me how to talk white like you. Why you doin' this? Why you foolin' with me?"

His earnest gaze touched me, and I was stung by his honest question. I turned away and felt for my handkerchief, then blew my nose. After folding my handkerchief, I was about to replace it when, without asking, Pan took it from me.

He leaned forward. "Look at me," he said, and with his small hand, he reached over and pulled my chin to face him. Then, with supreme care, he used the cloth to dab away a droplet of water that had slipped from under my eye patch. "That eye weepin'," he said. I was so touched that I rose and went to stand before a shelf of books, feigning interest while I composed myself.

He waited until I was seated again. "That eye hurt you much?" he asked.

"Does your eye pain you?" I corrected.

He gave a deep sigh. "Mr. Burton. You keep stoppin' me, tellin' me how to talk, I don' ever get a chance to hear what you got to say," he protested, then looked puzzled when I chuckled.

As TIME PASSED, Pan continued to help Robert around the house and Molly in the kitchen—Molly's only complaint now was his constant correction of her grammar—but increasingly, I called on him to assist me with my many projects. In his eagerness to understand, he was filled with questions and freely shared his observations. His carefree countenance broke through my guarded reserve, and over the next five years I came to care deeply for the boy.

But now he was missing! Could it be that he was stolen for a slave? It was a constant fear among the Negroes of Philadelphia, for it happened often. I imagined how desperate Henry must feel, as I recalled his own terror at being taken again for a slave. The thought of Pan meeting with this fate filled me with dread. He was quick-witted but had always been frail and surely could not survive the hard life of a slave.

If he had been stolen, he must be retrieved. And since I was traveling south for my work, could I not do so? Yet, the thought of it—the idea of deliberately exposing myself to people who bought and sold Negroes—terrified me. I had worked hard for the last fifteen years to move away from my past toward safety, and now the leaden ball of fear, one that had receded but had never truly left me, began again to grow.

CHAPTER TWO

1825

Pan

AFTER MY MAMA PASS, my daddy got no place for me to go, so one Sunday he brings me to Mr. Burton's house. How my daddy knows this white man, he never say, he just tell me to keep my mouth shut while he do the talkin'. We go 'round to the back door, where a black man, dressed slick, name's Robert, comes to the kitchen and takes us to what he calls the study. That place—I never seen nothing like it—is full of books and dead birds. While we's waitin', I take hold my daddy's hand to stop it from shakin', but I know him good enough not to say nothin'.

Soon as Mr. Burton walks in, I see he don't want nothin' to do with us. My daddy push me ahead. "Mr. Burton," my daddy say, "this here Pan."

Mr. Burton looks down at me, then looks back up at my daddy like he don't know what to say.

"I never ask you for nothin', but now I's askin' you to take in my boy," says my daddy.

"Henry, you know I am indebted to you, but he's too young, and I don't have need of more help. I would be happy to give you a purse, if that would help you out."

"I'm not here for no money! I'm here 'cause my boy need work and a place to stay. His mama die las' week and now she gone, he got no-body . . ." My daddy's voice start to shake and I grab hold a his hand. He still can't talk about my mama leavin' us without cryin'. He holds tight to my hand and starts talkin' again. "My boy can't stay in town by hisself, and I's still working outta town like before, so he can't stay with me."

Mr. Burton looks down at me. "How old are you?"

I'm guessin' this man only got one good eye, 'cause he got a black patch coverin' up the other one, but with the look he gives me, he only need the one.

"Tell him, boy," Daddy says, bumpin' my shoulder.

"I's eight years old," I say loud, knowin' my daddy count on me to speak up.

"You appear small for eight years," Mr. Burton says.

I don't wait for Daddy to poke me again. "Not too small to carry in wood," I say. "Carry in water, too, you needs it."

Mr. Burton look up at my daddy. "Isn't he too young to stay here on his own?"

My daddy talks quick. "He old enough to stay. He work hard, don' need nothin' but a place to sleep, somethin' to eat, and somebody to show him what to do. I come get him every Sunday mornin', see he get back by Sunday evenin', no need for me to come in the house." Then he looks down at me. "You ready to stay here an' work, isn't you, Pan?"

"I is," I say real loud, makin' my daddy nod to Mr. Burton.

Nobody say nothin' for a while, then Mr. Burton say, "Henry, I owe you. We'll give it a try, but if by next Sunday the boy doesn't work out, you must take him back with you, and I will give you a purse."

My daddy don't say nothing but turns and goes and leaves me standin' there. Him goin' like that makes it look like he don't care, but I know better. He jus' no good at sayin' goodbye.

Mr. Burton calls Robert in. They both stand there looking my way, like they's tryin' to figure me out.

I don't like it that quiet. "Where's the work?" I say. They look at each other, then Mr. Burton smile, like I say something funny.

"Can you find some simple tasks to keep him occupied?" Mr. Burton asks Robert.

"I'll have to give it some thought," says Robert, the slick man. "He's too young to be capable of much."

What he know! I been takin' care a my mama right through the week, till when my daddy gets back in town every Sunday. "My mama say I's real handy to have around," I say.

"But don't you want to stay with your father?" Mr. Burton asked.

"He try takin' me with him to the tavern, but they say he got to get rid a me or he's out a job," I say.

"And won't you miss him?" Mr. Burton asked.

"He come see me every Sunday, jus' like he do when Mama still here."

"Your mother recently died?"

"No, she don't die, she jus' release herself from her earthly body, jus' like she keep tellin' me she got to do. But she with me right now. We jus' can't see her."

The two men look at each other again. Mr. Burton take in air and let it out real slow. "Robert, take him in to Molly. Ask her to give him a room and set him up with a few light chores."

"I suppose you could learn to polish silver?" the slick man says, takin' hold a my shoulder and steerin' me downstairs.

THIS HOUSE SO big, I don't know how I ever gon' find my way 'round. The room off the kitchen that Molly puts me in to sleep is bigger than the room that I was livin' in with my mama. After Molly says to get to sleep and then closes the door on me, I start cryin'. I miss my daddy, but most, I miss the way my mama always kiss my face good night—smoochin' on me until I tell her to stop. I just want to feel her kissin' me one more time. I'm scared here by myself. This big house is too quiet. I's used to hearin' noise at night, those my age out runnin' the streets shoutin' each other down, men drinkin', gamblin', laughin' with each other, and women, too, that fool with the mens. Some nights they get to fightin' an' I get afraid they're comin' in, so after Mama throws the bolt she takes her chair an' sits in front of the door, tellin' me that anybody come in, they got to first get past her. Then I can sleep. My mama never was too big, but she got plenty of fight in her when it comes to lookin' out for me.

"Why don't we tell Daddy he got to stay with us?" I ask at those times.

"He doin' the bes' he can do," she always say.

"But why don't he stay?" I ask.

"Chil', he bring us his half dollar every Sunday that pays the rent. We got nothin' to complain about."

"He brings us the money, then why you got to take in all that sewin' the way you do?" I ask.

"How you think we gon' eat? How we pay for that wood to cook up the grits and to make us a fire when it get cold? You look 'round you. How many does you see shiverin' when it snowin' outside and they don' got the clothes to cover up? Don' you members las' winter, when we go over to see to Mr. Woods and he—"

"Don't, Mama," I say, "don't talk 'bout that." I don't like to think of that man we found layin' on the dirt floor of his room with nothing but a small rag covering his dead self and his woman sittin' there cryin' 'bout what she gon' do now.

"There lots a people out there like Mr. Woods," she said. "Your daddy always make sure we got a good room with a fire and a roof over our head."

"But why don't he live with us?" I keep askin', till one day she sits me down.

"Nex' time your daddy here, you watch the way he keeps on his feet. You ever see him sit? No, you don', and I gon' tell you why. He always be ready to go. He run from bein' a slave, and he still think they comin' to take him back. He got work outside a Phil'delphia at the tavern where all the coaches stop. By watchin' out who comin' into town, he think that he gon' see if anybody come lookin' for him. Here in town your daddy always afraid somebody gon' see him and send word to his old masta."

"So why don't we go live with him?" I ask.

"Out in the woods Henry keeps movin' 'round 'case somebody get wind a him. An' he don' want us there if he get picked up. He 'fraid they get us, too. Sell us for slaves."

"An' we don't wan' be no slaves, like Daddy. Sheila say slaves is low-down."

"Son! I don' wanna hear you say that no more! The word 'slave' don' mean somebody's bad. Plenty of folks 'round here come from bein' a slave. It mean that somebody got hold a you and you don' have no say. Your daddy can't help once bein' a slave. There no shame in that. There only shame in the man who use him like that."

THAT FIRST NIGHT in Mr. Burton's house, I'm wonderin' where my daddy is, but I go to sleep crying for my mama.

The next morning I wake up, sun's coming in the small window that sits over my bed. Real quick, I pull my clothes on and get myself out into the kitchen, but Molly's already working at the stove.

"You shoulda woke me up so I can get to my work," I say, afraid Mr. Burton will find out and send me back.

"Come over here and get yourself somethin' to eat," Molly says, and sits me down at the table, then sets a plate of two eggs with a big slice a ham in front of me. I sit quiet and wait for her to come back and take out what she gonna eat. She looks over at me. "Go ahead," she says, nodding at the plate.

"How much a this do I get to eat?" I say.

"That is all for you."

"I got to eat all this? What you goin' to eat? What Robert goin' to eat?"

"Chil'," she says, "we already got our food. You go ahead now and eat up. I give you some milk when you finish."

I dig in with the spoon, but when I lift the meat with my fingers, Molly comes over.

"Here," she says, "this is how we work it in this house." She cuts the meat with a knife, then gives me a fork to spear it.

I never do see two eggs on a plate like this before. Eggs is hard to come by, an' even though some folks keep chickens, they don't stay for long 'cause they get eat up.

I'm done eating, my stomach all puffed out, when Robert comes in. Quick, I get off my chair to show him I's ready to work. He looks me over, then goes over to a hook on the wall and takes down a big green apron that he ties around hisself.

"We have our work cut out for us," he says. "I've found some suitable clothes, but first we must get you scrubbed clean."

"But you washed me last night," I say to Robert.

"And today you shall have a full bath," he says.

I ask if I should start to carry in the water. Like he don't hear me, Robert jus' goes over and turns on a inside spigot that's right there in the kitchen, and water starts pourin' out! He puts it in two big kettles, and while he's waitin' for it to get hot he has me stand on a stool so he can cut my hair. I keep lookin' at that spigot. I'm glad if this means I don't have to carry in water, 'cause it gets heavy.

After Mama got sick and she couldn't lift no more, I carried the water in from the outside spigot that everybody get to use. The water for washing was always cold, and we didn't waste the wood just to heat it up, except for in the winter, when the fire was already going.

Carryin' in the water was heavy, so I brought in just a half bucket every time I made the trip, and Mama always said that was enough. Even though she'd stand at the door and watch for me, I didn't like to go out in the alley, past the heaps of dirt piled up and the rats big as cats digging in everybody's slop. The winters wasn't as bad, 'cause the piles was froze and the smell wasn't so strong. But when it got to warmin' up, the folks like Mr. Woods, who lived out there in the rooms close to the outhouse, they had a stink.

"Why you got to cut my hair?" I ask Robert.

"Because you've got hair that makes you look like a wild dog," he says.

"I do?" I say. "What kind a wild dog?" But he don't say nothin' and just keeps cuttin'. When he's done, I tell him my ears feels cold, but I don't know that he hears me, 'cause he's busy pourin' the hot water from the stove into a big washtub and then tells me to get in.

"You tellin' me to step in there?" I ask, watchin' the steam lift up.

"Remove your clothes," he says, so I take off my shirt real slow, not liking this one bit. "Now your pants," he say, and I look over at Molly. It don't seem like she's looking my way, so I get out of my pants and jump in the water, quick, but it's too hot to sit.

"Sit down," Robert says.

"I'm gonna cook," I say, tryin' not to yell out when he pushes me down.

"What you doin' to me?" I ask when right away he starts soapin' me and scrubbin' away, like Mama do with the pig's feet before she cook 'em.

"Stay still," he says, pouring water over me, but when my eyes start burnin' from the soap, I grab at him and pull myself up.

"I can't see nothin', I can't see nothin'," I say, forgettin' not to be loud.

He cleans the soap from my eyes, then gives me a big rag to dry myself off before he hands me my new clothes.

"Where'd you get these clothes?" I ask. "How'd you get 'em to fit me?" The white shirt and the brown pants, even though they's too long, look almost good as his. He don't say nothin' but leans down and rolls up the pants, and while I still got 'em on, he stitches 'em up. Then he stands back lookin' at me before he gives me some black shoes to put on. I never have shoes before, just a old pair of boots that Mama and me both use when we go out in winter. The shoes feel funny.

"They's too small," I say. "They squeezin' me in."

"They are fine," he say, "and I don't want to see you without them."

Robert takes me upstairs to show me how to clean out the fireplaces and to set a fire. There's five rooms we go to, and I stick close to him, wonderin' how we ever gon' find our way back, but he do. Back in the kitchen he sets me up in a small room where he shows me how to clean boots. First you got to take off all the dirt with a brush, then you stir up what's called the blacking, and then you use another brush to put it on the boots.

"What's in that stuff?" I ask, not sure if I like the smell.

"Some sweet oil, some beer, some molasses . . ."

"I already taste molasses," I say.

"Well, don't go tasting this," he says, then shows me how to finish up with the last brush that he calls the polisher. After he goes, I get to work and keep workin', even though my arms is 'bout to drop off, until Molly comes and tells me it's time to eat.

"We gon' eat again?" I say, 'cause it's the middle of the day!

"Come on," she says, and sets me down at the table with another plate of food. This time it's fried potatoes and a whole pork sausage. She sits down across from me and starts eatin' at her own plate, but I jus' can' take in all that food. I keep lookin' at it till I start snifflin'.

"You cryin', chil'," she asks. "What? You don' like Molly's cookin'?"

"I like your cookin'!"

"Well, then, what's troublin' you?"

"I'm thinkin' 'bout my mama. I jus' wish she was here to be tastin' some of this."

"Nothin' would make your mama happier than if you'd start eatin' so's you could get yourself back to work," Molly says.

"How 'bout I save it till later?" I ask. "I'm goin' to be hungry then."

"That be fine," she said, "but you sit here awhile, maybe you change your mind."

I don't know what to do, so I just sit there watchin' her eat and lookin' at the small green flowers on the red rag that she got tied up 'round her head. Molly's got a big head, but then she's a lot bigger all 'round, and I'm guessin' it's all the food she gets to eat.

"Mmm," she says, "I sure do like this sausage." She got big brown eyes and I like the way they look at me. "Potatoes good, too," she says. "The onions and the butter make 'em taste real good. You sure you don' want some?"

"No," I say, "I keep mine for later."

"Jus' so you know, long as you here, you get all the food you want," she says.

When she finishes her food, she sits back and drinks some coffee from a blue and white china cup. "You want some milk?" she asks, but I say, "No, my stomach is still big from eatin' them two eggs."

She tips up her cup and finishes her drink, then pushes back from the table and stands up. "Well, you go on, then," she says. "Get back to polishin' those boots."

That night when Molly sends me to bed, I ask if I can leave the door open so I can call out to her if I need somethin'. She say that fine by her, and not long after, I hear her snorin', so it ain't so quiet, and even though I still cry for my mama, I get to sleep easier. Next day I get up before the sun an' I'm waitin' for her and Robert in the kitchen when they show up.

"Give me some work," I say, afraid that if they don't get me goin', Mr.

Burton send me off. So Molly gets me to carry in wood and sweep the floor. When it's time to eat, she hands me a plate with two eggs and some warm biscuits that got butter drippin' off. I eat it all, even though my stomach rumblin' 'cause it don' know what to do with all this food, then she sets me up to help her wash the pots an' pans.

CHAPTER THREE

1830

James

I T WAS DARK after Henry left, and in my dressing room Robert had already put flame to the candle sconces on my tall cheval mirror. I slipped off my day coat and draped it carefully over the back of the tapestry-covered armchair, yet another fine piece of furniture that I inherited after Mrs. Burton died. But this night, appreciation for what my adopted parents had given me was overridden by my worry. In fact, I was so filled with concern that I, a man who is always punctual, sat down in the chair knowing full well I was already behind schedule and that tonight a late entry would not do.

To blend into this aristocratic society, through the years I had painstakingly studied the unwritten rules. Knowing when to arrive and, as important, when to take leave, was only the beginning. Whom to greet, whose hand to take, the clothes to wear, the gift to send, all reflected back, and that, for me, left no room for error.

But tonight, for the first time in a long while, I questioned if I could meet the challenge. This evening's event, hosted at the home of leading society members, Mr. and Mrs. Cardon, was meant as a celebration for artists awarded grants from the Peale Museum. Most of the attention would fall on known artists, and though I was one of the minor recipients, my appearance was required. I should have been eager to attend, yet I sat, head in hands: Pan's disappearance and Henry's visit had raised buried fears.

When the museum offered to fund an art excursion, I leaped at the opportunity. Their support was given so I might travel south along the coastline to study the natural habitat of birds native to that region. If, on my return, my work was approved, it would result in a small book for print, meant for travelers to better identify bird species. Now, after Henry's visit, I questioned my quick decision to accept. In the twenty years since I had escaped Virginia, time had dulled my fears, but when faced with Henry's alarm about Pan's disappearance, I was reminded of the dangers that might await me in those Southern slave states. Might I be recognized? Was it possible that patrollers were still searching for me? Why hadn't I considered my safety more carefully? Yet these worries came too late, for I was committed, and there was no turning back.

My anxiety about the evening only increased when I considered another concern, one as troubling as my first. It was Caroline. I was torn, for seeing her again would mean an end to the agony of our separation. But in what state would I find her? She had every right to be furious that I had stayed away.

I heard the clock strike and forced myself to my feet. Quickly, I removed my clothes, then shivered as I lowered myself into the bath, for though there was heat from the fireplace, the water had already cooled in the metal tub. I had no sooner soaped myself than Robert entered, bearing a large bucket of steaming water. "I was hoping you would wait," he said.

"I am already late."

"Yes, sir," he replied, slowly and carefully pouring in the hot water so I could rinse myself clean. I stepped out to catch hold of the bath blanket that Robert held, then dried myself while he stood by, ready with a fresh white shirt. As I pulled on my clean drawers and my dress pants, then tucked in my shirt, Robert clicked his tongue. "Sir, we have not done your manicure."

I glanced at my hands. "It will have to do," I said, buttoning my trousers. From behind, he fastened my galluses, then placed them over my shoulders so I could button them in the front. As Robert expertly tied my cravat, I took in some deep breaths. "I would cancel the whole trip," I said, "if I were not obligated to go."

"Yes, sir."

"And now I've promised Henry that I will search for Pan."

"I understand," he said, "though the boy was warned not to go down to the shipyards."

"Then why would he have gone?"

Robert hesitated while buttoning my blue satin waistcoat.

"What is it?" I asked. "Tell me."

"Molly said that he came to her requesting money," Robert said.

"For what purpose?"

"The boy said that he wanted to buy you a parrot."

"What? Why would he want to do that?"

"He told Molly that he wanted to see you happy again."

My chest thumped. Only Pan would have considered me in this way. That foolish, foolish boy! I had a sudden chill. Until that moment I had held out hope that he might safely resurface, but I knew that to find a bird, he would have gone down to the docks.

"Didn't Molly warn him?"

"She didn't consider that he might go to the shipyards. She thought that all birds were sold down in the market." Robert held up my black tailcoat, indicating that he needed me to hold on to my shirtsleeves. "If we hurry, you will not be that late," he said.

I held out my arms as Robert slipped my coat up and over my shoulders. He fooled with the collar until, impatient, I turned around to see myself reflected in the mirror. I stepped closer, using my fingers to pull my damp brown hair forward in loose curls, while Robert used a hairbrush to smooth the close-cut hair at the back of my head. I slipped on the black satin eye patch, though tonight I gave my useless eye little thought when I saw the lines of concern on my face. Those must be erased. This evening was meant to be a celebration, and I was expected to look the part of a joyous recipient.

I reminded myself again that traveling as a funded artist would allow me to gain entry into homes that otherwise would not have been open to me. And now I would need every opportunity to find Pan.

It was not until I was settled in the carriage and well on my way that I allowed myself to think of Caroline. Then my heart raced, for though telling my truth would likely end our affair, I could not wait to see her again.

CHAPTER FOUR

1825

Pan

I LIKE WORKIN' with Molly in the kitchen. We get along good. But Robert, he another story. All he cares is that I's scrubbed up like him and workin' hard. He don't let me go with my daddy on Sunday 'less I got on a clean shirt and my new shoes polished like his. I can tell my daddy happy to see me all dressed like I'm somebody, working big time for the white folk.

"You doin' all right, boy?" he ask every Sunday when he comes, and I tell him I is. Then I tell him about everything that happens to me. He listens good, 'cept when I start talkin' 'bout my mama. One day when we was sittin' in the trees and lookin' out over the water, finishin' up what Molly gives us to eat, I start wonderin' to him if Mama seein' us and what she's wantin' to say.

He shake his head an' look over at me. "You a talker, boy, jus' like your mama, an' that's all right by me, but I don' want to hear you talk about her no more. She gone."

"But Daddy," I say, "she always gon' be with us. She tell me all the time. She say—"

"Pan! I don't wanna hear nothin' 'bout her no more!"

"That fine, Daddy, I don't need to say nothin' more, just that she still here, that's all."

"You know she gone!" Daddy say.

"She still here! She say she always gon' stay with me!" My eyes start stingin', but I don't cry, 'cause my daddy don't like it when I do.

He gives me a look but don't say nothin' for a long time. "Jus' don' go talkin' like that to nobody else," he say.

"I already say so to Mr. Burton."

"You do?"

I nod.

"What he say?"

"Nothin'."

"Nothin'?"

"Nope, he don't say nothin'."

My daddy look out over the water. "Jus' don' go tellin' nobody else."

Some gulls dip down across the water. That reminds me how I'm helpin' Mr. Burton out with his bird, and I say so. My daddy look at me like I'm makin' up a story. "What bird?" he ask.

"He got this bird that talks good as you and me," I say. "Mr. Burton say that I'm good with birds and I got to help him out because Molly, she afraid that bird gonna bite her, and Robert, he don't want nothin' to do with it."

"What else they got you doin'?"

"Mr. Burton, he showin' me how to write."

"He do?"

"And he's showin' me how to read!"

"That's good, son. You watch close and don' talk so much."

"Mr. Burton say that askin' questions is a good thing. That's how you learn, he say."

"Well, that man don' get where he is today without bein' a smart man."

I nod. "He sure do know everything 'bout birds. And he tell Robert that I don't need to wear shoes all the time until my feet stop hurtin' so bad."

"How'd he know your feet was hurtin'?" Daddy asked.

"I tells him."

"You troublin' Mr. Burton that your feet hurtin' you?"

"No, just when I can't step right and he asks me why, I say 'cause

Robert says I got to wear shoes all the time and my feet ain't takin' to 'em the way they should."

Daddy shake his head. "Jus' don' go botherin' the man with too much talkin' 'bout yourself."

"Only time I talk 'bout myself is if he asks me somethin'."

"He ask you about me?"

"No, jus' why I can't stay with you, and I tells him that a tavern no place for a chil' and that you don't want me 'round the barns on my own. I tells him you take Mama's leavin' us real hard an' that I tell you not to worry 'cause I know she's watchin' out for us."

Daddy shoots me a look, then picks up the basket from Molly and stands to go. That's him tellin' me enough talk. We walk back with me quiet, but I take his hand and know he's not mad with me because he squeeze my hand real tight.

CHAPTER FIVE

1830

James

I ARRIVED AN hour later than the invitation called for. To say Mr. and Mrs. Cardon's home was magnificent would not be an exaggeration, yet the size of this Georgian home, their city dwelling, was said to be dwarfed by the size of their country estate.

"Mr. Burton, good to see you again, sir."

I thanked Felix, greeting by name their gray-haired Negro servant as I handed over my greatcoat, hat, and gloves.

"You know your way," he said, nodding toward the stairway.

"I do," I said, but hesitated while I tried to gather my reserves. How I disliked the feel of dampness around the stiff cotton of my collar. Over the years I had learned to hide uncertainty under the cover of sophistication, but tonight I was too unsettled, too shaken. I looked down the long hallway, and though I was not a drinking man, I wondered if I might go first into the back library to pour myself a quick brandy. However, with the arrival of another carriage and more guests about to fill the foyer, I decided to forgo the temptation and went instead to climb the broad and winding red-carpeted stairway that led to the ballroom.

The usual gaming tables were set up in the outer room, and many people were already at play. It was excruciating to hold back, so close to seeing Caroline, but I forced myself to walk slowly as I made my way around the room, greeting and accepting congratulations from those I knew. Finally, I allowed myself to go toward the ballroom. The vast room gleamed white tonight; masses of white roses and potted green cedars filled every corner and flat surface. I glanced about through the blur of a waltz, soft laughter, subdued talk, the swirl of colored silk, the slide of slippered feet across the white floor—and there she was!

Color rose to her pale face when she saw me, but she stayed in place, giving her attention to another who had already claimed it. Her blond hair, curled to either side and piled high in the back, emphasized her long white neck, made more so by the white low-cut gown draped stylishly off her shoulders. A pale pink rose, pushed deep into her swollen décolleté, matched perfectly her flushed face. She fanned herself prettily and could not keep herself from glancing in my direction.

I turned away just as her parents, the host and hostess for the evening, approached me. I gathered myself quickly, upset that I had been observed giving their daughter so much notice. "Mr. Cardon, Mrs. Cardon." I greeted them with a formal bow before lifting Mrs. Cardon's outreached hand. I could not escape what they both had seen, so I moved the conversation toward it. First, though, I paused for a deliberate review of Mrs. Cardon's person while she feigned disinterest yet awaited my approval. "I was just now admiring your beautiful daughter, but when I observe you, Mrs. Cardon, I see that she but replicates your beauty."

Mr. Cardon grunted. "Those are fine words, Burton, but I would remind you of my daughter's recent marriage."

"For heaven's sakes, Mr. Cardon!" Mrs. Cardon took her hand from mine and, with her fan, gave a light tap to her husband's arm. "Caroline has been married for three years. I wouldn't call that recent."

"What I was saying—"

"Yes, yes, my dear. She has a husband. We know. But surely you have a better understanding of women than that? We always want to know that we have admirers, especially after years of marriage."

"Where is he?" Mr. Cardon scanned the room for his son-in-law, his wife having adeptly shifted his attention.

"Oh, dear!" Mrs. Cardon murmured, noting the appearance of their son-in-law's parents. The oncoming couple moved so quickly toward us that they unfortunately hit their mark before I could make my escape.

The husband, a wealthy man I thoroughly disliked, was also a celebrated minister, well known for his dire sermons of fire and brimstone. In the past, when cornering me at a social occasion, he'd had the audacity to inform me that because of my "reputation with the fairer sex," he regarded me as a candidate for his words of advice. Astounded by his nerve, I had not replied directly but wondered aloud if his thoughts of my salvation might not be better directed toward his own son, who was often publicly battling the demons of drink.

Now, studying the couple, I noted how the wife, a bland pudding next to the great beef of her husband, was dwarfed. Here was an example of where a girdle, so popular with men today, might have suited a true purpose, had the man thought to use one, and I wondered where gluttony sat on his list of sins.

The alliance between these two families, resulting from the marriage between their children, gave catalyst to a merging of their fortunes, and as a result these two men now stood united as a mighty force in Philadelphia's world of logging and shipping.

From our first meeting, I thought Mr. Cardon something of a conundrum. A polished man, he was well versed in the ways of society and known to be generous, not just to the church but to many other institutions. In his earlier years, Mr. Cardon was involved in the fur trade, and accounts circulated of his ruthless behavior while living out among the Indians of the West. I myself heard him describe how to best kill and scalp a savage, a skill he claimed to have practiced more than once. When he spoke of the deed, from the flash of his eye and the grit of his teeth, I didn't doubt his story. Yet now he supported the museum's effort to collect Indian artifacts and often paid spectacular sums to help the members obtain what they deemed important. In fact, I suspected it was his money, and possibly his wife's influence, that had secured my upcoming ornithological excursion.

However, in the case of Mr. and Mrs. Cardon, I always remained aware of the treacherous waters in which I swam, for there was a dangerous duality in their views of slavery. The public knew Mr. and Mrs. Cardon as abolitionists. Indeed, they presented a good image, frequently citing their approval of the fact that in this city all of the Negroes were free. But in time I learned that Mr. Cardon had a holding in one of the largest cotton plantations in Louisiana, while Mrs. Cardon received a substantial yearly stipend from a wealthy father who owned a sizable farm in South Carolina worked by his enslaved Africans.

"So, Mr. Burton? I hear that you are soon to leave us?" the minister addressed me. I nodded, not caring to encourage a conversation. This offended him, which suited me. He drew back his coat and put his thumbs in the pockets of his waistcoat. Thrusting his significant stomach forward, he slowly surveyed the room. "I would suppose that some husbands and fathers will breathe easier while you are away," he said to no one in particular. His wife had the decency to give a faint gasp.

I was about to respond when Mrs. Cardon, always the expert hostess, addressed the minister and his wife. "Well, I'm afraid that Mr. Burton and I must leave the two of you to Mr. Cardon. Mr. Burton is, after all, our man of the hour, and we must give others their chance to wish him good fortune." She leaned in to me as she skillfully led me away. "You must ignore him," she said, "as I have learned to do."

I glanced down at her, but she was not smiling. She was what? Fifty years, give or take five on either side? Her bad teeth were a distraction, but her fair complexion remained, and though she carried extra weight, her corsets and beautifully cut blue silk gown enhanced her full figure. Considered one of the most powerful women in Philadelphia society, she used her quick wit and charm to rule from the throne of her husband's vast wealth.

As we moved away from earshot of her husband, she spoke over the music, and her voice held an edge. "Mr. Burton, you must know that it was because of my support that you were given this opportunity?"

"You know how grateful I have always been for your support," I said.

"Indeed," she said, thrusting her chin forward as she propelled us in Caroline's direction. "I promised my daughter to bring you to her. This is her last evening out, as tomorrow Caroline and I will leave for the country. I am concerned about her health." Her hand was clenched viselike on my arm, but she responded only with charm when various guests waylaid us to offer congratulations on my good fortune.

As we grew closer to Caroline, Mrs. Cardon leaned in to me once again. "It is too early in the season for Mr. Cardon and Mr. Preston—Caroline's husband," she added pointedly, "to be joining us at Stonehill, so they will be staying here in town. It is quiet in the country, so we shall have privacy. However, Caroline agreed to go to Stonehill only on the condition that I extend an invitation for you to visit. You will find time to do so before you leave?"

I met her penetrating gaze. "Nothing would give me greater pleasure," I said. "I shall await your invitation."

I could think of little but loosening my damp collar, but I quickly forgot that as we grew closer to Caroline and I saw how thin she had grown. Then I noticed her small waistline. Wouldn't the tight stays of her corset harm our child?

CHAPTER SIX

1830

Pan

B Y THE TIME I'm ten years old, I'm old enough to go on my own to see my daddy on Sundays. Because I'm dressed clean and I'm learning to talk like Mr. Burton, when I ask nice, the wagons going out of town give me a ride. My daddy always waits for me at the barns behind the tavern, then takes me to his shelter in the woods that he keeps moving around.

"Why don't you stay put?" I ask. "Then I could come find you on my own."

"I got to keep movin' 'case that ol masta come lookin' for me," he says.

"But Daddy, don't you think he forgot about you by now?"

"That old masta is sly, and I 'spect I see him any day. I's ready to head out soon's I catch sight a him."

"You'd just go and leave me?" I ask.

"Son, the best chance you got is stayin' with Mr. Burton. All we'd be doin' is runnin'."

"What was it like bein' a slave?" I ask.

"It nothin' I like to talk 'bout."

"But was it bad?"

"It bad enough that I'd sooner die as go back to livin' like that."

"But what if they ever get you again?" I ask.

"They never gon' get me again. They got to kill me before that happen," he says.

After he tells me that, when I go to meet him, my head is always hurtin' till I see him waitin' in the trees. Then I run to him, and when I give him a hug, I always got to stop myself from crying. I count on seeing him every Sunday, 'cause that's how it was all of my life. The rest of the time it was just me and Mama. The best times we had was when my mama's friend Sheila came by. Then I'd sit back and listen to the two of them talk. I liked to hear them laugh, even though Sheila had troubles of her own. Her two boys, both of them bigger than me, were always getting in a mess, and then her girl, just fourteen, goes out and gets her own baby.

One day after Sheila leaves, I ask Mama, "Why that girl of hers go out and bring in another baby? Sheila say she can't feed the ones she got."

"Those folks don' know no better 'cause they was slaves, comin' here to Phil'delphia from the farm where they don't have nobody tellin' them how to live free," Mama says. "It hard on them, tryin' to figure out how to make a livin' when they can't read or write. Mos' come from workin' in the fields and don' even know how to serve in a big house. Too, a lot a them still scared a the white folks."

I was six or seven when Mama first got sick. I did my best to help her out, but I was always happy when Sheila came over at night, sometimes bringing us food when we got none. One day she comes when I'm fussing over Mama, who was real sick that day. Sheila takes over and settles Mama, then pulls me on her lap and says, "Anybody tell you that you a good boy?"

Don't know why, but that gets me cryin'.

"That's fine, chil', you go head and cry," she says. "I knows this got to be tough on you."

I cry for a long time before she gives me a squeeze. "Come on, now," she says, "you got to be a lil man here. Your mama countin' on you."

"But I ain't no man," I say, "I jus a chil'."

"That's right," she say, "but sometimes we got to grow up fast. Why, when I was your age, I was takin' care of a whole house a white people."

"You was?" I ask, but I don't see her face 'cause her chin was on my head.

"Uh-huh," she say.

"When was you a chil'?"

"If I ever was, I forgot," she said.

ONE SUNDAY SHEILA comes over when my daddy's there and she gets to scoldin' him. "What you gonna do?" she asks. "This woman's not gonna make it through the winter. You can't leave the boy alone to take care a her like this!"

"What I gon' do here?" Daddy says. "I leaves the tavern, I don' have no money to help out. She gon' be all right, and the boy's doin' jus' fine!"

"You bes' get a job closer in," says Sheila.

"And where's that? You got somethin' lined up for me?"

Sheila don't have an answer, and she goes out slamming the door behind her.

UNTIL MY MAMA got sick, we went to church to get religion. The singin' and the callin' out to God lifts us up, but I always got my eye on the cake and milk they give you after.

After she can't walk that far no more, at night we sit together and ask God to help us out, but I don't like it when Mama starts tellin' me that she gon' have to leave me and go on to see the Maker. Every time I say, "Don't go, I don't want you to go," she tells me, "Baby boy, when I get the call, I got to go. You always 'member that even when you don' see me, I still right there, watchin' out for you. Come now, you tell your mama that you never gon' forget that."

I promise her over and over, but I forget all of that the night she passes. I don't care that I'm already eight years old, and I stay put on Sheila's lap, cryin'. When Daddy gets there, he stands at the door like he don't know if he's in the right house. "What goin' on here?" he says.

"She pass on," Sheila says, but there's no fight in her words.

Real slow, Daddy goes over to Mama, then starts shaking her and calling out to her like he can bring her back. I bust off a Sheila's lap and run over to push him away. "Don't fuss with her, can't you see she restin'!"

Daddy looks at me, then back at Mama, and he says real quiet, "I never think this gonna happen." Then he looks at me and grabs hold a my arms. "What we gonna do? What we gonna do?" he asks me, like I got the answer.

Sheila takes over then, and in the morning Daddy takes me back with him, but it don't work out, and the next Sunday he takes me to see Mr. Burton.

THE THING I like best about Mr. Burton is that he don't mind when I ask questions. That's just the way I is, full of questions. Quiet just isn't for me. I'm like my mama in that, where I like the sound of talk. I like the sound of singing, too, even if it's Robert when he don't think nobody's around. Then he lets loose. One day the slick man is working in the dining room, singing to the Lord like he's in church, when Mr. Burton and me come through to the study. Robert don't know we's there, and Mr. Burton just winks down at me, then heads on past like he don't see nothing.

About a year ago, this Miss Caroline shows up at Mr. Burton's art class that he gives on Saturdays. Mr. Burton was always a quiet man, but after a few weeks of Miss Caroline taking his classes, on the days she's comin' he goes around the house whistling, something Robert says I'm not allowed to do.

ROBERT TELLS ME that I got to learn to be discreet, a word that he says means not to talk so much. One Saturday afternoon I go runnin' for him. "Somethin's goin' on in the library," I say. "Mr. Burton is in there with Miss Caroline, and it seems to me like they need some help."

"Why are you bothering Mr. Burton?" Robert asks.

"Molly sent me to ask him if he wants some tea, like always. I know he and Miss Caroline went to the library 'cause I saw them go."

"Then what is the problem?"

"Well, the door is locked, and when I knock, they don't answer. Could be both of 'em is sick," I say.

Robert tells me to stay back and goes to listen at the door. It don't take him long before he comes back and gets us both into the dining room to do some polishing.

"They gon' be all right?" I ask.

"They are having a private meeting," he said. "You must never interrupt them during a private meeting."

"Never?" I ask.

"Never!"

"What if there is a house fire?" I ask.

"Then you come for me," Robert says.

"And what if you is burned up?" I ask.

He gives me a sigh. "I suppose at that point, you may knock on the door and shout, 'Fire!'"

"I don't think that's what I'd say. I think that I'd say, 'Mr Burton! Mr. Burton, you best stop your private meeting, because Robert is burnt up and the house is on fire.'"

"You could talk like this all day, couldn't you?" he asks.

"You mean about a fire?" I ask, but he don't answer me no more.

THEN COMES A DAY I walk into Malcolm's room and Mr. Burton and Miss Caroline is caught up in kissing. I'm so surprised that I just stand there until Mr. Burton sees me.

"Pan!" Mr. Burton says, like I do something wrong.

"I'm sorry, Mr. Burton, I come in here to clean Malcolm's cage," I say, but it's something to watch Miss Caroline's white face turnin' red.

"Will he tell Robert and your housekeeper?" she asks Mr. Burton, like I don't hear her.

"You know this is a private matter, Pan, that you must not speak to anyone of this?" Mr. Burton says.

"I don't say nothing," I say.

"Are you certain he . . ." she whispers loud enough for me to hear.

"Pan is most reliable, aren't you, Pan?" Mr. Burton says.

"I know how to be discreet!" I say.

Mr. Burton's eyebrows go up and then he gives me a smile. "Discreet, eh? We shall count on that, Pan," he says.

FOR MONTHS AFTER, Mr. Burton is whistling like never before, and I know why but I keep my mouth shut even when I hear Robert and

Molly talkin' almost every night at supper, both thinkin' that I don't know what's goin' on.

Then, all of a sudden, everything stops. Mr. Burton stops teaching his art classes and Miss Caroline don't come to the house no more. There's no more whistling and Mr. Burton spends most of his time closed up in his study.

One day I go to Malcolm's room with an apple that Molly gives me from the cold storage room.

"Hey, Malcolm," I say, "look what I got for you!" and when I toss the apple in the air and go to catch it, I bump into Mr. Burton, who is sitting quiet in a chair and looking down at his feet.

Malcolm flies over to me and I make him talk before he gets the apple, but this is the first time the bird's yapping don't get Mr. Burton to smile. I study the man for a while, then I say what he always says to me when I got trouble. "Mr. Burton," I say, "is there anything that you got on your mind?" I know he's goin' on a trip down into North Carolina to paint some birds, and I'm wonderin' if it would make him feel better if I was to go along to help him out. I'm about to say so when he looks up at me. "How old are you now, Pan?" he asks.

"I'm twelve," I say.

"You have always been wise beyond your years," he says. Mr. Burton is the kind of man who needs to think before he talks, so I stay quiet and wait on him. "I was thirteen when I first met your father," he says. "Has Henry ever told you about our first meeting? He saved my life, you know."

My eyes open wide. In all these years he's never talked to me about this, and my daddy won't say nothing about it, either, even when I ask. "How did he do that?" I say.

Mr. Burton puts his hands through his hair, making it go curly—not like mine, where it stands straight out if Robert don't keep it cut. "I'll tell you about my early years another time. For now I have too many things to sort out. It seems I've made a mess of things."

"Did you make a mess with Miss Caroline?" I ask.

He nods. "I'm afraid so," he says.

I try hard to think of something to say. "My mama always said, 'As long as you tell the truth, you got that to stand on.'"

Mr. Burton gives me a quick glance, then looks out the window. "Well, you've certainly hit on the problem."

I can see he's done talking, so I go back and finish cleaning up after Malcolm, then I hear Molly calling and I set out to find her.

FOR A COUPLE of weeks I keep waitin' for Mr. Burton to perk up, because I don't like to see him so quiet. He was never like this before. I keep tryin' to think of what to do, until one morning I remember how, before Miss Caroline was comin' around, he was always talkin' to me about gettin' a parrot with green feathers.

"Where you gonna find one like that?" I asked.

"They bring them in on the ships," he said.

I never been down to the docks. Robert and my daddy said for me to stay away because of slave catchers down there. But I'm old enough now to watch out for myself. Besides, my daddy's been talking all these years about gettin' caught by slave catchers and nothin's happened to him.

I got the money that Mr. Burton gives me, but I don't know how much a new bird is. I'm hopin' I got enough with what Molly gives me.

CHAPTER SEVEN

1830

James

I LEFT THE EVENING's celebration before supper was served; if I had stayed longer with Caroline, we would have given ourselves away. As it was, eyebrows were raised when she forgot herself and clung to my arm with both hands. When Mrs. Cardon was called away, I quickly walked us toward the supper room, hoping for a lesser audience there.

However, here, too, in this great blue room, there was a flurry of activity as waiters and chefs rushed about. Under different circumstances, I might have appreciated the abundant displays of red roses and tall strawberry topiaries massed together on the mantels, tables, and sideboards.

A confused waiter stood with a large covered dish in hand while two of the chefs squabbled.

"The sauce goes in front of the salmon!"

"Never! It must be presented from a side table," the other argued.

I led us to a corner and a large group of potted shrubs, tall as myself. Inadvertently, I stepped into the path of one of the servants, and we collided so firmly that the casserole dish he was carrying went flying. As the gold-rimmed china fell, splashing lobster Newburg across the carpet, Caroline reached for my hand and pulled me into a long dark corridor. No sooner were we alone than she was in my arms. I felt weak from wanting her, but I held her back. "Not here! Not here!"

"Why, James?" she begged. "Why haven't you seen me? Is it because of the child?"

"No, Caroline," I said. "No!"

"But why, James?" she asked. "Why haven't you sent for me? I disturb you, is that it? The sight of me with child disturbs you?"

"No, dearest, no!"

Her blue eyes shone with tears. "Then tell me! Why have you abandoned me?"

I pulled her close and spoke into her ear. "I have not abandoned you," I whispered. "I have been a coward, but I promise that I have not abandoned you!"

A servant startled us unexpectedly, and though he cast his eyes down as he hurried by, I was reminded again of the danger. I tried to put distance between us, but she would not release me.

"I must see you! When can we meet? Father is furious that I came here tonight, but I had to see you! I had to see you! Mother is insisting I go to the country. She said there are rumors and that I must go!"

"Your mother is right. It will be safer for you out there. But she has invited me out to Stonehill, and I will come," I said.

"You will? Truly, you will? Give me your word, James," she pleaded, clinging to my arms while dropping her forehead onto my chest.

My hand covered the nape of her soft neck. "You have my word. I give you my word. As soon as the invitation arrives, I will come," I promised. How terrible I felt at her obvious distress. What had I done to this poor girl? Why had I not given her more support?

Another waiter averted his eyes as he passed by.

"Come now, before we are discovered," I said, and drew her hand to my arm. Just in time, for no sooner did we appear in the doorway than a male cousin sent by Mr. Cardon swooped in and, with a haughty nod, swept Caroline away. She turned back and looked at me with such appeal that I took a step forward, then stopped myself. If I went for her, I didn't doubt she would come with me, but what then? I had no plan in place.

I stood back beside the potted shrubs, oblivious to the scurrying waiters. Why had I kept us apart for so long? If only I had told her the truth about myself from the beginning! But I loved her as I had never loved before, and always there was the fear of her rejection. Yet in not seeing her, I had missed her need for me. To learn that she saw my absence as abandonment filled me with shame.

And to think that there was the chance that our child could have color. How could I not have told her? Not only would she be horrified, she would be unprepared for potential danger. There were many stories of such situations that ended with rumors of murdered babies and mothers mysteriously disappearing. There was no way around it. The time had come. I must prepare her.

I would go to Stonehill, as promised, and there confess everything. I would plead her forgiveness and promise to provide the child a home, if that were necessary. Nothing would be more difficult than to lay this at her feet, yet tonight I had seen the suffering that my deceit had caused her.

A party of older women who had come early to assess the banquet were now staring at me. When I noted their attention with a nod, their fans flew open and they began to whisper. I needed no further encouragement to quietly depart.

CHAPTER EIGHT

March 1830

Pan

Friday morning I slip out and head on down to the docks. I'm scared to go, because if my daddy finds out, I don't know what he do.

The last time I talk to my daddy about going down to the ships, him and me was sitting downstream by his creek, catching us some fish. Nobody fries fish up like my daddy, and I tell him so. It's a good day when he can sit quiet—some days he's too jumpy and can't stop looking over his shoulder for his old masta.

"You growin' up, son," he says after I see him take a quick look at me. "But you never gon' be a strong one. It good you learnin' to work a big house for the white folk."

"You think I'm big enough now to go see those ships?" I ask, and Daddy gives me a look that means business.

"When I tells you to stay away from down there, I means that you stay away!" he says.

"Then how about you take me there?" I ask.

"Boy, you never gon' find me goin' close to that place. There some slave catchers that come up from the Carolinas and Georgia that get hold a you, tie you up on a boat, and take you back down, sell you for a slave. Nope, you and me got no business never goin' down there!" he says.

"If they'd take us, we'd just tell them we're free, Daddy."

"Once they got you, talk don' do you no good."

"I'm not afraid of them," I say. "They ever get hold of me, I can write to Mr. Burton, tell him to come get me."

I don't see his hand coming, and it catches me on the back of my head. He clips me so hard, everything spins. I grab hold of my head and can't talk 'cause I'm trying not to cry. He never hit me like that before, and I stand up 'cause it's no fun fishin' no more.

"Why did you hit me?" I ask, rubbing at my head. "Mama always said nobody should hit nobody else!"

He gets up, too, but he looks so mad that he's scarin' me and I take some steps back. "There's plenty more where that come from if I ever find out you go down there!" he says.

I got nothing to say, so I sit down again and go to pick up my fishin' pole, but I'm glad Robert makes me carry a handkerchief, because I got to blow my nose when I'm crying.

Daddy walks around for a while, then comes back and sits down, and I see his hands are shakin' when he picks up his pole. When I look up, I see his chin wobblin', like maybe he's gonna cry. I don't know what else to do, so I reach over and pat at his arm. "I don't mean no harm, Daddy. I always do like you say."

"Long as you don' go down there!" he says. "You don' never want to get took for a slave."

"What was it like, being a slave? Why won't you never tell me about it?" I ask.

He looks over the water, then all at once he sets his pole down and turns so I can see when he holds up both his hands to wiggle what's left of his thumbs. "This what they do to a slave," he said. "They cut you up in lil pieces."

Looking at his thumbs like that gives me chicken skin. "Why didn't you get out of there sooner?"

"Because I had a mama and a lil brother."

"What happened to your mama?" I ask.

"You don' want to know," he says, "you don' want to know!" With his hand he start pounding on his leg.

"You gonna hurt yourself like that," I say, reaching for his hand to stop him. "Don't do that."

He looks down where I'm holdin' his hand and then looks right into my face, something he never likes to do. His eyes look so scared that I'm glad when his pole starts jumping because I don't want him talkin' about being a slave no more.

"Let's just catch some fish, Daddy," I say, and we do.

THE SUN IS bright when I start out early in the day. Most of the snow is melted and I don't wear my big coat because I don't think I'll be needin' it. I won't be gone that long. I'm goin' down to the boats just once to get Mr. Burton his bird, and I'm hopin' my daddy don't find out nothing about it.

Mr. Burton got a map of the city up on his library wall, and I study it good before I set out. I know how to get to Market Street and from there I head toward the docks. I keep walkin' until finally, before I even get there, I hear the seagulls screechin' and my nose is filled with the smell of fish and water. When I go past the men sellin' fish, my heart starts poundin' because I know I should turn around, but I tell myself not to be a baby. I start to think I should a wore my warm coat because it's cold down by the water, but I keep walkin' when I see in front of me a boat tied up that is so big, it's got to be ten times the size of Mr. Burton's house.

On both sides of me is docks pointing out like fingers, and off them docks are boats lined up, one bigger than the next. At first I got to hold my ears for the noise. There is wagons and carts and men pitchin' stacks of boxes and barrels and the workers are yellin' to each other, one louder than the other, and the same thing is happenin' up and down the river as far as I can see. Out on the water there is already some ships moving out, with their sails puffed like big bellies full of wind. I forget about being scared because there's so much to see, and I move on in.

"Hey, you! Get outta the way!" I hear, and I almost get myself clipped when a wagon pulls up loaded with barrels. The driver stops his horses and hops down while men come over to unload his wagon. When they start workin' he looks over at me. "What you lookin' for boy?" he asks, none too friendly.

There's a sweet smell that I can't place. "What's in those?" I ask.

"Best brandy you ever goin' to taste," he says. "Boys," he tells his helpers, "I think we got someone here wantin' to buy a barrel a brandy!" Some of them laugh like they know somethin' I don't. The driver looks at me. "Hey, you got no business down here. You best get on home."

"But I come down here to buy a parrot," I say.

"You what?" he asks.

"I want to get a bird," I say. "Do you know where they sell birds?"

"Boys!" he calls out. "Any of you know where to find a bird?" One of the men laughs and points toward the seagulls that shriek and swoop down and around our heads. "Take as many as you want!" he yells, and this time they all laugh, but one of the men stops before he picks up a barrel. "You looking for those parrot types? Sometimes they bring them in down the line." He points forward. "Down a ways there's a tavern called Dockside. Go on in there. They'll tell you where they bring them in."

The driver jumps back up on his wagon. "Go on now. Get outta here before you get run over!" he says, and I have to jump out of his way when he swings his horses around.

Even though I got to walk a long time, I find the tavern easy enough, and I'm standin' outside wonderin' what to do when two men come pushin' out the door. The bigger one almost falls over me.

"Hey, boy, outta my way!" His face is burned red, and his yellow mustache, curled on each side like half a moon, moves when he talks.

"Sorry," I say, movin' back.

"You dressed fine for a nigga boy," he says. "What you doin' down here?"

"I want to buy a parrot," I say. "One that talks."

"You looking for a parrot, you say?" He looks around. "Where's your daddy?" He pulls a knife out from his belt and starts to cut at a fingernail.

"He works out of town," I say, wonderin' why he wants to know about my daddy.

"And your mama?" he asks. "She down here with you?"

"My mama pass on," I say, but after that something doesn't sit right the way the two men look at each other. I take a few steps back, thinkin' it's time to leave.

"Hey, where you goin'?" the man with the knife asks.

"I got to go home," I say.

"Didn't you say you was lookin' for a bird?"

I nod. "A green parrot."

"Well!" says the man as he slips his knife back into his belt, "if that don't beat all! Turns out we got one!" The two men nod at each other and I get a funny feeling up the back of my neck. I start walking away, but they both walk up beside me, one on each side.

"Say, boy! Don't you want to do business with us?" The one with the knife grabs hold of my shoulder. "Name's Skinner, what's yours?"

"Pan," I say, but now all I want is to go on home.

"Well, Pan, we got a bird for you!"

"I think I got to go home," I say.

"I think first you should come with us to see the birds," Skinner says, and his hand grips tight on me. "How much money you got to buy our bird?"

I tell him that I only got a few coins saved up.

"That'll do," he says.

I don't like his hand on me and try to pull away, but he just holds tighter to my shoulder and pushes me along. I'm scared and I want to leave, but I'm in between the two of them and I don't know what to do.

"How far up are we goin'?" I ask, and when they don't say nothin' I think maybe they don't hear me. We're moving fast, and I keep tellin' myself to set out at a run, but Skinner's hand is gripped on tight. I think maybe I should call out, but when a ship pulls out of the dock, there is so much creakin' and groanin' from the boat and so much yellin' from the men workin' that there's too much noise for anybody to hear me.

We get to one of the piers where there's a smaller boat tied up, and I want to say somethin' to the colored man that's sitting there smokin' his pipe, but when he sees me, he looks away, out onto the water. Skinner goes ahead and walks up a strung-up board that takes him across the water and onto the boat.

"Come on," he says, wavin' to me. The other man gets up behind me while I look around.

"Where are the birds?" I ask him.

"We got 'em on board," he says, then spits into the water, which looks almost black.

"I got to go on the boat to see them?" I ask.

"Yup," he said. "We keep 'em below, otherwise they're talkin' too much."

I start to tell him that I don't want to go on the boat, but he gives me a push and says, "Get on up there before I dump you in the river."

He sounds like he means it, so I move quick. The board stretched out over the water is wiggly and I got to hold on tight to the rope to get across. As soon as I get close, Skinner reaches for my hand and yanks me in. I yell out and try to pull away, but the rag he puts across my mouth has a strong smell, and then I don't remember what happens next.

WHEN I WAKE up, the boat is moving back and forth, back and forth, and all I can think of is that I got to get up on my feet and get outta there. When I try to stand, my feet slide out from under me and I land next to something that's making a noise. I'm so scared that my legs don't want to hold me up, so I just stay sittin' until my eyes get used to the dark and I see a small colored boy laying next to me. There's a bad stink, and when I look to see where the smell is coming from, the boy gets sick all over hisself and some of it lands on me.

"Stop it!" I say, and push away. My head hurts and my stomach don't feel good, but I stay sittin' up to try to figure out what's happenin'. It's like the floor is moving under me, and so I'm guessing that we're out on the water, but where are we going?

"What are you doing here?" I ask the boy.

"They took me," he says, then starts crying. "I wants my mama! I wants my mama!" He sounds like a baby, and the more he calls for his mama, the louder he gets.

"Stop cryin'!" I say. "You're hurtin' my head, yellin' like that."

"I wants my mama," he says, but then he gets quiet and vomits again. Hearin' him do that, I can't hold back no more and do the same, and we both keep at it until nothin's left in my stomach or in his. My head hurts so bad that I lay back and fall asleep.

I wake up to see him watching me. My head is still sore, but my stomach is quiet even though the boat is rocking. I sit up quick to look around. "Where are we?" I ask. "Where are we going?"

"I don' know," he says.

"What's your name?" I ask.

"I's Randall."

He looks so small. "How old are you?" I ask.

"I's five," he says, and when he looks at me, I wonder if I was that little when I was taking care of my mama.

"My name's Pan."

"How old you is?"

"I'm twelve years old."

"You big as my brother," he says. His voice starts to shake. "He was fightin' them an' they hit him on the head an' I don't know where he got to."

"I don't have no brother," I say, talking fast so his crying don't start up again, "but I got a bird."

"A bird?" he asks, but I don't answer when I start thinking of how a bird got me here. I got all kinds of questions, and when I think of them, each one scares me more. Who is that Skinner? Where is he taking me? Is he a slave catcher like my daddy said? Is he gonna sell me? Will I be a slave? Will they cut me up like they did my daddy?

"What gon' happen to us?" Randall asks.

"I don't know," I say. When he scuttles over close to me and starts to cry, stink and all, I start to cry myself. That stops him and he looks up at me. "Is you cryin'? Is you scared, too?" Then I remember my mama's friend Sheila and how she takes care of me when I was small as him. "I'm too big to cry," I say, and put my arm around him. "You just hold on till I can think of how to get us out of here."

We was just layin' there when Skinner comes down and slips in our sick and starts yelling so loud that Randall starts to shake all over.

"What kinda mess did the two of you make?"

"We got sick, is all," I say.

"Well, you're gonna clean it up!"

"Where are you taking us?" I ask. "Where are we going?"

"Never mind," he says. "I'm gonna bring you water, and I want this mess cleaned up!"

It don't take long before he comes back with a bucket and a rag. After he leaves, I wash the two of us down as best I can, then I clean up the floor. The only light that we got is from the trapdoor on top of our heads that got a ladder, and that's where Skinner comes down to bring us our food. Randall don't want the hard bread and cheese, but I know we got to get something in our stomachs, so I tell him, "I'll take a bite, then you take a bite," and that's the way I get him to eat a little bit.

The next time I see Skinner, I ask him again where we're goin'.

"None a your business," he says.

"But I want to go back home!" Before I know it I start yellin' at him. "Where are we goin'? You got to tell us where you're takin' us!"

He walks over and stands right in front of me and talks real quiet. "I guess you don't hear me the first time. I said it's none a your business."

I don't care no more. I got to know. I stop yellin' and straighten myself up and try to sound like Robert. "I believe that it is my business," I say. "You brought me here to see—" His fist winds up and catches me and I go down.

"Get off a me!" Skinner yells, and I see Randall, who's been hanging on to Skinner's arm, go flying against the wall, where he plops with a yelp like a puppy.

After Skinner goes, I try to sit up, but I can't and Randall crawls over. When I moan, he whispers, "Is you hurt? Is you hurt bad?"

While I lay there, Randall sits close beside me, waiting, his hands squeezed together tight in his lap, and I still can't believe that he tried to fight off Skinner.

"I wish I was brave as you," I say.

"I want my mama," he says, and even though he don't make no sound of crying, water is coming from his eyes.

"Tell you what," I say. "Soon as we get to land, I'll write to Mr. Burton. He'll come for us."

"You can get us outta here?"

"Yup," I say. "I'll send a letter to Mr. Burton, and he'll come."

Randall grabs at my hand. "An' you take me with you?"

"'Course I take you with me," I say. "I'm not goin' no place without you."

After that, I find what looks like a old sail and wrap us both in it, 'cause we's cold. Even when he's sleepin', Randall keeps hold of my hand.

The only time we see Skinner is when he brings us food and empties our slop pail, but I don't ask him no more questions.

It's hard to tell how many days go by, because after a while one day is like the next. I keep telling Randall not to worry, that as soon as I write to Mr. Burton, he'll come for us, and probably in his big carriage, too.

When Randall's cold, I tell him about the fur rugs that Mr. Burton keeps in his carriage and how we will use them to get warm on the ride home. He likes to have me talk, so I tell him about the house I live in and how it's my home and how good Mr. Burton is to me. I tell him about all the food I get to eat and how I take care of Malcolm and how Mr. Burton says that when I'm ready, he's going to send me to a school in New York.

I don't tell him about my daddy being a slave and how, every day we're on the water, I keep thinking of how Mr. Burton just got to come find us, because if Skinner's a slave catcher I don't want to be no slave. I think of what they did to my daddy's hands, and my fingers hurt just thinking about it, and when I feel Randall's hand in mine, I know for sure they can't cut nothin' off of Randall 'cause he's way too little to lose no fingers.

By the time the boat ties up, we both got a bad cough, and even though I try to get Randall to eat, he's too sick.

"The two a you shut up or you get my boot," Skinner warns when he brings us up out of the hold. It's warmer here, and someone at the dock says we're in Virginia. Right away I feel better, 'cause I remember from a map Mr. Burton showed me that Virginia is right close to North Carolina, and that is where he's comin' to paint his birds, and I'll bet he can find us easy!

The sharp sun hurts my eyes, but I make them stay open so I can see where we are when they load us on a wagon. There aren't as many docks as Philadelphia, but it seems like the same kinda men are yellin' and fussin', and there's bunches of them workin' the boats, but none of them look at me and Randall, and I can't call out anyway because Skinner's hand is squeezing tight at the back of my neck. He throws us up on the wagon, and when the wagon moves out, he starts cussin' at the driver because he only got one horse and it don't move too good. When the driver starts cussin' back, Randall takes my hand.

It's a while before we're away from the docks because we got to work our way past all the other horses and wagons coming and going. Most are piled so high with stacks of wood and barrels that you can't see over them. We finally get on a road, and after we travel out some, we take a turn that cuts through the trees, which is already greening up, but I don't look around much because we're bumpin' along so hard that I got to work on keepin' Randall and me in the wagon. Skinner is cussin' all the way until we get to a couple of small barns. When the wagon stops, Skinner pulls us down, but it's hard to stand after the boat.

The driver comes 'round to look at us. "This the best you can do? Together they ain't worth nothin'. One's too little and the other's too scrawny."

"The bigger one's got educatin', so he'll bring somethin'," Skinner says.

"That's not where the money is. They want 'em for the fields!"

"You know they're watchin' those docks in Philly real close now! Those niggas up there is gettin' a little too set up, organizin' with them Quakers. We had a better one, strong-built, but he went down too hard. Fish food now."

"You musta roughed him up too much again! I told you, they 's like handlin' money. When you gonna learn?"

I hold tight to Randall's hand and hope he don't understand what they say about his brother.

Just when I'm thinking of making a run for it, Skinner grabs us both by the neck and pushes us into a room at back of a small barn. They lock us in, and when the wagon thumps away, the two of them are still cussin' at each other.

"Now can you write to your man?" Randall asks when he sits down beside me on the dirt floor.

"I don't have no paper," I say.

"But you got to write to him to get us outta here," he says, his voice high and the next thing to crying.

"Shhhh," I say, looking back over my shoulder, "somebody might be listenin'.""

He looks 'round and moves closer to me, but after a coughing fit, he quiets down. Then, as though he's got nothin' left in him, he lays down and puts his head in my lap. "My head's hurtin'," he says, "an' I's cold."

"You sleep some while I figure this out," I say, and I rub across his bony little shoulders and wonder why he says he's cold when he feels so hot. I wait till he's sleepin' before I move, careful not to wake him. Then I go over to the window and try jumpin' up, but it's too high, and besides, it got some boards across it. I try the door, but it's locked tight, like I figured. I kick at it some until I hurt my foot, and when I limp around I start crying. Finally, I go back and sit next to Randall, 'cause he's coughin' so bad and shakin' in his sleep.

THAT NIGHT SKINNER shows up with the driver and another man. I jump up as soon as they come in the door, and it don't take a minute before Randall is up beside me and got a hold of me. "What they gon' do?" he asks me.

"Shhh," I say, trying to see past the lantern that Skinner holds up.

"They's both scrawny!" says the new one.

"Give me three hundred," says Skinner, "and you can have 'em both."

"Thomas doesn't take 'em when they're that small. Too much trouble. I'll give you one hundred for the older one."

"And give me twenty for the runt. You know you can sell him on the way down," Skinner says. "He'll bring you twice that."

"Deal," says the man, and when he comes over with the rope, I step back and Randall moves with me.

"If I give you my money, can he stay with me?" I ask.

"Let me see how much you got," the man says.

I unfold the rag that holds my coins, and with a swipe he pockets it. "And now you don't have none," he says with a laugh.

"But that's stealin'!" I say before I can stop myself.

He laughs again. "Sounds to me like you got some educatin'. You one of those mamby-pamby house boys? Won't take long for Thomas to work that outta you!"

"Can Randall please stay with—" I start, and before I can duck, the man sends his fist at me.

"I don't wanna hear nothin' from you after this," he says.

When I spit out blood, a tooth comes, too, and Randall starts screamin, but I don't shush him 'cause I'm cryin' too hard myself.

PART TWO

CHAPTER NINE

1830

James

O N MY RETURN from the event, Robert had the outdoor lamps burning when my carriage drew up to the house, and as usual, he was waiting for me at the front door.

"There is a fire in the library," he said as he took my greatcoat and hat.

"Any news of Pan?" I asked.

"No, I'm afraid not," he said, and without further comment, I went to the library, craving the solitude.

"Something hot to drink?" he called after me.

"Go to bed, Robert," I said, closing the door behind me.

It was past midnight. I went to the familiar chair next to the fire and sank into its worn leather, sighing deeply. This room always gave me comfort. How grateful I was to Robert for anticipating my need for a fire this evening. How I relied on him. I thought of him now brushing down my coat and hat and then finishing up his chores for the night. Lamps and candlesticks would be collected and carried down to the kitchen, where Molly would clean them in the morning. Then, if he hadn't already, Robert would go for a final assessment of the small parlor where I took my morning meal. There he would make sure that the grate had been cleaned and the logs set for an early-morning fire. He would check to see that the tea table was covered with a linen cloth, the crease set exactly down the center, and in the morning my tray would hold a crystal salt cellar, a porcelain egg cup with a soft-cooked egg, a slice of ham, and next to it, a small cruet of mustard. There would be butter set on ice in the gleaming silver butter dish, and after I spread it on my warm toast, I would clip off the top of the egg and dip the buttered toast into the warm yellow yolk. Then, while I enjoyed my tea and the morning paper, Pan would likely show up to ask some precocious question that would undoubtedly amuse me.

Pan! How accustomed I was to having him here. Robert was my mainstay, the one who established and adhered to a routine that gave me balance, but Pan—Pan was the one who gave me cheer. And where was he now?

I reassured myself that he was resilient enough to look out for himself until he was rescued. After all, he was already twelve, close to the age that I was when Henry found me. I rested my head back and closed my eyes, reviewing my own capabilities at that young age, but all I could recall was how helpless and utterly terrified I had been on my arrival in Philadelphia.

IT TOOK ME weeks to begin to trust Henry. All of my life, Grandmother had instilled in me that Negroes were sly and dangerous and not to be trusted. Now, though, I was not only eating and sleeping next to Henry, I was also relying on him to see to my needs.

His feral way of life was foreign to me, yet he taught me daily survival skills, and by the time my health was fully restored, I was beginning to enjoy the outdoor independent life. Under my grandmother's roof, I'd had servants to do my bidding, and my most difficult challenge had been to voice a request. Here, with Henry, I was expected to do my share of the work and was soon responsible for gathering the wood and tending the fire. Rather than viewing this as a hardship, I found it stimulating and woke each morning with renewed vigor.

In the early fall, Henry began to bring up the subject of my going into the city to find employment, but I avoided the issue, for the idea of leaving him petrified me. This man had not only saved my life but continued to provide for me, and daily I grew more dependent on him. Then one evening, after we had just finished a satisfying meal of wild onion and rabbit stew, Henry approached the subject again. We sat near the crackling fire, but the night around us had turned cold.

"The snow comin'," he said, "an' I got to move out."

"Where to?"

"I got another place a ways from here, place tighter for the winter."

I didn't look at him but shifted closer to the fire. "Can I come with you?" I asked. "I could pay you if you let me stay."

"An' with what you gon' do that?" he asked.

I hesitated but decided I had no choice except to trust him. "I have some jewelry," I said. "I can sell it." I glanced over to read his response.

"I don' suppose you keepin' it in that coat a yours?" he said with a half smile.

I nodded and quickly slipped off my jacket. Using my whittling knife, I carefully slit open one of the hidden pockets that sheltered a piece of jewelry. From inside I pulled out my grandmother's ring, set with a large blue sapphire and surrounded by sizable diamonds. My stomach clenched at the memory of her hand, only months before, smoothing my hair. Was it possible she was dead? I forced myself away from the dark thought and held up the ring for Henry to see. "We can sell this," I said.

"Boy, you got to use that to find yo'self a place to live. It time you move on. You stay out here, they gon' peg you for a nigga," he said. "No sense in that."

"But where will I go?" My voice rose high.

"You got to get yo'self into the city, look around. Not gonna find no work sittin' out here. There's lots a streets full of places where white people got business. We get over there and you go on in, tell them you lookin' to work. Any kinda work you good at?"

"I'm good at reading and writing, and I can do numbers. And I know how to draw and paint. Grandmother had two of my paintings framed." Sparks flew when Henry rearranged a log. I rubbed hard at my temples, trying to stop the thoughts from pushing through. "But they were burned up. Everything was burned up!" My voice trembled as I shook my head, trying to dislodge the memory of the great flames that had taken our home. I whimpered, remembering how I had scanned the smoldering rubble for remains of Grandmother, a woman I had always thought of as my mother.

"Boy," Henry said, "you got to let go a those things an' keep movin' on, or they take you down."

"But I keep thinking of the fire . . . of the pain she was in!" I tried not to cry.

"She don' feel nothin' now. She gone. It's you that feelin' somethin'. You think that's what she's wantin' for you? Feelin' the hurt that she's not feelin' no more?"

My throat was too choked to answer.

"I bin through enough to know you can't carry nobody's hurt. Hard enough to carry your own."

I nodded.

"Now we got to get back to figurin' out work for you. Is there any kinda work you can do with all that learnin' in books?"

"Well, I can paint and sketch pretty good."

Henry grunted. "I don' know nothing 'bout that. Best we jus' get you in there. It not gon' be hard for a boy that look white as you to find hisself some work."

The next evening Henry came home with news of a pawnshop where I could go to sell my piece of jewelry. "How 'bout we go in the morning?" he said, as easily as that.

I was so scared and angry with Henry for pressuring me to leave that I couldn't sleep that night. What if Rankin and the patrollers were still looking for me? Until now, out in the woods and under Henry's protection, I hadn't worried about anyone finding me, but what if they came looking for me in the city?

As dawn broke, Henry had me roll my few belongings inside a burlap feed bag. We were deep in a forest, and as Henry led us out through the towering oaks and pines, I started to mark a trail, bending back twigs as he had taught me to do in case I needed to find my way back, but Henry moved so quickly that I soon had to turn my attention to keeping up. We traveled for a good while before we arrived at the outskirts of the forest, where lay a well-traveled road that led into the city. There we set out on what would have been a long walk of some miles had a farmer, driving a one-horse cart, not stopped. "You wanting a ride?" he asked.

Henry nodded to me and I answered, "Yes, we would." The driver waved me up to my rightful place on the seat beside him, while Henry found room for himself in the back of the cart.

The driver slapped the reins and the horse moved out. Once under way, he glanced over at me. "You and your man going into town?" he asked.

"Yes."

"You from these parts?"

"No, I'm from Virginia," I answered nervously, until I remembered Henry's coaching. "If they start askin' too many questions, you start askin' some of your own."

"Are you from here?" I asked. "I mean, is this where you were born?"

"Yessir. Born and raised, but my parents come from Germany. They're gone now, but they left me a small farm. Me and the boys, I got two of 'em, we raise some cattle and crops like these potatoes." He nodded back toward his cargo. "We make out all right, bringing carrots and potatoes into the market whenever we got some."

The man pulled his battered hat low over his head to shade his weathered face, and he gripped the brown leather reins as he guided his horse over the rut-filled road. "That rain last week didn't help this road," he said. "Lucky it's dry today, though. That mud can be rough to get through."

I bobbed my head in agreement, though I had no experience with driving or difficult road conditions. Until my recent flight from Tall Oaks, I had been so sheltered by Grandmother that in all of my thirteen years I had never left our farm.

"First time in this city?" he asked.

I nodded again. Seeing that I had little to lend to a conversation, the man began to whistle, leaving me free to look about. The wagon bounced down the rutted road that cut through a dense forest, and I was soon sorry for having no gloves, fearing splinters as I gripped tight to the side of the wooden cart. We passed by a number of small farms where the fields had been cleared and chickens wandered about the gardens and apple orchards. The farmhouses were solidly built of stone or brick, and though most were not of large size, they looked sturdy.

However, my interest soon shifted as we came closer to the outskirts of Philadelphia. Large coaches raced by our small cart, and when our driver picked up the pace, joining the pandemonium, more than once I anxiously glanced back to make sure that Henry, clinging tight, was still with us.

As we entered the city, we slowed again to merge onto the gray cobbled streets, where I gaped in disbelief at the towering three- and four-story brick buildings that lined the streets. On my flight from Tall Oaks, I had been so frightened and then so ill that I had scarcely taken note of any town that our coach drove through. But now, wholly alert, I stared about at the frantic pace of the city as we passed row upon row of vast buildings, most of which had overlarge signs announcing their wares: tobacco and segars, coffee, boots and shoes. I had never imagined so many offerings all in one place.

When we arrived at Market Street, huge green awnings stretched out over brick walkways to shelter what was offered for sale. Men, women, and children, many burdened with multiple baskets, called out to one another, adding to the bedlam as they scurried among the stalls. We passed first the fishmongers, the smell of fish ripe in the air, and then the farmers selling their vegetables, heaped high in barrels and boxes. Next to them, women wrapped in white aprons sold butter, cheese, and brown and white eggs. From my wagon seat, I could see butchers in bloody aprons farther on down, cutting away at slabs of red meat while customers waited in line.

Our driver pulled his horse to a stop under one of the awnings, then leaped down to hitch his horse in such a way that the back of the cart could serve as a stall for his produce. After we thanked the driver for the ride, Henry led us away while I stumbled over my own feet as I gawked.

It took a while before we found Lombard Street, but the storefront sign displaying three prominent balls, the mark of a pawnshop, was easy to find. I hesitated at the door when Henry insisted I go in alone. Fingering the ring in my pocket, I felt a sudden reluctance to sell it.

Would Grandmother be angry with me for doing this? Yet I needed to find work and a place to stay. I reminded myself that I had other pieces of her jewelry sewn into the lining of my jacket, so I took a deep breath and stepped into the shop.

The vendor was eager to have the ring, and any hesitation I had quickly left when a good-sized purse was offered in exchange for the jewelry. It felt like a small fortune, and on my exit, I greeted Henry with a smile as I held up my gain.

He frowned. "You bes' put that away!" he said, and though I quickly put it in my pocket, he scolded, "What happen to you back at the tavern? You don' learn nothin'?"

"I just wanted you to see—" I said.

"I don' need to see nothin'," he said.

At another time I might have felt the sting of his criticism more acutely, but since I had achieved success with the sale, my mood was light. "Let's go back to where we came in—to Market Street," I said. "There was so much to see."

"Don't forget, you lookin' for work," Henry said.

"Today?" I said.

"Winter comin'," he reminded me.

Even though his words sobered me, I could not stop my growing excitement as I stared at all there was around me.

"Look at this!" I pointed out to Henry over and over again, and more than once Henry quietly reminded me to keep moving if I stopped short to observe shoppers or tradesmen at their work.

We were not far from Market Street when I caught sight of a beautiful window display. Through a large pane of glass, sun shone in on two silver birds, posed as though they were strutting about, their long tails dragging down behind them. "Look!" I said to Henry. "Silver peacocks!"

Henry moved in for a better look.

"Grandmother had two silver birds just like these. They always sat on our dining room table, but when I was younger, she let me play with them. She said that they had been purchased in Philadelphia!" I thrilled at the sudden remembrance. "Do you think they made them here?" I asked, but Henry only shrugged indifferently.

I looked up at the sign overhead. "Burton's Silversmith." Then I no-ticed a sign set to the side of the birds. "The sign says that they need help," I said.

Henry brightened. "You got to go on in," he urged. "I wait out here."

"You want me to go in there? Now?"

"Good a place as any."

With no job skills to offer, I was embarrassed to present myself, but I decided to at least make a show of it to appease Henry.

A bell startled me when it rang on my entry, and an older man, seated at a table behind a counter, looked up. Though he continued to polish a silver object, he glanced at me over spectacles that sat on the end of his short nose. He was seated beside a window, and the sun shone through his white hair that circled out from around the pale bald top of his head. I turned to the display case in front of me, filled with snuffboxes and watch chains, but something else had caught my eye. I went closer in and saw the same tubular whittling knife that I had taken from my home at Tall Oaks and now carried in my pocket. I leaned down to get a better view.

The man put down his polishing tool. "May I assist you?" he asked.

"I have one just like that," I said, enthused to see another familiar object.

"The apple corer?" he asked, giving it a name.

"Yes," I said, tapping on the case, "an apple corer. One such as this. I use it to whittle."

He scraped back his stool as he stood. "Would you like to see it?" he asked.

"No," I said, stepping back, alarmed that I had misrepresented my-self. "I . . . I saw those birds in the window. They are splendid! My grandmother has the same, although hers are smaller. Did you make them here?"

"We did," he said.

"How did you do it?" I asked, shaking my head in wonder.

"Are you interested in becoming a silversmith?" he asked, peering at me over his glasses.

"Is that what your sign is for? You want someone to help you make silver?"

"One doesn't make silver, young man, one works with silver. We pour it, we shape it, we hammer it, but we do not make it."

Though he was direct, there was a kindness to the man, and because of it, I dared ask my next question. "Could I learn how to make birds like that?" I asked, pointing back toward the window display.

"You are seeking employment?" He scanned my clothing and gave a quick look at my affected eye.

"Yes," I said. "I need to work."

"And what, sir, do you have for education?" he asked.

"I am good at reading and writing and mathematics. Oh, and I know some Latin." His close scrutiny made me uncomfortable, and I glanced back at the birds in the window. "And I can carve a true likeness," I said, quickly withdrawing from my burlap bag two miniature birds and a rabbit I had whittled recently. I placed them on the counter.

"Oh!" he said in surprise. He picked them up and held them to the light to study their silhouette. "These are quite remarkable," he said, but again he looked at my affected eye. "Does your eye give you trouble when you do close-up work? Does it tire easily?"

"No," I said, "my eye is good."

He set the rabbit down on the counter, then positioned the birds on either side of it. He fussed with their placement until he was satisfied, then stepped back to look at them again. "As miniatures, these are quite exceptional," he repeated.

Quickly, I dug out my sketchbook. "I'm good at drawing birds, but I can draw other things as well."

He took the small pad from my hand and slowly paged through, then closed it and handed it back to me.

"I didn't have paint," I said, "they would be much better—"

He raised his hand to stop me. "You have quite a talent, young man." I saw hope. "Could I work here, then?"

"Tell me, where are you from?" he asked.

The question so startled me that my mouth went dry. "I'm from Virginia," I said, "and I need to work."

He cleared his throat. "Well, let me put it to you this way. You say you wish employment, and it appears you have a great talent. I believe you could be well suited to this work. Your speech and dress suggest a certain refinement, but the scent of you and the outright dirt on your clothing have me questioning what you are about."

I looked down at myself. I had always been particular in my clothing and fastidious in my personal grooming, but in these past weeks out in the woods, I had forgotten my careful habits. I reached up and smoothed back my long hair, which had not seen water nor a brush since I had lost my satchel. What had I been thinking, to present myself this way? My face was hot when I turned away, but as I hastened for the exit, he called out, "Young man!"

I stopped to look back, my face burning.

"Cleanliness is what I am after. If you are interested, do as I suggest, then come back to see me before the week is up."

Wanting only to escape, I nodded, then made a quick exit. Henry caught up to me as I briskly walked ahead. "The man got no work?"

"He said that I was a filthy pig," I said.

"A pig!" Henry said. "He said you a pig!"

"Well, not in those words. He told me I need to get cleaned up."

"Then he gives you the job?"

"I'll never know," I said.

"Why you never know?"

"Because he insulted me! I'm not going back," I said.

Henry looked about to make certain that we were alone, then he spoke in a low voice. "Now you thinkin' like a white boy. How you get ahead like that? You want somethin', you got to fight for it! That mean you got to get cleaned up and go on back there."

Furious, I strode on, but as I began to pass by some clothing shops, my fury lessened. I finally stopped in front of one display window that featured a white shirt and a beautifully tailored green velvet dress jacket. The gold lettering on the window read "Gentlemen's Clothing."

"Go on in," Henry encouraged. "Get you some new clothes. You got the money."

Embarrassed now at my appearance, I was reluctant to enter, but smarting from the silversmith's insults, I went in, determined to clean myself up. On my exit, I carried a new leather satchel packed with three white cotton shirts, two pairs of dark breeches, a black jacket, some stockings, and a fine pair of black shoes. I also now owned scissors, a hairbrush, and a sandalwood-scented bar of soap.

I handed Henry a shining black satchel similar to my brown one. "Open it," I said.

He gave me a look of surprise as he dug though his bag to find a new muslin shirt, a bar of soap, and a wooden hairbrush. He smelled the soap and said nothing, but from his slight smile, I could tell he was pleased.

FOR TWO DAYS I could not find the courage to return to the city, but by the third day, Henry insisted I go. I had scrubbed myself clean and was dressed in my new clothing when Henry again led me through the woods, but this time when we came to the road, he handed me my satchel and encouraged me on my way.

"Aren't you coming?" I asked, alarmed.

"Time we cut ties," he said, avoiding my eyes.

I looked around, trying to think of an excuse to have him come with me. "Maybe I shouldn't go today. It looks like it's going to rain," I said.

Henry looked at the sky. "Rain or shine, you got to go," he said. I was about to plead, but his face hardened. "Go on, now. Time you git goin'. Go on, now, and do somethin' with yourself."

I didn't know what else to do, what else to say. My throat seized up, and fearing that I might start to cry, I abruptly turned and walked away. I knew why Henry was sending me away, but I felt he was all I had left of family, and I was heartsick at leaving him. When tears fell, I wiped them away, but hungry for a last sight of him, I turned back to wave. He was already gone, and it took everything in me not to run back into the woods to find him.

I waited awhile, hoping he might come forth to surprise me, but finally, I turned back to the road and forced myself on. By the time another farmer on his way to the market offered me a ride, my new shoes had rubbed my heels raw, and I was happy to accept. This wagon box was filled with baskets of alarmed chickens and I was grateful for the din, as it provided little opportunity for talk.

Once in town, I went in search of the silversmith shop. By the time

I found my way there, my feet were burning from blisters. Though the sign for help was still in the window next to the silver birds, I dreaded entering, sure of rejection.

I dusted my pants clean and brushed at the front of my jacket, then stepped in to meet the same man who had seen fit to tell me to bathe. Surprisingly, he recognized me and greeted me with some enthusiasm.

"So," he said, "you are back!" He came from behind the display case to look me over. "I see you took my advice."

"I did," I said, gripping tight to my satchel.

"I am pleased to see you," he said.

"You are?"

"I am! You have a talent, my boy. I was hoping that you would return. And now I see that you can accept direction."

I wasn't sure what to feel.

"So why did you return?" he asked.

"I need to work," I said.

"You would be willing to clean the floors?"

"Well, yes, I can clean floors if you show me how," I said, "but I would rather like to learn to work with silver."

"We could arrange for that, but it would take years to learn the craft," he said.

"Years?" I asked.

"Yes, but first you would have to start with cleaning the shop and running errands."

"Would you pay me?" I asked.

"Not if you are my apprentice." My face must have fallen, for he added, "But you will learn a trade, and while you are with me, I will supply your food and some coins as you might need them."

"I will need them," I said.

"Did you consult with your family?"

"I had only my grandmother," I said.

"Your grandmother? And where is she?"

I wasn't prepared for the question. "She was in a fire. She died," I blurted out.

"And your parents?" he asked.

"Umm . . . they are dead," I lied. "I have no one." Unexpectedly, for the second time that day, I fought tears, and when one slipped down my face, I quickly wiped it away with my jacket sleeve. "I don't like to talk about my grandmother," I said as explanation, though truthfully, it was more likely the strain of leaving Henry and now my fear of being caught in a lie.

The man gave me a moment before he asked, "And what is your name?"

I looked down at the floor and lied again. "James Smith," I said, calling up the name Henry and I had decided upon.

"And your age?"

I glanced up, and his expression was so unexpectedly kind that I told the truth. "I was thirteen years this past February," I said.

He nodded, then smiled. "Thirteen is a good age to begin." He stepped forward and offered his hand. "My name is Mr. Burton. Welcome."

Yet I hesitated. Where would I live? I had coins in my pocket, but I was reluctant to use them, as I hated the thought of selling more of Grandmother's jewelry.

"What is it?" he asked, noting my uncertainty.

"Do you know of a place where I could sleep?" I asked.

"Ah! Well, it is common enough to offer a new apprentice room and board," he said. "I can provide that for you in my home, where you will be downstairs with our household help. Your room will be small, but it will be warm and dry, and you will have enough to eat. Would that arrangement suit you?"

I was so relieved that I could only nod in reply.

CHAPTER TEN

1810–1811

James

Unspeakably grateful for the man's generosity, I was silent in the carriage that first evening when Mr. Burton took me along to his home. I had spent the afternoon cleaning up the silver shop, but I had left Henry early that morning, and I was dazed from the long day.

It seemed a short ride before the horses turned down an alley that led to the back of a four-story brick dwelling. After Mr. Burton and I left the carriage, the driver went on to the stables, and my host led the way into the house through a back door that opened into a small square entry where a welcoming lamp was burning.

From there I followed Mr. Burton down a short stairwell and into a large basement kitchen, where we were met by the scent of freshly baked bread and a simmering meat stew. The warmth and comfort of this large room contrasted sharply with the cold outside, but it was all so unfamiliar that I happily would have exchanged it for Henry and his outdoor fire.

Mr. Burton went ahead to a long pine table in the center of the room. There he lifted a blue-and-white-checked cloth. "Ah, Delia!" he said, breathing in the scent of fresh bread.

A thin Negro woman turned from the vast fireplace. "Done not two hours ago," she said without a smile, then went back to stirring the contents of the pot.

"Don't tell me that's my favorite stewed beef," he said, sniffing the air.

"Made just the way you likes it, with the cloves and extra onions," she said.

"Now, that's a meal to look forward to, Delia!" he said.

The woman placed the iron lid back on the pot, then picked up a small bucket and brought it over to slide the onion peels from the table. As I watched her work, her dark eyes kept darting in my direction.

"How was Mrs. Burton today?" my new employer asked.

"Oh, she have a good day," Delia said.

"She saw Malcolm?" he asked.

"Yessir, she go to his room. Like I say, she have a good day."

"Fine, fine." Mr. Burton looked back at me.

"We're trying out a new apprentice for the shop. This is James," he said, by way of introduction. He waved toward a dark hallway. "Can we get that back room cleared out enough to make room for a bed?"

"The one 'cross from the wine cellar?" she asked.

"That's the one," he said.

"I get Ed to take out some a those barrels what holds the apples and . . ."

"Fine, fine," he answered, already on his way to the stairway. Before he began to climb the steps, he addressed me again. "Delia will get you straightened out. Be ready to leave in the morning at seven."

"Yes, sir," I said, so grateful for his kindness that tears threatened. I soon sobered when Delia and I were left alone to stare at one another. Her brown muslin head rag was tied low on her forehead, and her face appeared to be set in a frown, though it might have been her low-slung jaw and heavy bottom lip that made it look so. Hers was not a handsome face.

"No white boy been put down here with us before," she said, clearly unhappy with my presence.

"And I'm not used to sleeping with servants," I said sharply.

She gave me a quick hard look. While I found her stare intimidating, I would not allow a Negro woman to speak to me in that way.

She picked up one of the lamps and, while mumbling to herself, shuffled slowly across the zigzag pattern of the brick floor and into the dark hallway. When she sensed that I wasn't behind her, she turned back. "You comin'?" she called.

I followed as she led the way to a small back room half filled with large barrels. In the lamplight, I saw there would be space enough to place a bed under the narrow window and away from the small fireplace.

"Set your bag down, and Ed see to get a pallet for tonight. Tomorrow we get a bed set up. What else you think you needin' in here?" she asked.

I decided it best to present a full list. "I suppose I shall need a desk," I said, "and a floor covering. Of course I will need a lamp and a wash-stand and a mirror—"

"I say what you needin', not what you wantin'," she said, then abruptly left the room. Since she had the light, I had no choice but to trail back after her into the kitchen. With nothing else to do, I sat on a stool and watched as she bustled around, preparing a supper tray for the Burtons. When she finished, she carried it to a corner in the room and there opened a small trapdoor to load the tray inside. After she gave a few yanks to a cord, which rang a bell on the floor above us, there was a low rumble as someone in the dining room above began to use a pulley to bring the meal up.

I couldn't stop myself. "Who is up there?" I asked.

"Robert," she said.

"Robert?" I asked.

"He the butler."

"The butler?" It was an unfamiliar word, one I could not recall having heard before, but I would not show my ignorance.

"That what I say," she said, then directed me to a corner of the table and set before me a large pewter spoon and a wooden bowl filled with the hot stew. Until now I had felt too drained from the day's events to eat, but the aroma awakened my appetite.

I was relieved to see that she was not joining me. It was one thing to share my meal with Henry out in the woods, but to sit at the table with a Negro house servant was another thing.

"Would you have a napkin?" I asked.

She went to a sideboard and opened a long drawer from which she pulled a folded white cloth that I suspected was used for drying dishes.

"This suit you?" she asked, setting it down beside me.

"Thank you," I said, shaking it out and folding it across my lap before digging in to the aromatic stew.

Delia spread freshly churned butter over a thick slice of bread and handed it to me. She was cutting another slice of bread when she gave me a sly look. "You know what a butler do?"

I dipped the bread into the sweet onion gravy, then took a bite and chewed it slowly before I replied. "I'm assuming he collects supper trays?"

"He don' collect no nothin'," she said.

"Well, then," I said curiosity getting the better of me, "I suppose that you had best inform me."

She glared at me. "After Mr. Burton, Robert the boss a this house, so you bes' mind him."

"Surely he doesn't have charge over Mrs. Burton?" I asked.

"Mrs. Burton don' do a thing without askin' me first," she said. "Ed and me was here before Robert."

As I took the second piece of bread that she handed me, I remembered the carriage driver. "Is Ed your husband?" I asked, more to make conversation than out of a need to know.

"Ed my baby brother," she said.

Her baby brother? How old was she? As though to answer my question, she said, "We both been here with Mr. and Mrs. Burton since they buy us, but we free now. We's here a long time."

I asked if the Burtons had children.

"One boy. They bury him back when the yellow fever comes through, back in '93." She looked at me and asked, "That before you was born?" Caught unaware, I didn't respond, so she asked another question. "Where was you born?"

I worried that I might say the wrong thing. "I prefer not to talk about myself," I said. Having finished the meal, I rose to take my leave, then remembered my manners. "That was an excellent supper," I said. "Thank you, Delia."

"That be Miss Delia," she said, and then went silent.

Fortunately, Ed soon came through with my pallet, and I followed him to my room. After he left, I sat down on the straw-filled mattress and looked around, dazed to find myself in this position. Until recently, I had known only luxury. Grandmother had raised me to be a gentleman, to have my own land and my own servants. Now I was sleeping in a storage room. What would Grandmother think to see me here? It had been weeks now, but still my heart clenched whenever I remembered that she was gone.

Fully clothed, I lay back on the pallet. Unexpectedly, exhaustion won out, and I fell asleep.

In the first months I served as an errand boy for Mr. Burton, picking up supplies and making deliveries. Gradually, the turmoil of the streets affected me less, and as I got to know the layout of the city, I grew more confident. If I earned a penny or two from a satisfied customer, I offered the coins to Mr. Burton on my return to the shop. When he assured me that those were mine to keep, I stored them eagerly.

When I wasn't out on deliveries, I was given the task of cleaning the three rooms of Mr. Burton's shop. Naturally, there was the storefront, where the glass cases and open shelves displayed some of the finest silver pieces, but Mr. Burton was as particular about his small office and the large room to the back where he and Nicholas, another silversmith, did their silver work.

Before I was introduced to Nicholas, Mr. Burton took me aside. "You should know that Nicholas has his peculiarities," he said.

"Yes, sir," I answered, wondering if he thought I had some of my own.

"He talks without thinking—that is, he seems incapable of censoring his thoughts. He has been like this from the beginning, but he means no harm."

Forewarned, I went with him to meet Nicholas, who was hard at work in the back room. The tall heavyset man paused only a moment when we were introduced, then twice slammed a hammer against a silver ingot. The muscles on his huge forearm bulged with the effort, and when he stepped back, he pulled a rag from under his leather apron to wipe dry his forehead as he considered me.

"You got an odd look about you with that funny eye," Nicholas said by way of greeting. I had been born with a useless left eye cloaked with a white film, but until recently, I had given it little thought. During my childhood, those around me seldom, if ever, made note of it, but since my flight, its oddity had been pointed out more than once, and its mention now made me shift uncomfortably.

"Well, I did warn you," Mr. Burton said after we left the room. "Fortunately, he does not aspire to a business of his own, as his forthright comments are ill suited to customers." He chuckled. "Oh well, it is my good luck that he wants only to be left alone to work at his craft, for he is the true artisan here." As proof of his words, he pointed out Nicholas's most recent work, an elegantly shaped teapot that even I, with no training, could appreciate.

"But here is how we make our real money," he said, opening two oversize drawers filled with silver pieces. "We supply these to fur trading posts for barter with the Indians." He invited me to examine the rings, wristbands, and round silver cloak brooches.

"Indians buy these?" I asked, excited at this news.

"Well, the fur traders buy them from me and offer these silver pieces as trade for pelts. The Indians wear them, particularly the men. There is a great demand for silver, and these are simple enough to make, but we can hardly keep up."

"Is it all right if I touch them?" I asked, and with his permission, I rifled through. I slipped a ring on my finger and moved my hand about in the air to better see the sparkle of the silver. "Will you show me how to make these?" I asked eagerly, but when he was slow to answer, I noted in surprise his moist eyes. "I'm sorry," I said, quickly slipping off the ring.

"No. No. You've done nothing wrong. It was the way you spoke just now. It was your excitement, you see. I had a son—you reminded me of him just then," he explained while using his knuckle to dab at a lone tear. "In answer to your question, yes, you will learn to make the rings, but you must be patient."

And so I was, dutifully carrying out my chores until a few weeks later, when Mr. Burton called me into his office. He sat at his large rolltop oak desk and had me take a seat across from him before he presented me with a document.

"James, I would like you to read this over and consider it carefully. If you sign, you are agreeing to be my apprentice. While I train you as a silversmith, I will continue to provide you with room and board. You will be with me for seven years, but I am hoping that with your artistic talent you will be established well before then."

"I don't need to read this. I will sign it," I said quickly, and handed back the paper.

"No, young man," he said, giving it back to me. "You must always read through anything before you sign your name. Your signature is the same as giving your word, and keeping your word is the mark of a man's character. In the end, it is the most valuable thing a man possesses."

His words cut deep. He had asked a few times about my past, and each time I led him to believe that I was orphaned, with no living relatives. Not only was I deeply grateful to him for having taken me into his home, I also respected this ethical man and I wanted only to tell him the truth. But I was too afraid. I avoided his eyes when I took the paper from him again and hoped he didn't see how my hand shook when I signed the document as James Smith.

ALTHOUGH MY DAY still included making deliveries, I now was given the opportunity to assist Nicholas in the back room. Initially, I only worked the bellows for the forge, and though my arms grew tired, I found it fascinating to watch the silver coin melt and harden again after it was poured into molds. But it was when Nicholas reheated the ingots and hammered the silver into shape that the artistry began. He did it with such skill that he made the craft look easy. When he finally relented and helped me craft my first silver spoon, I was unprepared for the physical stamina required. After the ingot was heated, it took both strength and dexterity to secure the malleable silver with tongs and then hammer it flat against the anvil. My arm was already sore when we placed the flattened silver over the mold, and when Nicholas handed me yet another hammer, I rubbed my shoulder. "Doesn't your arm get tired?" I asked.

"Nope."

"Mine does," I said, moving my shoulder up and down, expecting Nicholas to suggest I take a break.

But Nicholas was not like my grandmother, who had pampered me. Instead he dismissed my complaint with a grunt and nodded for me to continue until the silver began to take shape.

"Now, you got to use a light touch," Nicholas said, finally handing over a small hammer required to complete the finishing. Mr. Burton came in just then, and as I tapped away, he asked what I was doing.

"I'm doing the planishing," I said, quick to use the correct terminology, and when I saw Mr. Burton's approval, I forgot about my shoulder pain.

My admiration and appreciation for the man had grown each day, and my one objective was now to please him. True, I wanted to learn the craft, but more, I wanted Mr. Burton's good opinion of me, and because of it, I dedicated myself to learning. Likely because of my artist's hand and eye, the iron punches, chisels, and saws soon grew as comfortable in my hands as my whittling knife, and when Mr. Burton recognized and congratulated me on each progressive step, I was as pleased with myself as I had ever been.

Would that my transition into the Burton household had been as simple.

DELIA'S MEALS WERE of good quality and served to me in the kitchen, where I always ate alone, which suited me. One day when I saw the table set for three, indicating that I was to sit down with Delia and Ed, I said that I would take my meal to my room.

"Who that boy think he is?" I heard Delia ask her brother as I carried my food down the corridor. "He act high and mighty as that Robert!" she added more quietly. Curious, I stopped outside my door to listen for more.

"Now, Del, the boy white," Ed answered. "You know they don' eat with no colored folk."

"Well, for sure he act white, but he hidin' something, that much I know. He don' say nothin' 'bout where he come from or who his family be. He hidin' somethin'," she repeated.

"Del!" Ed said. "Even if that true, that his business."

"It my business to watch out for this house, and for sure it my business to care for Mr. and Mrs. Burton. I tell you, that boy hidin' somethin'."

Her insight terrified me, and from then on I was especially wary when fielding her questions.

"What you got in there?" she asked one morning, making note of my leather satchel that I carried with me each day to work.

"My personal things," I said, gripping tight my bag that contained Grandmother's jewelry. Mr. Burton had noted it as well, but with him I was more forthcoming and told him that it held some of my grandmother's things. He did not question me further and in fact provided me with a safe cupboard to store it in while I was at the shop.

"'My personal things!'" Delia repeated, mimicking my voice, and though I wanted to hit her, I pretended not to mind.

I was grateful that her brother left me to myself as he went about his business of running the stables and seeing to the gardens, and if we shared an exchange, he always spoke to me with deference, a behavior that I was accustomed to.

But then there was Robert.

BEFORE I MET him, Delia made it clear that though he ran the household, the two of them did not see eye to eye, and from the beginning I supposed it was because she resented the authority of a white man in her kitchen. One evening some days after my arrival, I met the man when he made an unexpected appearance just as I was finishing my meal.

"Yes?" I asked, setting aside my fork and knife.

"I am Robert," he said, speaking with a slight clipped English accent that I was to learn came as a result of his five years of butler training in London. "Might we have a word after you finish dining?"

This was Robert! He was not a white man, as I had assumed, but an impeccably dressed, carefully groomed, and well-spoken Negro. What would Grandmother have thought!

After I swallowed my surprise, I folded my napkin alongside my plate. "I am available now," I said, taking note of his starched white shirt and the spotless white apron tied around the waist of his dark trousers.

Delia, heating water for washing dishes, shot me a satisfied glance before she looked to Robert with a slight smile. She hesitated after he suggested she go upstairs to see to Mrs. Burton, but she reluctantly did so while he waited patiently for her to leave.

"I'll be in the pantry," he said, speaking in a way that left no doubt he was used to issuing orders. Irritated at being directed by a servant, I took my time to follow.

I found him seated behind a desk in a room off the kitchen, working figures in an open ledger. His tall, thin frame sat erect, and his long narrow feet, bound in shoes of black leather and polished to a high luster, set flat on the brick floor. It was difficult to assess his age, though when he looked up at me, I guessed him to be perhaps in his mid-thirties.

"Please sit." With his index finger, he indicated another chair across the table from himself. I declined to sit, stating a preference to remain standing. "As you wish," he said.

"How may I help you?" I asked, irritated by his assuming demeanor.

"As you might know, I am butler of this house," he said.

"Yes," I said.

"You understand, then, that I am responsible to speak to you about any household issues that arise?"

I could not imagine what he was referring to. I waited until, with only silence between us, I was forced to speak. "Go on," I said.

"I understand that you have been leaving out your coat and boots for Delia to clean."

"I have," I said. "That is the duty of a servant, is it not?"

"You are correct in believing that it is what one might expect from one's servant. However, Delia is not your servant. When you live below stairs, as they say in England, you are considered one of the staff."

"One of the staff?" I was outraged. It was true that I was lodging in servants' quarters, but surely I wasn't considered one of them. They were Negroes!

"Yes, one of the staff. You are expected to look out for your own outer garments and your boots. Of course, you may expect Delia to continue to do laundry for you, as she does for the rest of the household."

"I see," I said, and finding no rebuttal, I made a quick exit.

I found it almost impossible to settle that night. True, I was angry that this black man thought of me as a servant, but what also disturbed me was the forceful yet eloquent way he had spoken. I had never seen the like. His sophisticated conduct, educated speech, and overall deportment belied everything Grandmother had taught me about the Negro's limited capabilities.

SUNDAY WAS A day I had to myself. On those mornings Mr. Burton attended church services, and I generally took that day to stroll about town, but one Sunday morning in November I remained in bed, feeling under the weather with a cold. I heard Ed bring around the carriage for Mr. Burton and listened as the horses clomped away. I meant to rise then, but the weather outside had turned wintry, and I decided to lay abed a while longer. I suppose I dozed, for I was startled awake by cries for help from Delia. I hesitated to respond, for it was Delia, after all, yet her call sounded so urgent that I yanked my trousers on over my nightshirt and rushed from my room.

"Upstairs!" Delia called when she saw me. "Come! Upstairs!"

Expecting a house fire or a similar emergency, I followed as she hurried up the back stairs. There, in the hallway, light from a large fan window above the oversize front door streamed onto a chair where an older woman sat. She appeared to be struggling to breathe, but when I rushed to her side, she used her lace-edged handkerchief to wave me toward the dining room door. It was then I realized that though she was struggling for air, she was also laughing.

"Come, come," Delia called to me from the door to the dining room, and as she opened it, she pushed me through. No sooner did the door close behind me than a large white bird swooped past in a dive toward the dining room table. A feather duster slammed out from under it, further inciting the bird, and with a screech the bird dove in again. To my amazement, I saw Robert under the table, wedged in between chairs and hitting out with the duster in an attempt to protect himself.

"Throw the duster away," I called to him.

"But I need it!" he called back.

"Throw it away," I repeated. "The bird thinks that it's another bird attacking him."

The cleaning tool flew by me and crashed against the wall. As the white bird lit on it, I slid back two of the chairs. "Get out while he's distracted," I said.

Needing no further encouragement, Robert scrambled up and out the door, leaving me alone to face the bird. But I was more fascinated than frightened by this beautiful creature. Seeing bread on the table I made my way over to it and then sat quietly. When the bird took note of me, he flew over to perch on a neighboring chair. "Here," I said soothingly, and fed him a chunk of bread. He continued to squawk and complain, but his crest of bright red-orange plumes was no longer at full tilt, and I was fairly certain that meant he was calming down. Suddenly, he flapped onto my shoulder and, between bites of bread, began to gently nibble on my ear. Instinctively, I knew it to be a caress.

There was a soft rap on the door. "Hello! Are you alive in there?" a voice called.

"We are," I called back.

"I'm coming in," the woman announced, then slipped into the room. I rose from my chair, for I correctly guessed this to be Mrs. Burton.

She hobbled over to the chair nearest me, and with the bird still on my shoulder, I received the canes that she handed me before she sat down to regulate her breathing. She was a short, heavyset woman with a snub nose and a round pleasant face. Her gray morning dress, the exact color of her braided hair, did nothing for her gray pallor. "Sit," she instructed, and I did so. "You must be James Smith, my husband's new apprentice."

"I am," I said.

The bird squawked for her attention. She laughed and waved her finger at him. "Oh, Malcolm. You are a naughty boy, flying away from me like that!" She chuckled. "Oh my, I haven't laughed like that since I can remember. Poor Robert. I don't know why he is so afraid of this bird!" She dabbed at her eyes as she began to laugh again. Her merriment was so appealing that I began to laugh, too.

"What happened when you got in here?" she asked, and I described what I had seen of the bird's attack on the feather duster.

"Under the table? Oh, stop! " she said, laughing and gasping as she clutched my arm. "I cannot breathe as it is."

"Naughty boy! Naughty boy!" Malcolm offered. At that we both whooped, and that was how Mr. Burton found us when he opened the door.

"What is going on?" he asked, appearing bewildered to see me with Mrs. Burton.

"Oh, Mr. Burton!" His wife sighed, drying her eyes. "If only you had been here."

He came forward to kiss the top of his wife's head. "It is good to hear you laugh," he said to her, and smiled at me in thanks.

I rose to leave, but Mrs. Burton reached for my arm. "No, no, you must stay," she said. "Please stay. Come, husband, sit with us while we tell you."

"Could we have some tea while you do so?" Mr. Burton asked, stepping to the fireplace and rubbing his hands together. "It is cold and I am chilled."

I stood quickly. "I will go to the kitchen for it," I offered.

"Have Delia send up a pot of hot water and some cups. I have the tea caddy up here," Mrs. Burton said, nodding toward the sideboard. "And don't forget to have her include a cup for yourself."

I felt lighthearted when I left the room, but I sobered myself before I got to the kitchen. I had concern that Robert would be embarrassed and possibly angry at my having witnessed his altercation with the bird, but to my surprise, he greeted me as the conquering hero. Not so Delia. As Robert sang my praises, her face puckered in annoyance, and when she heard of Mrs. Burton's request that I join her for tea, Delia looked at me in disbelief.

"You sure she mean that you go back up?" she asked.

"Yes," I said, trying to curb my anger. "She said that you were to include a cup for me."

Delia clucked her tongue and shook her head. Her dislike of me only grew with each new encounter.

"And why should he not join them?" Robert said, addressing Delia. "They both need a distraction, Mrs. Burton in particular. A new face will be good for her." Then he noted my nightshirt. "But go," he said, "and dress yourself more appropriately."

So while Delia put together the tray, I went for a shirt and jacket. When I reappeared, Delia's look was so disapproving that when she carried the tray up, I kept a good distance behind her.

In the dining room, after Delia set out the cups and was then dismissed, Mrs. Burton waved me to the sideboard. "Bring the caddy and the sugar canister to me, would you, please?"

I recognized the silver sugar canister but was uncertain what held the tea.

"It is the wooden pear," she said, pointing to the small polished box, cut in the perfect shape of a pear.

"How pretty," I said as I brought it to her.

"Yes, isn't it?" she answered, smiling up at me, and I smiled back. I felt at ease with her. The way she looked at me reminded me of my grandmother.

The tea caddy was beautiful. "What kind of wood is it?" I asked, rubbing my finger over the polished dark grain.

"I believe it is rosewood," she said.

"Rosewood?" I asked.

Mr. Burton, who had taken a seat at the table, joined in. "It is a wood found in the tropics," he said. Addressing his wife, he went on. "This young man is quite gifted with drawing and also has a talent for carving."

"You do?" she asked, taking the pear-shaped box from me. "Perhaps I could see some of your work."

I flushed with the unexpected attention and stood silently by as Mrs. Burton fingered the chatelaine at her waist until she found the right key to unlock the tea caddy. Then, after carefully measuring out what was needed of the aromatic black leaves, she locked the box again and had me return the caddy to its place on the sideboard.

Mrs. Burton tapped at the chair next to her, and I sat. "Mr. Burton tells me that you are a quick study."

I glanced over at my employer. "I like the work very much," I said.

Malcolm squawked and Mrs. Burton turned to her husband. "Could I ask you to return Malcolm to his room? He has had something to eat, and I don't want to have to ask Robert to clean up after his enemy."

"Oh my!" Mr. Burton rose quickly. He held out his arm and spoke with authority. "Come on, you naughty boy. You've created enough of a stir for one day."

"Naughty boy. Naughty boy," Malcolm said to the room on his departure, causing another round of laughter.

As soon as her husband was out of the room, Mrs. Burton turned to me. "So, tell me now, do you genuinely enjoy your work?"

I answered her honestly. "Oh yes!" I said, but then became concerned. "Does Mr. Burton have a complaint?"

"Not at all," she said, giving me a smile.

I sighed in relief and again returned her smile. "I am relieved to know that."

"Malcolm certainly took to you," she said. "You like birds, I take it?"

"I do," I said. "I have been interested in them all of my life."

"When did this interest begin?" she asked.

"It began when I was a child and was given a book that had beautiful illustrations of birds. After I taught myself to copy their likenesses from the book, I spent hours and hours at the window, drawing birds that nested outside in our trees."

"Why did you not go outdoors?" she asked. "Were you ill?"

"No, I was in good health, but my grandmother needed me at her side," I said. "When she was very ill, I would draw and I could forget everything around me."

While Mrs. Burton checked the readiness of the tea, I looked around, and for the first time since my arrival in Philadelphia, I felt a stirring of content. This room reminded me of home—of Tall Oaks—with the high ceilings, the vibrant green walls, the tall windows draped in gold velvet, and the long polished dining table and sideboard. An attractive portrait of a young Mrs. Burton hung over the mantel, and on the opposite wall was a portrait of Mr. Burton, painted when he had a full head of hair.

"Were we not a handsome couple?" she asked, seeing my interest.

"You were very beautiful, but it is odd to see Mr. Burton with all of that hair," I said.

She laughed aloud.

"That was unkind," I said, feeling my face grow hot.

"It would have been insensitive if he were here to have heard it," she said, "but I see no need for either of us to repeat it."

"Thank you," I said. "Mr. Burton has been very kind to me."

"And how is it that you came to Philadelphia?" she asked. "Where is your family?"

My heart began to pound. When I was a child and Grandmother's hysteria frightened me, I learned to calm myself by quietly counting each finger before interlocking my hands. Now I did the same until, hands folded, I answered Mrs. Burton. "I am alone," I said. "My mother—that is, my grandmother—died."

"And your parents?"

I looked away. "They are both dead," I lied. "My grandmother raised me."

"I see," she said. "And was your grandmother's death recent?"

"Yes. There was a fire."

"In her home?"

"Yes. In our home. We had a farm."

"How unspeakably sad for you!" she said softly. My eyes stung from her unexpected words of empathy. How tempted I was to tell her the truth.

"And you were left destitute?"

"I have Grandmother's jewelry," I said. "But I don't want to sell it." I hung my head and mumbled, "It is all that I have left of her."

"I understand, dear boy. I lost my only son seventeen years ago, but his room stands as he left it. Even now, the loss is difficult for me to talk about."

Until this moment, no one had acknowledged my grief, and her words touched me deeply. Not only did she understand, but she had suffered the same. My attachment to Mrs. Burton began that day.

* * *

I WANTED TO see Mrs. Burton again. I had a plan. At work on Monday morning, I asked Nicholas for help in locating a paper and art supply store. He knew of such a place, and in the afternoon, with Mr. Burton's approval and coins in my pocket, I went out to find it.

I had not imagined a shop as wonderful as this. I had never seen embossed paint cakes sold for watercolor; nor had I ever imagined such an assortment of brushes and paper. A clerk helped me select what I required, and I was so excited on my return to the silver shop that I found it difficult to focus on the silver polishing that Nicholas had set out for me to do.

That evening I ate quickly, then, as usual, went off to my room. I worked late into the night and did so every night throughout the week. By Saturday evening I was satisfied, and on Sunday morning, after Mr. Burton left for church, I rolled up the small watercolor of Malcolm and gave it to Robert, asking that he give it to Mrs. Burton.

He eyed the roll with some curiosity, but he acted on my request. Later, as I had hoped, Robert returned with an invitation for me to join Mrs. Burton in what was known as Malcolm's room.

FROM THE KITCHEN I followed Robert up to a second flight of stairs to the third floor and there to a large and open landing. As we walked down the long hallway, past Mr. and Mrs. Burton's bedrooms, I noted a handsome tall-case clock. I had never seen one but had read of the pendulum workings, and I paused at the shining black walnut case, intrigued by the loud click-clock sound it made. When the machine suddenly bonged, I yelped in surprise, startling Robert. He gave me a sour look, for he was already on edge, having earlier voiced his concern about Malcolm being safely ensconced in his cage.

After Robert knocked on one of the doors, he gave me a look of relief when I offered to enter before him.

"Hello again, young man." Mrs. Burton welcomed me from a chair that sat next to the fireplace.

"Greetings!" Malcolm interrupted in a perfect imitation of Robert's voice. "I say, greetings!"

Robert gave a nervous glance, but Malcolm was in his large white metal cage.

Malcolm grew louder: "Greetings! Greetings!"

"You had best say hello to him. He won't stop until you do," Mrs. Burton said to me. "Robert, you go ahead. I'll ring if I need you," she instructed.

I was as intrigued by the bird as before, but when I reached my hand in to stroke his feathers, he put his beak around one of my fingers. "Careful," I said, lowering my tone. He held it, though he did not bite down. "Naughty bird," I said, and when he released me to repeat the phrase, I laughed aloud.

"Bring him out if you like," my hostess instructed.

Malcolm danced nervously while I worked to undo the enormous latch.

"Offer him your arm," Mrs. Burton said, and when I did, the bird hopped on. As I made my way over to her, Malcolm climbed up my arm to sit on my shoulder and there took hold of my earlobe.

"Ehhh," I warned in a low voice.

"Ehhh," he repeated to me, and when I laughed, he mimicked that, too.

I glanced to see if Mrs. Burton was enjoying this as much as I, and though she smiled, she appeared to have something else on her mind. She pointed to a red velvet wingback. "Come sit with me," she invited. When I did so, the bird flew up to a perch that swung in front of a window. "You have a remarkable understanding of him."

"He is beautiful," I said, settling myself into the chair.

"He belonged to my son," she said.

"Did Malcolm miss him after he . . ." I stopped myself, wondering if I should have brought up such a painful topic.

"When Gerard passed, Malcolm was as upset as I was. He wouldn't eat for days, and he didn't speak for months. For me, it was almost a consolation to see him so lost—he was as devastated as I," she said. As she spoke, the bird flew back and lit on my shoulder to nuzzle my ear with his beak.

She dabbed at tears. "Forgive me," she said. "It touches me to see him respond to you in this way. He was never the same after we lost Gerard, and he has been something of a problem for us, but I couldn't let go of him. Now, seeing him with you—well—this is how he behaved with Gerard."

"I don't want to make you cry," I said. "Should I put him away?"

"No! No, I've finished with my tears," she said, then blew her nose and gave me a tender look. "Thank you for being so thoughtful, though. Your grandmother certainly raised you well. May I call you James?" she asked.

"Or Jamie," I suggested.

"Is it the name your grandmother used for you?"

I nodded, afraid to speak.

Her voice was soft. "Well, then, I will call you Jamie." She studied me as though gauging my sensitivity about the upcoming subject. "Jamie, I have a personal question for you. It is about your eyes."

"Yes?" I asked, looking at her warily. Recently, with others noting it, I had become sensitive to the subject.

"Does your good eye pain you when you paint? That is to say, do you feel that you put a strain on it?"

"No," I said, "It doesn't bother me."

"Good," she said, "I was hoping for that. Pertaining to your affected eye, might I have a suggestion?"

"Yes," I said again.

"My husband has a friend, one who, in his youth, lost an eye. He wears a black patch to cover it, and I must say that all of the ladies considered it quite dashing. I was wondering if you would care to have something similar fashioned for you."

"Well, yes. I would give it a try."

"That is settled, then." She looked down at my painting in her lap. "Jamie," she said, "this is one of the best representations of a salmon-crested cockatoo that I have ever seen."

"I did the best I could from memory."

"It is so fine that I will have it framed. Have you ever considered attending some art classes?"

"Grandmother often spoke of it," I said. "But now . . ."

She smiled. "Well, dear, your grandmother was right. You have a God-given talent. We must have it developed."

Malcolm, seeking attention, gave a human chortle so true that he startled us both. We looked at each other and giggled, then burst out laughing when Malcolm repeated himself. "Oh dear!" Mrs. Burton said, drying her eyes, and then smiling at me. "You have no idea how good it is to laugh again."

But I did. I did! I had not laughed since Grandmother's death; nor had I felt this comfortable with another since fleeing my home. I liked and admired Mr. Burton for the man he was, but Mrs. Burton represented all I had lost with Grandmother, and I only wanted more.

THE FOLLOWING SUNDAY I was invited to join the Burtons for their Sunday dinner and there was no want of conversation. As soon as Robert served the soup, my host and hostess began to entertain me with stories of their earlier life.

Before their son was born, they had traveled to the West.

"She was fearless," Mr. Burton said of his wife. "You should have seen her. She rode—"

"I rode astride the horse," she interrupted. "If my parents had seen me! No sidesaddles were to be found. What freedom!" When she giggled like a young girl, I noticed Mr. Burton and Robert exchanging a smile. "Do you remember what I wore, Mr. Burton?" she asked.

"How could I forget? You wore my trousers!" he exclaimed, then addressed me. "I will never forget the sight of my young wife flying through the tall grass on that spotted Indian pony."

"It was brown and white and went like the wind!"

Mr. Burton beamed as his wife came to life, while I moved to the edge of my chair. "Was it a true Indian pony?" I asked.

Mr. Burton nodded. "It was given to her by the Indians."

"You actually met Indians?" They assured me they had, and my eager questions tumbled out, making our meal such a success that I was invited back.

The Burtons had lived a full life and became enlivened when they relived their stories. I was enthralled, not having imagined such lives of adventure, and I was filled with questions. Soon our Sunday dinners became routine. Increasingly, Mrs. Burton began to note aloud how similar some of my habits were to her son.

"Look, dear, how Jamie folds his hands when he speaks. That's exactly what Gerard always did, don't you remember?"

In the beginning Mr. Burton only nodded in reply, but gradually, he, too, made like references. With each mention I felt more included and, hungry for family, utilized every behavior to foster more of the same.

In time Mrs. Burton voiced concern that my room downstairs was too small, and though I assured her that it was fine, it was a happy surprise when, in spring of the following year, Mr. and Mrs. Burton announced that I was to move to their son's quarters on the fourth floor.

DELIA WAS OUTRAGED when she saw Robert assisting me with the move, and she didn't hold back. "This not right! What they doin' puttin' you in their boy's room?" she said.

"Delia!" Robert stopped her. "You should be pleased that Mrs. Burton has finally cleared out Gerard's room. Why shouldn't James take it over?"

From the kitchen, we carried my few belongings up three flights of stairs to reach the fourth floor. I had never been to this top story of the house, and as Robert led me down the long corridor, I glanced into some of the rooms that once served as the nursery and servants' quarters. Most of them were small and stood empty, though Gerard's room, at the end of the hallway, was spacious. The ceiling was low, but four dormers provided plenty of light. While the white-painted room retained the furnishings of a well-appointed bedroom, Gerard's personal belongings had been removed, and the space felt oddly empty and abandoned.

I began to have second thoughts about the move. "Robert, I don't know if I should do this."

"You must think of the Burtons," he said, straightening the blue coverlet on the bed. "You have brought happiness to this household again. They are doing this to please you, and opportunities such as this don't come often to people such as oursel—" He stopped himself. "I am always here to help you," he added before he quickly left.

I stared after him. Did he mean to say "ourselves"? What could he have meant?

I shook off the question and perched on the edge of the bed to look about. It was the quiet that struck me; this far away from everyone, the silence felt lonely. I looked across the room at the fine dressing table and the oak desk, and then I spied the large chest-on-chest. Although others might have appreciated the beauty of the burled walnut or the nine spacious drawers, for me it offered something much more precious. The bottom drawer held a lock and a key! Finally, I had a place to keep safe my belongings from Delia's prying eyes.

CHAPTER ELEVEN

1810–1812

James

FOLLOWING MY MOVE upstairs to Gerard's quarters, I came to dread the night. I had difficulty falling asleep, and when I did, nightmares were so vivid that I often woke myself calling out. Afraid to go back to sleep, I sat up late into the night, but in that state of fatigue, memories that I fought off during the day more easily broke through.

I was eight years old when, for the first time, I realized how Marshall hated me. It was a pleasant June day, and our small household was outdoors, enjoying a picnic under the large oak that stood back from the big house. It was unusual for Mother—that is, Grandmother—to be outdoors, but her daughter-in-law, Marshall's wife, Lavinia, had convinced her to enjoy the pleasant weather.

At this early age, I was infatuated with Miss Lavinia. That day she leaned down to place a large book in my lap, and when I couldn't resist touching a strand of her red silky hair that brushed against my face, she smiled, took my hand, and kissed it. It was her gentleness that made the abuse she later suffered under Marshall so upsetting to me.

"Jamie dear," she said, "this is for you. I ordered it months ago for your birthday, but it has only just arrived."

I read the title aloud. "*The Illustration of Birds.*"

"How lovely, dear," Grandmother said to her as I opened the book to stare at the pages.

Miss Lavinia patted my head. "I've never known anyone to be so taken with birds as our dear Jamie."

"It's the perfect gift. I wish I had thought of it," said Grandmother.

"But Mother, I loved the watercolors you gave me," I said, quick to reassure her so as not to have her upset. She reached down to where I was seated next to her chair and pushed back a lock of my hair that had fallen on my forehead. "I would give you the world if I could," she said, looking deep into my eyes.

I smiled up at her and waited until she sat back. Only then did I dare turn my attention back to the book—the one that in time became my most treasured possession.

But the memory darkens with Marshall's sudden appearance. We seldom saw him, for he was away much of the time. A tall, imposing man, he wore a permanent frown, and if he had a pleasant word to say, I never heard it. Until my final year at Tall Oaks, the year I killed him, I mistakenly believed he was my brother, while to him I must have been a miserable reminder of his unnatural coupling with a Negro servant.

Lavinia stiffened on her husband's approach. Marshall's disapproving glance went straight to Sukey, Miss Lavinia's much loved servant, who sat on our blanket alongside her mistress.

"Get her up," he began. "Teach her to stand when I—"

"Please stand, Sukey," Miss Lavinia quickly instructed. The young Negro girl leaped to her feet.

Marshall turned toward his mother. "Wine so soon in the day, Mother?" he asked.

"It helps my nerves, dear," Grandmother said, but her voice quavered and I hated him for how he frightened her.

"Yes," he said, "I'm sure it does." When his look finally settled on me, it was with such loathing that I turned toward Grandmother. What had I done? Why did he hate me so?

"And what in God's name is he doing here?" he asked. When he took a step toward me, Grandmother reached for my arm, and though her fingers dug in, I was so frightened that I didn't object.

At once Lavinia was on her feet, shaking out her skirts and standing to obstruct Marshall's view of me. "Marshall, won't you join us? I'll have the children leave. Please stay and have some of our cake?"

We had been having such fun. I hated to hear the strain in her voice. I resolved again that when I was grown, I would send this miserable brother of mine away from the place.

"I don't eat with nigras!" Marshall spat out, and he glared at me with such vehemence that I shrank back. He left as quickly as he had come, but Grandmother's nerves were so affected that she needed to go back to her bedroom for a strong dose of laudanum.

I was always relieved when the medicine put her to sleep, for I dreaded the times when her nerves took over. Her terror frightened me. As everyone scurried about trying to calm her, I retreated into my own world with my pencils and paints. There I sketched and colored, imagining myself in a forest, while convincing myself that Grandmother's screams were nothing more than the cries of a foreign bird.

Now, as memories surfaced in the still of Gerard's room, I spent nights of agony wondering if Grandmother had cried out like that when she died in the fire.

Finally, one such night I remembered my paints, and from then on, when plagued by memory, I would throw myself from the bed to sketch and paint. The distraction was so calming that when sleep did come, I almost always dreamed I was a bird in flight, with the sun warming my back and a gentle breeze cradling me in the air.

ON THE EVE of my fifteenth birthday, in February 1812, I awoke suddenly in the night to find myself drenched from a night terror. As I changed my nightshirt, I remembered that it was my birthday, and with that thought I remembered other birthdays celebrated at Tall Oaks. As pleasant memories came, my heart constricted with homesickness.

I felt a tug of guilt, for on the night of my departure, I had promised to send a note to my family to let them know of my safe arrival. Until now I hadn't done so, for I had been too afraid. Henry had cautioned me repeatedly to cut all ties to home, insisting that patrollers would be on the lookout. To reinforce this, he told me stories of runaways who were caught and returned to their owners after many years of hiding out. Thus, I hadn't dared send a letter, fearing that somehow it might be traced back to the Burtons. However, I had learned recently that I could obtain a post office box in my name, and given that anonymity, I felt it safe to make contact.

But to whom should I write?

I thought back to the night of my flight—when Belle, the slave woman, handed me my jacket wherein she had sewn Grandmother's jewelry. Before I left, she had attempted an embrace and I'd quickly turned away, repulsed by the recent knowledge that she was my mother. These two years later, I still cringed at the thought.

No. I would write to Miss Lavinia. She was the one who had cared for me through the years, and it was she who tried to protect me from Marshall. And so I wrote:

Dear Miss Lavinia,

I am writing to let you know that I am well. I live in Philadelphia and I am an apprentice at a silver shop. The owner tells me I have a talent for the work and he has given me a place to stay in his home. I hope that you are well and send my kind regards.

After some indecision, I decided to sign off using my new name, James Smith.

In the morning I took the letter with me, and later in the day, while making a delivery for the silver shop, I went to the post office. There I spent some of my remaining money to arrange for a post office box before I mailed off the letter.

MRS. BURTON SUFFERED from respiratory problems, but her chief affliction was arthritis that badly affected her hips. On her difficult days, when she was bedridden, I would send her a flower or a small sketch I had done, trying to cheer her in the same way I had my grandmother. Her response was always joyful surprise, and I was encouraged to continue when Mr. Burton repeatedly told me what a happy difference those small gifts made to his wife.

After Mrs. Burton learned that I did not find her invalid status off-putting, she requested if I was available that I bring Malcolm to visit her in her bedchamber when she was confined to her bed.

I don't recall the first time we went to see her in her rooms, but it was on a winter's day, for I was concerned about the cold draft in the hallway and how it might affect Malcolm, who was prancing excitedly on my shoulder. When we reached her bedroom, I was relieved to find a blazing fire warming the tall-ceilinged room, and although her carved four-poster bed was oversize, the violet and green draperies added a pleasant cozy feel.

After Malcolm entertained Mrs. Burton, I found him a perch on a folding screen, and she invited me to sit in a chair beside the bed. On her bedside stand lay a book. "Would you like me to read to you?"

"Do you read well?" she asked guardedly.

"Yes, I do," I said with assurance, for I had read aloud to Grandmother from the age of seven.

She smiled. "I'm quite particular about the way someone reads, so you must not be offended if I stop you."

It was light women's fiction, I don't recall the name, but I read, enunciating carefully, as Grandmother had taught. When I stopped for a rest, Mrs. Burton sighed. "Jamie, I must tell you, you have a delightful way of reading."

"I read to Grandmother all the time," I said, and then, forgetting myself, I went on. "And sometimes in the evenings the servants would come and I would read to them, too."

"That must have been wonderful," she said.

"It was," I agreed.

"Did you have a large library?"

"Yes," I said, "but it all went with the fire." I had learned that when I mentioned the fire, her questions about my past would stop, for she knew the subject was upsetting to me. In the same way, I did not mention her son unless she began to reminisce, and then I only listened.

"Well, I hope that you are making use of our library," she said.

"No," I said. "I would not go uninvited."

"Young man, consider yourself invited."

"Thank you!" I said.

"Jamie," she said, reaching for my hand, "I want you to consider this your home."

The look in her eyes was one of true caring, and I resolved that soon I would tell her the truth about myself.

As TIME MOVED forward, I began to feel more and more at home. Then one night at supper, the Burtons had a disagreement; as the subject matter came to light, I grew uneasy. Their argument regarded a visit from a lawyer who had come to inform Mrs. Burton of her brother's death. Apparently, the man never married and had left a sizable Carolina plantation to Mrs. Burton. Although it might have been a boon, after some inspection, the place was discovered to be heavily mortgaged. It would have to be sold to pay off debt.

The Burtons agreed that the estate, which included a good number of slaves, should be sold through auction. Anticipating this, the brother had made a request in his will that Mrs. Burton take special care in placing two of the house servants, a mother and daughter, who had been with him for many years. The dispute between the Burtons arose when Mr. Burton questioned if they were not obligated to make room for these two in the household. Mrs. Burton disagreed and wanted to sell them with the others.

Until this time, the subject of slavery had not been discussed. Because Delia and her brother had been given their freedom, I had assumed that the Burtons held anti-slavery views. Now, to my shock, I learned otherwise.

Mrs. Burton turned to me. "James, you said that you were raised with servants. What became of them when your grandmother died?"

I looked at her, quite stunned. "They were all sold," I said. It was the first thought that came to mind, and though the lie came easily, I shifted uncomfortably. In fact, I had no idea what had happened to those at Tall Oaks after I left.

"And were you attached to any of them?" she asked.

"I . . . I suppose I was," I said. "But there were debts."

"You see, dear," said Mrs. Burton, turning back to her husband, "there are debts here as well! We must sell the lot and be done with it!"

"But do you not think it unfair to include the two of them in the sale?" Mr. Burton protested.

"Unfair? Unfair!" Mrs. Burton cried, startling me with her level of upset. "For the past thirty years, I have been unable to visit my only brother. He insisted on having that unhealthy and illegal union with a Negress, and if that were not enough, he added an offspring! Imagine! To leave behind a Negro daughter who lays claim to his blood! And now he expects me to decide the future of these two. I will not do it! I will not take responsibility where he did not. They will be sold with the others."

I was horrified to learn Mrs. Burton's true feelings and I fumbled with a weak excuse before I hastily left the table. I had come so close to disclosing my own truth. What if they were to find out about me? What might they do? Should I leave before that happened? But where could I go? What would I do to support myself? Now that I finally felt at home, my stomach turned at the thought of leaving.

That night I lay on my bed, overcome with indecision, but by morning I had convinced myself to stay, certain there was no way the Burtons could learn of my past.

My one concern was Delia, for her resentment intensified as the Burtons and I grew closer. I did not trust her, for one day after she returned some laundered shirts to my room, I noted that the sketches and paintbrushes on my desktop were in disarray. On closer inspection, I saw that my top desk drawer had also been gone through.

I religiously kept the key to the bottom drawer of the chest-on-chest with me in the pocket of my waistcoat, but her suspicions alarmed me: not only did that drawer keep safe the jewelry, it also secured the letter I had received from Lavinia at Tall Oaks—one I clung to yet knew I should destroy.

Almost two months after I had posted the letter to Tall Oaks, a reply came. Although I had told myself not to expect a response, I found myself stopping at the post office whenever passing by on an errand. The day I received the letter, I was so stunned that I treated it like a hot coal and pocketed it quickly before hurrying back to the shop. For the remainder of the day, it burned against my chest. That evening, on our arrival home, I meant to go to my room to get cleaned up as usual before our meal, and there planned to read the letter, but Robert met us at the door. "Mrs. Burton had a difficult day and would like you to join her for an early supper."

"Of course, of course," agreed Mr. Burton, and since I had no ready excuse, I followed him to her quarters.

In spite of her confinement, or perhaps because of it, Mrs. Burton was in a talkative mood. I hid my distress when, after the meal, she asked that I bring Malcolm to her. The bird was overexcited, and for the first time I reprimanded him when he playfully nipped at my ear.

"Was your day difficult, dear?" Mrs. Burton asked when she sensed my irritable mood.

"No, it was fine," I answered abruptly, then checked myself. "I didn't sleep well last night," I offered as an excuse.

"Then you must have a good rest tonight. Take Malcolm back to his room and later go to Delia for a warm cup of milk before you retire. That always works well for me."

I thanked her, and when I leaned over to give her cheek my customary kiss for the night, I never felt such a traitor.

Once in my room I sat for a long time, fingering the letter and not daring to break the seal. When I finally did, I held my breath as I read the response that had come from both Miss Lavinia and Belle.

Dear James,

It is difficult to express how happy we were to learn of your safety. Countless times we've worried over you. How I wish I had the opportunity to speak with you before you left. I can only imagine your shock in learning the truth about your mother, and I regret my part in the deceit. If the need ever arises for you to have papers drawn up to verify your freedom, you must let me know.

I convinced your mother that you would like to hear from her and her note is included below.

If it is safe, please let us hear from you again.

Lavinia

My legs had gone weak and I sat down at the desk to read on:

Jamie,

Thank you for letting us know that you got there safe. You don't say in your letter that you is living white but I hope that you is.

I live with Miss Lavinia. The big house got built again and the farm we work is horses not tobacco.

Belle

I went to the fireplace, meaning to destroy the letter, but I could not let go of it. I read the words over and over until I was sobbing. Here was proof that there were people who cared about me. I did have a home, I just dared not return to it.

CHAPTER TWELVE

1814

James

OVER THE NEXT two years, I devoted myself to the Burtons. I applied myself so diligently at work that by my seventeenth birthday, Nicholas had me working on assignments consigned by some of our wealthiest customers. In the evenings, often over supper, Mr. Burton did not hold back his praise, and I basked in his approval. Mrs. Burton was ever warmer toward me, and though I did not forget her revealing words, her devotion was such that I could almost convince myself her feelings for me would not change should she learn the truth about me.

One morning a few weeks into my seventeenth year, in March 1814, I was informed by Mrs. Burton that at the end of the month, there was to be a celebratory evening dinner and I was expected to attend.

"Mr. Burton and I have an announcement to make," she said, "and we are having our friends in to celebrate."

I was surprised to hear of the social gathering, as the Burtons were solitary people, but when I asked to know more, I found Mrs. Burton unusually secretive. "It is to be a formal occasion, and everyone shall be in full dress. With Robert at the helm, we shall have a celebration that will rival any we have ever had!" She smiled at me. "And that, dear boy, is enough for you to know."

I was silent as I thought it over.

"Jamie?" she asked. "I know that look. You have a question?"

"I don't believe that I have suitable dress," I said.

She smiled. "And that is why I've arranged for you to visit Mr. Burton's tailor. You must consider it our treat." Thus, two days later, I went for my first fitting of formal attire.

IN THE DAYS before the celebration, a cleaning service was hired and strictly supervised by Robert, who saw to it that each room was scoured from top to bottom. Silver and china were taken from storage to be cleaned, even the chandeliers were lowered and washed. Additional servants were brought in, and the Burtons decided that in spite of Delia's upset, Robert was right to bring in another cook to preside over the kitchen for the elaborate meal.

Because of Mrs. Burton's hints that the evening had something to do with me, I began to think that it might be about my apprenticeship. Although Mr. Burton had recently suggested that I might soon be drawing wages, we had never formally discussed my future with his business. The more I thought about it, the more I wondered if this might be an occasion where he would offer me a position in his company. More than anything, I wanted to continue to work for him, though I worried that given a salary, I might be expected to live independently. How I dreaded the idea of leaving this home.

I had already begun to dress myself for the evening when there was a rap at my door.

"I have come to assist you," Robert announced formally.

"To assist me?" I asked.

"Yes, I have been sent by Mrs. Burton."

"How kind of her," I said. "But you have so much to do. Are you not needed elsewhere?"

"I am happy to be of service to you this evening," he said, as professional as ever.

"I appreciate your offer, Robert, but I believe that I have everything I need."

Robert studied my long black pants, which hooked down under my new polished black shoes. "This style suits your figure well," he said.

"Do you think so?" I asked. "I hope that Mrs. Burton approves."

"I am certain she will."

I looked back at the bed, where I had laid out my new silk waistcoat and dark blue jacket. Beside it was a crisp white cravat. The tailor had schooled me in the tying of it and I hoped I remembered the correct knot. "Actually, Robert," I said, going over to the bed and lifting up the cravat, "now that I think of it, I would appreciate a hand with tying this."

"What style were you considering?" he asked.

"What would you suggest?"

Robert didn't hesitate. "For this evening a Maharatta tie would do well." He placed the starched linen fabric to the back of my neck, brought the ends forward to join them as a chain link, and expertly fastened the remainder of the cloth in the back. As he helped me with my waistcoat, he voiced admiration of the embroidered blue flowers that dotted the ivory silk. When my jacket was in place, he tugged the tails straight and gave it a quick brush.

I slipped on the black silk eye patch that the tailor had designed to fit as flawlessly as a well-made glove, then I turned to Robert for his appraisal. "What do you think?" I asked.

Robert looked me up and down, then gave a rare smile. "It is a handsome look," he said. "Mr. and Mrs. Burton will be pleased."

"Do you think so, Robert?" I asked again.

He nodded. "I do," he said, then gave my shoulders a last quick brush before he held open the door.

THE DRAWING ROOM, just off the dining room, was already filled with guests when I entered. Mr. and Mrs. Burton were waiting for me, and together they took me on rounds to greet everyone. I already knew Nicholas and his wife and had met the family lawyer a number of times, but this evening I was introduced to his attractive young niece, a Miss Grewen.

When Robert opened the doors of the dining room to announce dinner, there was a collective gasp of delight. Candlelight from the low-hanging chandelier lit the glittering silver and crystal on the long dining table. Masses of white blossoms spilled over onto crisp white linen, and the scent of jasmine was thick in the air.

Robert, stylish in a blue body coat, blue trousers, and a yellow vest, stood at the ready alongside six assistants, all dressed like him, minus the yellow vest. A disgruntled Delia was positioned next to the sideboard.

When I was seated in the place of honor on Mrs. Burton's right, I had no doubt that this evening was about my promotion. But with so much attention on me, I had grown increasingly uneasy and wished the Burtons had not made this fuss. Yet I could see Mrs. Burton's excitement, so I forced myself to smile at her, for I had never seen her this happy.

When everyone was seated, Robert, much like a conductor at a concert, set the meal in motion. Delia ladled out a creamed carrot soup, then handed the bowl off to a waiter, while Robert gave a last inspection to make sure the waiter's thumb was enclosed in a white napkin before he served each bowl to a guest. Etiquette dictated that we not wait for the complete table to be served and those who began were quick to declare their approval.

The feast was served at a practiced pace, with the soup course leisurely followed by crab, picked clean and then roasted in its shell—a dish Mrs. Burton knew that I particularly enjoyed. Each course brought with it a new wine, and though I seldom drank, I did so this evening. I had two glasses in quick succession and was quite relaxed when another favorite dish of mine, roast lamb with mint, was served.

When the cheese and fruit were brought to the table, Miss Grewen, the young woman seated to my right, turned to me. "Would you care to share a pear with me?" she asked, blushing as though she had offered a true intimacy. Feeling friendly as a result of the wine, I smiled my agreement and adeptly speared the ripe fruit with my fork. I glanced over to see Mrs. Burton watching while I peeled the pear as she had taught. I gave her a quick smile and then a teasing wink. She laughed aloud, but then her eyes filled with tears. Before I could apologize, champagne had been poured, and Mr. Burton was rising with glass in hand. I looked again to Mrs. Burton and was concerned to see that her eyes still glistened.

"Are you all right?" I whispered.

"Yes," she said, reaching for my hand. She looked at me with such affection that I was reminded of Grandmother. In that moment my usual reserve fell away, and I spontaneously lifted and kissed Mrs. Burton's hand.

"We are here this evening to celebrate this young man." Mr. Burton nodded toward me. My face grew hot. By now I was convinced that he was going to offer me employment. Buoyed by the dinner wine, I quickly thought out some words of gratitude.

"Not only has he become a valuable member of our work team"—here he exchanged a nod with Nicholas—"but Mrs. Burton and I have come to care for him as we would a son."

I lowered my head. How unexpected were those words. I had come to care for each of them deeply, but to hear him use the word "son" touched me. When I looked up again, his eyes shone back at me. "And so, James, with our friends to witness, Mrs. Burton and I are asking you to join our family. We would like you to legally become known as our son, James Burton."

Stunned, I looked to Mrs. Burton, who now wept openly.

"James?" Mr. Burton addressed me again.

I tried to take it in. Could this be true? No! They didn't know me! An image of me holding a blasting rifle was quickly followed by another of Belle. I couldn't go through with this. What if they learned the truth? No! I wanted to shout. No! You don't know me!

"Do you accept us, James?" Mr. Burton asked, his voice choking back tears.

Mrs. Burton leaned over and grasped my hand. "Please say yes! Everyone is waiting."

Had she not been clinging so tightly to my hand, I might have bolted. Instead, when she urged me on, I rose unsteadily. "I don't know what to say . . ." I struggled for an answer.

Mrs. Burton began to laugh through her tears. "Oh, Jamie, please say yes! Don't you know that we already think of you as our son?"

I looked down at her. She wore a silk green gown made especially for the occasion, and though the white lace ruffle overpowered her, she had never looked so dear. How could I hurt her in front of all of her friends?

I felt light-headed and clutched her hand for strength. "Yes." I forced the word out. "Yes," I repeated. Nicholas's cheer of approval set off a round of applause.

"I would like everyone to raise a glass," Mr. Burton called out, lifting his champagne glass in my direction. "To our son, James Burton."

As everyone joined in the toast, no one else seemed to notice the crash of the tray when it slipped from Delia's hands, and everyone was crowding around me as she rushed from the room.

"You've made them so happy these past years. They are so proud of you." Those phrases were repeated over and over, and I did my best to respond appropriately.

As Robert directed the guests into the drawing room for coffee, the Burtons led me to the study. There, we sat at a table where their lawyer handed me a document enclosed in a beautiful folder of velvet indigo. As I scanned it, the lawyer explained that my signature and those of the Burtons were all that was required on this document to put my adoption in motion. The lawyer handed me a pen, but I set it down. I felt desperate to tell the truth. Yet, if I did, I would lose everything—this home, my job, and not least, the Burtons' support and love.

"What is it, James?" Mr. Burton asked, seeing my hesitation.

"I am not worthy," I murmured.

Mrs. Burton reached for my hand to kiss it. "Of course you are, my dear," she said.

"We are getting old, James," Mr. Burton said. "You understand the business, and what you don't yet know, you will grow into. There is no one better suited to take over for me one day."

"Don't you see, Jamie," Mrs. Burton asked, "how much we need you?"

"It gives me peace of mind to know that you would be here for Mrs. Burton should something happen to me," Mr. Burton continued.

Put this way, how could I not agree? I dipped the pen and signed the document. With joy, they both did the same, and after a thorough handshake from Mr. Burton and a tearful hug from Mrs. Burton, we left to join the others. Shaken to my core, I needed time away to gather my thoughts, so I excused myself, leading Mrs. Burton to believe that I had to accommodate nature. "Take your time, dear boy," she said. "Miss Grewen will be entertaining us on the harp, so slip in quietly on your return."

The stairs and long hallway were dark but so familiar that I didn't bother to take a lantern when I hurried toward my bedroom. As I approached, I saw light coming from under the door. Alarmed to think that I might have left one of the mirror sconces lit, I rushed ahead and threw open the door.

Delia was standing over my desk.

I was already so overwhelmed by the events of the evening that it took me a moment to comprehend what I was seeing. Delia took advantage of my surprise to push past me and hurry out. Immediately, I saw what lay on top my desk. In the excitement of the preparations, I had forgotten to pocket my key to the chest drawer.

I rushed over to the chest-on-chest to find the bottom drawer locked. I opened it and sighed in relief to see that the jacket was untouched. Then on closer inspection, I found Lavinia's letter missing.

I don't know how long I sat on the bed, trying to decide what to do, but when the tall-case clock bonged, I was reminded that the Burtons were waiting downstairs with their guests. I willed myself to stand and go back down. As I slipped into the drawing room, some of the guests turned to smile in my direction. I nodded to them as I lifted the tails of my jacket and settled into my seat next to Mrs. Burton, who reached over to pat my hand.

The melodious ripple of Miss Grewen's harp faded as my thoughts raced. I tried to recall the exact wording of the letter. My chest pounded when I remembered two partial sentences that would be incriminating— the first was Lavinia's offer to draw up papers to verify my freedom, and the second was Belle's mention of my "living white."

I seethed with fury at Delia. I knew that though she was once a slave, she could read and write, for I had seen notes she left for Robert. What did she mean to do with my letter? Was it enough to have it as a threat to me, or did she mean to show it to Robert or even the Burtons? Then how would she explain her thievery? Surely she realized that would put her own position in jeopardy.

I was left with the decision of whether or not to confront her. Naturally, she would deny the theft. In the end I decided to wait and see what she would do. If she dared present the letter to either Robert or the Burtons, and if I were made to leave because of it, I would not go alone.

CHAPTER THIRTEEN

1815–1816

James

ALONG WITH MY adoption, I was given a position in Mr. Burton's silver business that included a handsome wage. Determined to prove my worth to the Burtons, I applied myself more than ever. By the winter of the following year, there came an additional responsibility when, after working all day with silver, Mr. Burton and I began to stay into the evening so he could teach me his muddled accounting system.

"We all have weaknesses," he said with some embarrassment as we sorted through box after box of confusing paperwork, "and this, dear boy, is one of mine." He confided how much he had always disliked this aspect of the business, and after seeing the chaos, I could understand why. I knew there was another way, for as a child I had spent many hours assisting Miss Lavinia in keeping up to date the housekeeping accounts. Finally, after weeks of attempting to sort out Mr. Burton's accounts, I respectfully asked if we might use another system.

He agreed to try it, and when order began to emerge, we more happily faced the long hours necessary to get the job done. We were almost up to date with the records the February afternoon that Mr. Burton suggested that we make it an early evening, as he was suffering from a headache. Wanting to complete the task, I suggested that he go ahead without me and asked if he might send Ed back with the carriage later in the evening. "Or is that expecting too much of Ed to ask him to come back out in this sleet and snow?" I asked.

Mr. Burton's hand felt warm on my back. "I appreciate your diligence, my boy," he said. "I'm sure Ed won't mind coming for you." Wrapping himself in his long woolen greatcoat, he left. Nicholas also departed early and, after locking the front door behind him, I hastily ate a bread roll, then went back to work in the office, determined this night to put in order the last of the accounts.

It wasn't until the office clock dinged eight times that I realized the hour. Weary, I stood up to stretch. Where was Ed? I wondered. If he was waiting outside with the carriage, why hadn't he rapped at the door? Perhaps he didn't want to disturb me. I stretched my arms out wide, then yawned again and decided I was finished for the night. There was little enough left, and I could easily complete it tomorrow. I had rolled down the desk cover and was locking it when there came a banging from the front door. A voice called out for me, and I flung open the door to find our neighbor's servant.

"Robert sent me! You's to come home!"

"Where's Ed?"

"The carriage went over. They hurt bad."

"Who's been hurt?" I asked.

"Mr. Burton and Ed. They hurt bad! I helped get 'em in the house!"

ROBERT MET ME at the front door. He spoke low into my ear as he took my coat. "Mr. Burton is badly injured. The doctor is here."

"What happened?" I asked.

"We don't know. Ed took a corner too sharp, or maybe it was the ice, but the runner caught and the carriage tipped. When Mr. Burton tried to get out, the horses panicked and dragged him until—"

"Where was Ed? Why didn't he get hold of the horses?"

"He was thrown from the carriage. He isn't—"

An agonized voice called out in pain from upstairs.

"Dear God!" I said. "Is that . . ." I didn't finish and ran to take the stairs two at a time.

"Jamie! Jamie!" Mrs. Burton cried out from her husband's bedside.

"I just found out!" I said as she grasped hold of my jacket and began to weep. "Shh. Shh," I soothed. At the sound of my voice, Mr. Burton's eyes opened. When I reached for his hand, I tried not to react to the sight of his swollen and bruised face. "Don't worry. I'm here," I said, and gripping my hand, he closed his eyes.

The doctor motioned me to the door when Robert came in with a newly arrived nurse. "I've just medicated him," the doctor explained, "but his left hip is broken, and I don't know how much relief he will get. He has other injuries as well, but at this time they are difficult to assess."

"Will he survive?" was all I could think to ask.

"I don't know," came the reply. "Your driver downstairs won't."

"Ed?" I asked.

Robert nodded.

"What are his injuries?" I asked.

"It's his head. He's unresponsive," the doctor said, but I did not have time to discuss it further, as Mrs. Burton called out for me again.

TOGETHER SHE AND I remained in constant vigil. Laudanum gave Mr. Burton little relief, and his heart-wrenching cries could often be heard throughout the house. After two long days and nights, I persuaded Mrs. Burton to consider her own health; exhausted, she relented and left me to oversee his care.

It was almost two weeks before his condition improved enough that I was able to leave the house and go to the business, where I found Nicholas struggling to fill all of the orders.

I had been lent our neighbor's buggy, and during the ride home that afternoon I made the decision to purchase another buggy for the Burtons. On my arrival, I went to find Robert for his help with another driver and I was aghast to find him in the kitchen with his shirtsleeves rolled up, peeling potatoes.

"What are you doing?" I asked.

"Delia needs help," he said, nodding toward Ed's room.

"Then we must get someone in—someone to care for Ed."

"She won't have it. She refuses to have anyone else," Robert said.

"What is the latest from the doctor?"

"It is as before. Ed weakens daily. He will not live."

"Then we must find another cook! You cannot be expected to carry Delia's load. After . . . this is all over . . . it is time for her to go." Finally, I had found a way to get rid of the woman. What a relief to say those words! How I hated her and the threat she was to me. Before the accident, I thought daily of confronting her about the theft, but there was always the fear of what she might do in retaliation, so I kept my silence as my anger mounted.

The bell rang from upstairs, summoning Robert, who wiped dry his hands and hurried to answer the call. I was about to follow just as Delia appeared. She approached swiftly, grabbed the knife next to the pot of potatoes, and stabbed it into the table. "You think you get rid a me!" she hissed. "I hear what you say! We see what Mrs. Burton say! She my boss. Nobody else gon' tell me when I's done here."

"I'm afraid that you are mistaken," I said. "I am in charge now, and I say that a new cook will be hired."

"And what I gon' do then?"

"You will continue to care for your brother."

"And if he pass?" she asked. "What then?"

There was no turning back. "You will be given a stipend, and I will find you a room away from here."

"A room! You gon' find me a room! You think you gon' send me off, that you gon' send me away from here?" She glared at me and I glared back.

"Yes! You will leave!" I shouted, fighting to control my fury. "And before you go, you will give me back my letter!"

She flinched, but only for a second. "If I has a letter and you send me away, I tell you now that letter gon' find its way back. Matter of fact, you brings in another cook and I still here, maybe that letter show up!" She stared at me defiantly. We both knew that with those words, she had taken back the power. "And don' come looking for nothin', 'cause if there be a letter, Delia don' have it in her room," she said, her voice quiet but lethal.

I moved toward her, my teeth clenched. "If I leave here, you will leave with me!" I hissed before she turned and hurried away.

Any further dilemma I might have had with hiring another cook was resolved when, a day later, Ed passed away and Delia once again took her place in the kitchen.

Though I was ever alert to the threat of Delia, in the next months I was so taken up with my responsibilities to the Burtons that, of necessity, I set her aside as a leading concern.

MR. BURTON LINGERED for almost a year, and during that time I did my best to support both him and Mrs. Burton. As well, I worked diligently to keep the silver business afloat. Nicholas and I struggled to fill the orders, but at the beginning of January 1816, when Mr. Burton's health began to decline more rapidly, he spoke to me privately. "James, you must know that I'll never return to the shop."

I dropped my head. I didn't want to have this conversation, but I knew it was necessary. Mr. Burton's color had become an unhealthy gray, and the night before, when I had assisted him into bed, he had felt remarkably light.

"You must get some help for Nicholas," he said. "I would like to have you around here a little more."

I did as he requested, and in the next weeks Nicholas and the new man kept the shop running while I did my best to attend to the needs of both Mr. and Mrs. Burton. I had never cared for another man as I did for Mr. Burton and felt helpless as I watched him grow weaker every day.

Always, Robert was there to lend his support.

I WAS ALONE with Mr. Burton the night he passed away. He had been in a weakened state for days, yet this night was no different from the others. After Mrs. Burton went to her rooms for the evening, Mr. Burton reached out for me. "Sit next to me where I can reach you," he said, his breathing sounding moist. I moved my chair close to the bed and took his hand in mine.

"Son. Take care of your mother," he said, and later that hour he gave a final sigh. I was so stunned that it took me a while to understand he had left, but when I did, I dropped his lifeless hand and raced out to find Robert. On our return, the room felt cold and empty. My father was gone. I fell to my knees at his bedside, and though I was nineteen years of age, I sobbed like a child.

CHAPTER FOURTEEN

1817–1824

James

I N THE MONTHS following Mr. Burton's death, I was pulled under by a deep lethargy. Though I fought to free myself, I was left with such an exhaustion that I did not notice spring unfold. Every day I had to push myself to go in to the shop at the required hour. Once there, I might resume work on a silver piece but would soon lose interest. Offering the excuse of having to tend to Mrs. Burton, I would leave, turning the responsibility of the business over to Nicholas and the recently hired Mr. Taylor.

On my return home, the house was always quiet. Robert would immediately make himself available to me, but I would brush him off, and though I occasionally caught a glimpse of Delia, even my hatred of her was diminished in my grief.

In those long months, Mrs. Burton stayed to her room, but by the beginning of summer I began to find her in the back parlor, visiting with a neighbor, another widow, Mrs. Miller. One afternoon I came home to find the two of them playing cards. This soon became their habit, and though the two always invited me to join them in their games, after a brief appearance I would excuse myself. Then I would manage a short visit with Malcolm before I dragged myself to my room to lie down on the bed and sleep, only to wake as tired as before.

Because of my obligation to Mrs. Burton, I roused myself at suppertime, but where food was her comfort, it now repelled me. As my clothes began to fall loose around my thinning frame, Mrs. Burton became alarmed. "Something is not right with you, Jamie," she said. "Are you ill? Shall I call in Dr. Holland?"

"No!" I said. "It is just that my appetite is off."

"But you seem to require so much sleep," she said. Her eyes filled with tears. "I couldn't bear it if something happened to you."

I took her hand in mine. "Truly, I don't feel sick. I'm just tired. It will pass."

"But I worry about you. You are still so young," she said, "and you've had to take on so much responsibility. It might sound silly, but Mrs. Miller has been teaching me to play whist, and it has been such a boon to my spirits. Perhaps you need an outside interest. I have been thinking. You were always so happy when you were painting, but you haven't done it since . . . well . . . Why don't you consider taking an art class? We always spoke of it, but you've never had the opportunity."

"An art class?" I knew she meant to help, but the idea of drawing and painting—something that had always given me joy—now held no appeal.

"Yes, an art class! Mrs. Miller was telling me yesterday of her association with the Peale family. I am going to ask her if they would recommend an instructor," she said.

Too tired to argue, I abandoned the discussion, for I was certain that the Peale family, well known for their illustrious art careers, would have little concern for someone such as myself. But I had not taken into consideration the determination of these two women. By the next Sunday, a warm day in August, they had arranged for Mr. Leeds, an accomplished art instructor, to join Mrs. Burton and me for tea.

He arrived late, a tall lanky man, shaggy in appearance, and older than we expected. "Hello there!" he greeted us awkwardly when Robert brought him to the front parlor. He bowed formally to Mrs. Burton, then scooped his long gray hair back behind his ears before he yanked high each trouser leg and took a seat.

Small talk was not for him; the awkward silences were broken only by the slurping noises that he made while sipping his hot tea. To Mrs.

Burton's credit, she tried every avenue of conversation, only to be met with one or two words of reply. I was hoping he would soon leave, for I saw no purpose in this and was following through only to satisfy Mrs. Burton.

Finally, alone in her struggle for conversation, Mrs. Burton grew anxious enough to resort to personal questions. "It is too bad that Mrs. Leeds could not join us today," she said.

"I am not married," he said. "Never have been."

"I see," she said, and shot me a look of such desperation that I rallied.

"Mrs. Miller tells us that your work is on display at the Peale Museum?" I asked.

He nodded once. "A few watercolors of leaves," he said, then added, "and some pinned bugs."

"Bugs?" Mrs. Burton asked, clearly hoping to keep the conversation going.

"Bugs," he repeated. "They were dead," he said, as though to assure her. He looked at me. "Have you been there? Have you seen them?"

"No," I said. Of course I knew about the famous Peale Museum, but I had never been. It was a place that Mr. Burton and I had planned to visit, but our work at the silver shop had always taken priority.

With the mention of his work, Mr. Leeds came to life. After draining his teacup, he set it down with a clink, pushed up the sleeves of his ill-fitting brown jacket, then reached down for the portfolio that rested alongside his chair. Balancing the tattered leather thing on his lap, he untied a ratty cord, then rifled through some pages before he selected and handed over a small watercolor. "Here, take a look," he said.

I glanced at it, unprepared, and gasped aloud. It was black beetle depicted on a decaying log, painted with such detail, such vibrancy, that it might have been alive. It was such a true likeness that I wanted to touch it, to feel the movement. I looked up at him. "How did you do this? How did you achieve such detail?" I asked.

His gray eyes lit up. "I used a pinfeather. When I work in miniature, a pinfeather is best suited for that purpose," he began, and my interest stirred.

"A pinfeather?" I asked.

"Yes. Of a woodcock. I use the feather itself."

"But isn't that awfully small?"

He smiled a crooked smile. "That's the challenge."

At Mrs. Burton's insistence, I brought forth my now primitive-looking sketches of Malcolm and handed them over for examination. "I am fond of painting birds," I said.

Mr. Leeds took his time, sorting through my work. "You have ability," he finally announced, "but if you are to study with me, you must start at the beginning."

"What do you mean?" I asked.

"You need to study form," he said.

"Form?" I asked. "But it is the colors that I need help with. And I would like to learn to work in miniature, as you do."

"That will come in time. But first you must study form."

"But it is color that I—"

"Then do as you wish," he said. He slipped his work into the portfolio and stood.

Mrs. Burton looked at me helplessly. As frustrated as I was, I did not want this opportunity to pass. I rose and stood as tall as he. "Mr. Leeds, I will do what you ask me to do."

He looked me over as though trying to decide if I was worth the effort. "Are you free tomorrow afternoon?" he asked.

I looked to Mrs. Burton, and she nodded quickly. "Yes," I said.

"Then meet me at Bartram's gardens. You've been there?"

"No," I said, "I've never been to his gardens, but I have his book of travels at my bedside." I didn't tell him that this prized leather-bound book was worn from use. Before Mr. Burton's death, I had picked up the book nightly to read the accounts of the botanist's travels. Not only had William Bartram, a now famous botanist, written a fascinating account of his botanical explorations, but as well had included beautiful drawings of the plants and birds he had seen. In fact he had inspired a fantasy of mine wherein I imagined doing something of the same.

Mr. Leeds's white eyebrows lifted. "You've never been to Bartram's gardens?"

"No," I said, made uneasy by his incredulous look.

"He has had too many responsibilities to take leisure time for himself," Mrs. Burton said defensively, and I gave her a grateful glance.

"Tomorrow, then," he said to me, before offering a stiff bow of departure to Mrs. Burton. As he walked away, we both noted his white ankle poking through a hole in his bright blue stocking.

VISITING BARTRAM'S ESTATE was only one of many outings that I enjoyed with Mr. Leeds. In time, this eccentric but talented man taught me how to paint with a sable brush and then how to work in miniature with a woodcock's pinfeather. It was a relatively uncommon art form but one I had a talent for, and I became most dedicated to it.

As for my lethargy, after the first few weeks under the instructor's tutelage, Mrs. Burton noted happily how my energy had reappeared. And she was right.

I SOON FOUND that Mr. Leeds's insistence on paying attention to detail began to influence my work at the silver shop. Before, I had been satisfied to produce a solid and functional silver piece, but now I sought to enhance my work with detail.

A challenge presented itself the day Mrs. Burton called me into the back parlor, where she was playing cards with Mrs. Miller.

"Look," she said, "isn't this lovely? Have you ever seen such a fine vinaigrette?" She handed over a tiny silver box that measured no more than an inch long and three quarters of an inch wide. "Mrs. Miller had it sent from England," she said.

My thumb felt overlarge when I flipped open the monogrammed lid to examine the delicately punched grille. I sniffed it. "Whew! That holds a strong punch!" I held back the tiny box, which sent up a strong orange-vinegar scent. The two women laughed at my exaggeration, but indeed, the saturated piece of sponge tucked inside held a pungent enough smell to mask strong odors or bring a woman around if she felt faint.

"I carry it when I travel on the streets," said Mrs. Miller. "Especially in the summer. You know how foul the odors can be."

"I do," I said, pleased that I had not missed Mrs. Burton's delight in the piece. Her birthday was coming, and I decided that she must have a fine vinaigrette of her own.

Had I not been working in miniature with Mr. Leeds, I doubt that I would have attempted the task, but I drew a design and showed it to Mr. Taylor, the most skilled of us at crafting silver.

"You must be precise, but you can do it," he said, giving me the confidence I lacked.

Crafting the tiny box was not a challenge, but punching a dogwood design around the engraved image on the small cover was delicate work, and a steady hand was needed to solder the tiny hinges onto the grille. But it was worth the effort, for when I presented it to Mrs. Burton, she cried out in delight.

Naturally, she showed the treasure to her new circle of card-playing friends, and they were as taken with the trinket as she was. Days later, orders began to come. Because of the skill and time required to create each one, we priced the tiny boxes accordingly, but that did not deter these women. It only made the Burton-stamped vinaigrette more sought after and our silver business grew.

AFTER A YEAR of mourning, Mrs. Burton began to encourage me to accept some of the invitations that came our way. "I cannot go because of my health," she said, "but you must accept. How else will you meet others your own age?" Initially, I refused, but as a result of her insistence, I reluctantly attended a late supper held at the home of a family friend.

It was a long evening, for I was unfamiliar and therefore uncomfortable with others of my age. The men I found to be immature and pompous, while the women were much too gay and teasing, and their open attentions embarrassed me.

The next day word came back through Mrs. Miller, who was something of a gossip, that though I was thought of as conceited, the women considered me intriguing and attractive. "I also heard that after you left, someone said you had lost your eye in a duel, and you can only imagine how romantic the women found that!" she said.

"But that is not what happened," I said.

She laughed. "Oh, dear boy, it matters not. A rumor has begun, and it will stand." She picked up her red shawl, and before I could offer my help, she flung it around her wide shoulders. "And now I must go," she said.

"But surely . . ." Mrs. Burton called after her, ready as ever to defend me, but I shook my head and took the chair next to her.

"Now you see why I prefer to spend my evenings here with you," I said.

She reached her hand out for mine. "But Jamie, you are young. You should be around others your age."

I kissed her hand. "I like our routine. I look forward to our early supper and then to your company while I paint. I don't need others. I have you, I have Malcolm, I have the business, and I have my art. It is a good life."

Her look of affection filled me. "How fortunate I am to have you," she said.

"And I, you," I said, and the next few years passed quietly. Though Delia remained in the household, we seldom saw each other, and while she kept a wide berth of me, so, too, did I of her.

IN THE EARLY spring of 1822, Mrs. Burton, against my objections, began to plan a celebration of my birthday.

"Dearest! You are going to be twenty-five years old! At this rate I will never see a grandchild. It is time you met a young lady, and it appears that it is up to me to provide the opportunity," she said. Although her comment was said in a lighthearted way, it was not the first time she had expressed a desire for me to carry on the Burton name.

I felt some guilt whenever this subject came up; naturally, I had not told her that marriage, for me, was not a consideration. Given my ancestry, I would never chance having a child. I remembered well when, during one of my last years at Tall Oaks, the wife of a nearby plantation owner gave birth to a baby with Negroid features. When it was learned that a light-skinned house servant was the father, it was rumored that the child was murdered, and in despair, the mother took her own life.

That scandal happened when my grandmother's sister, Mrs. Madden, was visiting from Williamsburg, and her adamant declaration had stayed with me: "It only proves that no matter how light-skinned they might be, Negro blood will always show through!" How credible her comment was I did not know, but I had no intention of testing it.

However, I agreed to the birthday celebration. I had noted during the long winter that Mrs. Burton's spirits appeared to be flagging, and I hoped that a small gathering would give her something to look forward to. But the planning had no sooner begun than Robert was taken very ill with fever, and everything came to an abrupt halt.

Because of the yellow fever epidemic that had taken her son, Mrs. Burton feared the worst and begged me to keep my distance from Robert's sickbed. I did so for two days but finally went to visit, hoping to find him improved. Instead I found food and water set outside Robert's door, where he was too ill to access it. Inflamed, I strode to the kitchen, where I found Delia.

"Are you ill?" I demanded.

"No," she said.

"Then why are you not seeing to Robert?"

"I don' take care a those with no fever. I see how that boy of Mr. and Mrs. Burton die. No, sir, I don' have nothin' to do with no fever!"

"But you must! He needs care!"

"No! I don' go in there!" she said, staring me down.

I left to arrange for a nurse, but the rage I had suppressed toward Delia these past years was back in full blossom.

DAILY I CHECKED to ensure that Robert was cared for until he began to recover. The morning I found him sitting up in a chair, he asked the nurse to leave so he and I might be alone together.

"What is it?" I moved my chair closer to him.

"Where is Delia? Why is she not caring for me?" Robert asked.

"She refused. She said she wouldn't care for anyone with a fever."

His eyebrows shot up. "She refused? And you were required to hire someone in?"

"I had no choice."

He shook his head. "She goes too far!"

I saw my opportunity. "I don't trust her. I never have. I know you depend on her, but I would like her to be dismissed."

"It is Mrs. Burton who depends on her. I would be happy to see her leave," he said.

Now my eyes opened in surprise. "If you agree, I would be happy to speak to Mrs. Burton about discharging her," I said.

Robert looked toward the closed door before he leaned forward to speak quietly. "On my arrival, Delia was already employed with the Burtons. She resented my taking over the household and went to Mrs. Burton with a rumor that regrettably followed me from Europe." He leaned his forehead on the tips of his long fingers and closed his eyes. After a long minute, he straightened to look at me. "The rumor was true, but fortunately, the Burtons were open-minded. On the promise that I would give no further cause for gossip, they kept me on."

Robert, too, had secrets! And such a damaging one that the Burtons might have dismissed this wonderful man! What a relief to know that I wasn't alone in this. His candor gave me the courage to speak more openly about Delia. "I don't trust her. Years ago she stole something from my room."

His dark brown eyes looked at me carefully. "Why didn't you tell Mr. and Mrs. Burton?"

My face grew hot. "It involves my past," I said. "They . . . it . . . would have been upsetting to them."

"I see," he said, avoiding my eyes as he smoothed the blanket that covered his lap. "I should have told you this before. Years ago I overheard a conversation wherein Delia told Ed that she had information—damaging information—about you. Ed was upset and made her promise to stay quiet."

"Weren't you concerned?" I asked. "Didn't you wonder what it was about?"

Robert met my eyes. "I knew that you did not mean to harm the Burtons. In fact, you brought this household back to life, and Mr. Burton died in peace because of you."

My gratitude to him brought tears to my eyes. "Thank you, Robert," I said.

"I am not an innocent," Robert said. "We all carry burdens from our past, but it is not for others to exploit them."

I breathed in deeply. It felt as though a large weight had been lifted off my shoulders. For the first time since Delia's theft, I felt some measure of relief; now I knew I had Robert's support. "As soon as you are well, I will see to it that Delia is removed," I said. "It is my responsibility."

"I will leave it to you, then," he said. "But tread carefully. She can be ruthless."

I WAITED UNTIL Robert was back in good health before I sought Delia out. On an early morning before I left for work, I startled her just as she was sitting down to enjoy a cup of coffee.

"I would like you to give my letter back!" I said, approaching her.

"I don' know what you's talkin' 'bout," she said, setting down her cup with careful precision on the weathered table.

I glared at her. "The letter that you stole from me years ago. It is mine, and I want you to give it back to me."

She stood up hurriedly and began to gather the morning dishes. "I never say nothin' to nobody. I don' know why you comin' at me like this now."

"I want that letter back! It is mine!" My hands clenched in fury.

"Delia don' got no letter."

"Then where is it?" I asked.

"She never do have no letter," she said, continuing to stack the dishes.

"You are lying!" I grabbed her wrist and sent a blue and white saucer spinning to the floor. "I said I want it back now!"

She jerked her arm free and backed away. "That letter make sure I stay in this house. You best forget about it."

"You will regret this!" I said, and inflamed, I turned to go while I still had control of myself.

That day I was useless at work. I spent the bulk of the morning pacing. How should I proceed? Did she still have the letter, or had she gotten rid of it? When I dismissed her, what might she do? Would she go to Mrs. Burton?

I left for home in the early afternoon, deciding to go directly to Mrs. Burton and tell her that Delia must leave. However, on my arrival, I didn't find Mrs. Burton resting in her room, where I had expected her to be. Instead I found her sitting with Malcolm in Mr. Burton's room.

"Oh, Jamie!" she greeted me with reddened eyes. "You are home! I didn't know if I should send for you! I don't know what to do!"

"Greetings! Greetings!" Malcolm shouted in Robert's clipped accent, then flew across to sit on my shoulder. He clung there as I pulled up a chair next to Mrs. Burton.

"I am home now. All is well." I took her hand as she began to weep. "Tell me," I said, "what is the trouble?"

"I promised Delia . . ."

"Promised her what? There is nothing you can't tell me."

"It involves you. You wouldn't believe . . ."

"You know Delia has resented me ever since I came here as a young boy."

"But she said that you mean to harm her?"

Malcolm nipped my ear, and for the first time I smacked at his beak. He squawked in surprise and flew off to perch at the window. I loosened my damp collar and leaned back in the chair. "Harm her? And why would I do that?"

"She said that she had read a letter of yours. Of course I asked her immediately if you had given her permission to do so, but she did not reply and went on to say that she fears you will make her leave."

"And this supposed letter," I said, "did she mention the contents?"

"Oh, the accusation she made was so vicious that I am reluctant to repeat it. She accused you of—Oh, it is too ugly. Really, Jamie, I'd prefer not to say."

"Please tell me," I said.

"But I promised."

"I must know the slander so I might address it," I said, gripping the arms of the chair while fighting to stay calm.

"Oh, dear boy, let us forget it!" she said, seeing my growing fury. "It is really too ridiculous to repeat something so outrageous!"

"Please let us get this over with," I demanded.

"She said that you are a Negro," she blurted out.

I leaned over to brush some supposed dirt from my pant leg, needing the time to steady my breath. After I straightened again, I gave a short laugh. "She is off her head," I said. I held out my hands, then turned them over to expose my palms. "Which part of me, exactly, does she suggest is Negro?"

"I know how foolish this must sound to you, but she held to it so strongly that it was most upsetting."

"Surely you couldn't have entertained . . ." I said, moving to the edge of my seat.

"James! Of course not! I could never believe such a thing! Please! Do not take offense. I don't believe any of it! You? A Negro? It isn't possible!"

Anger suddenly took over. Was her love for me so limited that my tainted blood would destroy it? Dreading the answer, I could not contain the question. "And if I were? If it were true? What would it mean to you if I said I was a Negro?"

An unmistakable look of revulsion crossed her face as she shook her head. "But it isn't possible!" she said.

"So you would no longer care for me?" I asked, rising from my chair. My worst fear was true.

"James! Jamie, dear," she said. "Please sit!"

But she had given herself away, and I could not stop. "What upsets me is that you will not answer me! To think that you would not care for me if . . ." I couldn't breathe! That her love was conditioned on my race struck me so profoundly that I could not take in air.

She called out to me as I fled the room and left for the outdoors. My thoughts circled, and I noted nothing as I walked for hours that warm mid-May afternoon. What should I do? Should I tell her the truth? But what was the truth? Would I call myself a Negro? Surely there was not enough Negro blood in me that I should be cast as one of them. Nor was I one of them! How many times had Grandmother pointed out what a lesser race they were—so eager to be taken care of, so willing to be subservient. How many times had I heard of their nonexistent morals; they thought nothing of bedding each other and producing offspring they abandoned. And they were a thieving people—as evidenced by Delia taking my letter. How could I be one of them? Nothing in me fit the description. I carried none of their traits! I was not one of them!

Yet I could not forget that look of disgust on Mrs. Burton's face. Twice I ran to an alley to empty my stomach when it heaved at the remembrance. Why could she not love me as I was, Negro or no? I had loved her as I loved my own dear grandmother.

How wrenching it was to think of leaving this safe and beloved home, but by nightfall I had come to the sickening conclusion that I had no other choice.

I was exhausted when I returned to the house and there went straight to my rooms. I had just pulled out my leather bag, but before I had a chance to begin packing, Robert came with a note that bore Mrs. Burton's seal. After Robert left, I opened the note.

Delia has been asked to leave this house. I beg your forgiveness for questioning you about her slanderous accusations. The subject is forgotten. You have my word that I will never doubt you again.

I sat with the note long into the night, unable to make a decision.

In the early morning Robert came to tell me that Delia had been put out of the house and Mrs. Burton was waiting to see me. I went then, terrified of the task at hand.

I found her seated in a chair beside her bed, still dressed in her night-clothes. She looked so frail and shaken, so frightened and alone, yet I knew what I had to do. At the very least, she deserved to hear the truth.

I went to her chair and knelt by her side. I tore free my eye patch, wanting her to see all of me. Her hand trembled when she smoothed the ridge on my face that my eye patch had made. My head pounded and tears burned my eyes.

"I must tell you—" I began.

Her hand slipped down to cover my mouth. "No," she said. "We shall never speak of this again. Let us leave it at that."

In relief, I dropped my head in her lap and wept, while she soothed me as a mother might her son.

*   *   *

BUT THE DAMAGE had been done, and because the truth was never addressed, it festered like a thorn. Where before Mrs. Burton and I were easy and relaxed around each other, now our relationship was strained, and while she became more solicitous, I, in my guilt and need, grew more distant.

THOUGH I WAS years into my art study with Mr. Leeds, I continued on as my passion for the work grew. Malcolm's room overflowed with watercolors—miniatures, mainly—that covered every surface and were pinned to every wall. Birds were my main focus, but now I painted flora and fauna as well. I had become so adept at miniatures that Mr. Leeds suggested I consider creating a small handbook, such as Bartram's, for amateur botanists. However, to undertake this task, travel such as Mr. Bartram had done would be required of me, and with the silver business and the responsibility of Mrs. Burton, I did not see it as a possibility.

Over the years, Mr. Leeds had become a friend to both Mrs. Burton and me, and he proved a pleasant distraction. On Sunday afternoon it became habit that, following my art instruction, he joined us for tea. Lemon-glazed pound cake was a favorite of his, so it was always served, and we were then assured of his entertaining company until the last of the cake was gone.

Thus, Mrs. Burton and I were dismayed to learn later that summer that Mr. Leeds was facing health issues and must abruptly end his teaching.

"I would like you to take over a small class that I teach in my home," he said to me. "The students could benefit from what I have taught you."

"But I am not qualified! I know so little—"

He laughed aloud. "I believe that some would say otherwise," he said, referring to the two sales I had made recently. They were small pinfeather renderings and had sold for quite a sum. "I think teaching would benefit you as well," he added.

"Is it a watercolor class? Would the students be using sable brushes?"

"Of course! What? You thought I meant that you should teach them to work with a pinfeather? Good luck to find students with that kind of talent!"

"Why don't you consider it, James?" Mrs. Burton asked enthusiastically. "You could hold the classes where you do your work now—up in Malcolm's room. It is large enough, and it would be nice to bring new life into this house."

And so, because it offered Mrs. Burton and me a further distraction on a Sunday afternoon, I accepted.

I WAS RIGHT to do so, for the art classes proved a boon to our strained relationship. My adopted mother knew many of the students' families, and their family histories were often a topic of conversation for us. In time we grew more comfortable again with each other, though we never did recover the intimacy we once had, for neither of us could cross the divide: she, who needed to deny the truth, and I, who longed to have her accept it and love me for it.

There is one deep regret I carry from that time. On a number of occasions Mrs. Burton asked me to clear out Mr. Burton's rooms and to take them as my own, but I always declined. Was I punishing her, or did I not want to feel more the imposter than I already did? I still do not have the answer. However, when Robert came to me on September 4, 1824, to tell me that Mrs. Burton had unexpectedly passed away during the night, I was grief-stricken.

I had loved her as a mother, and though she had put forth her best effort to love me as a son, a difference existed after she learned the truth from Delia. Yet I did not hold her responsible; how could I blame her for an inability to love the part of me that I, too, loathed?

CHAPTER FIFTEEN

1824–1828

James

THOUGH I HAD inherited everything and the house was mine, months passed before Robert could persuade me to move down to Mr. Burton's quarters. I knew the sense of it, but I felt an intruder and relented only after Robert convinced me how much easier it would be for the household staff to serve me.

When we went down to look over Mr. Burton's rooms, I wondered aloud if the house was perhaps too large and too elegant for me.

Robert frowned. "And why would you not be suited for this home? The Burtons chose you as their son, and as their heir, you must claim it."

Because he believed it, I tried to convince myself to do the same.

THE WINTER WAS long and lonely, and I spent so much time at work that I grew weary of it all. Then, in the spring of 1825, a woman swept through the door of my silver shop and demanded to see the proprietor.

Nicholas summoned me from my back office, where I had been looking over the accounts. After Christmas, work had fallen off, and though I knew I should find a way to encourage more business, with both Mr. and Mrs. Burton gone, building the business no longer interested me.

When I came out, I immediately recognized the visitor. "Mrs. Cardon!" I exclaimed in surprise and walked around to greet her. I had met this socially prominent woman through Mr. Leeds, a longtime friend of the Cardons. It was she who had purchased the two paintings of mine.

"You remember me!" she said with a smile.

"How could I not?" I said, pleased to see her. In the past two years we had met twice at Bartram's expansive gardens. I remembered well her casual demeanor and lighthearted ways, which put me at ease. Because she was twenty years or so my senior, her teasing was less threatening than had she been of my age, and she laughed gaily when I uncharacteristically quipped in response to her repartee.

Now, as she gave a quick look about the shop, she let slip from her shoulders a patterned paisley shawl to expose a green day dress that snugly fit her comely figure. When she abruptly turned back, one of the many feathers from her large-brimmed hat dislodged, and we both watched it slowly float to the floor. I picked up the wayward adornment, blew it free of any dust, and presented it to her with a flourish. "Madam, your feather," I said.

"Oh, you may keep it," she said, laughing, "as a memento of my first visit here."

I followed her lead and placed the feather in my waistcoat pocket, then patted it. "I shall treasure this always," I said, smiling as I gave a small bow.

She laughed again and tapped my arm with her fan, then tilted her head as she studied me. "So! James Burton!" she said. "I've been hearing rumors about you."

"You have?" I asked, and when my heart gave a sudden thud, I brushed at an imaginary spot of dust on the display case. "Are they at least interesting?"

"Well, certainly. One involves a duel!" she teased.

Surprised at her reference, I involuntarily touched my eye patch, then saw I had embarrassed her. I planted my feet firmly and deepened my voice: "Mrs. Cardon, the rumor is false! I did not lose my eye in a duel! In actuality, it was such a spectacular event that I am afraid I have forgotten the details."

She laughed and tapped my arm again with her fan, but before she could continue, I spoke. "No, I'm afraid that you will find all of the rumors are false. Naturally, you will not be surprised to learn that I have heard rumors about you as well."

"Oh, I am sure that you have," she said, "but mine are all true!"

We laughed together.

"You are fun," she said. "You must come to some of our evenings. Rumor has it," she said, offering a sly smile, "that you are quite reclusive."

"Yes, I will concede that is true. Mrs. Burton was an invalid, and I didn't want to leave her," I explained.

"I was sorry to hear of her passing," she said.

"Thank you. I miss her a great deal."

"Well, then, I must introduce you to my friends."

"I would be pleased to have you do so," I replied, knowing full well the significance. At the least, here was an answer to my business dilemma. Many were competing in the silver trade, and a client such as Mrs. Cardon would mean not only survival to my silver shop but added prestige as well.

Many times I had heard the Burtons speak of Mrs. Cardon and the power she wielded. In this large city of Philadelphia, the topmost echelon of aristocracy included only families who could trace their lineage back to the earliest Quaker settlers. They considered themselves an exclusive group and denied entry into their tight circle to those of new wealth. As a consequence, socially aspiring merchants and businessmen—those who had more recently acquired their fortunes—developed their own elite society, and it was headed by none other than Mrs. Randolph Cardon. Now she stood before me in my shop.

There was a pause as she again looked about.

"Might I show you something?" I asked.

"Actually, I came with a specific request. I have seen some of your vinaigrettes, and I would like you to craft one for my daughter. But it must be exclusive. It is a gift for her eighteenth birthday."

"Do you have a particular design in mind?" I asked. "What are her interests?"

"Well, she likes to paint—Oh, and she is interested in anything that has to do with birds. She has a parakeet that she dotes on."

"She likes birds?" I asked.

"Yes," she answered.

I thought for a moment. "I have an idea," I said, "but it will take time, and the cost of the finished piece might be—"

Her hand brushed the air, dismissing my concern. "The cost is incidental, but you must complete it within four weeks so she will have it for her birthday."

"I will have it done for you," I said.

"Don't disappoint me," she warned.

EACH WEEK MRS. Cardon dropped in to ask about my progress. Because of our light flirtation, it was always a pleasure to see her, but the day she arrived for the completed piece, she bore a more subdued air.

I invited her into my office, a small room made smaller by the oak rolltop desk that took up a quarter of the space. The cleaning woman had left the room in good order and smelling of fresh lemon, so I seated Mrs. Cardon there before I hurried off to retrieve the package.

On my return, she was holding a miniature painting of Malcolm that had been propped on my desk. "You painted this?" she asked.

"I did," I said.

"It is exquisite. Would you allow me to purchase it? You know how I love the others that I've purchased!"

But I was impatient. "Before we discuss that, I would like to show you this. Come," I said, waving her over to the window, where I opened the small blue box in the sunlight. As I knew it would, the tiny silver parakeet gleamed against the dark blue velvet, and the small ruby in the eye of the bird sparkled. Mrs. Cardon gasped as she lifted it from the box, then opened the bird's miniature wing to expose the ornamental grille. "Oh! Mr. Burton! It is beautiful! Caroline will love this."

"Do you think so?" I asked, enjoying her pleasure.

"Oh yes! She will!" When she caught my smile, her eyes filled.

"What is it?" I asked, concerned at her sudden change of mood.

"Forgive me," she whispered, handing the silver piece back to me before reaching into her soft leather reticule for a handkerchief.

I went over and closed the office door. "Please, sit," I said. "You must be forthright. Do you not like the piece?"

"Oh, no. No. I love it! My problem is . . . that is, it is more . . . personal." She glanced at the closed door.

"What you tell me will not leave this room," I assured her.

"You give me your word? It will stay between the two of us?" she asked.

"Certainly!" I answered.

"Just this morning, as I dressed to come here, Mr. Cardon informed me that he had finalized arrangements for Caroline's marriage," she said. She looked at me, her eyes pained. "The match is wrong, all wrong, but he is insisting on it."

"You do not approve of the young man?" I asked, trying to better understand.

"I do not! And neither will Caroline!" Bitterness coated her words.

"Can she not refuse?"

"Refuse? Caroline? No one refuses Mr. Cardon. Least of all his daughter."

"And your husband has no regard for your opinion?"

She looked at me in disbelief. "My opinion? His opinion is our opinion. It is as simple as that," she said. With her elbow on the arm of the chair, she leaned her head into her hand. "This marriage will destroy my daughter's life."

I tried for words of comfort. "But at least she will be here with you in Philadelphia," I reminded her.

"No," she said, staring up at me with stricken eyes, "they are to go abroad. For two years! It is part of the arrangement. The boy's father wants him to travel, and my daughter is to go with him."

"I see," I said.

She turned on me. "No! No, you don't see! The boy is already a ruin. And this is my only child—my only daughter! Can you understand what this means to me? What it will mean to her?"

She looked so lost that I rested my hand on her shoulder, then quickly removed it. "I do," I said. "I do understand."

"Oh dear." She straightened her shoulders as she struggled to collect herself. "I am sorry, so sorry, to have burdened you with this."

I was struck at her difficult position and wanted to console her, but I could find no words. I rose and went for the small painting of Malcolm.

"I want you to have this," I said, handing it to her. "It is my gift to you."

"Oh!" She stood when she reached for it and held it to her bosom. "How dear of you."

"I only want to see you smile again," I said, but realized too late the intimacy those words invited when she stepped close and placed her hand on my arm. "Am I to understand. . . . ?" she asked, her voice soft and inviting. "Perhaps next Wednesday afternoon? I am free."

"I . . ." I stumbled over words as I tried to reestablish a boundary. "I wish I had the time, but I'm afraid my days are taken up with work." As though on cue, my pocket watch pinged, marking the hour.

"Of course," she said, pulling back her hand. "You are busy. How foolish of me to think otherwise. Naturally." She laughed lightly as she busied herself and tucked her handkerchief away.

"I am sorry," I said, knowing that I had insulted her. "Perhaps dinner?"

"Certainly," she said. "I shall send you a dinner invitation. You must meet my husband."

"It would be my pleasure," I said, hating the distance now between us.

Before she left, she opened her reticule. "You have created two pieces of art," she said. "Now tell me, what does my husband owe you? I will always consider the painting a gift, but I must insist he pay for both."

LONG BEFORE I received my first invitation to Mrs. Cardon's home, friends of hers began to frequent my silver shop. These were women of enormous wealth who were not opposed to spending extravagantly, and because of them, the silver business again flourished.

That autumn, when an invitation arrived from Mrs. Cardon, I was happy for the distraction, for my own home was a lonely place. I missed Mrs. Burton more than I could have anticipated, and sometimes, in my loneliness, I visited her rooms with Malcolm. There I sat at her bedside, fingering the books we once read aloud to one another, while Malcolm flew about distractedly. Usually, though, he did not settle, and we would have to leave when he, in his frustration at not finding her, would chew at the engraved bedposts.

I had come to dread the solitary meals served in the large dining room, until Robert suggested I take them in the small back parlor. There, in a more intimate setting, Malcolm and the crackling of a small fire gave me some company while I ate.

I looked forward to teaching my Sunday art students, not only for the company they provided, but for the stimuli of my own artwork. Many evenings I found solace in painting as I worked to perfect the technique of using a pinfeather, often dreaming of the day I might travel and create a small handbook similar to Bartram's.

I DID NOT see Mrs. Cardon after our last meeting at the silver shop, but throughout the summer I heard through her friends about her daughter's extravagant wedding.

In the fall, Mrs. Cardon sent me an invitation for a dinner. Though a month away, it presented a dilemma, as it included an evening of dance, a skill I had not yet learned. After Robert made some discreet inquiries, he found a dance master who agreed to come to my home and teach me not only how to dance but also the required etiquette of the ballroom.

I was surprised at how much I enjoyed the exercise. The dance master's handsome young wife laughed as we giddily circled the room. "I prefer the waltz to any of the other dances!" I called out above the music, enjoying the easy rhythm and liking the idea of having only one partner.

The dance master suddenly stopped playing the spinet that Robert had moved from the back parlor into the more spacious front parlor. "It is not good form to hold your partner that close," my instructor sniffed. "And though the waltz is done at Mrs. Cardon's affairs, you will not find it so in the more conservative ballrooms. The intimacy of it is considered quite scandalous," he said, glaring first at his pink-faced wife and then at me over his spectacles.

I ARRIVED AT the Cardons' home that first evening to find I already knew some of the other guests, as they were now my customers. Nonetheless, Mrs. Cardon took my arm and introduced me around, and though her voice remained cheerful, her hand stiffened when we came to her husband. "Mr. Cardon, this is the young man I was telling you about. He is the artist—the silversmith artist James Burton. Do you recall me speaking to you of him?"

"I certainly recall his bill," he said. He laughed then, as though to dismiss the insult, and when his repeated glance at my eye patch alerted me to his curiosity, I ignored it, knowing with some satisfaction that good manners prevented him from asking the question he most wanted answered.

Dinner went by smoothly as our skilled hostess kept dinner conversation light and free of controversy. After the meal, I was disappointed to learn that dancing was canceled; instead we were led into a large parlor off of the dining room where chess and backgammon were set up. As a child, I had become quite skilled at these games, so I readily took a seat, and the rest of the evening passed pleasantly enough.

Because of Mrs. Cardon's sponsorship, invitations from her friends followed, and as they served as a distraction from my loneliness, I began to attend. Most of these evenings followed the same pattern: guests were liberally doused with spirits as elaborate meals were presented. Because more liquor was served later in the drawing rooms, the games that then took place were enjoyed more freely than they might have been otherwise. Occasionally, a small orchestra provided music for dancing, and in this way I put to good use the skills that my instructor had taught, but it was over cards or backgammon that the more intense flirtations abounded, and when Mrs. Cardon was in attendance, her attention was always on me. More than once she hinted at her availability, but I skirted the issue, and because there was no outright rejection, she did not appear to take offense as she had that day back in the silver shop.

Curiously, it was she who introduced me to eligible women, and it seemed that she took perverse pleasure in their interest in me. Some of these women caught my eye, and the more forward of them maneuvered to be alone with me to offer up a kiss or two. A few offered more, and though I participated, I did not push for these interludes. I had not forgotten who I was, nor what was at stake, but I was a healthy man, and the frustrations that followed were uncomfortable. In time I learned through the men who gathered in the smoke-filled drawing rooms for heartier drink and easier talk that houses existed where men could visit to relieve themselves of this primal tension. I gave some thought to it, but afraid of disease, I stayed away, though as the next few years passed, I began to give the possibility more consideration.

Then, in the summer of 1828, I met Caroline, Mrs. Cardon's daughter.

IT WAS AT a dinner hosted by a close friend of Mrs. Cardon's to welcome Caroline and her husband home after the years they had spent traveling abroad. Only twenty or so had been invited to the dinner, held prior to a large reception. Though the dinner number was restricted, I was accustomed, as an eligible man, to being included when seats were at a premium. I had been to this home before, and though it was not as grand as the Cardon residence—few were—this one had a large drawing room that opened to a magnificent rose garden.

It was a mild June evening, and dinner was served outdoors in the lush blooming garden, where hundreds of suspended candles and lanterns flickered in the twilight. When the guests of honor arrived, they were too late for introductions, and we were all seated immediately, as the reception was soon to follow.

Caroline's husband, Mr. Thomas Preston, took his seat across from me, and as he nervously adjusted his spectacles on his long thin nose, he acknowledged those around with a stiff nod of greeting. His neck was restrained by an exceptionally tall white shirt collar and held in place by a wide cravat, and when the woman seated next to him complimented him on what she referred to as his European fashion, his pale narrow face flushed with pleasure.

Caroline was seated farther down, so I didn't take notice of her right away, but what I did note was that before we had finished the vichyssoise, Mr. Preston had already consumed more than enough wine.

It wasn't until the oysters were served that I looked down the table and saw Caroline. I had been looking forward to meeting her, expecting to see a younger version of her mother, but how wrong I was. Though Mrs. Cardon was handsome enough, her daughter was a true beauty. Dressed in a pale gray-blue silk, Caroline leaned in to better hear the man seated next to her, and when she tilted her head up in my direction, her dark blue eyes locked on mine. I stared, and when she offered a slight smile, I became flustered and turned away. Had she taken me for someone else? Unable to deny myself another look, I turned back. Still in conversation, she again met my gaze, and she repeated her sweet smile. A toast was offered, and when she lifted her glass of wine, her long fingers cupped the bowl so gracefully that I found I was again staring and forced myself to look away. With some guilt, I looked to her husband, but his attention was on having his wineglass refilled.

With dinner over and the dancing begun, Mrs. Cardon brought over her daughter and son-in-law for introduction. She scarcely had time to present them before a small crisis occurred and the hostess sent word for Mrs. Cardon's assistance. As she left to give her help, Mr. Preston mumbled something unintelligible, and then he, too, swayed off, leaving Caroline alone with me.

"I apologize for my husband's behavior," she said. Close up, she was even more beautiful, and I struggled to make conversation.

"I am sure coming home is an adjustment," I said, offering her an excuse.

"Yes," she said. "He hated to return."

"And you?"

"I never wanted to leave home in the first place," she said.

"You didn't?"

How vulnerable she looked as she stared up at me. I had asked too intimate a question, and I tried to think of something else to say. "Might I ask if you had opportunity to use the vinaigrette I fashioned for your birthday?"

"Forgive me! I meant to mention it first thing after I recognized you at dinner."

"But we've never met."

"No, but your eye—" She caught herself. "I'm sorry, that was unkind."

"Don't be sorry. I am quite used to it, and I suppose it is a distinctive enough feature."

"It is," she relied honestly, then adeptly changed course. "Please know how I treasure my vinaigrette! It is a true work of art."

"Thank you," I said.

"You also paint?"

"How did you know?" I asked.

"Did you not paint that beautiful miniature of a cockatoo? The one Mother has?"

"Oh. Yes. Yes, I did," I said.

"It is so tiny yet so detailed. I've studied it many times. However did you achieve it?"

"Instead of a sable brush, I used a pinfeather," I said, surprised at her interest.

"You painted it with a pinfeather? Of a bird?"

"Yes. It is a very old craft."

"And where do you find these pinfeathers?"

"Hunters shoot woodcock as game and bring them to the market. Through the winter months, I purchase all I need."

"How remarkable! In England I heard of a woman who used a bird's pinfeather to paint on ivory."

"You did? I must tell Mr. Leeds, my art instructor. He believes it a lost art."

"Mr. Leeds is your instructor? Perhaps he will teach me as well."

"I'm afraid he has grown old and no longer teaches." She was so breathtakingly beautiful, and I was so drawn to her, that her nearness felt dangerous to me.

"Oh," she said, "how unfortunate for me." She tilted her head while her fingers played with a small curl that hung to the back of her neck. "Might you consider giving me a few classes?" She smiled with her full pink lips, and though I knew the danger, I was lost.

"When would you like to begin?" I answered so quickly that Caroline laughed, as did I.

"Perhaps in a few months? I should have my house in order by then," Caroline said, just as her mother, panting and short of breath, rejoined us.

"Your husband is holding forth, and he is quite inebriated," Mrs. Cardon scolded.

"Yes, I am sure he is, Mother," said Caroline. Mrs. Cardon pursed her lips and stared back in the direction of Mr. Preston. "Mother," Caroline went on brightly, "Mr. Burton has agreed to give me some painting instructions."

Mrs. Cardon turned her attention toward us and assumed a smile. "Oh, darling," she said, "when will you find the time? You have your home to set up."

"Mr. Burton has agreed to wait until the fall. By then everyone will be tired of seeing me, and I shall have something to look forward to when the snow comes."

Mrs. Cardon patted her daughter's arm. "Well, if it is an art class that will make you happy, then we must find you an art instructor. Mr. Burton is a busy man. Surely you won't impose on his time."

"He already has agreed, haven't you, Mr. Burton?" Caroline smiled up at me. Caught in the cross fire, I had no choice but to agree with Caroline.

"I see." Mrs. Cardon looped her arm through her daughter's and flashed me a smile that lacked warmth. "You will excuse us, Mr. Burton. Others have yet to greet Caroline."

"Naturally," I said, and after they walked away, I soon left for home, where I tried to make sense of this uncomfortable fascination I felt for Mrs. Preston.

CHAPTER SIXTEEN

1828

Caroline

FOR WEEKS I vacillated over sending a note to Mr. Burton reminding him of the art classes, until one day we met by chance. Early in October I agreed to accompany Mother and her gardener, Phelps, to visit the greenhouses at Bartram's gardens, but on the morning of our intended visit, Mother was struck with headache and had to forgo the trip. It was a lovely day, and as I knew the place, I decided, rather than spending the afternoon alone, I would accompany Phelps. I packed my sketchpad with the idea that I would visit the gardens while our gardener went about his business and made his selections.

Phelps and I were easy company on the carriage ride over. I had known him all my life, and he had always been my most reliable source for botanical questions. He laughed still in remembrance of the time when, as a child, I asked if the wings of his dark mustache were meant to attract butterflies.

On our arrival, as planned, Phelps went to the numerous greenhouses and hothouses while I took to the gardens. It was a Tuesday, and there were few about as I ambled through the red and yellow gardens of dahlias and chrysanthemums. When I saw the river, I felt something akin to joy and hurried toward the blue water. The air was still summer-warm, and as I approached the shade of the maple and dogwood trees and saw no one about, I removed my hat. My new maid, try as she might, had no talent for dressing my hair. The pins were too tight, and I sighed with relief as I pulled them out and swung my hair loose. When I felt a tickle on my neck, I rubbed at it only to hear the buzz of an angry bee. My reaction was involuntary when, afraid of a sting, I swatted it and then fingered it from the tangle of my hair. "Oh no!" I said aloud when I found that I had killed it, for I had a particular affinity to bees. I wrapped the bee in my white handkerchief, meaning to take it home, but as I was doing so, a stern voice startled me: "And what might you be doing?"

I swung around only to be met with Mr. Burton's teasing smile.

"Oh, it's you!" I said in surprise.

"So, Mrs. Preston. What have I found you illegally pocketing?" he asked.

His playfulness unnerved me, and when I fanned my face with my hat, my handkerchief dropped. He stooped to pick it up.

"Be careful," I said. "It will fall out."

"And might I ask what treasure it holds?"

"It holds a bee. I killed it accidentally."

"You killed it! And why would you do that? I happen to fancy bees."

"It was in my hair," I explained.

"Oh dear. Did it sting you?"

I fingered my neck. "No," I said. "But I was afraid that it might. I should not have removed my hat."

"And why did you?" he asked, his manner playful.

"Because my pins were pinching," I said.

"*Mrs. Preston, Seen in Bartram's Gardens with Her Hat Off.* I can see the newspaper headline now. The scandal of it!"

I laughed, and so did he.

"I was sitting over there, under that pine," he said, pointing to a bench. "Would you care to join me?"

I had no reason not to do so, and after he lifted a sketchpad to make room for me, we sat together in silence, looking out over the water.

"Mrs. Preston?"

"Yes?"

"Why exactly are you keeping the bee?"

"I am taking it home to sketch it."

"I see."

"I would not intentionally kill a bee, but now that I have, I don't want to waste the opportunity to use it."

"And what is your process?"

"Well, I'll study it first, the color, you know, and then I'll paint it. But first I'll draw it over and over—until I get the details right."

"Ahh," he said. "Like this?" He picked up his sketchpad and flipped it open to a page filled with quick sketches of a common sparrow.

"May I page through?" I asked.

He handed the pad over, and as I leafed through, I was curious to see it filled with sketches, not only of birds, as I had expected, but of pinecones and acorns and a multitude of various leaves and branches. I asked him the purpose of this.

"I hope one day to produce a small book of bird illustrations. If I am to authentically represent birds, then I must realistically display them in their natural habitat."

"And your book would include our local birds?" I asked.

"No, my idea is to provide a handbook as a reference for those traveling down along the eastern coastline."

"How wonderful! Is there one bird that particularly interests you?"

"I must say that I am drawn to the Carolina parakeet."

"Oh, I love parakeets!" I said.

"I know," he said, and his smile was so genuine that I looked away. "Your vinaigrette," he reminded me.

"Of course!" I said, and embarrassed at my forgetfulness, I steered the conversation away. "Will your books be for sale?"

"I'm afraid I am far from that," he answered. "Getting it into print is a very expensive proposition."

"I would be the first to purchase one," I said, and he laughed at my enthusiasm.

Again we looked out at the water. It took me a while to work up the courage before I addressed him. "Mr. Burton?"

"Yes?"

"I must ask, are you still willing to teach me how to paint with a pinfeather?"

He picked away a golden leaf that had fallen on his jacket sleeve. "I wondered if you were still interested," he said.

"Oh yes, but I didn't want to impose on your time."

"I already teach a class on Saturday morning. It is in watercolor. Your medium?" he asked, and I nodded. "Good," he said, "but the students use traditional brushes. If you would like, you might join that class. We can see how you do and then proceed from there."

"That would be wonderful!" I said, but held tight to my excitement.

"I have one hesitation," he said.

I leaned over to better see his face. "And what is that?"

"I'm afraid that it has to do with your mother. I sensed she had an objection?"

I sat back. "I am not a child, and I do not need her permission."

When he laughed, his face wrinkled in a most pleasant way. "No, you are not a child. Quite the opposite," he said. "But I'm afraid that I was only thinking of protecting myself. Your mother can be quite formidable."

It was my turn to laugh. "Leave her to me, Mr. Burton," I said. "I will see to it that you come through this unscathed."

CHAPTER SEVENTEEN

1828–1829

Caroline

O N A SATURDAY morning, at the early hour of ten o'clock, I entered the foyer of Mr. Burton's home. There, to my dismay, I discovered that I was the only woman attending his class and that the three other young male students were from the university. I felt so intimidated that I would have left had not Robert, the butler, already begun to lead our small group up the stairwell. As we made our way through the rather dark house, my tension increased. What had I done! What had I been thinking!

I was getting ready to bolt when Robert ushered us into a room so charming that at once I relaxed. The walls were painted my favorite shade of yellow, and when Robert drew back the blue and white draperies, light filled the room. It streamed onto an old pine table loaded down with pints of water, glass jars filled with upended brushes, ceramic palettes, and boxes and boxes of paint cubes. Heaven!

The other students, after selecting supplies, made their way to the easels. As I moved in and gaped about, I tripped on the heavy canvas cloth that covered the dark oak floor, but I saved myself when I grabbed hold of the fireplace mantel. In an effort to cover my clumsiness, I leaned in to smell the sweet fragrance of the yellow roses that poked out from the fingers of a quintal. At that moment Mr. Burton entered with a large white cockatoo perched on his shoulder.

Previously, I had been as curious as any about his black eye patch, but this day it only lent to his handsomeness. He was a tall man, well proportioned, and his close-fitting waistcoat, patterned in blue and black, was set off by his white shirt and his black cravat. I wished I had worn something more attractive than my dark navy day dress.

He paused when he saw me, then turned toward the students when they hailed him. What he might have said or done next, I know not, for the entire room was distracted when his bird lifted off and flew to my shoulder. There, testing me, the bird gave a small nip to my ear.

I tapped his beak, as I had learned to do with my own spoiled pet. "No!" I said in a firm tone. "I don't like that."

The bird cocked his head to look at me. Miffed that I had corrected him, he flew to a perch by the window and from there squawked out for all to hear, "Naughty boy!"

"You *are* a naughty boy," I said quickly, and all the young men laughed.

Mr. Burton was not amused and came forward. "Did he hurt you?" he asked.

"No," I said, cupping my ear with my hand, for I guessed it was red. Mr. Burton looked uncertain.

"I'm fine," I reassured him. "I am familiar with birds. I have Rodger, my own parakeet. He, too, can be quite naughty," I said, smiling.

Just then a young colored boy entered the room carrying a large blue bowl of red and green apples. "Pan!" the students all greeted him enthusiastically, and his large brown eyes sparkled in response.

"Go ahead," Mr. Burton encouraged him, and the boy carefully made his way to the front, where he placed the full bowl on a table set up to be used as a prop for a still life. Next to me, Mr. Burton spoke quietly: "Mrs. Preston, if you would please take what you need from the table and go to an easel, our class will begin."

I FEARED I would not be skilled enough to keep up with my classmates, but in the weeks to follow, I was happy to see that I could hold my own. Meanwhile, though he knew of my earlier studies, Mr. Burton expressed surprise at my talent, and I privately reveled in his praise.

However, I was disappointed to find that he was not the same man he had been that day in Bartram's gardens. In the classroom he held himself back, not only from me but also from his students. Perhaps because of that, we all worked hard to earn his praise.

THE ART CLASS soon became the focus of my week. Here I lost myself in the joy of painting, and the time flew by. Yet it was not only art that drew me to Mr. Burton's home.

At my home, Mr. Preston's comments about my art were so disparaging that I increasingly kept it from him. My marriage had failed so desperately that my husband and I scarcely managed civility with each other. Mr. Preston cared no more for me than I for him, and we had not been intimate since early on in the marriage, when I had found him in a compromised position with another man. However, bound together as we were, we continued to make the required social rounds, where his inevitable inebriation and resulting behavior left us both humiliated.

At these affairs, Mr. Burton and I were cordial, though I was ever careful to hold myself at a distance. Yet there were moments during these events, inescapable moments when our eyes met, and what passed between us was so powerful that I was often left profoundly shaken.

This tension, this draw, followed us into the classroom, but as it grew for me, he became more aloof. I held myself in check, but when I was away from him, I spent hours imagining that he longed for me as I did him. In those hours I traced his mouth with my fingers and imagined his smile as he clasped my hand and then kissed me.

Soon gaining his attention became my focus, and my days were filled with the effort. I canceled some of my routine engagements with Mother and used my extra time to paint. At the same time I found a new maid who was more skilled at dressing hair and could guide me with my clothing. The challenge of winning Mr. Burton's notice gave me new life, and with my happiness, my mother became curious.

SOME MONTHS LATER, Mother and I were in my carriage, returning from the shops. Squeezed between piles of boxes and packages, I was quiet while fingering the package on my lap that held my new blue shawl. I wondered if Mr. Burton would see how well the color suited my eyes.

"And how is your artwork progressing, dear?" Mother asked casually.

"Very well," I said, happy for the subject, "but I am impatient to begin working in miniature. I cannot wait! I only hope that when it comes time, I do not disappoint Mr. Burton."

"You must think well of Mr. Burton if you do not want to disappoint him."

"Oh, I do!"

"He is a good instructor, then?"

"I have never known better. He is so encouraging." I could not keep the warmth from my voice.

"Be careful, darling," she said, touching my hand.

"Of what, Mother?" In my guilt, I drew my hand back.

"You are a married woman," she said. "You do not yet have a child. Until you do, you must be especially careful of how you conduct yourself."

"What do you mean?"

"You know, darling. First the heir, then the affair."

"Mother! How horrible!"

"I know," she said, covering her mouth as she gave an embarrassed laugh. "It's just that . . . I know your situation at home is not—"

"I've done nothing inappropriate! You forget. You yourself agreed that I should take the art class!"

"Of course I did. I'm only suggesting—"

My guilt fed my anger, and I cut her short. "I know what you are suggesting, Mother, and what you suggest insults me! How could you insinuate such a thing!"

"Caroline," she soothed. "You know I only have your welfare in mind." She gave a slight laugh. "Besides, I forgot. He must be at least fifteen years older than you are."

"Nine," I said angrily, "nine years!" I caught myself. "Not that it matters," I added. I pulled loose the purple ribbons on my bonnet, and as I looped and retied them, I fought back tears. Of course it mattered! It was all such a mess. I had no way out of my dreadful marriage, and

I was in love with another man. As much as I wanted to confide in Mother, I could not, for she would insist that I stop the art classes, and I could never do that. Seeing Mr. Burton gave me life. All that mattered was him.

Mother watched as I fussed with my ribbons. "Are you all right, dear?"

I didn't answer but looked out the window as our carriage pulled up to Mother's house. When the driver held open the door, Mother hesitated, then leaned in close and whispered, "Be patient, darling. I've been trying to convince your father that your marriage is unsuitable and that it would be better for you to return home. You know how stubborn he is, but I feel I am making progress."

"Thank you, Mother," I said, but her words startled me. As much as I disliked my husband, marriage had at least given me some freedom, and if I were to return to my parents' home, I would again be under the controlling supervision of my father. To continue on the path that I was taking, my marital home was the easier of the two to navigate.

CHAPTER EIGHTEEN

1829

James

I HOPED MY infatuation with Caroline would pass, but as the weeks went by, it only grew stronger. Not only did I see her on Saturdays, where I fought to keep my attraction for her hidden, but we also attended the same social events. There I often overheard others sniping at her beauty and laughing at her embarrassment when the inebriated Mr. Preston urinated in the palms or vomited in the shrubbery. In Saturday's class, when she appeared as gracious as ever and spoke not a word of her troubles, it infuriated me to think of the marriage she had to endure.

The first day Caroline requested to stay after the art class so that she might complete her project, I assured her that I was only going to continue to work myself and she was welcome to remain as long as she chose. After the other students left and we were alone, I felt so drawn to her that I wondered if I could trust myself. For that reason I said not a word. We both worked silently until Robert came to ask if I would be in for dinner. Then Caroline, claiming surprise at the hour, rushed off.

The following Saturday, I was the one who invited her to stay. After the other students left, I addressed her. "I thought I might start teaching you to work with the pinfeather."

She set down her brush. Her look of delight undid me, and needing time to steady myself, I went toward the door.

"I have some early works of mine to show you," I said. "I will get them. They are in the library."

"Might I come with you?" she asked unexpectedly.

"If you like," I said, stepping back to let her pass through the doorway. Her small waist was within reach, and I fought to keep my hands away.

When Malcolm screamed his unhappiness at being left behind, we smiled at each other, but something other than amusement—an urgency, perhaps—passed between us.

The library was dark, though the mid-July sun beat against the drawn curtains. This was one of the rooms I had not yet redone, and I hoped that the brown velvet drapes didn't look too worn as I hooked one of the panels back. When I turned around, Caroline, bathed in the light, appeared a mirage.

"Caroline. Caroline!" I came toward her, whispering her name as one might a prayer.

She stared up at me. Her eyes had gone the same shade as the blue silk she wore. When she began to weep, I reached for her. "Don't cry," I said. "Please don't cry." She dropped her head on my chest. "I am desperate for you," I whispered.

She looked up at me. "And I for you," she breathed.

When she offered me her mouth, all reason left, and I was lost.

CHAPTER NINETEEN

1829

Caroline

WE HAD REACHED the point where James had offered to teach me to paint with a pinfeather, but art was forgotten when we were alone together, for time was limited and our passion was strong. We met every Saturday after class, but soon, too hungry to wait out the days, we arranged to meet during the week as well.

I lied to Mother, using one excuse and then another about why I had less time for her. Though she never questioned me and likely guessed the reason, I was beyond caring.

My time with James was always too brief, but on the occasional glorious afternoon when time was not as critical, I relished what little I learned about him. Though he was guarded about himself, he encouraged me to chatter on. He inquired of my childhood, and I spoke willingly of that lonely time. When I shed a tear in the telling, he kissed it away. Yet he did not question me about the circumstances of my marriage, and I soon guessed that he placed such boundaries so I would not cross his own. Though he did not verbally share himself, his loneliness was palpable and as great as my own. It was in our lovemaking that we completed each other, and parting was anguish.

One Saturday afternoon, both spent, we lay across his tall four-poster bed. I was cradled under his arm, and from there I lazily studied the carvings on the dark oak bedposts, then the thick green-and-cream-colored fabric of the bed curtains. On his dressing table, reflected in the mirror, were several bottles of cut glass, each capped with an elaborate silver stopper. To the side sat two black eye patches, and I realized I had never seen him without one.

"James, will you tell me what happened to your eye? Why do you wear the eye patch? I have never seen you without it."

He gave a light laugh. "There is nothing much to say. I was born with the affliction. I have no sight in the eye, and Mrs. Burton suggested I cover it with a patch. I've become used to it."

"Will you show me your eye?"

"Sit up," he said, and when I did so, he lifted the patch and looked at me. The white glaze that covered his affected eye made him look more vulnerable.

"Can you see anything with it?" I asked.

"Just shadows," he said. I reached for his head and gently kissed both his eyes before I snuggled back under his arm. There I turned my head onto his warm chest, wondering which of his toiletries he had used, for I loved his fresh scent. In the intimacy of the moment, I wanted to know everything about him.

"How did you come to be adopted by the Burtons?" I asked.

He stopped stroking my head. "I needed a family, and they adopted me," he said.

"But what of the parents before them?" I asked. "What happened to your first parents?"

"Both of them died," he said abruptly.

"Oh, dearest! It must have been difficult, losing both. How old were you?"

He was silent. I circled my hand lightly on his chest and flattened it across his heart. I felt the steady rhythm, and though I sensed he was uncomfortable, I wanted to know more. What had he been like as a child?

"Jamie," I said, trying out a pet name. "Jamie, dearest, I know so little about you." There was such a long silence that I feared I had crossed a line.

Then suddenly: "You called me Jamie," he said.

"Yes."

"Mother called me Jamie," he said. "Well, I thought she was my mother, but in the end I discovered that she was my grandmother."

"Your grandmother! Where was your mother?" I asked. "Had she already died?"

Again he was silent, but his breathing had turned shallow, and my hand felt the increasing thump of his heart. I raised myself up on my elbow to look at him. "What is it, dearest? What is upsetting you?"

He looked away. "Caroline, there are some things that I need to—"

I sat up. "Tell me everything! I want to know everything about you."

He gave an odd laugh. "You only think that you do."

"But I do! I do!"

"What if I told you that I not only have feet of clay but that I am made of it? Dark brown clay."

It was my turn to laugh. "Oh, James. I often think of myself the same way. Well, not so much me, but that my marriage is covered in mud. Although—and forgive my obscenity—my mud is more like manure."

He laughed. "Manure, is it? My Caroline is stuck in manure! Whatever shall I do?"

"Since your feet are already of clay, you can't object to rescuing me." We laughed, and when he reached for me, I playfully pushed him away while I noted the time. My husband cared little for my whereabouts, but that evening we were expected for supper at my parents' home, and for that we dared not be late.

As I rushed to dress, I asked James again about his childhood.

"I will tell you another time," he said briskly, drawing his pants up over his shirt. His collar had doubled back, and I took the time to go over to him to fix it.

"There is nothing about you that I would not love," I whispered and was rewarded when he pulled me to him and kissed me with such tenderness that I wept.

IN THE FOLLOWING months I cleared my schedule as much as possible so I would be available whenever James could find the time to send for me. If my husband suspected anything, he said nothing.

What I could not escape were certain weekly visits with Mother. Every Tuesday and Thursday her carriage arrived at eleven, and together we set out to satisfy our obligatory social calls. I was overflowing with love for James, and though I said nothing, Mother noted my newfound cheerfulness.

One Thursday morning, she arrived all a-flutter. "We are late," she fussed as I climbed in. After I settled back, I pulled my new pocket watch from my reticule to check the time.

"Oh, Mother, it is as I thought. We have plenty of time."

She noticed the glint of new silver. "How pretty! Where did you get it?" she asked, reaching her hand out to receive the watch.

"It was a gift," I said, handing it over to her.

"From whom?" she asked.

"From one of my many admirers, Mother," I teased.

She ignored my jest as she examined the underside of the tiny silver piece. "I've never seen one this delicate," she said. She turned it around. "It has the Burton stamp. Only he could do something this fine. Was it a gift from him?"

"It was," I said. There was something in my tone of voice, some pride, perhaps, that clearly caused her concern.

"Oh, Caroline!" she said. "You must be more careful."

"Mother—" I began.

"No! Listen to me. This is a worldly man! You are easy prey. I know the difficulties you are having in your marriage, but you must be patient. Every day I appeal to your father to have you return home, but until he agrees, you must protect your name."

Her words alarmed me. It was only because my husband cared so little that I was able to visit James as spontaneously as I did. That would change if I were to return to my parents' home.

"Mother. Please! Don't worry about me. I am fine. Can't you see?"

"You must know how concerned I am about you," she said.

"But you see for yourself that I am well."

"That is my point, Caroline. As your husband's reputation grows worse, you seem to have become happier—which, forgive me, darling, leads me to believe that you—"

"Oh, Mother! Please don't accuse me of—"

"I am not accusing you of anything! I am only expressing my concern."

"Well, don't!" I spoke sharply.

"Please, dear, let us not argue," she said, then hurriedly found another topic. "Did I tell you that I convinced your father I need six new gowns?"

I was relieved to have her change the subject and responded with a quick laugh. "Six gowns, Mother? Six!"

"That is exactly what he said. 'If your finances cannot bear the strain,' I said—you know how he hates me to say that—'then I will have to make do with two.'

"'Mrs. Cardon!'—you know the voice he used—'Do not imply that I cannot provide what you need! If you need six gowns, then get yourself six gowns!' Of course I did not tell him that I intend three to go to you. How soon, dear, can you schedule the time so we might go to Geraldine for our fittings?"

CHAPTER TWENTY

1830

Caroline

J AMES AND I were lovers throughout that glorious summer and fall, but by the end of January 1830, I could no longer deny my pregnancy.

"Can't you lace this corset tighter?" I asked Mary, my new maid. "Begging your pardon, but I think you are already too squeezed in," she said, coming around to the front to rest her eyes on my stomach. "You don't want to hurt what's in there."

"Shhh," I said, putting my finger to my lips. I set my hands on my expanding waist. "Can you see that I've gained weight?"

She gave a nod.

"Oh dear," I said, and sat back on the edge of the bed. These past months I had ignored the cessation of my monthly flow and the increasing tenderness of my swollen breasts, but I could no longer hide the truth, especially from myself.

I was not a fool, and from the start knew a pregnancy could result, but I was so in love with James and so caught up in our passion that I refused to steal from my happiness by dwelling on a possible complication. Faced with the reality, I was not altogether unhappy. The idea of having James's baby rather excited me. I didn't foresee a problem presenting the child as Mr. Preston's, and since he was not in a position to judge, I felt certain of his support.

I fully expected James to be pleased with the news, for it was, after all, his progeny. Should he have hesitation, I would assure him of my health, for I had never felt so alive. Furthermore, other than needing a few weeks for recovery following the birth, I saw no reason why the pregnancy should impact our affair. Yet before I presented James with my condition, I decided it would be helpful if I came to him with my husband's support.

Approaching Mr. Preston with the news did not overly concern me, for he once said that he would like to have a child, and we both knew that if it were left up to the two of us, we would never have one of our own.

Since my affair with James had begun, my husband and I had grown more civil, and during the day we might share an exchange about the weather or have a word or two about attire for some upcoming event. But civility was lost when alcohol was introduced. Then he almost always overindulged, and if his mood turned belligerent, his fury was often directed at me. "If you were more a woman," his rant would begin, and I would try to make my exit before he began his accusations of how my father had coerced him into this marriage.

Following these nights, apologies were few, but his remorse was often evident. I decided that should he object to this pregnancy, I would use his guilt to settle my case.

In the morning I had my maid deliver a handwritten note to my husband. Though he and I seldom shared a meal at home, he agreed to join me that night for an early supper.

I had our cook prepare my husband's favorite Italian dish of macaroni and cheese and, for dessert, a bread pudding with his favorite custard sauce. I dressed for the evening in my new pink silk, though I was soon sorry, for it was somewhat oversnug. I might have changed, but the downstairs maid had come to tell me that my husband was waiting.

After our meal was served in silence, I dismissed the servants so we might be alone. My husband's eyes were wary, but enticed by his favorite food, he began to eat. I tried some banter. When that failed, I fingered the heavily worked pattern of silver cutlery that Mother had chosen for us until I finally blurted out, "I am going to have a child."

His eyes lifted. "Is it Burton's?" he asked.

My face went hot. "How do you know?"

"I have my ways," he said, smirking at my surprise.

I felt nauseated as he forked in another bite of the macaroni. "I don't know what to say," I said.

"You say nothing," he said. "We will raise the child as our own."

My dress restricted a deep sigh of relief. "I was hoping you would agree to do so," I said, grateful enough for his unexpected generosity that I was close to tears.

He drained his glass of wine, then looked up at me after he poured himself another. "Naturally, you will stop the affair," he said.

I stared at him. "What do you mean?"

"You must end the affair."

"No. Certainly not!"

He drained the fresh glass of wine. "Yes, you will! I will not have the child's paternity questioned."

I braced myself against the table. "But I love him! I must continue to see him!"

"You love him! Caroline! Simple as you are, surely you know that he is using you, just as he has used half of the women—"

I partially rose from my seat. "He has not! How dare you!"

"Caroline, don't act more the fool than you are. Sit down!"

I dropped back into my chair. "He isn't using me!" I felt weak at the thought.

He gave me a pitying smile. "He is known for it!"

"Don't say that! That is not who he is!" I flung my napkin onto the table and began to sob.

"For pity's sake!" he shouted. I winced when he rose from his seat so forcefully that his chair flew back. "Don't start with those damn tears! Always! Women and their damn tears!" He straightened his dinner jacket before he picked up his chair, then reached for the unfinished bottle of dinner wine before he left the room.

My tears! How dare he! The only time he saw me cry was during his alcoholic rages.

When I flung my knife across the table, the weight of the silver caught the edge of his crystal water goblet and sent shards of glass to the floor. Stunned by my own outburst, I sat for a minute before I burst into wild tears.

THE DAY FOLLOWING that dreadful supper with my husband was a Tuesday. James and I regularly met on Wednesday and Saturday afternoon, and until now I had kept to this pattern. However, all day Tuesday, I grew increasingly concerned that my husband might contact James about my pregnancy, and by the evening, frantic with worry, I made a rash decision and went unannounced to my lover's home.

I had not slept the night before, wondering if it was possible that what my husband had said about James was true. Had he been using me? Were there other women? After all, hadn't Mother suggested the same months before? And how would that affect the way he would feel about my pregnancy? I had been so certain of him, but now the questions haunted me.

Snow was falling heavily when I arrived at James's house, so I didn't have my carriage go around to the back as I usually did; instead I had it pull up to the front door. Robert sensed something amiss and led me directly to the library before he went to fetch James.

Faint from upset and my tight corset, I sat on the edge of a chair to wait. When James rushed in, I was so relieved to see him that I could not find words.

He knelt at my side. "What is it?" he asked. "Caroline, this is foolhardy, coming here like this. My lawyer will be here within the hour."

"Your lawyer?" I asked stupidly.

"I'm arranging to sell my business," he answered, as though he, too, could think of nothing else to say.

"Sell your business?" I felt light-headed from fear. "Are you leaving Philadelphia?" I gripped the arm of the chair, prepared to hear the worst. So my husband had already been here!

"No! Of course not! I meant to surprise you with this. I'm selling my business, and I'm finally going to illustrate that book of birds." He reached for my shoulders and looked into my eyes. "But tell me, what has happened? You are too pale. What is it?"

"Do you love me?" I whispered.

"You know I do!"

I was trembling. He was my whole life! What would I do if he turned from me? I could not live without him! "I am going to have a child," I whispered.

His hands gripped my shoulders before he suddenly released me. He stood and dropped his head into his hands, then lifted his head again to stare at me. "You are certain of this?" he asked.

"Yes," I whispered.

He looked about as though searching for words.

"James, it is your child," I reminded him.

"Of course it is!" he said sharply. "That is the issue!"

I had not expected his anger. Surely he had known this could happen. Why did he so hate the idea of a child? Would it restrict him with other lovers?

He walked to the window, then came back and stood beside me. I could not look at him, terrified of what he was about to say. Did he mean to end the relationship? I couldn't bear it!

"Caroline, there are some things I must tell you about myself. I have been unfair to you."

Dear God! Here it was! My husband was right! Now he would confess to the other women. He would say that he had never loved me. I couldn't suffer those words. I covered my ears and shook my head as a child might. "No!" I said. "No! Don't tell me! I don't want to know!" I lost all restraint and sobbed so desperately that he knelt beside me and pulled me into his arms. When a clock bonged from the upstairs hall, announcing the hour, I felt him tremble as he held me away.

"Caroline, you must go now. He will be arriving any moment. I will see you soon, and then we must talk. I will tell you everything."

I shook my head. "Please, James," I begged. "I don't want to know! Please! Leave it as it is."

"All right," he soothed, but his face was pained and troubled as he helped me into my carriage.

THROUGHOUT THE FOLLOWING day, I awaited a note from James, as per our routine, telling me to come for our Wednesday appointment. But nothing came.

On Friday I received an impersonal note announcing that the art classes were discontinued until further notice.

Against my better judgment, I sent James a return note:

Please, please, let me come to see you.

His response:

Be patient. In view of everything, we cannot risk it while I am in the middle of negotiating the sale of my silver business. I will be in touch as soon as the transaction is secured.

I felt sick from needing his reassurance, and each day that passed without further communication filled me with increasing anxiety. I canceled all my engagements, unwilling to leave my home should a summoning note arrive.

I waited every long day for all of that dark February. I refused visitors and made constant excuses to my mother until, at month's end, she brushed by both the housekeeper and then my maid, Mary, to appear unannounced in my bedroom.

Weeks before, when I had told Mother of my pregnancy, her response had been to the point: "Pardon me, darling, for saying this, but Father and I were under the impression that you were not having relations with . . . Let's just say this is something of a surprise."

"Yes, it is, for me as well," I said.

"You are happy?" she asked, trying to read my eyes.

"I've never been happier," I said, smiling.

"And?" She nodded toward my husband's study.

"He is pleased as well."

"What a relief," she said, though her stiff congratulatory embrace did not convey the feeling.

But now, this day in late February, she greeted me with an unhappy look. "Darling! Have you lost weight?"

"I don't know," I answered listlessly.

"What is wrong? Are you feeling unwell?"

"I suppose it is the winter . . . or perhaps the effects from carrying a child."

"But you must be about six months along," she said. "You should be feeling quite well."

I pulled my shawl tight around my shoulders; though there was a strong fire warming my bedroom, there were drafts, and I couldn't feel warm. "Don't frown so, Mother," I scolded, uncomfortable with her stare.

Mother sent Mary to the kitchen for some tea, then tossed her red wool fur-lined cloak on the foot of my bed. "I don't like the way you look, Caroline," she said. "You look ill."

"I am only tired," I said. What else could I say? I couldn't very well tell her of my abandonment.

"And that is all?" she asked. "There is nothing else wrong?"

"I suppose I'm afraid," I offered.

She dragged a chair to the side of my bed and sat. "Of course you are," she said. "Every woman fears childbirth. But you must pull yourself out of this mood for the sake of the child. You must look for other things to distract you." She paused. "Does Mr. Preston support you? Has he . . . been unkind?"

"No, Mother," I said, sighing, "all is as usual." I did not tell her that it was I who was cool with Mr. Preston, for I strongly suspected he had played a role in James's staying away. "I like your new dress, Mother," I said, changing the subject before she had time to quiz me further.

"Do you?" she asked as she pulled and puffed out the enormous sleeves on her costume. "What do you think? Are the sleeves too extreme? They are called gigot and are the latest in fashion, but in winter, with my cape, it is difficult for them to hold their shape."

"The red flowers in the fabric look pretty with your cape," I said, though soon her primping made me irritable. "So tell me, Mother. What have you been doing? What is the latest news?"

"Well!" she said, satisfied with her frock and settling her hands in her lap. "I'm quite excited, my dear. Your father and I have been asked to host the museum's annual event in our home!"

"Oh," I said, trying to sound interested, "tell me about it."

"Do you recall the annual ball given to celebrate the artists who are to receive funding for their projects? I'm sure you've already heard the news about James Burton." She avoided my eyes as she turned again to her sleeves.

I clutched the covers. "What about him?"

"I believe he was one of those selected by the museum to receive a grant for an art project. Something about a book and funding for an excursion."

I worked to stay composed. "I know about the book, but an excursion? What do you mean?"

Her eyes were on me as she explained, "Apparently, he submitted a proposal for a book of bird illustrations, and the museum decided it was worthy of funding. I'm not certain of the details, but I believe he means to travel south, where he will study and paint birds."

I sat forward. "And he is expected at the event?"

"Well, yes. All those selected are expected to attend." Her voice had grown cautious.

"When is it to be held?"

She hesitated.

"When, Mother?"

"A few weeks from now."

"When, Mother!"

"In the second week of March," she said reluctantly.

Finally! A solution! I could meet James there! Warmed with excitement, I threw the covers back. "I am going to attend," I said.

"Oh, darling! You cannot possibly hope to do so. You are too far along to appear in public."

"I shall corset myself!"

"Caroline! There are rumors! In fact, because of them, I was well pleased to hear that Mr. Burton was leaving."

"Rumors! What do I care of rumors, Mother?"

"Dearest. You must take care. Everything that your father has ever done has been to ensure your future and the future of your children. You must protect that! If your husband ever questioned . . . If he ever alerted your father or pointed a finger, the consequences could be extreme."

"My husband! You say my husband could point a finger? How would he dare to point a finger at me! He, the one who prefers men . . ."

Mother's face went white, and when I saw her shock, I forced whatever else I might have said back down my throat. She looked away while struggling to regain her composure, but in my need, I pressed her further. "Please, Mother," I begged, "I will go whether or not I have your help, but please say you will give it."

It was a while before she turned back to me, her eyes moist. "Pardon me, dear, what did . . . What did you say?"

I was intent on one purpose. "I said I want to go to the event, and I will need your help to do so."

"Oh, Caroline! My dear girl," she said, drawing in a deep breath. "If you insist on going, I will give you my help, but you must then promise me one thing."

"What is it?" I asked.

"After the event, you will come away with me to Stonehill, and we will stay there until the child is born. That should put a stop to any further rumors. Will you give me your word?"

"Stonehill? It is so far away from here!"

"That is my point," she said.

"But I must see Mr. Burton before he leaves on his trip. Will you give me your word that you will invite him to Stonehill?"

I had never seen her look so weary. "I will," she said.

"And what about Father? Won't he say it is too early to open Stonehill? Won't he object to the cost?"

"I will insist," she said. "But I will leave the house staff here in town so his routine won't be interrupted, and I'll hire outside help to take with us."

Thus we agreed that after the event, we would go to up Stonehill, where I would give birth to my child in our country house.

CHAPTER TWENTY-ONE

1830

James

CONFRONTED WITH THE news of Caroline's pregnancy, I was so struck by fear and indecision that I put her off, not wanting to add to the nightmarish position I had put her in. How could I tell her that she might give birth to a child of color? On the night of our last meeting, I wanted to confess, but Caroline was already so overwrought that I worried what action she might take if I forced this news on her. At the worst, I feared that she would go to her mother, who, naturally, would involve Mr. Cardon. And that would be disastrous.

I needed a month or two to put my affairs in order. If the truth about my ancestry became known now, the sale of my silver business would fall through, I would never see Caroline again, and my future as an artist would end. Everything hung in the balance.

A few months previous, with Mr. Leeds's encouragement, I had submitted my name to the Peale Museum for consideration for one of their esteemed grants. To my amazement, in January I was notified that I had been selected for a subsidized excursion into the Carolinas. On my return I was to present renderings of birds, flora, and fauna native to that area, and based on approval, funding for an illustrated handbook of birds would follow.

When the offer came from the museum, I had rethought the course of my life. Since Mrs. Burton's death, I had worked diligently at the silver shop but had grown weary of the long hours; the bulk of my time was spent in the office balancing figures. Along with the silver shop, the Burtons had left me a sizable estate, and as my interest in the business faded and the opportunity of the excursion came, I went to my lawyer to arrange selling the silver shop.

I had not told Caroline of my plan to sell the business, for I was saving it as a surprise. It would allow us more time together—something I felt certain would please her. As for news of the excursion, I was waiting for a favorable moment to tell her, for though it meant we would spend some months apart, I wanted her to see the opportunity that it was for me.

But then she came with her own news, and there was no time to explain the decisions I had made. And now that I knew of her condition, what was I to do? Naturally, she would remain with her husband, but how could I best support her? Dread followed that question, for the one thing I did not wish to do was to add to her dilemma. Yet she must learn the truth, for if the child had color, we would have to arrange to have it cared for.

I decided it was best to keep a distance, for I suspected that her husband was on high alert. The man already disliked me and now would not hold back on destroying my good name.

But the sale of the silver business was slow, and one week followed another until the whole of February had passed. Much to my regret, I stayed away from Caroline.

IN THE FIRST week of March, a letter came from Lavinia in response to one that I had written while flush with excitement about the grant.

In the years following Delia's theft of my letter, too afraid of another interception, I had not corresponded with those at Tall Oaks. Soon after I received the award from the museum, while studying the map and planning the route I might travel on my excursion, I was surprised to see the proximity of Tall Oaks, located in southern Virginia, to the parts of North Carolina where I meant to journey. Though twenty years had passed since I had fled that home, I still dreamed of seeing it again. Now, with Delia out of the way, and believing that my safety in Virginia was no longer in question, I wrote a letter to Lavinia and asked if I might visit.

Two months later, that first week in March 1830, came her response. It was not what I had expected.

My dear James,

What news! How proud we are of you! You always had such skill with a paintbrush. All of your childhood paintings were lost in the fire, but I remember so well how vividly you captured the cardinal and bluebird. I cannot imagine an improvement.

Pardon me for the delayed response to your letter, but Belle and I only just returned from a visit to Williamsburg. There we visited my daughter Elly and her cousin Meg Madden. The two have successfully established the Madden School for Young Girls. Can you believe that my Elly is already twenty-seven years old? She was so young when you left, but early on was made aware that the two of you share Marshall as a father. Perhaps that is why she is so free-thinking.

You may remember Meg, who is as independent in her thinking as my Elly. Because of their liberal views, should you ever need friends, I believe you might be warmly welcomed if you find yourself in their vicinity.

Which brings me to the visit you requested here at Tall Oaks. How it breaks my heart to refuse you, but because we are such a small community and word travels so quickly, I do not think it wise. You might recall our former overseer Rankin and his son Jake and how determined they were to locate you. Though they are no longer under our employ, I have heard rumors that they are still about, and I believe that should those two learn of your presence, they would mean to harm you. Given the time that has passed, I doubt that you would be recognized, but your distinctive eye gives me concern.

Please take care and know that both Belle and I want only the best for you.

Always your friend,

Lavinia Pyke

I sat down after reading the letter. To learn that Rankin and Jake were still around stunned me, and though it was already the first week in March, I began to question my wisdom in going ahead with the excursion. But a few days later, when Henry came with the news that Pan was missing, I knew I had to go. Now I had until my departure to tell Caroline the truth and see what our love could bear.

CHAPTER TWENTY-TWO

1830

James

I RETURNED HOME from the event at Mr. and Mrs. Cardon's, shaken to have seen the effects of my procrastination on Caroline. That night I resolved to set things right. I would meet with her the next day, tell her the truth, and offer to provide for the child, should it have color. But in the morning, when I sent a note to her home requesting to see her, it was returned with a note from the housekeeper stating that Caroline had already left for Stonehill with her mother. Not knowing what else to do, I waited uneasily for Mrs. Cardon's invitation.

Meanwhile, I worked to find Pan. The theft of young Negro children was very common, but it was a complex problem. I hired a man familiar with the shipyard to investigate. When he learned that Pan had likely been sold into North Carolina, I kept the man on, hoping he would uncover more detail.

March and then the first weeks of April passed, and my departure date grew closer. Still I heard nothing from Caroline. Daily I waited for a summons from Mrs. Cardon. I could not understand why it was not forthcoming. There was always the possibility that Caroline had confided in her mother and her mother had convinced her not to see me, but that idea only made me more desperate to see her. My greatest concern was for Caroline's health, for she had looked too pale and thin when I saw her at the event. I struggled against taking matters into my own hands, but the situation was already so tenuous that I dared not.

In the third week of April, while I was signing the final papers for the sale of the silver shop, Robert interrupted my meeting to present a note from Mrs. Cardon requesting that I come to Stonehill as soon as possible.

STONEHILL WAS WIDELY known as the Cardons' magnificent country home, set high on the banks of the Schuylkill River. Had I not been so worried about my mission, I might have enjoyed the scenic two-hour carriage ride there.

The home was the most luxurious I had yet encountered. Georgian in style, it was a massive two-story brick house, easily fifty feet square, with a hipped roof of such low pitch that it gave the appearance of being flat. To the back of the house were a number of handsome brick outbuildings, among them the stables and a large greenhouse, while to the left a two-story outdoor kitchen was connected to the house by a covered walkway.

A manservant I did not recognize met me at the door and, after taking my coat and hat, led me to a front parlor. There, as I waited, I walked about the room to calm myself. I felt sick with my upcoming disclosure, but as I paced the light-filled room, I couldn't help noting the extravagance. The walls were covered in a yellow and gray silk stripe that traveled up to the high ceiling and there met with wide white detailed molding and plasterwork. Four bergère chairs covered in yellow silk surrounded a marble-topped table and I might have taken a seat had I not been so nervous.

I was tinkering on a harpsichord when Mrs. Cardon rushed in. On seeing me, she paused and, with a sweep of her hand, brushed back her unkempt hair before waving me through tall pocket doors into a smaller connecting parlor. There she closed us in. "For weeks I've tried to dissuade her from seeing you, but she insists!" Her voice was so shrill that I was taken aback. She swung toward me. "Do not act the innocent! She has told me that you are the father of her child!" The words drained the fight from her, and she sank into a chair and began to weep. "She is so ill, Mr. Burton! She is so ill."

Alarm broke my silence. "What do you mean? Is it her time?"

She looked up at me, her face drawn and afraid. "No, but she is due very soon. The doctor has been here, and his concern is that she weakens more every day. He has bled her over and over, but nothing relieves her."

Now my voice turned harsh. "How long has she been ill like this?" I asked.

She became apologetic. "Almost from the moment we arrived. I wonder now if the carriage ride was too difficult. We should never have left town; we are so isolated out here. She is too ill to return. I am so afraid. I have not left her side."

"Is she alone now?" I asked, concerned at the thought.

"No. There is a housemaid with her, but she is new to us." She shook her head. "I made such a mistake. Mr. Cardon hates to have our town house disrupted, so I left him with our staff and hired new to come with us. I—"

I spoke over her to cease her rambling. "The doctor?" I asked. "When was he last here?"

"Two days ago. He is due again tomorrow, along with Mr. Cardon."

I walked to the door. "Please take me to her," I said.

"I don't know! If Mr. Cardon should ever discover that you—"

I interrupted again. "Mr. Cardon knows of my involvement?"

Her eyes grew wide. "Mr. Cardon? Oh! No! No! He must never know!"

"I agree," I said, "but we will speak of that later. Now please take me to Caroline."

She stayed sitting and shook her head as though arguing with herself. "If he ever finds out . . . he will kill both of us!"

"He won't find out," I said.

She studied me for a brief moment before she pushed herself to her feet. "Come," she said, "but you must be gone before Mr. Cardon arrives tomorrow afternoon."

"Yes," I said.

The decision made, she moved quickly up the massive staircase and down the vast hallway, the dark red walls lined with massive gold frames outlining portraits of family ancestors. At the door to Caroline's room,

Mrs. Cardon straightened her shoulders and filled her lungs. "We must stay calm," she said as though to herself before she opened the door. A young Negro maid came forward, silencing us with a finger at her lips. I stood back, waiting for direction from Mrs. Cardon, for under ordinary circumstances, I would not have been given entrance to this room.

When she saw that Caroline was sleeping, Mrs. Cardon directed me to take a seat. The maid, while bringing over a chair, bumped into the bedpost and jarred Caroline awake.

The circles under my beloved's eyes were as violet as the color of the room, and the pink in her face had been replaced by alabaster white. On seeing me, she struggled to sit, but her swollen stomach made her movements difficult. Forgetting all else, I rushed to her bed. She grasped hold of me as she might a savior. "James," she cried. "Oh, James! You've come!"

I held her to me and forced soothing words past the pain in my throat. How could I have failed her so? What a coward I had been!

I heard Mrs. Cardon's muffled sobs before she left the room, and I set Caroline back against the pillows. "Hush," I soothed, "hush, darling. I am here now, and I will stay."

"Oh, James, do you promise?" she asked. "Do you promise?"

"I will not leave you again," I said. "Rest now."

"What about Father?"

"I will speak with him, and then I will make arrangements. After the baby comes, we will go to New York, where no one will know us."

"Yes." She sighed, resting her head back. She gave a weak smile and closed her eyes. "Yes. We'll go to New York," she whispered.

THOUGH SHE SLEPT, Caroline clung tightly to my hand, and as I sat with her, I came to terms with what I needed to do. One thing was certain: I would not leave her side again.

When Mrs. Cardon brought in a tray, Caroline tried to eat to please me, but the food came up soon after, and the episode left her exhausted. When she slept again, I went to her mother, who sat dozing in a chair. "Why don't you get some sleep while I keep watch. I will call you if she needs you," I offered.

Mrs. Cardon, who appeared dazed from exhaustion, agreed to rest.

When she appeared again before daybreak, she looked more herself, and when she saw that Caroline was sleeping, she directed me to a bedroom down the lengthy hallway.

"I'll send a maid with some coffee and rolls in a few hours, and you can visit with Caroline before you leave," she whispered. I nodded and, not wanting to upset her, didn't tell her of my intentions to stay and meet with Mr. Cardon.

Wall lamps flickered and lit my way along the long dark hallway. The room I had been directed to was vast, though the chill had been taken from the air by a satisfying fire in the fireplace. I sat on the massive bed to review my plans. First I would cancel my trip and stay with Caroline until our child was born. After seeing what I meant to Caroline, I now believed her love was strong enough, and that if a choice needed to be made, she would choose me, regardless of my ancestry. When Caroline was well enough for travel, I would take my new family up to New York City, where we would begin anew. Robert, I hoped, would come with us, and as for Pan, I would hire someone who knew the South well enough to retrieve him. Then Pan, too, if he chose, could join us in our new home.

Exhausted but satisfied with these plans, I removed my jacket, waistcoat, and boots and lay back on the bed. I had been awake since five o'clock the previous morning, and because I knew what was in store for me on Mr. Cardon's arrival, I closed my eyes to rest.

I fell into a deep sleep, until I heard a rap on the door and then smelled fresh coffee when the maid entered with a tray. She added new logs to the fire, and as they cracked and sizzled, I forced myself awake. I swung my legs over the edge of the bed and rubbed my face as thoughts of the upcoming day rushed in. When I looked up, the maid turned back from the fireplace. We stared at each other in shock. Then Delia ran from the room.

I WAS STUNNED. Finally, I drew on my boots, splashed water on my face, and combed my hair. There was a light rap on the door, and thinking it was she who had returned, I drew on my jacket before I called for her to enter. But it was the manservant who had met me at the door on my arrival.

"Mr. Cardon is in his study," he announced. "He insists you come with me now."

"Mr. Cardon! Is here now?"

"Yes. His arrival was earlier than expected."

"Might I see Mrs. Cardon first? Would you send word to her?"

"Mrs. Cardon is not to be disturbed. You are to come directly to the study. Please, sir, follow me."

I KNEW MY life was in danger seconds after I entered the room. Behind me, Mr. Cardon's carriage driver, a large Negro man, moved to the doorway to block my exit. Caroline's father sat at his desk, one arm resting next to a pistol. He was fingering a glass paperweight, and on my entry, he stood and hurled it at me. I jumped to the side in time to avoid it, and the glass shattered when it struck the marble fireplace.

"Let me explain—" I began.

He strode across the room and, with the back of his hand, struck me across the face. "Explain! Explain! You want to explain how you seduced my daughter? My daughter!" he said. "Dear God!" His face twisted with hatred. "You nigras are all the same! You will not leave the white women alone!"

I had no words. How could he know?

"Explain this!" He went back to his desk and from it thrust out a letter that I recognized as my own. "Is it yours?" he bellowed.

This felt like a nightmare with no escape. "It is," I admitted.

"So it is true. You are a damned nigra!"

"It is claimed that my mother is part Negro," I said, still floundering with the truth.

"Part! Part!" he began to yell. "There is no such thing as part! Nigra is nigra!" Without warning, he stuffed the letter in his pocket and reached back for a knife. Lunging at me, he grabbed hold of my shirt collar, twisting it to cut off my breathing. The tip of the pointed knife pricked into the skin behind my ear. "I'll scalp you like a red Indian!" he growled. My legs went weak. I doubted not that he was about to do so when Mrs. Cardon burst into the room.

"Mr. Cardon!" she shouted when she saw the knife. "No! What are you doing? Don't harm him! Caroline needs him! She will die—it would kill her!"

"Then Caroline will die!" he shouted.

"Oh, you cannot mean that!" his wife cried out as she sank into the nearest chair.

"I mean every word I am saying," he said. "I would rather see Caroline dead than with this nigra bastard."

"Please!" Mrs. Cardon pleaded. "You make no sense. What are you saying?"

"Silence!" He flung me aside and went to stand over his wife. "Are you not aware that this—this thing of theirs will be colored?"

"What are you saying? What do you mean?" Mrs. Cardon asked, staring up at him.

"He's a nigra, is what I mean." He pulled the letter from his pocket and thrust it into her face. "Here is your proof. His mother is a nigra!"

"Surely it is a lie!" Her eyes begged me to agree.

Her enraged husband grabbed hold of her face and forced her eyes on him. "The thing will be taken before Caroline has a chance to see it. She will be told that it died. Do you understand?" he roared to his terrified wife.

"I will take the baby!" I called out, and in three long strides, the man was back at my side, the blade of his knife at my throat. "I've promised Caroline I'll take her to New York. I'll come back after she's—"

He growled before his knee shot up between my legs, and I doubled over. "If you ever see Caroline again, I will kill you both!" He heaved me upright. "You will leave Philadelphia. You have a week—no! Five days! Salvage what you can in that time, but you will not return to Philadelphia. If you breathe a word of this to anyone, or if you are fool enough not to leave, I will kill you. You have five days. Now get out of here before I kill you now!"

CHAPTER TWENTY-THREE

1830

James

As my carriage sped away, my thoughts were of Caroline and how desperate she would feel to think I had abandoned her once again. However, I knew well that her father was capable of carrying out his threat if I did not leave.

"Nigra!" he had called me. I had been called that name before, and the sound of it brought terror. Fighting the wretched memories, I closed my eyes and leaned back against the seat; when I felt something moist on my waistcoat, I glanced down to see blood on my fingers. I had an aversion to blood and fought for control as I unraveled my cravat to press it against my neck wound.

I opened the carriage window to take in gulps of cold air while reminding myself that soon I would be home, where Robert would be waiting for me. He would know what to do.

An alarmed Robert took me straight to the study, where he removed the bunched-up cravat to study the wound. "It is a small cut and has stopped bleeding," he said reassuringly. I gratefully swallowed the brandy he handed me, but it wasn't until I drank the second one that my breathing came more naturally.

"Come." Robert led me to my favorite wingback chair. "Sit by the fire."

I sank down, head in hands. Everything I had worked for was gone. All of my carefully guarded secrets were exposed! I was ruined. "I don't know what to do, Robert! I don't know what to do."

"I will do all I can to help you. Is it Miss Caroline?"

"Yes! Yes, she is so sick! But her father . . . I have to leave Philadelphia. I have five days."

Robert took a step back. "You must leave?"

"Her father threatened to kill me if I did not leave."

"For good?" he asked.

I nodded. "There's more," I said, staring up at him.

"More?" Uncharacteristically, he sat down.

I worked to clear my thoughts. "I need to tell you everything, Robert," I said. "You need to know who I am!"

"You're upset. This isn't necessary—" he began.

"Yes, it is necessary!" I shouted. I needed him to listen. He had to know the truth. If I lost him, at least I would know where he stood. I began to speak before I lost my nerve. "When I was thirteen, I found out that my mother was a mulatto. Before then, I thought I was white. Marshall Pyke owned the plantation where I was born, and I had no idea that he was my father. My grandmother raised me to believe that I was her son and that my grandfather, who had died, was my father."

It was as though the words released a lid from a fermented jar of memories, and those most fiercely suppressed spilled out. I was a child of six again, back at Tall Oaks.

"Marshall was an awful man, Robert. I was hiding under the bed when he pushed Miss Lavinia into the bedroom. He kept hitting her. 'Please, no, Marshall,' she said over and over. I put my hands over my ears, but I could still hear what else he was doing to her. I was so scared I wet myself, and after he was gone, I was too ashamed to crawl out and comfort Miss Lavinia."

"That must have been terrible," Robert said.

"It was!" My voice sounded strange—high and childlike—and I gripped the arms of my chair. "Only days after I found out he was my real father, he had me tied up and taken down to the quarters so I could be sold for a slave. That night there was a house fire, and Grandmother died in it. I heard her calling me for help, and I couldn't get to her, Robert! The next morning, when I broke free, I found a gun."

"You don't have to continue," Robert said, but I silenced him with a wave of my hand.

"Before I shot him, I wanted him to look at me, and I called out to him, 'Father! Father!' When he looked at me, I pulled the trigger. He just blew apart. And then, oh God, bits of him stuck to me!" I felt again the damp bloodstain on my chest and gave a shuddering sob.

"Come now. That is in the past. It's best we leave it there," Robert said, rising and coming over to me. "Come, stand up and we'll take off your waistcoat. I'll clean it later."

His help brought me back, and by the time I sat again, I felt more myself.

"Would you care for some tea?" he asked.

"Did you hear what I said? I killed my father."

"I understand," he said. "There are circumstances that might drive us to do things that appear wrong, but who is to judge? You were fighting for your life."

"Do you think so? Do you believe that?"

"I do," he said.

"I was! I was fighting for my life."

"And you were only thirteen."

"But now I've ruined everything. Caroline's father . . ." With that, I told of the debacle at Stonehill and of Mr. Cardon's ultimatum. "I had to leave Caroline behind. I had no choice," I said. "And now I have to leave here. I don't know where to go, and how can I leave without Caroline?"

"Who is to say that Miss Caroline won't join you after she is well?"

I looked at him. Was that possible? It was at least a ray of hope. "And will you come with me?" I asked, though I dreaded his answer.

"Whatever you decide, I will be there to assist you."

"Even now?" I asked. "With everything you know?"

"I'd already guessed at your burden," he said.

I stared over at him. "How did you know?"

He met my eyes. "I recognized in you the struggle I have within myself."

I looked at him with new eyes. Of course! Why had I not seen it before? "Are you half white?" I asked.

"I am," he said. "I am also half Negro."

"You speak of this as though you carry no shame," I said.

"There is no shame in who I am," he said. "There is only shame in how I came to be, and that is not my burden to carry."

"So you don't blame me for—"

"Your road is one I might easily have taken, given your coloring. Your choices are not for me to judge."

I might have stood to embrace the man, so grateful was I to him. Instead I offered him the only words that came. "Thank you, Robert, for being my friend."

EARLY THE NEXT morning a sealed envelope arrived. Inside was a card with only two boldly printed words: "Day One." There was no question that Mr. Cardon meant to carry out his threat. A message from the museum came later in the day to inform me that my funding for the excursion was withdrawn. I doubted not Mr. Cardon's involvement.

Though I was desperate to get word to Caroline, I could think of no safe way to reach her. I had no choice but to leave and get myself settled elsewhere. In a few months I would send funds and a carriage in hopes that Caroline and the child would come to me.

It was Robert's suggestion that he stay on until the house was sold. After the sale, he would release the staff and join me. New York seemed the most likely destination.

WE MOVED QUICKLY and purchased a small house nearby in Robert's name. There we stored some of the best furniture, the portraits of the Burtons, and the finest of the china and silver.

Mr. Cardon's envelopes continued to mark the days, but on the morning of day four, the usual morning message did not arrive. In the late afternoon, a black-edged note came from Mrs. Cardon, stating that both Caroline and the child had died.

I took the note into my darkened study, where I sat throughout the night, holding tight to the printed words, too shocked to make sense of it.

* * *

THE FOLLOWING MORNING, day five, I was still in my study, staring about the oak-paneled room, now stripped bare but for the dark blue draperies shielding the sun and the worn leather chair in which I sat. I could not believe that Caroline was gone. Surely it was a lie. But it had come from Mrs. Cardon. I wanted to go to Stonehill to see for myself, but I remembered only too well Mr. Cardon's threat, and I dared not chance it.

There came a quick rap on the door, and from behind Robert, Henry rushed in. "I jus' found him! Pan down in the Car'linas! I's right! They sell him for a slave! But I found him! He at a place in the Car'linas," he said excitedly. "Place called Southwood."

Caught up in my own tragedy, I had forgotten about Pan. "Henry, I'm not—" I began, but in his wild enthusiasm, he cut in.

"I find out where my Pan is at! He at a place called Southwood in North Car'lina, up from a place they call Edenton. Here," he said, handing me a brown piece of paper with a hand-drawn map. "They show you here."

I roused myself enough to study the piece of paper and recognized a clearly drawn map of the North Carolina coastline. How had Henry obtained it?

"Henry, I've had a man working on this for weeks, and he's come up with nothing. How do you know that this is not someone taking advantage of you?" I asked. "For the right amount of money, some people will tell you anything you want to hear."

"I know it's my Pan by the things they sayin' 'bout the boy!"

"Henry," I said reluctantly, "I won't be traveling down there. My trip has been canceled."

"What you sayin'? You say you not going after my boy? Then who gonna bring him back?"

"Henry. Surely you know it is not that simple."

"I know that my boy gone and we got to get him back!"

"I have funds. We can send someone else—" I began.

"No, no! How they gonna know it my boy? You the one who got to go for him! They sell him back to you. You got to go get him!"

"Henry . . ." I began, trying to find the best words to reason with him. Unlike before, when he would not look me in the eye, now he stared at me, his eyes overflowing.

"I's askin' you for help. I's comin' to you 'cause you know what it mean to be a slave. That boy think more a you than he do a me, but I don' mind. You can't jus' leave him be!"

I walked over to the window and held back one of the drapes. The light from the spring sun was so bright. Was it possible that the redbuds were actually in bloom? On the street, a couple strolled by, she laughing up at him. How could this be? Over and over the thought struck me like a blow: Caroline was gone. What was the point of anything?

Henry's voice broke through my dark thoughts. "Mr. Burton, I got nothing left. I already give everythin' I got. If you not goin' to get him, will you give me the money to go get him?"

I turned back from the window. "You propose to go by yourself?" I asked, taken aback. I knew the terrible fears that governed him, yet he meant to face even those. I met Henry's desperate eyes, and in the determination shining there, I recognized Pan. I spoke before I could dissuade myself. "All right, Henry," I said. "I will go for Pan."

"And you take me with you? I don' have no money, but you gives me the papers sayin' I's your slave, we come back with my boy, an' I stay your slave till the day I die."

"You owe me nothing, Henry. But coming with me—do you think it is safe? Aren't you afraid of being taken again?"

"Far as anyone takin' me, we tell them I your slave, that I belong to you."

"But all of these years you feared that—"

"I got to get him out!" His eyes filled. "That boy don' have it in him to be no slave!"

I made another quick decision. "All right. Then we will go together."

It felt good to have a purpose, and I began to plan aloud. "I will take my supplies and travel as an artist," I said. "You will come as my manservant, and we will go on the pretext that I am there to paint birds. That will be our reason to travel to the area, and once there, we can find our way to the plantation. Then we shall see."

PART THREE

CHAPTER TWENTY-FOUR

April 1830
Southwood

Pan

WHEN I COME to, there's a colored woman sittin' over me. She got her hair tied up in a brown rag and she got a nice round face but her mouth is set and she don't look none too friendly. It hurts when she starts working on my head, but when I go to touch it, she catches my hand and gives me a dirty look, then shakes her head. Why don't she talk? I wonder. Then I remember Randall and try to sit up and look around for him, but my heads hurts too much and I drop down again.

"Where is he? Where's Randall?" I ask. Last I saw of him, he was holding on to—And then I remember.

We was in the wagon. He kept throwing up and throwing up until it was red. His head was hot when he put it in my lap, and he didn't even cry no more, just made noises like a puppy when the wagon bumped over those ruts. I tried to tell him to hold on, but I guess he couldn't. When I knew he was gone, I just keep talking quiet to him, telling him to go look for my mama 'cause she'd watch out for him. Skinner turns around to tell me to shut up, quit my talking, but when he gets a look at Randall, he starts cussin'.

"We got to bury him," I say, and when they stop the wagon, Skinner hops down. He comes back for Randall, grabs hold a him, takes him to the side of the road, and drops him there.

My hands are free, but they got one of my legs in a metal ring that's hooked to the side of the wagon. "Take this off my leg. I won't go nowhere. Just let me down," I say. "We got to say a prayer over him before you cover him up."

Skinner comes back, and I'm thinking he's coming for the shovel that sits in a pile of work tools next to me, but he jumps up on the wagon. "Boy, you got to pray all right, but you better start prayin' for yourself. You get to Thomas's place, you're going to be needin' those prayers," he says.

When the driver slaps the reins, the horse starts moving again.

"Hey!" I yell. "Hey! You forgot to bury him! You forgot to cover him up!" They don't say nothing. It's like they don't hear me. "Hey!" I say. "Hey, you got to bury him! You got to bury him!" I start crying then because I can't get loose and go back to help Randall.

Skinner looks back at me. "You shut up! What you crying for? I'm the one who lost my money!"

"You can't leave him there," I say. "The dogs will get at him!"

Skinner snorts and turns around to look at the road in front of him. Before I can stop myself, I get hold of the shovel and use everything I got left in me to shove it into Skinner's back. It feels good when he tips right off the wagon.

"Whoa!" The driver pulls the horse to a stop, and after Skinner gets himself back in, he grabs the shovel away from me. When he swings, I duck, but the shovel gets me in the head.

THE WOMAN TAKING care of me comes over a couple times a day. My head's not right, and it takes a long time before I can stay awake. When I start feeling good enough to look around, I see that I'm in a big room made out of wood with no paint. There's no pictures hung, but it got windows and is filled with beds, maybe five along each side of the wall. Most of the Negroes in the beds are women having babies. I wonder where I am and what's going on, and I ask that woman who looks out for me, but she don't say nothing and I don't know why.

The woman is built big, like my mama's friend Sheila, but Sheila liked to laugh and this one don't. When she's working on my head and it hurts, sometimes I tell her to quit it, but it's like she don't even hear me.

I got a long cut down the back of my head where the shovel hit me. When the woman's not looking, I touch it and can feel it drying up. When I'm awake, I try to figure out how to get back home, but then I go to stand up and everything gets shaky and I got to lay down again.

One night after I've been there a while, the big woman comes to work on me and sits on the side of my bed heavy, like she's tired. She always moving around, but this time she looks done in. She works on my head, but in between she keeps rubbing on her belly. I see it's round and I wonder if she eats a lot or if she's having her own baby. Her hands are so dried out that they rub rough on my head.

I try to get her to talk to me. "If you use some lard on those hands, they'll smooth right up," I say.

She looks at me and then at her hands like she don't believe what I just say.

Across the room there's a man they brought in last night who got beat up so bad that all he does is moan. I'm glad that he isn't calling out like he did before, but a woman who's having a baby is startin' some yelling of her own. The big woman goes over to her, and when I see how that baby comes out, I felt like yelling myself. Thing is, after the baby comes, the mama starts to love on it, and that makes me cry. I want my own mama, and I wonder if she and Randall is together yet. And what's my daddy gonna say? When I get home, he's gonna whoop me good, but I don't care. I just want to go home.

CHAPTER TWENTY-FIVE

1830

Sukey

THEY BRING IN a boy that looks so much like one a mine that I can't hardly stand to look at him. His head is so cut up I don't think he'll make it, but I stitch it and clean it up, all the while trying not to think of my own boys.

For a couple weeks this one don't move, don't do nothing, until one day when I'm cleaning his head, his eyes open and he gives me such a pretty smile that it hurts to see it. Then he goes right to sleep again. Next time he wakes up, he stays awake longer. He's scared and he keeps asking me to come sit with him. But I got my work to do, and besides, I don't let myself favor no boy like this when I know what's coming down the road.

Every time I get around him, he asks questions. "Where am I?" he asks, and when he talks, I can tell he has schoolin', maybe as much as me. I don't say nothing, but that don't stop his questions. "They gonna sell me for a slave?" I got to look away because he got those big eyes, and sometimes they still got a smile left in them. But he keeps talking. "I'm no slave. I'm free and I got took from Philadelphia. My daddy was a slave and it was bad for him. He's gonna whoop me for sure when I get back." I put my finger up to my mouth to shush him. Everybody I'm caring for in this sick house has big ears. That's how Thomas keeps everybody in line, paying off the ones with the biggest mouths. Keeps everybody scared of everybody else.

"My head hurts and I want to go home," the boy says, and then he turns away like he don't want me to see him cry.

One night he tells me to bring over my can of lard, and when he starts rubbing my hands with the grease, I just sit there staring at him. Where'd he come up with that idea? I want to ask, and no sooner do I think it than he tells me how his sick mama liked to have her hands rubbed. He is some kinda chil'!

"Are you a slave?" he asks.

I nod.

"My daddy was born a slave. You born a slave?"

I don't say nothing and he don't ask again, just keeps rubbing my hands. I close my eyes and think about how, for the first years of my life, that word didn't mean nothing to me.

I was born at a tobacco farm in Virginia where the mistress, Miss Lavinia, raised me from a baby and was like my own mother. We'd go out riding together, me dressed smart as her. She had me reading some and writing, and I had my own bed in her room. That's how close we was, with me living up at the big house right there with her. She always kept me away when Master Marshall was around because he had no feel for slaves, but then he was mean as a snake with everybody, even her, and he was her husband. That last day when he come in all fired up, in all my thirteen years, I never see him mad like this. I was sure he was settin' to kill her.

The first time he slap her, she stays sitting up. The next time she goes down. When he goes for her again, I jump him. He tries to shake me off, but I get ahold of his arm with my mouth and hang on. After he works me loose, he sends me flying against the wall. When Master Marshall comes at me again, Miss Lavinia starts crying for him not to hurt me. "She is only a child! She did nothing wrong," she say.

"Your nigra bites me and she did nothing wrong?"

When she get to her knees in front of him, he look down at her so ugly that I think he gonna kill her.

"Marshall, I'm pleading with you not to harm her," she say.

"Get this nigra out of here!" He pushes me at Papa George, his best slave, who runs things down at the barns. "Get her down to the quarters!"

"Please, Marshall," I hear her say, "she's like my own child."

"Like your own child!" he yell. "The titles you give these nigras! You talk like she's kin to you!"

When Papa George takes me down to the quarters to stay with Ida, all the while he talks to me. "You do what Ida say and you get along jus' fine. In time Masta Marshall forget you down there and they bring you back up. And don' go cryin' and carryin' on, so's you don't have Rankin payin' attention to you."

Hearing Rankin's name make the hair on my neck rise up. The only man on that farm that I's more scared of than Master Marshall is Rankin.

When Papa George hands me over to Ida, I get scared and start calling out to him, "Don't leave me, don't leave me!" Two times he turns 'round like he's comin' back, and when Ida waves him on, I only yell for him louder. Ida hits me hard and tells me to hush up! That quiets me. Nobody never hit me before.

Ida's a tall woman but skinny like a post. Even for a slave, she got a hard look about her, and I wonder if it's because all she ever raised was boys. She sure don't give off no warm feelings to me.

"You want Rankin in here?" she asks. Her eyes show worry when she says that, and I wonder how she can be scared of him when she had all those babies with him.

Two days pass and still no one from the kitchen house or the big house comes down to see me. I don't have none of my nice clothes and I got only one pair of shoes and no combs for my hair. Still I keep thinking that any day Miss Lavinia will send Papa George down for me.

Everything at Ida's is different from up at the big house. She lives in one room, and at night I got to sleep beside her on a dirty floor pallet. Then two of her boys come in and sleep across the room from us. One looks about my age and the other is older. In the days I's there, they don't say one word to me but watch me when they think I don't see. I got on a pretty green dress of Miss Lavinia's that was cut down to fit, but what they most keep looking at is the soft leather shoes on my feet. They don't have none.

I do my best to help Ida out. It's winter, so she don't work out in the field. Instead she spins wool. She good about showing me how to card the fiber by pulling the wool through long nails. Even if it's not a hard job, my arms and shoulders get tired real quick. But Ida don't let me stop. She keep me going, saying, "You never know when Rankin's gonna show up, and we better be working."

One afternoon I ask about her children. "I only got boys. My older two was sold," she says, not looking in my eyes. "Rankin say they was troublemakers, but"—she whisper—"it just that Masta Marshall needin' the money. Now I got the two you see at night. My other one, Jake, he workin' with Rankin and live with him at the overseer's house."

"Why does Jake stay with him and not with you?" I ask.

"Jake's the only one almos' as white as his daddy. He was just a little one when he sees his big brothers get sold. When he see them go, he don' stop carryin' on until Rankin tells him if he don't shut up, he's the next one. After that, Jake change. He don't call me Mama no more, and one day he says, 'Ida, you'll never see me get sold. If I do anythin', I'll do the sellin'. Then he goes to live with his daddy in the overseer's house, and after that he do everything he see his daddy do."

"Would they ever sell you?" I ask.

She stops the spinning wheel and works the wool in her hands. "Maybe so," she say real quiet.

THREE DAYS AFTER they take me from Miss Lavinia, the slave traders come. Ida and me jump awake when Rankin and Jake bust open the door in the middle of the night. When Rankin starts tying up my wrists, I yell to Ida, "Go get Miss Lavinia!" but Ida just stands there quiet.

"Shut up!" Rankin talks to me in a way that makes my mouth go dry. He grunts at me. "Nigras, acting like white folk! There's one more up in that big house that needs sellin'," he says to Jake. "That Jamie the next one to go."

"You mean the one with the bad eye?" Jake asks.

"Yah, he's the one."

"He's white as me," Jake says.

Rankin snorts. "He's white as you, but that don't mean you both not nigras."

The dark look that goes across Jake's face scares me so much that I start to call out again for Miss Lavinia. That's when Jake takes a rag that was tied around his neck and comes at me.

"Don't let them take me," I say to Ida before Jake ties the rag tight around my mouth. Ida is pulling on her dress, but she stays quiet. She follows us outside and watches as they tie me to three other men who all look done in. They sit as soon as I'm tied, and the rope pulls me down to the ground with them. I start to cry, but with the rag in my mouth, I choke. My tongue burns when I work to loosen the rag, and I keep looking for Ida to help, but her head is down and turned away. When the traders go off for a drink with Rankin and Jake, Ida comes over.

"Remember who you is," she say in my ear when she loosens up the rag. "You no slave like me. You raised like a white girl. You knows how to read and write. You 'members that and hold your head up like a white girl. That way they buy you for the big house someplace."

By now I's too scared to cry. I keep looking up toward where the big house is and wonder why nobody's coming to get me. Where is everybody? Where are they taking me? Nobody's telling me nothing.

When the traders come back, one of them slaps at the air with his whip, and the men I's tied to jump up like a gun goes off. Before I know what's going on, they start out walking, and I get jerked along so fast that I can hardly keep up. When the trader whacks his whip again, it cracks down beside me. I'm so scared that my water start running down my legs.

"Keep a good eye on her," Rankin call out to Jake, and that's how I find out that Jake is coming along with the slave traders.

IN THE NEXT days we stop at other farms. They got slaves to sell, so others are tied up with us, but I's the only girl. It's cold and I's too scared to cry and all the men stay quiet as me. They keep their heads down and move ahead, and I wonder why they don't have no fight. Then I hear two of them talking at night and find out that one man was already killed for getting loose and trying to run.

In those next days Jake don't leave me alone. After he takes the rag from my mouth, he keeps talking smart until I finally sass back. He laughs. "Oh, listen to this one from the big house! Don't she think she's somebody! I guess we'll get to find out what she looks like when they take those fine clothes off and set her up on that block for everybody to see."

That scares me enough to start me crying, and after that, every chance he gets, Jake rides up beside me and tells me about what's going to happen to me up on the block. I keep telling myself don't pay him no mind. Miss Lavinia won't let that happen. I know she's sending Papa George for me any time now.

In the end it's good that Jake is there. At night the traders talk rough about me being a woman and what they wanting to do to me, but Jake tells them that his daddy sent him along to make sure I get to the auction without no man on me. "She'll bring more money, never been used yet," he tells them.

They keep me tied at the end of the line. One of the men has a bad foot, but that don't stop them from making us move fast. I keep up good enough, but after three days of walking, my feet are so puffed up that when I take off my shoes, I can't put them back on. The man tied next to me watches me when I set them to the side. Before we get up again, he clicks his tongue and nods at my shoes and then at my feet, letting me know that I got to put them on. "I can't," I whisper, "my feet is too sore." But he nods again, and when I shake my head, he pushes his legs out for me to see both his feet swoll' up and bleeding. I see what he's telling me and put my shoes back on, and after that I don't take my shoes off no more no matter how sore they get.

Sometimes we stop for food and water, but tired as we are, we's always ready to get going again. None of us has warm clothes to keep out the cold, and when you move, you work up a heat. At night they give us some blankets.

After about three days, my bowels start moving on their own. Up to then I don't let myself go like the men do when the drivers tell us to squat. We's all tied together, and I turn my head when the men do their business, but I hold on. Then a couple of days in, my stomach starts hurting, and before I know it, I don't have no say. The worse part is it gets all over my skirts and then the smell starts coming off me. Soon as Jake picks up on my trouble, he starts in on me, but I don't let him see me cry no more.

"So, Miss Sukey, they don't teach you how to use a privy up at the big house?" he say.

Cold as I is, my face gets hot.

He makes pig sounds. "You sure do stink like the pigs down at the barn. You dressed like a lady, but you just a pig!"

My bowels keep running, and after two days my legs and my private parts is so sore that I don't care no more. All I want is to get someplace to wash up.

On our last night out, I'm shaking from the cold and I feel so sore all over that when everybody is sleeping, I can't hold myself back no more and I start to cry. The man who's tied next to me is the same man who tells me early on to keep my shoes on my feet. Now he slides closer and talks to me: "What yo mama's name?"

I's so surprised to hear him say something that I stop crying. "Dory," I whisper, "but she's dead."

"Den who raise you up?" he asks.

"Belle and Miss Lavinia," I say, but that starts me crying again.

"Dey do a mighty fine job a raisin' you," he says.

I's so cold my teeth is chattering.

"Ol' Ernest here gon' come close to you. He don' mean you no harm. He jus' gon' keep you warm," he says.

"But I stink!" I say.

"You stink, but it ain't nothin' that won't come off with a good dose a water," he says as he moves beside me.

He stays there all night, but I can't sleep because his being nice to me makes me cry even more.

CHAPTER TWENTY-SIX

May 1830

James

MY FEAR WAS that Mr. Cardon would be at the door before I was able to take my leave. The night of the fifth day, as Robert packed my trunk, I studied the map on which I had originally planned my excursion. I set it next to the one that Henry had given me. Though his was crudely drawn, they both directed me to the eastern shore of Virginia and then down south into North Carolina. On seeing this, I decided to follow my original plan, going first by boat to Norfolk, then by coach, traveling south from Virginia alongside the canal that ran down through the Great Dismal Swamp into North Carolina.

As a boy, I had read of the Great Dismal Swamp and dreamed of the exotic wildlife rumored to live there. Previously I had anticipated a visit, though now I cared nothing about my earlier plans and studied the map solely to locate the fastest way down to Pan.

Henry was at my door before sunup, wearing an optimistic smile and carrying the small black leather bag that looked as new as the day I had given it to him years before.

Robert was there to see us off. Though he was always youthful-looking, this early morning his face was lined and gray. We had spoken the night before and solidified our plans. I understood the burden I had left him with, but he assured me that all would be seen to and as soon as matters were taken care of, he would join me wherever I decided to settle.

"Godspeed," Robert said as I turned to the carriage. I nodded, wishing mightily that he were coming with me.

Though it was before dawn when we left for the shipyards, I kept a sharp lookout for Mr. Cardon or one of his men, and when long lines and chaos met us at the docks, I pushed through to pay double the going rate so Henry and I could more quickly board the steamboat.

Once under way, the huge boat, pumping and puffing steam, moved swiftly through the Delaware, and in under three hours we arrived at the canal that cut through thirteen miles of land to meet the Chesapeake. Here we disembarked to climb aboard a lesser boat, where horses, hitched to the small craft, pulled us along a scenic path that I might have appreciated had I not been so anxious to put Philadelphia behind us. As I looked about nervously, Henry, unaware of the threat of Mr. Cardon, gave me a questioning glance more than once.

To my great relief, when we reached the Chesapeake River, another boat was already waiting to take us to Baltimore. On this we traveled for six more hours, but luck was with us, for no sooner had we disembarked in Baltimore than we were able to find passage on yet another steamboat—one that kept night hours and was bound for Norfolk.

I secured a small cabin for the two of us. When we were finally alone and well under way, Henry spoke his mind. "You got to settle down," he said. "You actin' like somebody on your tail."

I was uncertain how much to tell him, for he knew nothing of Mr. Cardon. "I might have been in trouble if I had stayed back in Philadelphia," I admitted.

"Might do, you tell me 'bout what you got goin' on, so I knows what you lookin' for."

"I was with a woman and she became pregnant," I began. "Her father found out about my . . . past . . . and threatened to kill me if I didn't leave Philadelphia."

"The girl white?" he asked. When I nodded, he blew air through his teeth. "Then it good you gettin' outta town."

"I don't know what I was thinking to get involved with her. I knew better, but I couldn't help myself."

"Yup. It like that for me first time I see Pan's mama. She got hold a me and no talk was gonna get me out. Thing is, now she gone, she still got a hold on me."

"Caroline died, too," I said. It was the first time I had said those words, but they still had little meaning.

"She do? When?"

"Day before yesterday."

"Uh," he grunted as though I had kicked him.

"She was married," I added, deciding to confess all.

He rubbed his face before his next question. "And what 'bout the husband? He lookin' for you, too?"

"I don't know. I didn't ask her about him. I didn't want to know. We didn't even discuss what could happen if she had a child. She knew nothing about me—nothing about my past."

"You 'fraid she find out, she walk away?"

I nodded. He had hit the mark.

"Mr. Burton, I got to sleep now. My head's hurtin' and I's done in," he said before he lay back on his bunk.

Though Henry soon slept, I couldn't. When I had sat beside Caroline at Stonehill as she slept, I had imagined the two of us living a life together. It was so sweet a dream that now it would not quit me. Why hadn't I planned it sooner? Would she be alive had I done so? And would the child be alive? I thought back to the black-edged note from Mrs. Cardon. How I wanted to believe that it had been a lie, but I had seen for myself how ill Caroline was. No. She was dead. The word now struck me like a hammer to my chest.

THE NEXT MORNING Henry sat back a distance, as a manservant would, while I stood on deck staring out at the Chesapeake coastline. The weather was mild, and as we drew closer to Norfolk, familiar Virginia scents came in on the soft breeze. Unexpectedly, wave after wave of homesickness struck. Nostalgia for my old home swept over me. I thought again of how close Tall Oaks was to the area of North Carolina where I hoped to find Pan. Perhaps after I found him, when he and Henry were safely on their way back to Philadelphia, I could travel the day or two it would take me to arrive at my childhood home

206   *Kathleen Grissom*

in Virginia. Surely Lavinia had been overcautious in her warnings about Rankin. Wasn't he already an old man when I fled twenty years ago?

As the boat docked, Henry rushed over to push me aside and vomit into the water. Others attempted to disregard his miserable retching as they filed off, while I gathered our things and Henry tried to recover himself.

On the next part of our journey, we were to board a stage, but Henry was unfit for the road, so I got us settled into a tavern close to the water but on the outskirts of town. There I hoped to give Henry a chance to recover before we set off once more.

On the second day, late in the afternoon and while Henry slept, I walked into town to seek out the post office. Enveloped by the warm spring sun, I felt such a sense of longing for my childhood home that I wanted to weep. Though my home was now in Philadelphia, everything about Virginia felt like mine. Here was May as it should be, thick with honeysuckle scent and lush trees bursting with green. As I neared the post office, I quickened my pace. Robert and I had agreed that if he heard any early news, he would post it to me in Norfolk. Though I knew that was unlikely, I was nonetheless disappointed to find no letter from him.

On my return to the tavern, I found Henry had worsened; his eyes were glazed with fever and his speech was incoherent. I sent for a doctor who suggested only that Henry be given rest. Five days later, his condition had worsened to such a degree that I left him only for meals and to walk out for the mail.

One afternoon, concerned and frustrated, I left for the mail earlier than usual and went the short distance into town to join a small group of farmers and tradesmen who had gathered to await the mail's arrival. We first heard the shout and the whip, then the steady dull thudding of what I thought were horses' hooves. But I was wrong. A coffle of slaves came around the corner, driven forward by two men on horseback, one who whipped the air as though driving cattle.

The double row of chained Negroes thumped by at a slow but steady pace. My chest began an aching pound when, in the midst of the dark-skinned prisoners, I saw a face almost as white as my own. He was stumbling in his struggle to keep up with the others, and when a whip caught him on the shoulder, I flinched as though it had landed on me. Outraged, I looked toward the slave driver who had dealt the blow. He was a small man, and his dirty brown hair hung clumped around his face. Though his hat sat low, there was something about the set of his jaw that looked familiar. The closer he came, the more certain I felt I knew him.

Taller than many, I stood above the crowd, and as though he felt my stare, the rider looked up and met my one good eye—or was it my black eye patch at which he stared? When I clearly saw his face, I caught my breath. It couldn't be! Although our last encounter had taken place some twenty years before, it took only one brief moment to recognize Jake, Rankin's son. To judge from his openmouthed expression, he recognized me, until a stumble of his horse and a shout from the other driver had him turn back to his duties.

The coffle soon rounded the corner, but I was left with the memory of my last encounter with Jake.

THE AFTERNOON WHEN Marshall had me removed from the big house, Rankin took me down to the quarters where, mute with fear, I was bound to a row of other slaves. We were mercifully left to sit under some trees and out of the direct sun but were watched over by a heavily armed slave trader until evening, when another man took his place. Although he looked as rough as the first man, Jake was younger, and because of that I appealed to him. "Listen," I said, "there's been a mistake, and I need your help."

"There's been a mistake?" he said. "And what kinda mistake is that?"

"They're calling me a Negro, but that isn't the case. Just look at me. Do I look like a Negro?" I pulled open my shirt to expose my white throat and neck.

He shifted uncomfortably, then turned to walk away.

"I say," I shouted after him. "I insist that you release me! I am not a Negro and therefore cannot be treated like this!"

He came back and stood above me, looking down. "You that Jamie from the big house?"

"I am," I said hopefully.

He gave a low laugh. "Then you just a dirty nigga like the rest of 'em."

One of the slaves to whom I was bound suddenly growled. "And how you know this, Jake? How you know he a nigga?"

Jake stared at the man. "You shut up!"

"He as much a nigga as you, Jake? It looks to me like he even whiter than you. Uh-huh, he sure do! This boy look even whiter than you!"

Jake kicked out, his booted foot connecting with the man's head; the man righted himself from the blow and spoke again. "But then he don' sell his own brother, like you do me, do he, Jakie?"

I wasn't certain what might have happened had the slave trader not pulled Jake back. Later in the day, when Rankin made his return, I saw the unmistakable likeness between Jake and his father. Then I looked at Jake's darker-skinned brother, bound with the rest of us to be sold. Rankin was selling his own flesh and blood.

AFTER THE COFFLE was gone, one of the townsmen spat into the silence and then asked a question. "Anybody know who that was bringing them through?"

"Man named Jake. Has that tracker Rankin for a daddy. You know the one. He's older than dirt, but he's the one to call, you got a man missing. His boy Jake takes the rough ones from up here and then sells 'em further on down, far as Georgia."

One of the men gave a chuckle. "They weren't going to slow down for that yella one."

"It's the yella ones that give the most trouble."

"Those the ones that got a little education. You don't see none on my place. I don't like to deal with 'em."

"Simple enough," said another. "Ya just gotta work any notions outta them. You get heavy-handed enough, they come 'round."

It was a warm day, but I was cold from fear. Had they not seen the look of recognition that Jake and I had exchanged? How much time did I have before Jake told Rankin about me?

I dared not draw attention to myself by leaving before the mail arrived. When it did and brought a letter from Robert, I hurriedly slipped it into my pocket before I rushed off to tell Henry that we needed to leave.

* * *

BUT HENRY'S CONDITION had grown more critical. After the doctor arrived a second time to examine Henry, he took me aside. "Look," he said, putting his hand on my shoulder, "sometimes we get attached to these old buggers, but this one isn't going to make it. Don't bother to call me back here or what you'll spend is more than what you'd need to replace him." Hearing the little value he placed on Henry's life, I was reminded how I had done the same. Though I had taken Pan in, I had not involved myself further with Henry, always afraid that my secrets might be discovered.

Still, I doubted the doctor's words. Though I was concerned for Henry, after the doctor left, all I could think of was Jake. Had he recognized me, and if so, was it possible that he would get word to Rankin, or worse, double back and come looking for me? I crouched down at Henry's bedside. "Henry! You need to get up. We need to get out of here!" I said. When he didn't respond, I clutched his shoulder and gave him a shake. "Henry! Henry!"

Slowly, his eyes opened.

"Henry! We need to leave!" I repeated. "We have to get out of here!"

He tried to force himself onto his elbow but failed, and I had to lean down to hear his whisper: "You go. You go for my boy." He closed his eyes.

"No! You have to come with me!" I said stubbornly. Again he tried to lift himself, but even with my help, he was unsuccessful. His extreme weakness forced me to reconsider the doctor's words. Was Henry dying?

All of my life I had felt trapped but never more so than now. My instincts were pushing me toward the door, telling me to save myself. But this was Henry—the man who once saved me. I had abandoned Caroline. I could not do the same with Henry.

I paced the small room as I fought mounting anxiety. Finally, when Henry slept, I left for the outdoors to walk aimlessly while trying to formulate a plan. I knew I should go back, but the idea of sitting with Henry as he lay dying was almost more than I could bear. If he did pass, what was I to do? Did I have the courage to go on my own to find Pan?

When I found myself at the water's edge, I stood in the thick mist coming in off the waves. The grasping cry of seagulls only deepened my dark mood—the blackest since Caroline's death. I couldn't swim, and I had the thought of giving myself over to the water. Yet there was Henry. I remembered again how he had rescued me. He had asked for nothing in return, save my looking out for his son. No, if Henry were to die, I must see that through. That much I owed him.

Meaning to wipe dry the mist from my face, I reached into my jacket pocket for a handkerchief. There, I found the unread letter from Robert. I broke open the seal and read:

> *Dear Sir,*
>   *There is no easy way to say this. I am in possession of your child.*

I read again the words. Finding it difficult to breathe, I sat on a nearby log to fill my lungs with the thick sea air. Then I began again:

> *Dear Sir,*
>   *There is no easy way to say this. I am in the possession of your child. Without the knowledge of her husband, Mrs. C. brought her to your home the evening of your departure. The lady implored absolute secrecy but requested that you write to her in a year's time to let her know of the child's health. She wept so fiercely and then left so abruptly that I had no time to inform her of your absence.*
>
>   *Immediately I sent out word for a lactating mother and found one who was willing to stay with us under these unsettled circumstances. She is a Negro, discreet and healthy, and having lost her own child, she is a willing nurse.*
>
>   *Your child is a girl and as fair as was her mother. Because of it, I call her Miss Caroline, and will do so with your permission until you decide otherwise. I assure you that she does not leave my side but for the nurse's necessary care.*

I had a daughter, and she was alive! It was no longer the mist that dampened my face. I used my handkerchief to wipe dry my tears before I read what remained of the letter.

There was still no offer on the Burtons' home. Thinking it prudent, Robert had settled the nurse and the baby in the small house that we had bought under his name, and he wanted my approval on the monies spent.

Then I could read no more, for I was running to tell Henry of my news.

OUR LODGING DID not cater to the elite. I had purposely found a place that cared little about who shared my room. As I rushed through the tavern, I waved off the few patrons I had met who called out for me to share a drink. Our room was up two flights, and because I took two steps at a time, I was panting when I threw open the door. Across the small room, Henry sat slumped on the rough pine floor a few feet from his low bed. While I was out, he must have roused himself, for he was partially dressed, as though preparing for travel. His head lifted when I called out to him, but then dropped again. How wretched I felt at the sight.

"Look here," I said to Henry as I helped him settle back in bed, "I shouldn't have said what I did. I was upset. We'll wait here until you get better—until you have your strength back."

I propped him up higher in bed so he might breathe easier, but that seemed to have little effect. Through rasping breath, he begged me to go for Pan with or without him.

"I will," I said.

He held out his hand. "Swear on this," he said, weakly pointing to his missing thumb. I took his disfigured hand in mine and made a promise. Then I sat, his hand clasped in both of mine, until Henry breathed his last.

I STOOD SILENT at Henry's grave site. He had died so quickly, much as Caroline had. Had I failed him, too? I was free to go and though everything in me wanted to bolt, I had promised Henry that I would go for Pan. I tried to argue myself out of it. It was too dangerous, and now I had a daughter to care for. A daughter! Caroline's child! My daughter! Wasn't she my first responsibility? Yet I knew that the baby was as safe in Robert's hands as she would have been in mine. True, I needed to arrange for them to leave Philadelphia, but Pan was the one most in danger, and I had given Henry my word.

I flinched when the grave digger threw the last bit of dirt on Henry's grave, and when he struck at it to tamp down the soil, I reached out as though to stop him.

The man leaned back on his shovel. "You wantin' to say somethin' over him?" he asked. I looked about this remote cemetery located outside of town, meant only for Negroes. Here stones and sticks served as markers, and I thought of the large granite headstones that marked the Burtons' resting place. I remembered, too, the eulogies given my adopted parents, but words for Henry failed me, and I shook my head. "But he was a good man," I said, not wanting the man to misunderstand.

He studied me for a moment. "You needin' me to say somethin' for you?" he asked.

I nodded. What harm could it do?

The old colored man set down his shovel and straightened up. "What you call him?" he asked.

"Henry," I said.

"Jus' Henry?"

I nodded again but was somehow embarrassed for Henry's lack of a family name.

The man folded his dirt-stained hands in front of him before he lowered his head. "Lawd, You got Yourself a good man. Keep him safe in Your place a glory." The man gauged my reaction from the corner of his eye, then assured himself of coins when he quickly added, "And Henry wants to thank You, Lawd, for providin' him with this good masta what looks out for him down here."

BACK IN THE room, I set Henry's small bag in a corner next to mine. That evening, after having secured passage on a stagecoach for the following morning, I paced the small room.

What was I to do about the baby? Now that I knew there was a child, I was surprised by the feelings that I had about her. I had never imagined myself as a parent—in fact, because of my parentage, the idea was not a consideration. But now that she was here, I felt protective toward her. I feared leaving her in Philadelphia, for what if Mrs. Cardon were to change her mind? Should she demand the baby's return, Robert had no way of refusing her. No, the baby must be removed, but where could I send her?

The only place that came to mind was Williamsburg. I dug into my trunk to find Lavinia's letter and reread it once again. She had written of her daughter, Elly, whom I remembered only as a willful redheaded child. But she was grown now, and Lavinia had stressed that both Elly and her cousin were independent and freethinking. As well, they ran a school for girls, and I hoped their caring might extend into sympathy for a young baby. In the end, I had little choice. I sat down to write a letter, addressing it to the Madden School for Young Girls, Attention: Miss Eleanor Pyke, Williamsburg, Virginia.

Dear Miss Pyke,

I have recently been in contact via letter with your mother, Mrs. Lavinia Pyke. She informed me that you are aware of our personal connection. Thus I dare write to you with a request that, because of the extreme circumstances I find myself in, would surely appear to be taking advantage of the situation.

I will come straight to the point.

I am on my way south to North Carolina to carry out a mission that is not of my choosing. Because of a promise made, I am bound to go. However, I have just learned that my motherless infant daughter must leave Philadelphia at once. I find I have nowhere else to turn, and I humbly ask that you open your door to my manservant, who has my daughter in his trusted care.

I set the letter aside to pace again about the room. According to Lavinia's earlier words, Elly was aware that Marshall was my father, but was she also aware that I had killed him? And had Elly been told that Belle was my mother? Would she then see my child as Negro and, if so, might that influence her consideration of a safe haven?

I forced myself to sit. I would take the chance. If Elly did not take the baby in, I would have to trust Robert's ability to formulate another plan. I could think of no other solution and ended the letter with Edenton, North Carolina, as a post station whereby to reach me. After some thought, I signed off as James Pyke Burton.

Next I wrote to Robert with instructions to hire a carriage and bring the baby and the nurse to Williamsburg, where they were to find shelter with Miss Elly Pyke until my return. I included a letter of passage and another of introduction for Robert, then added a last note for my lawyer with instructions to transfer all available funds to Williamsburg.

In the early morning I posted the letters, then waited anxiously to board the stage for North Carolina.

CHAPTER TWENTY-SEVEN

1830

Pan

FINALLY COMES A day when I can stand up some. Then I start to wonder how to get home. I figure if I can get hold of Mr. Burton, he'll come for me.

I can't get the woman who takes care of me to talk, but one night after she finishes working on my head, I ask her to bring over a can of lard. I don't think she will, but she does. When I ask her to sit down beside me, she keeps looking at me like she don't know what's coming next.

"I'm just gonna do what I always do for my mama," I say, and I take one of her hands and start to rub it in with grease. I work her hand just like I did Mama's, and in a little while she closes her eyes. While I'm working on each finger, I start to talk, and I tell her about my mama and about how good I took care of her when she was sick. I tell her how Mama had to go when the good Lord called, but that she said she would always look out for me. "I don't know where she was when I got took, but I'm expecting that she'll get Mr. Burton to come any day now."

The big woman is quiet and her eyes stay closed, but it looks to me like she's listening, so I keep going. "Mr. Burton is the man who's coming for me. If he knows where I'm at, he'll show up."

I reach for her other hand and this time she gives it over easy. "Can you tell me what place this is so I can write to Mr. Burton?" I ask. The woman opens her eyes and starts looking around to see if anybody's awake. Then she holds her finger up to her mouth so I stay quiet. Later, after she checks to make sure nobody is awake, she goes into her own small room where she sleeps and comes back with a old quill and a bottle of ink and a piece of paper. At the top it says:

You at Southwood in a sickhouse in North Carolina.

The ink is still wet. I stare at her. "Did you write this?" I ask, but quick she puts her finger to her lips. Then she grabs hold of my hand and on the inside of it spells out S, U, K, E, Y, showing me how she don't need to use paper and ink.

"Is that you? Sukey?" I ask, and she nods. "My name's Pan," I say, and I'm excited now I know her name. I want her to write some more on my hand, but she keeps pointing to the paper for me to get started on my note to Mr. Burton, so I do. My hand is shaky, but under what Sukey wrote, I print out real careful: *Mr. James Burton in Philadelphia.*

Mr. Burton, they got me in the sickhouse at a place called Southwood in North Carolina. I need you to come get me. I got whooped on the head but I can stand now. Come quick to get me. I want to get home. I'm scared.
    Pan

I give the paper over to Sukey, who waves it around to dry it out, then folds it and puts it inside the top of her dress by her big chests that hide the paper easy.

I want her to talk some more, so I ask her what's going to happen to me if I get took for a slave, but she only shakes her head and goes back to her room. After a while, when she looks out and thinks everybody is sleeping, I see her take my letter out from her chests. Then with a long stick she hooks down one of the baskets hanging from the ceiling. It's filled with weeds, but she takes them out. Then she turns the basket upside down and taps at the bottom until it lifts out. From what I can see, it looks like the basket got two bottoms. She slips my letter in, then closes up the bottom, and after she puts the weeds back in, she hooks the whole works up again onto a rafter. I count three baskets over from the corner and wonder if she'll remember which basket she put it in.

It's hard to see in her room because she's got so many baskets of weeds hanging all over, but squeezed in there she has a chair and a small bed with a brown blanket, just like we all got. There's nothing on the wood floor and no window, but she got a table with some quill pens and some ink with some paper sitting to the side.

Later I find out that she uses the paper to write down who is sick and how many babies get born, and every week she gives that over to the two white men who come to see her.

I wonder when she's going to send my letter off. I don't like this place and I want to go home.

CHAPTER TWENTY-EIGHT

1830

Sukey

EVEN THOUGH I say that I don't want nothin' to do with this boy, I never seen nothin' like him before. Almost every night now he rubs my hands down and I don't remember somethin' ever feeling so good. Trouble is, he got that sweet way about him, and while he's rubbin' my hands, he keeps asking me questions. I don't give no answers 'cause there is none. One night he say, "What happens if I get took for a slave?" I keep my eyes closed like I don't hear him, and I try not to think about it. He's small in size, but he's 'bout the same age as me the first time I got sold, and thinking back on it, I don't know how I come through.

I FORGET HOW many days we was tied up and traveling, but on our last day, when they drive us through the town, I hang my head because people stop what they're doing when they see us coming. Some laugh and poke fun but most only get quiet when they look at us. Some shake their head and look away. One of the slave men that's tied can't take no more and starts yelling at the town people watching us, "What you lookin' at? What you lookin' at?" The trader slaps the whip at him, but that don't stop him, and he starts to laugh in a way that scares me. It's like he can't stop hisself.

I's feeling so low that I don't look up no more. I just want to get to the auction yard, and when we do get there I almost feel good. The place has a high wood fence around it and they got to unlock a big door to let us in. We don't have no time to look around before they free us from the line. When they untie me from Ernest, I see his hands shaking, and that makes my stomach knot up. I never see him look scared like this before, and I's wondering what he knows that I don't know.

They hand me over to a old woman, and I think maybe she's a slave herself because she's rough in her talk when she takes me out to a small wood shed. There she brings two buckets of cold water, a rag, and a chunk of soap. She has me take off my clothes and shoes and tells me to wash myself, all the while shaking her head as she watches. But I don't care. Let her look. When I start to wash, my sore skin burns like it's on fire. I don't stop, but I soap up and scrub the stink away. Real nice, I ask the woman to bring me two more buckets of water. When she does, I soap up again, then rinse myself over and over. The cold water bites at me, and I keep catching my breath with each dose, but at least I feel clean. The woman hands me a big rag to dry myself with, then gives me a old and mostly clean brown petticoat and dress. We don't talk, but she keeps watching everything I do. Now that I's clean, I start to feel more like my old self.

"Please," I say, "I need to write a letter. Could you help me?"

She sighs and shakes her head. "I jus' know that you was somebody's pet! It was those clothes and those shoes. And now you talkin' 'bout writin'. I see this over and over. Young ones like you startin' to look too good to the masta, the wife sell you off. That what happen?"

She brings over a brown rag to tie around my head and talks low into my ear. "Don't you go tellin' nobody here that you can write." She steps back with her hands on her hips to look me over. "You been with a man yet?"

I shake my head, pretty sure of what she's saying.

"You start your bleedin' yet?"

I nod, wishing she'd stop asking me these questions.

She makes a face. "Till you sold, you keep your eyes down, you keep your head down. Don't go smilin' at no mens. They ask, you say you trained for the big house."

Then she hands me a gray blanket and takes me out to a stall.

* * *

INSIDE THE HIGH wall that hides the slave pen, a dirt yard runs down the whole side of what looks like a long barn. The big building has rooms that look like stalls in the horse barn, with doors that have bars across the windows. In time I find out that they need those windows so buyers can get a look at us before they put us on the block.

Inside the stall I get put in, there is a dirt floor with clean hay spread out. There, a woman and a small child sit on a bench against the wall across from the door. The woman looks up at me when I come in but doesn't say nothing. Her girl is asleep with her head in her mama's lap.

"What happens to us now?" I ask when we are alone.

"Now we gets sold," she say real quiet.

"Who will buy us?"

"Some mens come. They look us over. I gon' tell them I got to take my Jenny or I don' go. I jus' don' go noplace without my Jenny. No, sir, I don' go noplace without my Jenny. No, sir, I don'."

I don't like the way she keeps saying the same thing over and over, so I sit on the other bench, but when I sit on my sore parts, I get up again. I stand up until I can't no more, and then I wrap the gray blanket around me and I lay down on the hay. The dirt floor underneath stinks like a privy, but I shut my eyes and right away I sleep.

EARLY THE NEXT morning I hear men talking outside the window. One of the voices is Jake's. "She's trained for the big house," he says. "Worked there all her life, but she knows her place. She's good with little ones and knows how to cook good, too. Only lived in one place, been treated right all her life, but with the crops last year, Mr. Pyke's needing to sell some off. She's one of his best, and he's looking for a good price."

"You say she's good with children?" another voice asked.

"All by herself she took care of the three little ones at the big house," Jake said.

"Let's take a look," the unknown voice said.

The door squeals open. I sit up, feel the soreness on my bottom, and quick get to my feet. The other woman gets up from the ground and moves fast to sit on a bench and pulls her daughter onto her lap.

"Sukey." Jake comes strutting to me, full of hisself. "This here man is looking to buy you before I even have a chance to put you up on the block." Jake talks like him and me is friends.

The man looks me over, turns me 'round two or three times, then asks me to show him my hands. My hands are clean, but my nails are all broke up. He turns them over to look at my palms. "It don't look like you do much heavy work," he say.

"Like I said, she was only used for the big house," Jake say. "Mr. Pyke spoils his house nigras. She never lived down in the quarters."

"Can you sew?" the new man asks. I look up to see that he's older than his voice sounds. His clothes are cut good, but he isn't dressed like a man from a big house. Later I find out that he's a buyer for the farm he works on. His eyes are waiting on me.

I nod. "I can sew," I say.

"Jake pokes me on my shoulder. "Speak up!"

"Yes, I can sew real good," I say.

The man grunts. "Talk like you might have a little book learnin' in you, too."

"No, she don't," Jake says. "Mr. Pyke don't allow no nigras on his place no book learnin'."

"You know how to read or write?" the man asked.

Yes, I can read and write, I want to say. I can read good! But I know what I got to do. I drop my head and shake it.

"I think they're going to want this one," he say. "I'll give you seven hundred for her."

Jake almost falls over his own feet as he goes for the door. "I'll get the papers on her," he say.

"Hold on," the man calls. He points to the woman's child, Jenny. "Let me have a look at her. They want another girl, one they can teach from small on."

Jake goes over and pulls the child off the mother's lap to stand in front of the buyer. The girl is maybe four or five and looks up at the man with her small round face like she's trying to understand what's going on. The mama comes quick and pulls her girl against herself. "She don' get sold 'less I go with her," she say.

"We don't need nobody for the fields," the man says. "I'm just here to buy two young ones for the big house. Your girl here will work out just fine for that."

"I kin work the big house real good," the woman says, doing her best to smile at the man.

The man grunts. "You know you never worked a big house. I saw the papers on you. Only place you worked was the fields."

"Please, mister! I work like three peoples, you put me up in the big house."

"They ain't lookin' for nobody like you."

"My Jenny don' go if I don' go." The mother says it like she means it. "Please, mister!" she say, but she can't hold back her crying.

"Listen! You can make this easy or hard on your young one. She's getting a chance to work in a big house with good people. They treat their people fair. You let her go, she got a chance to make a place for herself in a big house. Otherwise she's going to end up a field worker, just like you. And you know once you're on that block, they don't care about keeping you with her. Chances are you get sold apart anyway."

It looks like the mama's going to start bawling, but when her girl looks up at her, the woman works her mouth against itself. She looks me over good, then quick, she puts her girl's hand in mine. "Jenny, you go with this nice womans. She take good care a you. I come find you some day, and then you gon' be runnin' a big house jus' like your mama always wanna do."

The man sees this is a good time to get going, so he picks up the child and slings her over to me. "Find the owner and get the papers," he says to Jake, and nods me toward the door. As we go, the girl figures out what's happening and starts to call back for her mama. My heart turns over when I hear the mother doing her best to sound happy.

"It gon' be all right, Jenny. You go along now. Yo mama gon' come find you."

As we make our way out of the auction yard and into the man's wagon, the child puts her arms around me and holds on tight. It's like she knows that crying won't do her no good, but her lil heart is pounding so fast and hard that I can feel it against my own.

* * *

WHEN WE GET to our new place, they think that Jenny is my sister, so I don't say nothing different. Fact is that's the way I come to see her. She was a good girl, and when she ask when her mama's coming I always say, "Any day now, Jenny girl. She coming any day now." If I was ever looking to find the child, all I got to do was go out to the front of the house where she'd be looking down the road watching for her mama. It got so that I'd a done anything for the girl. Looking back, I wonder if caring for her took out some of the sting of my own worries.

At our new place the people was good enough to their slaves. There was plenty of food, and Jenny and me slept in the kitchen house with the cook. The mistress had four young girls, and we helped her out with them, but we was there no more than four months when the two youngest got the fever and died. Not two days later, the mistress goes down with the same thing, then Jenny. We try to save them, but even with the doctor coming, there's nothing we can do to keep them going. They both go, first the wife, then Jenny, one right after the other. When Jenny goes, the cook tells me if I don't stop cryin' I get sick myself, but that chil' was like my own. Some nights I still wake up wondering what I'm going to say if Jenny's mama ever shows up.

After the wife is gone, the master walks around like he can't remember his name, then sends his other two girls to live with his own mama up in Washington. I guess he don't have no more need of me, 'cause he sells me off by the end of that month. All told, I was there about six months.

The next place they sell me to is a preacher's farm . . .

CHAPTER TWENTY-NINE

1830

James

I N THE EARLY morning I posted the letters, then anxiously boarded the stage. My destination was Edenton, North Carolina, located some ninety miles south of Norfolk. According to the map, Southwood—the plantation where Pan hopefully awaited me—was located some miles north of Edenton. How Henry had obtained the details of where his son was taken he had not said, though he did suggest a strong underground connection by which messages were passed. How reliable this information was, I did not know, yet it was all I had to go on.

I planned to stay in the town to uncover information about the owner of the plantation and hoped that freeing Pan would be as simple as offering a heavy purse. I dreaded the transaction, for I would be obliged to go to a plantation that owned slaves, the thought of which petrified me.

As the coach moved along, I forced myself away from these thoughts and tried to put my focus on what was out the window. At any other time, the road we traveled would have had my full attention, for it ran alongside the canal that had been dug through the Great Dismal Swamp. This waterway was now the major thoroughfare connecting the Chesapeake Bay in Virginia to the Albemarle Sound in North Carolina, and it had been dug by slaves who inched their way through twenty-two miles of impassable jungle. Now large barges, sloops, and schooners all traveled the route, carrying trade and passengers to and from the Norfolk region down into North Carolina.

This vast swamp was so huge that it was said to cover over a million acres. What had interested me since childhood were the numbers of unrecorded botanical and birds species said to be found in the region. So it was that as we rode along, in spite of all my anxiety and emotional turmoil, I began to take note of my surroundings.

Seated at a window on the right of the carriage, I was able to look out onto the canal and was struck again and again by the multitudes of turtles basking on logs that bobbed on the water's edge. It was already mid-May, and I might have opened my window for some fresh air had I not been so concerned with giving entry to the swarms of biting flies and mosquitoes. I peered across the waterway and into the swamp, but it was impossible to see through the tangled reeds and bushes and into the dense and dark stands of juniper and cypress that reportedly sheltered bear and bobcat and the cottonmouth snake.

Four other passengers were in the coach with me, along with their excess luggage. A middle-aged father and his two daughters, accompanied by a female servant, were returning home from a visit to Williamsburg. Shortly after our journey began, introductions were made, but I soon turned again toward the window and paid little attention to them until, sometime into the ride, I became aware of the older of the two girls making whispered comments to her younger sister.

"Oh, Addy, you don't think—"

"I do!"

The younger one, dressed in pink-and-blue-flowered calico, looked to the father, whose attention was focused out the window. "Oh, Papa, are we truly in danger?" she asked.

"What?" he asked, shaking himself as though out of a reverie.

"Addy said that we are in danger! Is that true?"

"Certainly not!" he said. "Addy, you must stop frightening your sister." He frowned at his eldest daughter.

"Father, you know as well as I that there are escaped slaves who hide out in these parts, and that should they ever stop our coach, we would be murdered for our clothing alone." She rose slightly from her seat to adjust her full skirts, also of calico, but hers of a green color and a larger pattern.

"Addy, I asked you to stop this talk!" the father said.

I glanced over at the Negro servant and guessed she was not yet as old as Miss Addy. Though she did not speak, the young servant's eyes told me that she, too, was frightened.

"Father," Addy said, "I would rather we were all prepared to meet our death than to sit in ignorance, should the worst present itself."

The three girls sat opposite the father and myself; now the youngest of the sisters lurched over to sit between us. As bags between us were set to the floor, the young girl removed her bonnet and handed it to her father before she settled herself against his shoulder. "Oh, Papa," she said, slipping her arm into his, "you would not let them kill us?"

"Of course not, Patty. I am well armed," he said, making a show of thumping the traveling bag that sat wedged between his feet. He settled her bonnet on top of the bag. "Any renegades would learn in short order who they were dealing with."

"So I see, Father, that you acknowledge there is danger?" Addy said.

"Is there, Papa?" the young one asked. "Are there bad slaves hidden out here?"

He sighed unhappily as he gave a dour look to his oldest daughter. "It is rumored so."

Patty leaned across his lap to stare out the window. "But why here, Papa?" she asked. "Why would anyone come here? Just look! See how dark it is in the trees. And look at the water. It is so brown that it looks like coffee. Why is that, Papa? Why is the water brown?"

"I've heard it said that it is because of all the dead Negroes," Addy said. "The snakes got them."

"Adelaide!" the father said. "Stop teasing your sister! You know full well that the water is the color it is because of the tannin from the cedars. One more word from you, miss, and that new gown coming from Williamsburg shall be returned."

Addy gave a light laugh. "Daddy, you know that you would as soon see me naked as without my new dress."

Patricia gasped, and the servant girl gaped openmouthed while her father shook his head at his daughter. "What would your poor dear mother say . . ." His voice broke, and Addy, who recognized that a line had been crossed, spoke up.

"I apologize to you, Father, as well as to everyone present." She nodded toward me. "I do believe that the danger we face has me over-excited. I do not like the feeling that this land gives off, and the sooner we are through it, the happier I shall be." She sat back, satisfied for the moment. She sighed and then removed her bonnet as her younger sister had done. A pale green ribbon held her black hair in place, but when she tossed her head, the ribbon slipped free. She shook her head again and did nothing to restrain her long hair when it fell loose around her shoulders, but her dark eyes glanced over to see her father's reaction to this demonstration of impropriety. When he did not appear to notice, she left it as it was. Then she looked at me and gave a bold smile.

Catching her smile, the father, as though to apologize for his daughter's forthright behavior, addressed me. "Do you have children?" he asked.

"I do," I said spontaneously, surprising myself with this easy acknowledgment. "A girl. I have a daughter."

"What is her name?" Addy asked.

"Caroline," I responded, but upon using the name, I felt strange. There was only one Caroline, and she was dead. I must find another name for the baby.

"So you have an understanding of young women?" the father asked.

"Mine is but a babe," I said, forcing myself to recover quickly, "but"—I smiled and nodded at Addy—"I see what is to come."

"Sir." Addy straightened herself. "I am not a child! I shall be sixteen before the end of this year, and I am generally quite mature for my age."

The indulgent father smiled. "That might be an exaggeration, my dear."

"Oh, Papa," she said, sighing, "I dislike it so when you tease."

"He wasn't teasing, Addy." Patty reached her brown square-toed shoe across and poked at her sister's leg, causing Addy to yelp.

"Girls!" the father corrected, while I, having enough with their foolishness, turned away to catch a glimpse of the land we passed through.

Addy was right to say that the place was dark and foreboding, for it was that. And I supposed she was right to say that many slaves had died here—from snakebites alone, since copperheads and cottonmouths were said to await their prey in the moss-covered trees. Her final assertion, that slaves were hidden out within the treacherous confines of this dangerous swamp, I guessed might also be true, but I wondered what level of desperation it would take for a man to live in a place as forbidding as this.

"Sir," Addy said, pulling me back, "may I ask you a question?"

Her father inhaled sharply.

"Certainly," I said.

"Was it a duel?" she asked.

"Pardon me?" I said. "Was what a duel?"

She raised her hand to touch her eye. "This," she said, making reference to my eye patch.

"Adelaide Matilda Spencer!" her father said. "I see now how right your mother was in wanting to send you off to a school! Where are your manners?"

"That is a personal question!" the younger sister corrected.

"One I am happy to answer, Mr. Spencer," I said, giving him a slight wink before turning toward Addy. "Yes, it was a duel. Although I was injured, I'm afraid that he was the one who did not survive."

"And was the duel because of a woman?" she asked. The coach was silent but for the bumping and jolting of the road. I glanced at the father before I answered Addy. "It was," I said, knowing it was time to end the charade, yet I was reluctant to let go of this distraction that kept me from my own gloomy thoughts.

"And she waits for you now?"

"No. I'm afraid that she died, too."

Miss Addy stared at me, and when I felt the father's frown, I addressed his daughter. "I must apologize, for I'm afraid that I've have been having fun with you. The truth is, since birth I have been unable to see from my left eye, thus my eye patch, and though a duel did not take place"—here I addressed the father—"I did recently lose my child's mother."

"Oh! You poor man," Addy said with genuine feeling.

The conversation was skirting too close to the truth, and hoping to put an end to it, I turned to look out the window.

The father, sensing my discomfort, changed the subject. "You are traveling down for business?" he asked.

"I am here to paint birds," I said, lying with the same ease that I had done for so much of my life.

"An artist!" Miss Addy exclaimed. "How exciting!"

I gave her a slight smile before turning back to her father. "I am here to study the birds and their habitats in this region."

"Are you funded, then?" the father asked, rather to my surprise.

"I am," I lied again. "By the Peale Museum in Philadelphia." I crossed my arms and sat back, hoping this uncomfortable line of questioning would end soon.

"Very good." He nodded his approval. "There are many in our area who have ties up there. I am sure they will be happy to welcome you."

My heart thumped at the idea of word traveling down from Philadelphia, but I reassured myself that I would soon find Pan. Meanwhile, I would avoid most people and hope that word of any scandal involving me would not reach these rural parts.

"And where will you stay?" Addy asked.

"That has not yet been decided," I said. "I was hoping to find an establishment outside of Edenton where I might observe the birds in the wild. Perhaps I could find lodging on a farm or a working plantation."

"Well, Father," she said, "why don't we have Mr. Burton stay with us?"

Caught unaware, I looked nervously at her father and then at her. "That is kind, Miss Adelaide, but I am looking to board somewhere within the vicinity of a place called Southwood. It is located—"

She gave me an open-eyed stare. "The land is next to ours!" she said.

Startled, I mumbled something to her about the coincidence.

The father turned to me. "It is true, we are neighbors of Southwood." His eyebrows lowered. "But why Southwood?"

While traveling with Henry, I had already planned this lie, and now it came easily. "Apparently, it is a region that has an unusually large collection of birds I wish to study."

"Well, we do have plenty of birds in the area," he said, "though I've never given them much thought."

Then came a sudden idea. With a personal introduction, this ordeal might be over with sooner that I had anticipated. "Are you familiar with the owners of Southwood? Are they friends of yours?" I asked hopefully.

"We have been neighboring farms for many years, but I'm afraid the owner is not in residence."

"So it is not a working farm?" I asked, wondering why, then, slaves were needed.

"Oh, no, it is a working farm. Cotton, wheat, flax, they grow it all on a large scale. The owner and his wife live in Raleigh, but it is managed and overseen by Bill Thomas."

"Is it a place where I might seek lodging?"

"I'm afraid it is not set up for visitors," he said.

"I see," I said, disappointed.

"Father, I insist that we invite Mr. Burton to stay with us," Addy said. "Perhaps he can be persuaded to give us some art lessons?" She turned to me with the question, then looked back to her father. "You know how Mother always wanted that for us." From the look on the father's face, I saw the trump card that Addy played by invoking her mother's name.

"Adelaide. I was about to extend an invitation, had you not spoken for me." Mr. Spencer shifted his position in my direction. "Mr. Burton, what do you say? We are within walking distance of Southwood, though I am certain we have the same birds on our land that they have on theirs. If you decide otherwise, I will take you over myself and introduce you to Mr. Thomas, though I warn you, he is not the type to have you tramping through his property."

I could not have wished for a more favorable resolution. If all went well, my imposition would be short-lived. "Well," I said, speaking aloud as I thought it through, "I don't know. I wasn't expecting this kind offer. I don't want to take advantage, but it would certainly serve me well, particularly if you would be kind enough to give me an introduction to . . . Mr. Thomas, did you say?"

Mr. Spencer gave a quick nod.

"Do come! It would make the house cheerful. Since Mother . . ." Addy trailed off.

I looked to the father. I said, "I will do so if you would allow me, in exchange for a bed, to offer some watercolor classes to your daughters while I am in your home."

"How wonderful!" Miss Addy sank back against her seat.

"And you, Miss Patricia?" I asked. "Are you in favor of learning to paint?"

She looked at me shyly with her deep-set brown eyes. "I am," she said, "although of course you cannot expect me to do as well as Addy. I am only nine, and she is—"

"I'll soon be sixteen," Addy interjected.

"Art is not a competition," I said to Patricia. "If you have a natural inclination for it, art is a gift that you may choose to develop or not, regardless of age."

"Well put," said their father. "It was our good luck to share this last leg of our journey with you, Mr. Burton, and we welcome you to our home. Be assured that your presence will provide a much needed distraction. It will be difficult not to have Mrs. Spencer at home to greet us." He turned his head to gaze out the window. Patricia clutched her father's arm and dropped her head against it, as Addy turned to stare out the opposite window.

WHILE THE COACH rolled on and the girls napped, Mr. Spencer told me of his wife's recent death in childbirth. Taking the girls to visit relatives in Williamsburg was his attempt to help them all with their grief. Needing some time alone to adjust to his sorrow, he had intended to leave the girls in Williamsburg for the summer months, but when it came time for his departure, they had carried on so that he felt he had no choice but to bring them back home, in spite of the summer's heat.

"Patricia most feels the loss," he said. "Adelaide, although she was with her mother when she . . . Well, she seldom mentions her. I suppose she is older and more capable of understanding the realities of life."

He went on to say again how grateful he was to have me return with them to their empty home, where my presence would serve as a buffer for the girls and a distraction for him as well.

CHAPTER THIRTY

1830

Pan

WHEN I FINALLY get my feet under me and feel good enough to start walking around, I ask Sukey to put me to work. I remember working hard for Mr. Burton and how he keeps me on. I think maybe I can do the same with Sukey and work for her until Mr. Burton gets here.

Sometimes if my legs get shaky, she makes me lay down, but I don't like to lay back, 'cause then I start to worryin'. It scares me thinking about how mad my daddy'll be that I went down to the docks and got took, just like he said. But I don't care. He can whoop me if he wants to. I just want to see him again. I worry, too, why Mr. Burton don't come. What's gonna happen if he don't find me? I want to get home!

I don't mind helping Sukey out with the women who have babies, but one day they bring in a man they call a runner. Right away Sukey washes down his back, but when I'm wringing out the rags and handing them back, I can't hardly look 'cause he's so tore up. I'm holding a jar of her weed medicine that she's going to put on his back when in walks two white men. The room goes quiet. The runner stops his moanin' and even the two women having their babies don't call out no more. It feels the same way like after the thunder when you wait for the hit of lightning. The quiet scares me and my legs feel shaky, so I sit down on one of the beds. The men come on over to see what Sukey's doing, then they start telling the runner what's gonna happen next time he tries to leave the place.

The two men are laughing when the one with the missing teeth sees me and walks over. He makes me stand up and then he starts poking on my head. It hurts and I want to tell him to cut it out, but the way Sukey's got her lips squeezed together, I know to keep quiet.

"Is he getting steadier on his feet?" he asks Sukey.

She shakes her head.

He pushes me and I fall back on the bed. "Talk about a waste of money!" he says. "A runt, and now he's sick to boot. Won't never get no decent kinda work outta him. Better off he'd a died with the other one. Less trouble all around."

I get scared and stand up. "I'm a good worker for my size," I say.

He takes a good look at me. "Oh! You don't say?"

"Yes, sir," I say. "I know how to lay fires and how to polish silver and—"

"Well," he says, smiling at the other man while he's talking to me. "Sounds to me like you work like a girl."

"No! I'm no girl! That's what I did for Mr.—"

Sukey gives out a loud grunt at the same time the runner lets out a yell that makes all of us jump. The two men tell the runner to shut up, but he keeps callin' out for Jesus Lawd to help him with his pain. Sukey's standing beside his bed and waves at me to bring the medicine for his back. I take over the jar while the two men start walking away.

The one missing his teeth looks back at me. "I'll talk to Thomas about selling him off. Trader's coming through. Least we'll get a little somethin' for him that way."

Soon as they go, the runner stops callin' out, but Sukey gives me a look that says I done wrong. "What did I do?" I ask her. She pokes the runner's hand and he speaks for her. "You got to learn to shut up, boy," he says, sounding mad as Sukey looks.

My head is hurting and I go to my bed to lay down. I didn't do nothing wrong. I was just talking up for myself. And now what? They were talking 'bout sellin' me off? What if they do it before Mr. Burton gets here? Then how will he find me? When nobody's looking, I start to cry.

* * *

THAT NIGHT WHEN the cook brings in the food, the grits look like they always do. I set down the wood bowl 'cause I don't feel like eating. I lay back on my bed, wondering how I can get myself out of here before they sell me for a slave. I'm crying when Sukey comes over with the can of grease. After she sits, she surprises me and grabs hold a my hand and starts rubbing it down. Least she isn't mad at me no more, but I still can't stop crying. I want to go home! I want to see my daddy. And where is Mr. Burton? Don't he know I'm waitin' on him?

She keeps rubbin' away until I settle down some, and then I figure out that she scratchin' out words in my hand. I'm a good speller, but it takes a while for me to figure out what she's saying. Why don't she just talk like everybody else?

"You got to be strong like my boys," she writes.

Soon as I figure out what she's writing, I sit up! She got boys! I wonder where they is. When she sees I'm going to talk, quick she holds her finger to her mouth. "You got boys?" I whisper.

She nods and squeezes her eyes tight before she looks at me again. I look around, and even though everybody's sleeping, I whisper: "Are they here?"

She shakes her head.

"Are they slaves?" I ask. She nods again, but then she looks away and her chin starts wobbling like she's gonna cry. Before I can say something, she gets up and goes to her room and shuts the door, and then I think I hear her crying.

All night I wonder where her boys is at and what's going to happen to me.

CHAPTER THIRTY-ONE

1830

Sukey

P AN KEEPS ASKING if he's gonna be a slave. What he don't know is that he already is one. Now they're saying that he'll get sold. How's he gonna make it through that? I wonder.

He asks me about my boys, but I don't talk about them. It's hard enough to think back to the good times when I met their daddy at the preacher's farm.

AFTER JENNY DIES and they sell me away, the preacher's nephew buys me and tells me he's bringing me to an old couple because they need the help. They have a small place and don't have no slaves but me, so I do all the cooking, and cleaning, and working in the garden.

The first while I don't say much, but I watch how they are with each other. All that old man does is try to make his woman happy, running around, trying to please, but nothing he can do is good enough. One day I ask her why she don't show him some kindness.

"You think that he was showing me kindness when he got that last girl—who you happen to be replacing—with a child?" she asks.

I don't know what to say to her, so I just stand there looking at her.

"That's right! That old fool!" she says. "We were never able to have children of our own, but he lays down with a servant one time, and when he gets up, she's with a child."

Again I stare. The longer I'm quiet, the more she keeps talking. "He said he was with the girl only one time." She snorted with disgust. "One time! Who would believe that?"

My face gets hot.

"Don't you worry," she says, like she knows what I'm thinking. "I've told him that if he lays down with another woman, he'd best enjoy it, because the next time he'll burn up in his bed."

Her eyes blaze with the thought, and I decide then not to tell her that her husband has already taken a liking to my bottom. He pinches at it whenever he thinks he has me alone, and I learn to move fast when I see him coming. In time, though, I learn to beat the old man at his game. As long as I let him have a pinch now and then, at night he lets me sit by the fire when he reads the Bible to his old woman. She always falls asleep, but he keeps reading until his eyes get tired. One night just when the reading was good, he starts falling asleep himself.

"You want me to read?" I ask, taking a chance.

"Sure thing," he says, and hands me the book like he don't know any better. I start to read then, and every night after he hands me what he calls the Good Book. I read till they both drop off, and then I just keep going as long as I want.

I don't know how, but seven years pass this way, each year the two of them moving slower, him trying to please her while pinching at me, and her happy with nothing he does.

One morning the nephew shows up and sees how slow the old man is getting and that the farmwork isn't getting done. He tells his uncle that he's going to buy him a Negro man to help with the farmwork. The two old ones go along with whatever the nephew wants, so the next day the nephew brings over the man he calls Nate. When I go to the well to pull up water, that Nate man is already at work fixing a plough. The old man and his nephew are in the house, and when Nate sees me pulling on the rope, heaving the water up, he comes over to help lift out the bucket. I see his arm muscles working that rope, and from then on all I know is I want that man for my own. I could say it was his laugh that got to me, sweet and deep, but that isn't the truth. After I saw his working arms, what got to me was his eyes. He looked into mine and there was no way out.

AFTER I TELL the preacher's wife that I'm carrying Nate's baby, she tells her husband that it's only right that we marry, so there we are, September 1815, when I'm already twenty-three, standing in front of that old preacher, who reads from his Bible before telling us we're married.

I wear a blue calico dress that I sewed up from some new fabric that the old woman gave me. I made sure to cut it big so I could wear it right up until the baby comes. At least that's what I planned, but as time goes on, my stomach pushes out so far that Nate laughs every time I try to make that dress fit. When two babies show up, I get worried that the old man and woman will think there's too many to feed, but sometimes we don't know nothing. When the old woman holds first one, then the other, you'd a thought they was hers. She looks up at me and says they was the prettiest babies she's ever seen, and I have to say that she's right.

We had two boys, and they both looked just like Nate. I won't say too much more about that time except that we had five years where I forgot everything except how to be happy. The old woman and even the old man cared about our babies almost as much as Nate and me. They each had a favorite, and my boys knew which one to go to when they wanted something extra.

Nate and me ran the place, and we was good to those two old ones. The old man still pinched me if he could, but I never told my Nate, 'cause I was afraid he might do some pinching of his own. The nephew came every few months, but as long as things were moving along, he didn't have no complaints. Fact is, Nate had the place running better than I ever seen it, and the nephew saw it, too.

When the day came that the old woman dies, we were all standing 'round her bed, one crying louder than the next. Not one month later, the old man goes down too. All along he was telling us that he was gonna give us our freedom, but when the nephew came, he said he didn't know nothing about that and sold Nate and me to two different farms.

My Nate, a proud man, started cryin' and asked the nephew not to do it, but that nephew didn't care that we was a family. It takes two men to tie up my Nate and get him onto the wagon. That's all I's saying about that.

CHAPTER THIRTY-TWO

1830

James

I T WAS LATE afternoon when our coach deposited us at the Hornblower Tavern in Edenton. There we spent the night, and in the morning the Spencers' driver awaited us with their personal carriage. The girls were excited to be going home, and as we made our way to their farm, they eagerly pointed out landmarks. The land, though heavily treed, was as level as any I had ever seen.

"Look! Look! There is the house!" Both girls looked eagerly out the window as their home came into view. We had traveled an hour or so, and as we neared the farm, the young Negro maid joined the girls in their merry chatter.

Clora had not been formally introduced to me, but through the girls I learned her name, her age of thirteen, and that she had early ties to the Southwood plantation.

"When Father bought Clora's mother for our housekeeper, he bought Clora as well, but of course he had to pay a substantial sum for her—"

Addy was interrupted by her father. "That is my business you are discussing," Mr. Spencer said.

"Yes, Father, but this is about our Clora, and I am only telling of your generosity in watching out for her," Addy explained. "I don't see how that—" Surprisingly, she stopped herself after exchanging a look with her father.

So they did sell slaves from Southwood! How helpful to learn! And surely this must mean that Mr. Spencer had a good relationship, or at least a working relationship, with those at Southwood. Yet I saw how upset he was with Adelaide for bringing up what appeared to be a sensitive subject, so I decided to rest any questions I might have put to him.

I HAD EXPECTED the Spencer house to look more like Tall Oaks, but though this white clapboard house appeared well built, it was much smaller in size. The terrain surrounding the home was flat, and the soil, I was told, was rich and fertile. Mr. Spencer was a farmer, but he operated on a small scale and owned, counting Clora, four servants. Although he appeared to be a kind and fair man, that he spoke of owning Clora in her presence did not escape me; nor, I believed from the lowering of her head, did the meaning of it elude her.

What a relief it was to finally arrive and leave the carriage, with one of us more travel-fatigued than the other. At the door, a middle-aged Negro woman welcomed all three girls with open arms amid exclamations of how they had grown in their two months away. Clora and Patricia wept in her embrace, while Addy encouraged me to follow her indoors, where I was soon shown around the house. While the other bedrooms were up a flight of stairs, I was led down a stairway to the simple but well-furnished bedroom offered me. What struck me—what pleased me—was that the room had its own entrance to the outdoors. Here I could come and go without question, and because I was uncertain what lay ahead, I welcomed the freedom.

After I was left to myself, tired out from traveling, I was tempted to lie down on my bed, but instead I opened my trunk. First I removed the soiled clothing from my travels and set it aside, hoping that the woman who had met us at the door would see to it. Next I set my leather traveling case atop the dresser. Finally, I brought out my jackets, pants, and shirts and made use of the pegs on the wall. On removing my last pair of boots from the trunk, I found the heavy packet of coins that Robert had tucked into a bottom corner. Next to it was a package, one he hadn't mentioned. I opened it curiously, wondering what Robert had included that warranted a double wrapping. Of course! It was my old jacket, the one with my grandmother's jewels still sewn in place. I fingered it to feel for the jewels, then tucked it back in the trunk. How well Robert knew me.

I lay back on the bed and closed my eyes. Was Pan really only a short distance away? Impatient to retrieve him, I reminded myself that I had one chance, and I must plan his rescue carefully.

And where was Robert? I wondered. Was he on his way to Williamsburg with the baby, and what kind of reception would they receive there? The thought that I was a father still surprised me, but it also made me feel uneasy. From the beginning I had questioned my ability to care for a child, but since I'd met the Spencers, any confidence I might have mustered was waning. After observing Mr. Spencer with his two daughters, I saw more readily what awaited me as a parent. The responsibility of raising a daughter on my own was beginning to feel overwhelming. I knew nothing of children, and the more immediate problem was that I had no home for her. How could I care for her when I was homeless myself? And yet she was all I had left. My throat tightened at the thought of Caroline, and a dark wave of grief threatened, just as whispers and then a knock sounded on my door. I leaped up to slip on my jacket before I invited my visitors to enter. When the door opened, the three girls presented themselves as one.

"Father is in his study, but he said we might invite you to take a walk with us, or would you prefer a rest?" Addy asked.

"Please, come in," I said.

"Father said that we are only to stand at the door. It is not proper for young women to enter a man's bedchamber," Patricia announced importantly.

Adelaide stepped in, pulling her sister along. "I'm sure he meant that we had to be invited," she said, her eyes eagerly darting about. Clora waited outside the room, but when I waved her in, she did not hesitate to join the other two.

Addy tried to restrain herself as the two others gaped openly at the small oak table and my case of art supplies on the table. Then curiosity won out and Adelaide, drawn to my open traveling case, moved in to take a closer look. "Oh, what is in that one?" she asked. I withdrew the cut-glass bottle and unscrewed the silver top to let her sniff my Bay Rum cologne.

She closed her eyes. "Heavenly, Mr. Burton!"

I offered the experience to Clora, who put her face too close. She sputtered and coughed, then looked at me as though I had tricked her. "Here," I said, showing her how to better take in the scent by wafting the bottle under her nose.

"You are a patient man," Adelaide said. "I wish I shared that virtue."

I chuckled at her outspokenness. When she smiled back, I reminded myself to use caution. The girl was immature and had lived an insulated life, and because of it I supposed that she might misinterpret much.

I threw on my old straw hat and slung a pair of field glasses around my neck. "But now you must take me for a walk," I said. "Do you think we might spy a Carolina parakeet? Are we far from Southwood? I hear there are many in that area."

"Oh, we don't have to go as far as Southwood. I have seen them everywhere!" Adelaide said.

"When did you see them? What do they look like, Addy?" Patty asked innocently.

Adelaide blushed as she scowled at her sister and then looked at me. "I believe they are . . . colorful, are they not?"

I took pity on her. "You are so right," I said. "They are exceptionally colorful. Their forehead and upper cheeks are orange, while their neck and head are yellow. The rest of their plumage is green, and their legs and feet are a pinkish brown. Imagine that."

"Exactly so," agreed Adelaide. "Those are the ones I have seen!"

"But have you seen the purple ones?" I teased, and when the three looked at me in disbelief, I winked at Patricia. For the first time Clora spoke up. "We don't see no purple birds 'round here," she said emphatically.

"I might have seen one or two," Adelaide said.

"No, you don't," Clora answered.

Addy shot her a dark look. "You shouldn't sass, Clora."

Patricia reached for Clora's hand. "She's not sassing, are you, Clora?"

Clora shook her head.

"Might Addy have seen a purple bird, Mr. Burton?" Patricia asked.

"I believe that Miss Adelaide will see things that others might not," I replied, and was rewarded with another smile from Adelaide. "And now for our walk," I said, holding open the door to let the three of them dance out before me. "Could you show me the direction of Southwood from here?"

I DOUBTED WE would sight the bird, for the colorful parrot, the only species of its kind known to have existed this far north, had become scarce. The girls cared little if they saw the parrot but squabbled over the use of my field glasses until I took them back for myself. I asked again about the Southwood plantation border, and they pointed to the property that appeared less than a mile or so away. Was it possible that Pan was really this close? Again I had the thought of going directly over to claim him, but reminded myself that this was not Philadelphia and here he was considered someone else's property. No, I must approach this carefully.

Later in the day I was back in my room debating my next move when Clora's mother, Hester, came to ask for my soiled clothing. She seemed pleasant enough, and because of her connection to the neighboring plantation, I hoped she might have some useful information. "I must say that your young charges are a credit to this household," I began, gathering the clothes that needed laundering.

"Mrs. Spencer raise them right. Mr. Spencer gon' be lost without her. They all good girls," she said, "but that Miss Addy, she somethin'."

I smiled at her honest observation and decided to risk raising the subject of Southwood. "I believe you came from Southwood?" I asked, and recognized my mistake when she scooped away my garments. "I don' talk 'bout that," she mumbled, and made a quick exit.

NEWS OF A traveling artist from Philadelphia must have been intriguing to the local gentry, for within days of my arrival, servants from the surrounding plantations began to arrive by horse or buggy to deliver social invitations. Fortunately, I managed to avoid attending these affairs by using as excuse my respect for Mr. Spencer's recent loss of his wife.

However, with each new invitation I became more anxious to retrieve Pan so we could leave.

Though I doubted the museum would have made public the news of the withdrawal of their funding, or that Mr. Cardon would have told anyone of the intimate and sensitive details of his family crisis, I did fear the gossip of servants, which often traveled faster than fire into the wealthy homes of Philadelphia. My chief concern was avoiding this select Carolina group of merchants and planters, with their strong business and personal ties not only to one another but to Philadelphia as well.

There was a second concern, and it grew daily. With these Southern plantations so interconnected, I was afraid that news of my whereabouts might alert people such as Jake or Rankin. If only my eye weren't such a distinctive feature.

I had not heard from Robert and I tried my best to set that concern aside, but my tension mounted. As etiquette dictated, I was obliged to wait for my host to arrange a meeting with his neighbor, but Mr. Spencer appeared to be in no hurry to do so. Keeping to my end of the bargain, I began art classes with the girls; finding them receptive, I included some penmanship as well. Meanwhile, Mr. Spencer, clearly suffering the loss of his wife, sat for hours alone in his study or rode off by himself for long stretches of the day. When he was home, I saw how easily his daughters found their way around him and noted, too, how at a loss he appeared with them. Finally, one evening at the beginning of June, the two of us were alone in his study, and I could hold off no longer.

"I understand that you purchased Hester from Southwood," I began.

He folded down his newspaper as he guardedly eyed me. "I did," he said. "And as a Northerner, you object?"

"Actually," I said, "I do not have a strong opinion on that subject."

"I see," he said. "I presumed otherwise."

"In fact," I said, closing my own book, "in these recent days I have come to believe that it might be wise for me to purchase a young Negro, one perhaps more familiar with this heat than I. He could travel with me and give me assistance when I am out in the woods. I was hoping that Southwood might have some possible candidates."

He stared at me with a strong look that I could not interpret.

"But I will need an introduction," I said. When that was met with silence, I resorted to the manipulation I had seen Addy use. "Yet you are reluctant? Do you think me somehow unsuited to meet with this Bill Thomas? Are you concerned that I might act in such a way as to embarrass you?"

"My dear man!" he sputtered. "You are badly mistaken!"

I had hit my mark and might have felt some guilt had I not had such genuine need. "I cannot imagine another reason," I said. "Perhaps I ask for too much?"

"No," he said, "you do not. But I see that I must be frank. The truth is, I do not like to visit the place. Thomas is an unfriendly man, and he and I have had words on more than one occasion. I do not like the way he runs things. That is how I came to purchase Hester. She made her way over to us one day in such a state that Mrs. Spencer would not allow her to return. Of course, I paid a heavy purse for her and then one as heavy for Clora, though she was but a small child." He mopped at his forehead. "No, Mr. Burton, there is no love lost between Mr. Thomas and myself. But you are right to say that I offered you an introduction, and I mean to stand by my word."

Instantly, I saw my chance. "Then you would support me in obtaining a manservant from him?" I said.

His eyes opened wide. "So you are indeed looking to purchase?"

"I am," I said. "I don't believe I have a choice. In these past weeks, whenever I've ventured out in the fields, I've seen that if I am to work in this heat, I will need assistance. Especially when I consider further travel. I was thinking a younger boy, one easier to train."

"Perhaps in town. In two week's time, there is an auction . . ."

"No, I would like to purchase a boy as soon as possible."

"But from Thomas?"

"Yes, why not? It will give me time to train him before I leave."

"You are thinking of leaving us?" he asked.

"Certainly that day is coming," I hedged.

"Be assured that your time here is not measured. Your presence in our home has benefited this family in many ways. This has been more difficult than I expected. Mrs. Spencer was everything . . ." His voice thickened with tears.

"I understand," I said, and did not tell him how I grieved at night for Caroline.

He blew his nose. "I only want you to know that you need not rush away. If you feel that you need an assistant for your work while you are here with us, we can see about obtaining someone for you within the week."

"Are you of the mind, then, that Mr. Thomas would be open to a sale?"

"Bill Thomas continually buys from auctions, and if they don't settle in, he sells again to the traders who stop by his place when they're heading down into the lower states. Some—including myself, as you know—have bought from him, though he commands a high price."

"It is settled, then. When would you suggest we make our visit?"

"I suppose that tomorrow is as good a day as any. We will go early, to avoid the heat, and with some luck we will return with your man."

I felt almost light-headed with relief and fear.

CHAPTER THIRTY-THREE

1830

Pan

I'M POURING OUT a slop bucket the day the two white men who bring in the runners show up again. I get inside quick, but they follow me in, and the one with no front teeth grabs hold of my ear so hard that my eyes get watery. "Look at her, cryin' for her mama," he says. I want to tell him that I'm not crying, but I know to keep quiet.

"His head looks better, but he still ain't worth nothin'," says the other one, who's poking at my head. "When's that trader comin' through?"

"Sometime in the next couple of weeks."

"Good. Looks like Sukey put him to work. We'll keep him in here till then. Sukey," he calls across the room. "You got enough work to keep this one busy for another couple of weeks?"

Sukey gives a nod but looks away again, like she don't have no time for me.

After the men go, I walk around all day wondering what to do. What if they take me from this place before Mr. Burton gets here? And why don't he come? I know my daddy don't come 'cause they'd take him for a slave, but why don't Mr. Burton come? After a while I get so worked up that I can't eat and I got to go lay on my bed.

That night Sukey already got on her nightdress when she comes out of her room and waves at me. I follow her into her room, wondering what's going on, because she never does this before. She grabs down the slate board hooked to the wall and then points for me to sit on the edge of her bed. After she puts the lantern on the table, she grabs a small rag from her desk and sits beside me. "We getting you out," she writes, and soon as I read it, she spits on the rag and wipes it off the slate.

"What do you mean?" I get so excited I stand up. She puts her finger up to her lips and waves me down again. She stands up and goes to the door to look out. When she sees that everything is quiet, she comes back with her finger at her mouth.

"What do you mean?" I whisper. "That you gonna get me home?" She nods. It feels like the sun come up inside of me. "How? How will you do that?" I ask.

"Some runners coming through and you go with them." She spits again and wipes the words away.

Chicken skin comes up all over my arms and on the back of my neck. "Runners?" I whisper.

She looks at me deep and then nods.

"Do you know them?" I ask.

She shakes her head. "We just know that they need our help." She writes so fast that I hardly have time to read before she erases.

"Does that mean I'll be a runner?" I ask. She nods. I can't help it. I stare up at her. "What happens if they catch us?" I ask.

She nods to the other room and I know what she means. By now I understand what they do to runners.

"They're gonna sell me away if I stay here, right?" I ask.

She nods again.

"Then I want to go," I whisper, but I'm so scared I got to pee.

"You got to do what they say."

"I will," I agree.

"They catch you, you can't say nothing about who help you."

I don't need to be told that if I am caught and they find out Sukey helped me, they would hurt her bad as me. I shake my head. "I'd never tell on you." She does something she never done before—puts her hand 'round my shoulders and gives a squeeze. It feels good. Now I just got to ask. "Sukey?" I say.

"Uhh?" she grunts, real quiet.

"Can't you talk?" I ask her.

She shakes her head.

"Didn't your mama teach you how to talk?" She looks at me like she wants to say something, but instead she opens her mouth big and points inside. It takes me a while to figure out that her tongue is gone. My stomach flops over when I think about her having no tongue. Where'd it go? I look around the room, trying to think of something to say; then it comes to me. "Why don't you come, too?" I ask.

She takes my hand and holds it on her big belly. Quick, though, I pull back when I feel something in there bump at my hand.

"It's moving!" I say, and even though I'm still thinking about her tongue, I can't help but smile at her stomach. I touch it again. "You got a baby in there!" I whisper, but then I see she's crying. I wait for a while before I ask, "Don't you want this baby?"

She shakes her head.

I look up at her because I wonder what kind of mama don't want her baby. Then I'm thinking that she won't need to spit no more to clean the slate because of how wet she's getting the rag by wiping at her face.

"Why not? Don't you like babies?" I finally say when she stops.

"They sell them," she writes, crying at the same time.

I don't know what to do because I never see her like this. "Don't cry, Sukey," I say, and put my arm up around her shoulders as far as I can reach. "After I get to Mr. Burton's, we'll come back for you and this baby."

She sends me back to bed then and closes the door to her room. In the morning her eyes is all puffed out. I feel bad for talking about her babies and making her cry, but mostly, I'm too scared to worry about her. During the night I remembered that sometimes they shoot the runners.

CHAPTER THIRTY-FOUR

1830

Sukey

WE HEAR THERE'S a strong runner coming up from Georgia. He's been through before and didn't make it, but those that try again got a better chance 'cause they know more of the places to find help. I'm sending Pan off with him 'cause that trader's coming through, and who knows what'll happen to him then.

I'm making the boy carry out slop pails and work his legs whenever I got the chance, and I see he's getting stronger, but we don't have much time left. Pan reminds me of my own boys, maybe 'cause he's so full of questions, like my own used to be. "Mama, why this? Mama, why that?" He's sweet, too, like my boys was. Trouble is, worrying about what going to happen to Pan makes me wonder where my own boys got to.

AFTER THE OLD couple die and they take Nate away, they sell me and my boys to a new place. It looks like the farm I grew up at, but this one is easy five times the size of Miss Lavinia's home. Here there is also a mistress in the big house, but I never see her. Her three children are all away at school, and from what I know, she is most often away herself.

They put me in with Hester, a woman who is head of the kitchen house. Three overseers run the place, and from what Hester tells me, I got to be careful of them because they don't stop at nothing. They live down by the quarters and don't bother with the big house or the kitchen house unless there is a problem they have to work out.

At this farm they grow cotton, but for the fieldworkers it's all the same. Cotton or tobacco, hard work is hard work, and nobody here gets finished without knowing there is plenty more behind it.

The master of this place I see only two times. The first time I'm working in the kitchen house, putting up peas with Hester, when he stops by with an overseer to look at me. He asks me if I have any questions and if I know the rules. "Yes, sir," is all I say, and that seems enough for him. The second time I see him is after they take my boys.

THEY WAS GOOD boys, but they was only five years old when they took us from the preacher's place. After a couple of months living at the new place, they start fussing at me to take them back home to find their daddy. I can't keep watch over them 'cause I'm working in the kitchen house, and during the day they are looked after down in the quarters. At night they come back to me, but then they keep pestering me, where is their daddy and why don't I take them home. They even cry for the old woman and the preacher man. They tell me they don't like staying down at the quarters. The other boys fight rough, they say, and if I don't take them to find their daddy, they're going to go without me. I get scared and tell them about the patrollers out there and what they do to small colored boys if they find them out on the road. I don't hold back and I scare them enough so they stay put, but soon after, they start getting into trouble. With another boy, they break in to the springhouse and help themselves to milk and a whole kettle of pudding. They's lucky that Hester is the one who finds them, even though she paddles them hard.

"You bes' get those two in line before they put them out in the fields!" Hester tells me. She only has one girl, a little one, Clora, who is easy-going, so Hester don't know what I'm up against. I tell her maybe she don't know how hard it is to raise up those two on my own.

"Don't you go gettin' on me!" she says. "I'm just tryin' to do right by you. Those boys a yours need shapin' up, and you don' want the overseers on this place doin' the job for you."

I know she's right, but I don't know what to do. I talk to them again, but they cry and say that they want their daddy back and they want me to go find him. I get mad and say they can't talk about him no more. He gone, and that's the way it is! They get quiet and stay that way because they never do see me cry before.

I'm glad to go to work in the morning, because when I'm working hard, I have no time to think. I like to cook, but I miss working outside in the gardens like I did at the preacher's house. Here the vegetable gardens are the biggest and best I ever seen, but Hester warns me against going in. She tells me that Emma is in charge of the gardens, and nobody crosses Emma. She says on a good day Emma isn't friendly, but on a bad day even the overseers watch out for her.

"Truth is," Hester says, "Emma don't have no scare left in her. She even takes on the mens that are beatin' on their woman. She goes right on up to them. 'You wanna fight?' she says. Then she lands a good one. Everybody says she's crazy, takin' on the mens like that."

The day Hester spilled a pot of stew on her foot, she screamed so loud that I didn't wait but took off running, pulling her with me, down to the slave sickhouse. There old Tony, who runs the place as good as any white doctor, came to help us right quick. After he got a good look, he called across the room to a big woman who was standing next to a shelf of glass jars. "Emma, bring the med'cine in the blue jar," he calls. When the woman came over, old Tony points her toward Hester. "Put some a that on that burn," he says, then goes to help out a woman a few beds down who's having a hard time with bringing in a baby.

Emma sits down, big and heavy as a stone, and I try not to stare. The woman was ugly-looking, there's no other way to put it, with her eyes bulging out and no eyelashes and no eyebrows. With hands as big as a man's and nail beds twice the size of normal, she spread the herb grease over Hester's burn, and when she's done, I help her wrap a clean rag around the foot. Hester feels a whole lot better with the grease and cloth taking the air off the burn.

A couple of weeks after Hester's burn is cleared up, Emma comes up to the kitchen house, looking to talk to me. "They tell me to take somebody from up here to help out ol' Tony in the sickhouse, and when he don't need you, you can help me out in the gardens. You was good with Hester, so I'm takin' you."

"You sure you got to have her?" Hester asked. "She's working out here with the cookin' real good."

"They told me to get somebody from up here, and I'm pickin' her," Emma says, then leaves the kitchen house with me standing there.

"You best go," Hester says. "Emma gets what she wants. Jus' stay out of her way and do what she says."

So that's how I start working with Emma. Some days we work the garden, some days I work with old Tony, it just depends on who needs what the most. I move my things down to a room off of Emma's hut, and the boys come there to sleep at night, but they don't like it 'cause they was just getting used to sleeping at the kitchen house.

The man that lives with Emma comes in and out, but I don't ever hear them saying two words to each other. I'm guessing he's the daddy of the baby she has. Right from the start, I don't like Emma for the way she don't take care of it. The only thing I see her do is give it her milk. Seems like that baby cries all day. I'm not there two days when I can't take it no more. I don't care what Emma's goin' to say, I go pick up that baby and clean him up good, and after that I take it on myself to see that he stays clean. I get some grease from old Tony and put it on that baby boy's sore bottom, and after that he don't cry as much.

"Why you do that?" she asks when she sees me cleaning his bottom. "He jus' dirty hisself again." But I remember what it feels like to have that dried on you and to have it stinging sore. It ain't right to let babies feel that, and I tell her so.

The first time I sing to that child of hers, Emma look at me like she gonna grab that baby away. Instead she goes stomping off, but she don't stop me. I never know a mama like this who don't have no feelings for her own baby.

One day when Emma and me is sitting beside the house and shelling beans, real careful, I ask her why she don't care nothing about her baby.

She turns her head at me, her eyes half closed, and shoots me a mean look. I don't look back at her, I just keep shelling.

"They gonna get them anyway," she say. "'Sides, I don't like babies. The only baby I ever care for was my first one. She was four years when they took her. She was nothin' like me. She was little and never did nothin' but laugh. Four years old and she talked like she was a growed woman. When they took her, I was working the fields. When I come back, she was gone. Nothin' I could do about it 'cept have the one I was carrying. Now don't ask me no more."

I don't ask her no more, but I still take care of her baby. In time I start to notice that she stops leaving him by himself and brings him along in his basket to wherever I'm working, so when he fusses, I'll go to him.

Then one day, after she's talking to some others down in the quarters, she comes stomping over to me. "I's hearin' that your boys is trouble. You best watch out. They send them off if you don't get hold a them."

First I think to tell her that my boys is none of her business, but I think better of it and keep quiet. That night I sit them down and try to talk to them; when they start sassin' back, I know that I got to paddle them. When the moon comes up, all three of us are crying ourselves to sleep.

In the morning both of those boys is curled up next to me. I kiss their baby hands that still got some fat on them. I know about the God in the old preacher's Bible, but I'm thinking maybe He only looks out for white folks. I talk to Him anyway and ask for His help.

The boys are seven years old the summer they are put to work bringing water to those in the fields. A couple of weeks in, I don't know what went wrong, maybe one got to sassin' and the other one stood up for him, but that night they both come back with a beating. Monday afternoon of the next week, Emma comes running up from the quarters to tell me they are sold and the cart is heading out.

I run, but when I get there, they are gone and dust is all I see. I run down the road, and when I think I hear them calling for me, I start screaming for them. One of the overseers gets ahold of me—"Stop your screamin'!" he say, but I can't. Two overseers got ahold of me, pulling me back, but that don't stop me. Some of the workers from the fields stop their work and are walking over, carrying their hoes. Then a couple of the women start calling out for them to let go of me.

One of the overseers shoots his gun up in the air and tells them to get back to the field. I's still yelling for my boys, and they pull me back behind the quarters, where one of the men knocks me down, stands over me, and tells me to shut up, shut up! When the other one starts kicking me, it's like he's lighting a fire, and something lets loose in me. I jump up. I go after the first one, catch hold of his hand, and bite down, his blood tasting good in my mouth. He gets loose and I grab hold of a stick. Then I go after the other one. I run at his face, and before he can stop me, I get it into his eye. All the while I'm calling out for Nate! Nate! Nate!

Why I start yelling for him after all this time, I don't know. Maybe something in me knows that I never get to say his name again, 'cause after they tie me up, they take my tongue.

First I get lost in the pain, then I get lost in the fever. The master comes, takes a look, and Emma say he's not happy about what's been done, but it's too late to fix it. For a couple of weeks my mind don't know where it's at. After the fever passes, Hester and Emma get me up walking, and slow but sure, those two bring me 'round. Emma gets me to drink a mix that softens the burn, but I choke on it because I don't know how to drink with no tongue. After I start keeping the drinks down, in the next days Emma comes at me with mashed sweet potato. She steps back when I bring it up. That night she comes with more. This time the sweet potato got molasses.

It takes a long time to work it down 'cause every swallow makes me feel like it's going to get stuck. One night I figure out that I can die if I don't let no food stay down, but Emma works so hard to get it in me that I wait for her to go before I bring it up again.

And that's what I do every time Emma leaves, until one night she catches on. I lay down and make like I's going to sleep so Emma will leave, but instead she comes over to my pallet. "Scoot over," she says, then lays down beside me. "I gon' stay the night."

What's she doing? I wonder. We lay there looking at each other. "You got to cry, girl," she says. I look at her real long. I don't feel like crying. I don't feel nothing but that my babies are gone and there's a fire in my mouth. Besides, what's Emma doing telling me to cry? If there's one woman on this place who don't cry, it's Emma. Everybody knows that.

So Emma and me just lay there looking at each other. She takes a rag to wipe my mouth. I'm still so sore that I don't know there's spit and maybe some blood dripping out the side. I close my eyes, hoping she will go so I can throw up the potato.

"Suk," she say real soft, but I keep my eyes closed like I'm sleeping. "Sukey," she say again, "you got to live, girl. They never should a done this to you. What my baby boy gonna do if you gone?" When I hear a noise like she's choking, I open my eyes. I never hear that sound coming out of her. Then I see her whole face is wet, and I know she's crying the best she remembers how. My arms feel like logs, but I reach over and take the rag she got and I wipe down her face. More choking sounds come from Emma until her whole body is wet and shaking like she got a bad fever, so I put my arms 'round her like she one of my babies.

I hold her like that till we both fall asleep. In the morning I get up when she's sleeping, her eyes swollen bad as one of the times she's been drinking and fighting. I get myself up and go to old Tony and let him know that I need two cups of his healing tea. I take them back and give one to Emma. She don't say nothing when we drink it together, but since that day we watch out for each other. And when she needs to, Emma does the talking for me.

I work in the garden, but more and more old Tony needs me to help out in his hospital. He starts teaching me about the herbs that help in the healing, which ones do what, and when I start to write down the mixes, he sees that I can read and write, and it's not long before I find out that he can do the same.

On the day I find out where my boys is at, someplace down in Georgia, I set it in my mind to go find them. A few nights later I try running, but I don't get far before they catch me. They give me a lashing that puts me down for a couple of weeks, and they tell me I go again, they kill me.

Maybe a year goes by before one of the field men, drunk, gets ahold of me and takes me back of the barns. First I fight, but when he gets rough, I just let him finish up. He catches me two more times before I write a note to old Tony. He goes to Emma, and that night the man who's bothering me gets to know what Emma's like when she's not happy. When I start showing a baby, Emma shakes her head, then puts her arm around my shoulders and says not to worry, she'll help me when the time comes.

"Don't give him a name," Emma says when the baby shows up, but in my head I call him Nate. After that I take care of him right along with Emma's boy, before they move the boys down to the quarters and then sell them off. The day they go, Emma does the fighting for me. She goes too far, and the beating that she gets shoulda done her in, but Hester and me bring her through.

After that time the three of us watch out for each other until the day when Hester and her girl, Clora, and me gets sold up here to Southwood plantation. They don't buy Emma.

AT SOUTHWOOD THEY need somebody to run their new hospital, so they put me in there, thinking I know more than I do. I don't say otherwise; lucky for me I got all of old Tony's medicines writ down. It don't seem to bother nobody that I can read and write, and they like that I don't talk.

There's a man at Southwood who right from the start was good to me. When he got the fever, I treated him, and after he got back on his feet, we get together and he the daddy of this baby. It take some time before he lets me know that he helps colored folk that are running, and it don't take long before I'm helping him out. He got a big job on this place, heads up some of the field workers. The two of us talk about running one day, but we know we can't go together. They'd track us till we was dead.

Almost every time another runner comes through, my man says, "Sukey, girl, you wanna take this chance, you go." But even though I want this baby free, I guess I'm just too scared. Where am I gonna go? I used to think I could try to find my way back to Virginia and Miss Lavinia at Tall Oaks, but then Masta Marshall would just sell me again.

Even if I never get away, I feel good helping others make it out. We never know for sure when the next bunch of runners is coming through. Sometimes it's only one, sometimes four or five. One more scared than the next, but that don't stop them. I keep hoping that one of these times Emma or maybe even one of my boys is going to come through.

CHAPTER THIRTY-FIVE

1830

James

IT WAS ALREADY June, the Monday morning we set out for Southwood. I used great care to dress, taking it upon myself to polish my tall brown boots and brush out my best dark brown jacket. Hester provided me with a clean and pressed white shirt and cravat, and before donning it, I gave myself a close shave. As I patted on my Bay Rum, I peered into my traveling case mirror and was relieved to see that wearing a hat had served its purpose, and the sun had not affected my complexion.

Surprisingly, Adelaide joined us at the morning table, dressed prettily in a pale green riding costume. When she announced her decision to accompany us, her father first objected, but she pouted in the way he could not resist, and with a shrug meant for me, he gave his assent. In fact, I was happy to have her along, thinking she might prove an added distraction if anyone looked me over too carefully.

The horse provided me was a gray thoroughbred. I was anxious to leave and did not use the mounting stone but made the leap up onto the horse's back.

"You see, Father! That is how it is done." Adelaide nodded at me approvingly.

"Well, maybe if I were ten years younger and a few pounds lighter," Mr. Spencer said, patting his round stomach, but he did not smile at her as usual, and I realized then how tense he was. In fact, he appeared as anxious as I felt. All I desired was to get hold of Pan and to leave this place. I had my purse in the saddlebag, and with any luck, by tomorrow, Pan and I would be on our way up to Williamsburg. There I could only hope that Robert and my daughter safely awaited my arrival.

Adelaide chattered merrily as the three of us rode together toward our destination, but as we approached the drive leading up to Southwood, my horse shied, setting off skittish behavior with the other two horses.

"I'm afraid these horses haven't been worked in a while. Use a heavy hand if you must," Mr. Spencer directed. "Here, Addy, let me take your reins," he said as she worked to calm her horse.

"No, Father!" she said, using her crop to take command, while glancing at me to see if I noted her accomplished riding skills.

As we approached Southwood, we moved our horses out of the brutal sun and into the shade of the tall cedars that lined the long drive. Past the trees on either side lay open fields with workers bent over vegetation. We were approaching one of the largest cotton plantations in this northern Carolina region.

I looked about hopefully, wondering if I might see Pan out in the fields, but my horse, sensitive to my nerves, began to sidestep.

"Use your crop!" Mr. Spencer instructed, but I knew the problem was with me and not the horse.

"He'll be fine. He'll settle down. How many acres do they have in cotton?" I asked as a means of distraction.

"That is a question you might ask Thomas," Mr. Spencer said, his attention on his own spirited horse.

The night before, Mr. Spencer had warned me to tread carefully with Bill Thomas. My host explained that for years Thomas had complete run of Southwood and the absentee owners relied on him exclusively. No one in the area could dispute that this was one of the most efficiently run plantations and that the cotton production was enviable. However, Mr. Spencer said, "Bill Thomas is a man who runs his place by his own rules."

I knew what he insinuated, for I remembered Tall Oaks and the absolute control Rankin had enjoyed. His actions were seldom, if ever, influenced by the law, and as a result he was ruthless.

THE FIRST BUILDING that came into view was a fair-sized clapboard house set at the head of the drive. It had a balcony protruding from the second floor, a place where a man might observe all of the many buildings under his jurisdiction. I was not surprised to learn that it was Bill Thomas's home.

A wide brick path was laid parallel to the drive and both ran up and past a row of neatly constructed whitewashed buildings. Farther down, the two trails divided, and while the road wound around to the right, the brick path turned left toward a handsome house set in the center of a heavily treed garden. This house, too, was white-painted clapboard, but it was easily four times the size of the first, and from it protruded three large balconies.

From atop my horse I could see the entire plantation laid out on flat terrain, with a river at the far end creating a natural boundary. A good distance from the main house, set back from the riverbank, was an extended row of small but orderly gray cabins that constituted the quarters.

Another boundary was set to the left of the house by a canal that intersected with the river and traveled down the property out and away as far as I could see. I later learned that this waterway was used to transport the cotton via a series of rivers and other canals that wound their way down to Edenton.

We stopped in front of the manager's home and before Mr. Spencer had time to dismount, a woman came to the door. Although she was white, her faded homespun dress, worn face, and disheveled hair alerted one to the fact that she was not a woman of leisure. She dried her hands with a rag, then tossed it over her shoulder as she squinted at us. "You looking for Bill?" she asked in a hard voice. Not waiting for a reply, she pointed toward the big house. "He's up there, workin' on something. But he don't have no time for sittin' around talkin'."

"We've come on business," Mr. Spencer answered.

"You'll just have to go on up, then. Ask any of the niggas you see where he is. They'll tell you."

My horse was prancing and so agitated that I decided to dismount. "Give him the crop!" Mr. Spencer directed, but my feet were already on the ground.

"I'll straighten him out tomorrow," I answered.

"We might as well join you on foot." Mr. Spencer slipped down from his horse and handed me the reins, thereby freeing himself to assist his daughter.

"I'll get Alfred from the barn to take your horses," the woman said. Without warning, she put her fingers to her mouth and gave a shrill whistle for help. Addy was preparing for dismount when her horse, startled by the whistle, jumped back. Addy, tossed forward, flew through the air and landed hard on the brick path. With her scream of pain, her father rushed to her side. As Mr. Spencer helped her stand, her face went white. "Daddy," she cried, clutching at her arm and falling against him. "Daddy! My arm!"

He scooped her up and frantically looked about. The woman hesitated but then opened the door of her home and waved the two of them in before she looked back at me. "Give Alfred your horses," she said, nodding toward the newly arrived servant, "then go on to that building up there, the sickhouse, the one with the glass windows. Get Sukey. She's a nigga, but good as any doctor hereabouts."

I did as directed and moved swiftly past the washhouse yard where women boiled and scrubbed and slapped at the air with wet laundry. Though concerned for Addy, I hadn't forgotten Pan as I hurried up the road. I glanced into the next building, where the door stood open and inside a lone woman clanked away at a room-sized loom. I kept moving, and in the shade of the loom house, I startled a group of women who looked up, grim-faced, from their spinning. I greeted them with a nod, but they did not respond. This might have been a peaceful scene, but something was amiss. Unsettled by their silence, concerned about Addy, and growing more desperate to get a glimpse of Pan, I left the drive to cut through a yard and found myself at the back of the cooper's shop. I brushed past some dozen or so newly constructed wooden barrels and rounded the building so quickly that I almost tripped over the cooper. The man worked like one possessed. Wood shavings flew as perspiration dripped from his face, and even as I greeted him, he didn't take note of me. Then I saw why.

In front of him, in the center of the work yard, set a type of stockade. There, seated on a thin wedge of board, a nude Negro man was locked into a wooden contraption. With his feet tied straight out and his hands secured behind him, he had nothing to support his back; the pain of the wood cutting into his buttocks must have been unbearable. Added to his torture were the scorching sun and the clouds of flies and mosquitoes that surrounded him. His head lolled to the side and his eyes were glazed with pain, while his breathing came in short guttural grunts.

Because of his location, all of the yard workers were witness to his torment yet almost certainly were forbidden to do anything to relieve his suffering. I stared, sickened, before turning away.

I ran then toward the building with glass panes and rapped heavily on the door. When there was no response, I pushed in and closed the door behind me. My breathing finally quieted as I looked about the sparsely furnished hallway, and when I heard voices, I followed the sound through another door. The large room I entered had at least twenty pallets lining the walls, and though most were empty, it was well built to serve this community of more than two hundred slaves.

The floorboards creaked when I stepped across the doorsill. A young boy, assisting a Negro woman who was caring for a patient, turned at the sound of my entry. He stared for only a moment before he dropped the wooden bowl he held. "Mr. Burton! Mr. Burton!" he called out as he ran toward me. "I knew you'd come for me! I knew you'd come for me!" He clutched at my waist, his whole body trembling. It was difficult to believe that this sad, emaciated boy was Pan.

As I patted his shorn head, I felt the long jagged scar. What had they done to this gentle boy? How had he been so badly injured? In those moments, my fear for myself turned to rage for this child. I wanted to snatch him and go, but after what I had already seen, I knew that now more than ever, I needed to hold myself in check. I had been warned that this place was governed by its own law, and guards were likely everywhere.

All eyes were on us as I pried Pan loose, then set him back and looked directly into his eyes. "Listen to me!" I said, speaking as low as I could. "Do not say another word! You must not address me. Do you understand?" I held both of his frail shoulders and looked into his eyes. "Your leaving here will depend on this."

He nodded, but he reached for my hand again as though for reassurance.

"No!" I said, pulling back. "You must go back to work." I turned him around, then directed him toward the large homely woman who watched silently. "I'm looking for Sukey," I said.

Pan pointed to her. "That is Sukey, Mr. Burton!"

"Pan! Do not use my name!"

The boy's shoulders slumped. "I'm sorry," he said, his eyes enormous in his drawn face.

I forced my attention away from him. "Are you Sukey?" I asked the woman.

She nodded, then slowly came forward as she readjusted her faded head wrap and smoothed out her brown skirt. She was a heavyset woman with plain features, and as she approached me, her black eyes kept darting to my eye patch.

"She can't talk," Pan said.

"Tell her that she is needed at Mr. Thomas's house," I said.

"She can hear, she just can't talk," said Pan when the woman shot me a look. Did she mean the boy harm? Would she tell Thomas what she had seen the boy do?

I wanted to ask her for help, but she moved quickly. As I left, I glanced back at Pan and put my finger to my lips, reminding him of silence. His eyes sparkled when he nodded his understanding.

By the time we reached Thomas's house, he had come and gone and the doctor had been sent for. It appeared Addy's arm was broken, and the decision to take her up to a bedroom in the big house had been made. When Mr. Spencer requested that I go to fetch Hester so she might attend to Addy, I could not ride out fast enough, wanting only to head for the north. But I had found Pan, and now I had only to extricate him.

CHAPTER THIRTY-SIX

1830

James

ADDY WAS TO remain at Southwood for seven days. Her arm had been set, and though it was a clean break, the doctor insisted that she not be moved. She was made as comfortable as possible in a guest room of the big house.

Following her first day of confinement, Mr. Spencer returned from seeing her and called me into his study. "Hester will remain with Addy for the duration of her stay. I will spend the mornings with her and go back every evening, but I need some time in the afternoon to see to my work. I realize this might be considered unusual, but I wonder if I might ask you to visit with her in the afternoons. I can't say that I like to leave her and Hester alone on the place without someone to oversee to their welfare. Perhaps you would be willing to check in with her and read to her for an hour or so?"

"I would be happy to do so," I said, feeling some obligation but also realizing the access it provided me to Southwood.

As though reading my thoughts, Mr. Spencer continued on. "I know you want to get yourself a man," he said, "but I'm asking that you wait until Addy is back home. Thomas's moods are too unreliable, and I'd like Addy out of there if you decide to carry through with a purchase."

"Certainly," I said, and though frustrated with his request, I thought it best not to press my need.

* * *

WHEN I VISITED the following afternoon, I found Addy sitting up in a chair with Hester by her side.

"How well you are doing! It is wonderful to see you sitting in a chair," I said.

"It's my first time up! I almost fainted," she said with some pride. "It was fortunate that Hester's friend Sukey was here to help catch me."

I looked at Hester. "She is your friend?"

Hester promptly busied herself straightening the bedcover.

"They came to this place together," Addy said. "Isn't that true, Hester?"

Hester kept her attention on the red quilt that she was smoothing. "We know each other a long time," she said.

"Hester won't tell me why Sukey won't speak," Addy complained.

There was an awkward silence in the room. "I don't talk about that," Hester finally said.

"All I want to know is why she won't talk," Addy argued.

"She jus' can't, is all," Hester said.

"Does she not like me, or is that the way she is with everyone?" Addy asked.

"She don't talk to nobody," said Hester.

"But why won't she?" Addy persisted.

"'Cause she can't," Hester said, her tone of voice issuing a warning that Addy disregarded.

"But why won't you tell me, Hester?" she pushed.

"That none a your business!" Hester said in a voice so harsh that the girl sat back in surprise. When Addy's eyes watered, Hester spoke more gently.

"Miss Addy, I don't mean to talk to you like that. I'm just wantin' you to get better so we can get home, is all. I don't like being back at this place."

Addy was ready to take advantage of the opportunity. "All I wanted to know was why that woman won't talk to me," she said, actually sounding contrite.

Hester looked at me helplessly before she turned back to Addy. "She won't talk 'cause she can't. They take out her tongue."

In the heat of the room, a chill traveled the length of my body. Addy's mouth opened and then closed again. "I want to go back to bed," she said weakly.

I HONORED MR. Spencer's request and returned to visit with Addy over the next couple of days. On my way to the big house, I passed by the hospital where I knew Pan waited, though I dared not make contact with him.

I struggled with fear for my own safety and continually fought myself over wanting to make a quick escape on my own. But then I would recall the knotty feel of the long scar on Pan's head that marked his abuse, and fury would renew my resolve. As soon as Addy was home, I would meet with Thomas and offer a purse he could not refuse.

On Thursday afternoon I was with Addy longer than usual and stayed to play chess with her until her doctor arrived. It seemed he would never come, but when he finally did, I made my exit. It was then, while hurrying down the back porch steps, that I met Bill Thomas for the first time.

Thomas was a tall man, and his stride corresponded to the length of his legs. Had I met him in a public square, I might have given him notice, for he was a strikingly handsome man who carried himself with an authority that reflected undisputed power. Clothed in various shades of brown, he wore a low-slung leather belt from which hung a handgun and, next to it, a treacherous-looking sheathed knife. He nodded in my direction but would have kept on walking had I not stepped out in his path. "Good day," I greeted him.

"And who are you?" he asked.

"My name is James Burton. I am an artist, and I am visiting with the Spencers."

"I see," he said.

"And you are Bill Thomas?" I asked in a friendly voice, for he did not appear the brute I had expected.

He nodded, then looked toward the house. "How's the girl?"

"She appears to be doing well," I said. "I believe that we will be able to take her home soon."

"Sooner the better," he said.

I duly noted the cold comment but saw an opportunity and took it. "I've been wanting to meet you," I said.

"And why's that?"

"As I mentioned earlier, I am an artist, here to paint birds for the museum in Philadelphia."

"What's that got to do with me?" he asked.

I mustered as optimistic a tone as I could. "I was hoping to solicit your help. Since my arrival, I have come to realize that I will be needing some assistance when I am out in the field. I specifically need someone to tote my supplies and help me out when I travel, as I foolishly left my valet at home. This summer heat is more brutal than I expected, but your Negroes seem to be able to tolerate it well."

He grunted.

"I thought that I might be able to purchase a young man from you," I added quickly.

He smirked. "I thought you people up there didn't believe in payin' money for nigras."

"Not everyone thinks along those lines," I said.

"Uh-huh," he said. "So what are you wanting from me?"

"When I was down in your hospital the other day, I saw a young boy who I thought might work out," I said. Made uncomfortable by his stare, I glanced toward the building.

He waited for me to turn back. "And which one is that?" he asked.

I tried to sound as offhand as I could. "He's small, thin, but I didn't get his name. He was helping that Sukey woman out."

"Ah, him. Hmm. Got him a couple a months back. Sickly. Isn't broke in yet."

"I'm hoping you'll sell him to me. He's of the age I was considering, and he won't be expected to do much heavy work. I'm prepared to pay."

"He'd cost, that's for sure."

"Just give me a number," I said, and knew that I sounded too eager. Thomas eyed me as I removed my hat to wipe my forehead dry.

"I have a couple others that might work out," he said.

I knew this ploy, for I had seen this same strategy applied when trading for a horse. He meant to get a feel for how determined I was

to buy this particular boy. I had no desire to haggle over price. "Pan—"
I caught myself, but not before he noted it. "I believe the boy's name is
Pan," I said, my chest tightening as I realized my mistake. "I think that's
what that woman Sukey called him. No, it couldn't have been her. She
doesn't speak, does she?" I hastily sought to recover. "It's unimportant.
All I need to know is how much you want for him."

Thomas leaned over and snapped off a tall blade of grass, then put
it between his teeth and began to chew. He looked me over, then spat
out the grass. "I'll see you another time," he said. "I got some thinkin' to
do." As he turned away, so sure of his position, dark fury shot through
me. How dare he dismiss me as though I were one of his Negroes!

He had no sooner disappeared than a pebble struck the back of my
head. I swung around to see Sukey peering out from the corner of the
house. She waved me over, and as soon as I rounded the house, she
pulled out a slate and began to write. "You Jamie Pyke?"

I was so startled that I thought I had misread the words. I reread
them. I had not.

She quickly erased the board with her skirt and scratched out, "I am
Sukey. Tall Oaks."

My stomach dropped, and my mouth went slack as I stepped back.
What did she mean? Surely it wasn't possible. Was she trying to say
that she, this aged, worn woman, was Lavinia's favored servant from
Tall Oaks? And if she was, how had she so easily recognized me? I
stared at her, searching her face, while she scrawled again. "Get Pan
out," the slate read.

I forced myself to stop staring at her. "I will," I said. "I'm going to
buy him."

She shook her head violently. "Trader coming for him," she wrote.

"I'm arranging to get him," I repeated, wondering if her hearing was
impaired as well as her speech.

She was about to write something more, but when two Negro men
rounded the corner, the startled woman fled.

MY HORSE HAD free rein, and as he galloped for home, my mind raced.
I fought to control my rising panic. What had Sukey meant when she

said that a trader was coming? How soon, and was he coming just for Pan? And what of Sukey? She was older than I, and my memories from Tall Oaks were vague, but I recalled well the terrifying day when she had been sold. What were her memories of me, and if she knew of my lineage, would she use it against me to benefit herself?

Perhaps it would be best if I tried to buy her along with Pan. But Thomas was already suspicious. What if I were to approach him from another angle and state that both Pan and Sukey had been stolen from me? But I had nothing to offer as proof, and I understood the man well enough to know that if he suspected my desire, he would refuse me. I had already made that error! Because of it, I worried that I had already jeopardized the sale of Pan.

My horse whinnied at an approaching gig. I reined him to the side of the road as Mr. Spencer and Patricia wheeled up.

"I cried until Daddy said he would take me to see Addy!" Patricia called out happily.

Mr. Spencer glanced at me with a sheepish grin. "You have two letters waiting for you. Sam went into town today and has just returned with the mail," he said.

Finally, some word from Robert! "Wonderful!" I said. Though hesitant to let him know that I had gone against his wishes, I brought up my meeting with Bill Thomas. As I explained our exchange, Mr. Spencer lost his pleasant look. "I'm sorry for not waiting," I quickly added, "but the meeting was so fortuitous that I felt I had to take advantage of it."

"And does Thomas have a man for you?"

"There is a young boy I have seen around. He works with that woman Sukey in the hospital. He is the one I want."

Mr. Spencer looked at me curiously. "I see," he said. "And Thomas has agreed to the purchase?"

"Not yet," I said. "I'm afraid he's taken a dislike to me. I wonder if you might put a good word in for me."

He frowned and shook his head. "Once Thomas decides something, nothing will convince him otherwise. He is that way in all matters and believes himself above the law. Unfortunately . . ." He looked over at

Patricia and thought better of what he was about to say. "My suggestion is to let it go, and we will go to an auction next week. There are plenty of others for sale."

"The thing is, I have settled on this one boy. He would be perfect for my needs. And I'm thinking of purchasing that Sukey woman, too. She seems to know a lot about—"

"Forget about her! She runs that hospital for him, and he isn't about to let her go. I say to forget about the boy as well."

"But he is the one I want," I argued.

He leaned toward me, and though his voice was quiet, it was deep and commanding. "Listen to me! Thomas is not a man to fool with. There is a lot of swampland in these parts, and you would not be the first to go missing after a disagreement with him." With that, he slapped the reins and put a quick end to our conversation.

WHEN I FOUND the two letters addressed to me on a tray in the front entry, I took them directly to the privacy of my room.

The first letter I opened was from Robert.

Dear Mr. Burton,

We arrived safely in Williamsburg and have been well received by both Miss Madden and Miss Pyke. Rest assured that your daughter is cared for and in good health.

Though the Philadelphia house has not yet been sold, I have hired a reliable caretaker, and Molly will stay on until such time as a sale takes place. As per your request, your lawyer has seen to the transfer of your monies to Williamsburg, and I have included a record of what has been spent to date. I have been as judicious with expenditures as possible.

I await your safe return and remain a devoted servant to both you and your daughter,
Robert

Satisfied to learn that the baby and Robert were safe, I tore open the second letter.

Dear Mr. Burton,

How surprising it was to receive your letter.

Your lineage in this family is well known and because of it, Aunt Meg's mother, Mrs. Madden, who is elderly and old-fashioned, quite disapproved when Aunt Meg and I agreed to honor your request. However, please know that your Miss Caroline is kept safely under our wing and will remain so until your return.

As well, your man Robert has been given our protection.

We eagerly await your arrival,

Eleanor Pyke

I reread both letters several times until the words blurred. My half sister Eleanor's short note told me little, but what seemed clear was that I needed to get to Williamsburg as soon as possible. But first there was Pan.

THE NEXT AFTERNOON, as I rode again to see Addy at Southwood, I decided that if I were to encounter Bill Thomas, I would override Mr. Spencer's warning. Though I didn't doubt his words were true, I believed that when it came to money, every man had a tipping point, and I meant to offer a purse that Bill Thomas could not refuse. Pan and I needed to leave as soon as possible.

On my arrival, Addy had the chessboard set up, but I spent most of our game lost in my own thoughts. "Mr. Burton! It's your turn," Addy finally scolded.

I forced myself to focus on the chess game. "Sorry, sorry," I mumbled, and picked up a pawn to make a quick move.

"Oh, we might as well stop playing!" she pouted.

"Why?" I asked.

"Look at what you did! Are you intentionally letting me win? And before, when I said that I was coming home on Sunday, you didn't say anything kind."

"I didn't? Forgive me, Miss Adelaide," I said. "Of course it will be wonderful to have you home again. I'm having one of those days when I can't seem to get my feet on the ground."

She tilted her head to look at me. "I'm surprised to learn that about you. You are always so sure of yourself."

"It is all a fine act, Miss Adelaide," I said.

"You mustn't feel bad," she said. "Even I have days when I don't feel myself."

"Is that right?" I teased.

"Yes, especially since Mother . . ." Her eyes welled up. "I miss her, you know, but I daren't say so. Father and Patricia are both so unhappy. I must stay strong for them."

"I understand," I said.

"And one mustn't dwell on sadness," she said. "As Father's friend would say, 'A stiff upper lip, don't you know.'" She mimicked well an English accent. We exchanged a smile and then returned to the game. Under an hour later, as I was preparing to leave, word came that Bill Thomas was waiting outside to see me. My heart racing, I headed to the stairway, where I ran into Sukey. She reached out as though she wanted to say something, but I didn't want to keep Thomas waiting and shook my head. "Later," I whispered, and left.

The man was standing in the shade of the house, one foot resting casually on a back step. "Mr. Thomas," I greeted him as cheerfully as I could. "It is good to see you again."

He nodded in response, then took off his hat, wiped his forehead with his sleeve, and ran a hand through his thick blond hair. He replaced his hat, then studied me while setting it right.

"Are you ready to do business?" I asked.

He looked down at his feet. "What kinda business you wantin' to do?" He leaned over and slapped at some dust on his pant leg.

I knew that I had one chance. "I'll get right to the point. I want to buy that woman Sukey and the boy Pan. I'll give you what you ask."

"'Fraid you wantin' two that's not for sale. I have a few others you can have a look at." He eyed me with a smile.

From the upstairs rooms, I heard Addy call out for Hester and wondered if Thomas knew that Hester and Sukey were likely at the open window, listening to our conversation.

"It is the two from the hospital that I am wanting," I said.

"They ain't for sale."

"Name the amount," I said.

"They are not for sale," he said.

"All right. Then I'll settle on Pan."

"Nope. Not for sale."

"And what if I were to tell you that he was stolen from me?"

If I expected a surprised reaction, it was not forthcoming. He remained as composed as ever. "And you have papers on him?" he asked.

"He was free! He didn't have papers."

"So you say." He smirked.

"Look," I said, anger seeping in, "if you don't sell him now, I will return with papers that say he is free, and then you'll get nothing for him. Why not just sell him to me, and that will put an end to all of this!"

"Why you wantin' him so bad? Seems you got some other kind of interest in him. You get yourself with a nigra? He your boy?" I glared at him, and when his blue eyes glinted with pleasure, I realized I had lost. Nothing material would substitute for the deep satisfaction that his power provided him. Threats were all I had left.

"Unless you sell him now, I make a promise that I shall keep. Stealing Negro children from Philadelphia is illegal, and if you do not hand him over to me now, I will prosecute you. I will not stop until I see you—"

"I've heard enough! The boy is already sold."

I took a step back to stare at him. "So he is no longer here?"

"Trader's comin' by to pick him up."

"You've actually sold him?" I asked, moving closer again.

"That's right," he said. "Once he's gone, I'll forget I ever saw him. Funny thing is, everybody on this place is gonna forget about him, too. You come back here with those papers, nobody's gonna know who you're talking about."

An armed overseer, fingering his gun, watched from a nearby position. Thomas scanned the fields. Finally, he looked back at me. "I take it, then, that you don't have no interest in any of the others?"

"You know who I want!"

"Something tells me you didn't come here just for that boy. What I'd like to know is what you're doing here, anyway? When you started askin' for Sukey, now, that got my attention. Why her?" He peered out from under the brim of his hat. "Something's just not sittin' right. I've got to tell you, soon as you came over here looking for that boy, I've been wonderin' if you're actually from Philadelphia. I got a man in town lookin' into you right now. From the start, somethin' about you don't feel right to me." Casually, he placed his hand on top of the gun slung from his waist. "Now, Mr. Philadelphia, you got time to get your horse, and you got time to get up on him. Then I'll give you enough time to ride out. But I'm warning you right now, don't come back!"

I had no weapon, and even if I had, I was outnumbered. My chest pounded with impotent rage as I walked down the brick path that led me out of the garden and past the hospital. Was Pan still there, or had they already taken him?

I spurred my horse for home and pounded into Mr. Spencer's yard, where he and Sam were standing outside the barn. Fury had me lose good sense. "Thomas already sold the boy!" I shouted. "And he told me to get off the property!"

The two stared up at me.

"The boy was mine!" I continued to shout. "Months ago he was stolen from me! He was free, but he was under my care."

Mr. Spencer looked grim. "I was beginning to wonder about your interest in the boy," he said, then turned to Sam. "Hitch up the farm wagon. We've got to get over there." He hurried toward the house and waved me with him. "Help me get the wagon fitted out so we can fetch Addy."

I didn't understand his need to remove his daughter. Surely Thomas would not harm the girl. "He was upset, but he won't involve Addy," I said as we pulled pallets, pillows, and blankets from the house and heaped them into the wagon to create a soft nest in which to cradle the patient.

"I've seen Thomas when he's riled. He takes it out on others, and I don't want her on the place if that starts to happen."

When we finished, Mr. Spencer climbed up on the wagon alongside Sam. "Do you want me to come?" I offered, but Mr. Spencer gave me a grim look.

"You stay here, and when I get back, we'll talk this through. Right now I've got to get over there."

Sam slapped the reins and set the two horses off at a trot. Before they were out of sight, I went into the house to begin packing. With Thomas's men asking questions about me in town, I had to leave as soon as possible. With a sick heart, I realized that I would have to leave Pan behind.

CHAPTER THIRTY-SEVEN

1830

James

ADDY WAVED TO us with her good arm as the wagon rolled up to where Patricia, Clora, and I waited on the front steps. Sam pulled the team to a stop, and Mr. Spencer leaped down with more agility than I had seen previously. As he made his way back for Addy, the pounding of hooves and then a stream of dust alerted us to two approaching riders. One of the horses, a dark brown gelding, galloped forward and was brought to an abrupt halt in front of the wagon. From atop the horse, Bill Thomas glared down at Mr. Spencer. "I'm missing the boy!" he shouted. "They're tellin' me he's gone!"

I stared, disbelieving.

"And which boy is that?" Mr. Spencer sounded as angry as I had ever heard him.

Thomas looked over at me. "Should I be askin' you?"

My look of surprise was genuine. "I have no idea what you are talking about."

"That boy Pan!" he said. "What do you know about him runnin' off?"

I had the horrifying thought that if Pan had escaped, he might have come looking for me. Was he hiding somewhere on this property? "I know nothing," I said as calmly as I could. "I thought you said he was sold."

The other rider spoke up. "He was meant for me. I just come for him!"

Thomas swung himself off his horse. "I don't suppose you'd mind if we have a look around."

Mr. Spencer turned red in fury. "You doubt my word? Go on! Take a look through the barns. And while you're at it, you may as well search the house!" He turned to me. "Mr. Burton, do you object to this man going through your room?"

"Not in the least," I said. But was this wise? Was it possible Pan had found his way into the house?

"Then, Mr. Burton, I ask you to accompany Mr. Thomas to see that everything is left as he found it. I will wait out here with my family." Mr. Spencer turned back to Addy. "It's all right, dear. As soon as this invasion is over, we'll get you in the house."

The trader, accompanied by Sam, went to search the barns. When Thomas climbed the steps to the house, I followed, while Mr. Spencer shouted after us, "Thomas, I'll tell you now, you have one chance to do this. You insult me with this accusation! I am not a thief, and neither is my guest! This one time you have my permission for access to my property, but I warn you, it will not happen again!"

I led Thomas through the house, and each time he peered under a bed or opened a cupboard, my heart hammered. But Pan was not found, and Thomas's fury was palpable when we left the house. I stood next to him on the porch as he surveyed the property, and my eyes followed his when they rested on the wagon.

Adelaide was propped up with pillows and quilts and looked quite comfortable, but when Thomas suddenly jumped off the front porch and strode toward the wagon, she grabbed hold of her arm and stiffened. Hester had already stepped down and stood next to Clora and Patricia, but on Thomas's swift approach, she clutched the girls to her. When I moved forward, Mr. Spencer stopped me with a glance and a quick shake of his head. Thomas reached the wagon and began to yank at one of the quilts. Addy's shrieks were so piercing that he stepped back. "Daddy! Daddy! He's hurting my arm! He's hurting my arm!"

Mr. Spencer clapped his hand on Thomas's shoulder. "You will not hurt my daughter!" His voice was so dangerous that I did not recognize it. "You have accused me of thievery, you have searched my house, and you have insulted my guest. But you will not assault my daughter. She is ill, and I will harm you if you do not leave at once."

Addy's wrenching sobs filled the air. "My arm, Daddy! My arm! Make him go away, Daddy! He's hurt my arm!" When Patty began to screech for her sister, Thomas moved away, but he shot me a last look before mounting his horse.

Addy's cries continued as the two rode away, though they quickly ceased when the riders were no longer in sight. Patricia, concerned for her sister, began to climb into the wagon. Mr. Spencer caught her by her waist and set her down beside Clora. "Hester, I need you to take Clora and Patty up to Addy's room and wait for us there. Make certain the girls stay with you. I might have to carry Addy up, and I don't want to trip over anyone."

Addy exhaled after Hester quickly ushered the two young girls away. "Oh, Daddy!" she said, her face blotched pink from crying.

"You were brave, my dear. Very brave," her father said. "But now let's get you into the house."

I came forward to help just as Addy moved her feet to the side and pulled back the pink and green quilt. "Are you all right?" she whispered, looking down into the wide eyes of a frightened boy.

I stared at Pan in disbelief. I was about to shout my relief when Mr. Spencer barked out, "Cover him up!" and Pan ducked under the covers once again. "Boy! Can you hear me?" he asked.

A muffled "uh-huh" answered him.

"Listen to me," Mr. Spencer said. "First we will get Miss Addy into the house. You stay right where you are, and we will drive the wagon into the barn. Later we'll roll you up in blankets and bring you into the house. You hear me?"

The "uh-huh" was barely perceptible. I could have wept in relief at knowing Pan was with us.

As we helped Addy from the wagon, she looked at me and gave a thin laugh. "Oh, Mr. Burton, I was so frightened for the poor boy! My legs still feel weak," she said.

"I don't wonder," I said, offering her a grateful smile. What bravery she and her father had shown! But why had they risked so much? What was Pan to them? Yet now was not the time to ask.

"Do you want me to go to the barn with the wagon?" I asked Mr. Spencer.

"No, I'll go with Sam. It's best that you go inside. Can you take Addy in? Hester is waiting for her in her room. The two younger girls know nothing about this," he warned.

"I understand," I said before offering Addy my arm and leading her into the house.

She sighed when we came to the inside stairway. "I don't know if I am strong enough to climb all of those stairs, Mr. Burton. I believe I might be too weak."

"Miss Adelaide, do I have your permission to carry you?" I asked.

"You do," she said, and when I scooped her up, she dropped her head against my shoulder. Her hand rested softly against my chest. "This is really quite romantic," she said, sighing again, and in spite of the trauma of the day, I fought back a chuckle.

"Well, today you are a heroine," I said.

"Do you think so, Mr. Burton?" she asked as I carried her to her room.

"Indeed I do," I said.

The patient was welcomed into her room with great fanfare. As Hester settled her on her bed, Addy pulled her down to whisper in her ear: "Did I do well, Hester?"

Hester smoothed Addy's hair back from her face while giving her a soft look. "You did real good, Miss Addy. You did jus' like your own mama woulda done."

Patty stood back, nervously observing her older sister. "Did he hurt you?" she asked. "It sounded like he hurt you."

"Come here, dearest," Addy said to her, tapping the bed. "Come here beside me. I've missed you, Patty Pat." When Patricia burst into tears and ran to her, I left them to Hester.

Downstairs, I met Mr. Spencer on the way to his study. He motioned for me to follow, and once there he poured each of us a double measure of whiskey. He tossed his down and I followed suit, welcoming the hot surge.

"Sit," Mr. Spencer commanded as he removed a pistol from the interior of his jacket and set it on his desk, but I remained standing, anxious to see Pan.

"Do you want me to bring the boy in?" I asked.

"No," he said, pointing to a chair as he took a seat. "At this moment he's as safe in the barn as he is in here. But we need to get him away from this property as soon as possible."

"I'll leave with him tonight! We'll get down to Edenton and sail out from there," I said.

"No, they'll be watching for the two of you. Thomas will have his men all over the place. You must remain here at least for a few days after the boy leaves. That way you'll avoid suspicion. The boy will stay here tonight, but by tomorrow we'll have to get him up to Norfolk."

"How will we do that?" I asked.

"I have my ways," he said.

I studied the man I thought I had known. Why would he risk his life and his family's safety for a young Negro? After all, he was a slave owner himself.

I had to ask. "Why are you—"

He anticipated my question. "Look, I believe in minding my own business, but there are times when one can't look the other way. Weeks ago, after the boy first arrived, Sukey sent word to Hester about getting him out. She had taken a liking to him and was afraid of what Thomas would do to him. This morning, after Sukey heard the trader was coming today, she hid the boy. Fortunately, Thomas didn't think we were coming for Addy until tomorrow, and he was out in the field, so after we got Addy settled in the wagon, we stopped at the barns where the boy was hidden."

"So that's why Sukey kept trying to tell me to get him out!"

"If Thomas ever finds out how many that woman has . . ." He stopped himself, then looked me in the eye. "I have told you more than might be wise. Now you must tell me what your interest is in this boy."

"I would be happy to tell you everything, but might we first get Pan into my room?"

"As you wish," he agreed, and heaved himself up from the chair.

We found the frightened boy in the safety of the barn, still hidden under quilts in the wagon. I kept him wrapped when I scooped him up, as though carrying a bundle of quilts down to my room. Free of the blankets, the boy was wet with perspiration. When I had him remove his clothes in exchange for a dry nightshirt of mine, I was shocked to see how frail he looked.

Hester brought some bread and cheese. Pan refused the food but greedily drained a mug of milk. I took the empty cup from his quivering hand.

"I'm sorry, Mr. Burton," he said, "but I can't make myself stop shaking."

"That's all right," I said. "That can happen when you've had a fright." I had him climb into the bed and pull the covers up around himself.

"I was so scared," he said. "I thought you'd go without me."

"Don't you worry," I said, trying to insert conviction. "We're going to get you home safe."

He studied me with sunken eyes but managed a smile. How unlike he was from the carefree boy I had known. I had to tell him about his father, but now was not the time. "You rest," I said, and left then for the study, where Mr. Spencer awaited me.

He was seated in his worn armchair and lifted a glass toward me. "Pour another for yourself," he invited, but I declined as I took a seat. Now more than ever, I needed clarity. How much should I tell this man? And what was he about? Not certain where to begin, I looked around to give myself time.

The room was comfortable enough but not furnished in a lavish way. There were a few good pieces, a highboy to the side and a red settee that showed age; a stack of books that appeared to be accounting records rather than literary works rested on a large but simple oak desk. The windows were covered by green wooden shades, tilted open to allow in an early-evening breeze. One of them rattled, startling me. Quickly, I glanced toward it but, reassured that it was only a breeze, I turned back to my host.

"Mr. Spencer, let me begin by apologizing for my deceit. My true purpose down here was to find Pan. A few months ago he was stolen from my employ in Philadelphia and brought down here and where he was sold to Thomas. Pan's father, a man to whom I was deeply indebted, was once a slave himself, and somehow he was able to locate his son at Southwood. How he discovered this, I have no idea."

Mr. Spencer nodded. "They have their ways."

"Yes, apparently so. My trip to these parts had already been scheduled. I was given a grant by the museum to do a study of birds, that part is true, though before I left, the money was withdrawn. But I had made a promise to Pan's father that I would find the boy and bring him back." I took a deep breath. "So here I am. I apologize again for all of the untruths, but until today I was uncertain of your . . . views."

"I can't say I like to be lied to, but under the circumstances . . ." Mr. Spencer paused, and my conscience pricked. Should I tell him more? Should I mention my connection to Sukey? Did I need to? No, I had said enough. Divulging more would serve no purpose.

"Now that I have the boy, I would like to leave with him immediately. I must get to Williamsburg, where my daughter awaits. Yet you think that unwise?" I asked.

"There's no way you could leave this property with the boy and not be discovered. Like I said earlier, you've got to sit tight for a few days until we get the boy out. That's going to be hard enough. Chances are, Thomas has already called in Rankin."

My heart thudded. Was it possible? "Rankin?" I asked.

"He's a tracker out of Virginia, well known in these parts for finding runaways. He's mean as a skunk and deadly, too—known to bring back only body parts, just so he gets paid."

I was finding it hard to breathe. "Should we call in the law?" I asked. "Surely Thomas is not above the law."

"The minute we bring the law into this, Thomas will lay claim to the boy. Before you have the legalities worked out, he will have the boy either dead or shipped out." He took a long swallow of his drink.

I fought rising panic. "What do we do?" I asked.

"No doubt Thomas will have this place watched. Fortunately, with Addy's arm as an excuse, I can send for old Doc McDougal. He and his man have a wagon that is outfitted for . . . situations such as this.

It's damned uncomfortable for a grown man or woman, but your boy should fit in with no problem. I've already sent word, and with any luck, Doc will be here by the morning. We'll have to get the boy back into the barn before daylight."

"And where will this man take him?"

"Old Doc lives close up by the Great Dismal. He has people there who will pick the boy up, then get him on board a ship, and send him back up to Philadelphia."

"How about Williamsburg? Can they send him on there?"

"Is that where you're heading?"

"Yes. My sister lives in Williamsburg, and I will send Pan to her. I have money for his passage," I added.

"Good, that always helps," he said, then nodded toward his desk. "Could you write down your sister's name?"

I did so with some reluctance, for I had no idea how another imposition would be received by Miss Elly. I wrote down Robert's name as well. "He is my valet and the one to get in touch with. He will care for the boy until I get there. Robert is the most trustworthy man I know."

"I understand," said Mr. Spencer. "Sam is the one I would trust with my life."

I stood. "I think that I will try to get some sleep," I said, and went toward the door, then turned back. "I can't thank you enough for your understanding and your help."

My host nodded. "Let the boy rest, then get him back out to the barn before daybreak. Sam will be waiting for him."

PAN WAS ASLEEP when I arrived back in my room. Not wanting to disturb him, I sat in a chair and dozed until later that night, when Mr. Spencer alerted us that it was time for Pan to return to the barn. As the boy dressed, I told him of the plan for his escape. Not wishing to burden him further, I decided not to tell him of his father's death.

"I wish you'd come with me," Pan said plaintively.

"You're going to have to be brave," I said.

"I'm scared," he said.

"I know. I was only a year older than you when I set out for Philadelphia all on my own. I was afraid, too, but I was determined to be a strong man. And now look at me." I postured for him, puffing out my chest and flexing my arms until he smiled. It was true, I had been his age, but I had been in robust health, and he was far from it.

Pan was close to tears when I left him in the barn with Sam. It pained me to see his distress, so I turned to leave quickly.

"Mr. Burton! Mr. Burton!" he called out in a loud whisper.

"Yes, Pan?"

"Don't worry, Mr. Burton. I'll be strong, just like you." He puffed out his small chest and flexed his thin arms.

I couldn't trust myself to speak, so I just waved back.

CHAPTER THIRTY-EIGHT

1830

James

Doc McDougal was a thin, stooped old man who appeared to have a difficult time getting down from his wagon. Warmly received by Mr. Spencer, the old man removed his worn hat from atop a mane of long white hair before he nodded in my direction. After our brief introduction, he straightened himself as much as his body would allow, then slowly took the stairs to find Addy, leaving me to wonder how this arthritic old man could help Pan escape.

I did as Mr. Spencer said and stayed indoors while he got Pan settled in the doctor's wagon. I paced until Doc's return downstairs, where he found me in the study. The old man went to the sideboard and helped himself to a sizable portion of whiskey, then looked me over as he drank it. He set the empty glass down with a thump.

"Mind if I ask why you come all the way down here for him?" he asked.

"I promised his father I would find him," I said.

He grunted. "You best take care. Thomas is going to have it out for you. By now he's got to know that you're involved."

"Thank you for the warning," I said. "I plan to leave by tomorrow."

"I wouldn't do that. Sit tight for another week or two. Let Thomas's suspicions die down."

I already knew I wouldn't do as he suggested. By tomorrow I planned to be in Edenton, on the first coach out. "Can you tell me where you're taking the boy?" I asked.

"The less you know, the better. All's I can say for now is that we're gonna try to get him out of here in one piece. Spencer said the boy's got a place to go in Williamsburg?"

"He does," I said. I wanted to say more to thank this man, but he left abruptly, and soon after, his wagon rolled away. I watched from behind the slats of the window blinds and wondered how they managed to cram Pan into the hiding place under the wagon seat. I hated to think of how uncomfortable and frightened the boy must be, but I reminded myself that he was on his way to freedom. And tomorrow, in spite of Doc's warnings, I would leave, too.

As I watched the dust from the wagon settle on the empty road, Clora called me from the head of the stairs. "Mr. Burton! Miss Addy wantin' to see you."

I found Adelaide propped up in her bed, with Patricia and Clora on either side, eager to serve her. Although the patient was smiling, her face was drawn, and she soon sent the two other girls off on a chore. "Has the wagon left?" she asked as soon as we were alone.

"Yes," I said. "A few minutes ago."

"Oh, good." She sighed. "Doc McDougal is such a fine man, don't you think?"

"I do," I said. "He is a family friend?"

"He and my grandfather grew up together," she said. "Daddy knew him when he was a little boy. Now he and Daddy often work together." She looked at me from under her lashes. Where before I would have thought she was playing at being coy, now I saw she was trying to read me.

"I see," I said. "And you help them as well?"

"Mr. Burton, I have been told," she said, looking at me sideways, "the less said, the better."

"Of course." I smiled. "And we must respect that."

"Unless you have a question that I feel obliged to answer?" She raised her eyebrows.

"Miss Adelaide!" I chuckled and shook my head. "You are a prize!

After I leave, you must promise to write to me, and you must not stop those letters until after you are safely married. I can only imagine the havoc you will wreak and the hearts you will break. Your letters will be more intriguing than any novel."

"Indeed!" she agreed, giving a sly smile, but I sensed that underneath her facade, she was as worried about the safety of Pan as I was.

OUR CONCERNS WERE justified. In under two hours, Doc McDougal's carriage returned. When Mr. Spencer rushed out, he found Doc slumped to the side with chest pains severe enough that he could not continue on. Mr. Spencer and I helped the old man into the study while Sam drove the carriage into the barn. "Give me a stiff one," Doc directed Mr. Spencer.

The old man downed the whiskey, then held out his glass again, but before it could be refilled, Doc slid to the floor. For a long moment, Mr. Spencer and I stared in disbelief and, though we were soon on our knees beside him, the old man was already gone.

AN HOUR OR so later, a shaken Mr. Spencer laid out his plan to me. He would take Doc's body to his son's home some two hours away. "The boy will have to stay hidden in the barn," he said. "I'll try to make it back here before sunrise. Then I might have to drive him out myself." The strain had drained all healthy color from his face.

"Is that the only option?" I asked.

"I need some time to think it through," he said, "but I'll have it figured out by the time I return. Meanwhile, you stay inside this house. Don't go out to see the boy, and whatever you do, don't bring him in with you. It's too dangerous." He handed over a pistol. "Keep this on you," he said. "If there are intruders, use it. Sam will be on the lookout in the barn, and he is armed as well."

When the wagon left, there was some relief in knowing that Pan was not on it. Though dark clouds were gathering, it was so beastly hot that I doubted the boy could have survived the heat under the wagon seat.

Alone in the study, I paced, desperately trying to think of a way out. I hated that I had put Mr. Spencer in the middle of this dangerous mess. Might it be best if I just took Pan and left? But where would we go, and how would we get there?

It was raining heavily by nightfall, when Hester and I secured the house. She took Clora upstairs to stay the night with the girls, but I was too restless to sleep, so I went to the study. I wanted nothing more than to reassure Pan, but I had given my word to stay away from the barn. I thought to distract myself with a book, but I could not settle myself. My thoughts flew between concern for Pan and then for myself. Had Thomas already sent for Rankin? Would Thomas's description of my eye patch alert him? How long would it take for him to come here looking for me?

Finally, I took the lamp and went to my bedroom, but there, too, I moved about restlessly, fingering my things while trying to decide if I should begin to pack. A loud clap of thunder and a bright flash of lightning lit up the room as I unlocked and lifted the lid of my trunk. There, at the bottom, I saw again the old jacket that hid my grandmother's jewels. I lifted it out and felt at the bulges, wondering if it wouldn't be safer to take the jewels out and secure them in a small money pouch.

I found my silver apple corer in my traveling case, thinking that the sharp edge of the small knife would work well for opening the stitches, then sat on the edge of the bed. Just as I was about to slit open the first stitch, there came a rap on the door. Thinking it was Hester, I set the jacket aside, but when I opened the door, I found no one there. I stepped out into the dark hallway and looked about but still saw nothing. Back inside, I convinced myself that it was a noise from the storm, but when I sat again to pick up the knife and jacket, another, more urgent rap came, quickly followed by another and then another. Then I realized my mistake. The persistent knocking was coming not from the interior door but from the door that opened to the outside.

I slipped the knife into the pocket of the old jacket and tossed it on the bed, then grabbed hold of the pistol from atop the dresser. The knocking grew more insistent, and after a short hesitation I pointed my pistol forward and swung open the door. It took me a moment, between the heavy rain and the dim lamplight, to recognize Sukey.

SHE PUSHED IN and slammed the door shut behind her. She waved her trembling hands in the air, indicating that she needed paper to communicate.

"We got to go now!" she wrote. "They find out it was me who got Pan out. Trader come in saying that Jake see you in Norfolk and tell Thomas that you a nigga. Patrollers getting together, but Thomas all fired up and send for Rankin!"

She kept clutching at my arm and trying to pull me toward the door, making it difficult to read what she had written, but when I made out the words, I went numb with terror. As Sukey frantically tugged on me, I stood rooted in fear. Where could I hide? Then I thought of the barn. "Sam is armed," I said. "We can hide out in the barn!"

Sukey shook her head vehemently as she scribbled. "They think nothing a killing him. We got to get to the swamp." Again she pulled on my arm, but I yanked my arm away as I tried to gather my thoughts.

What should I take? I flung the gun on the table and grabbed my small satchel. Frantically, I looked about, wondering how to best fill it. Seeing the jacket on the bed, I dropped the satchel and lifted the jacket, intending to lock it away in the trunk. As I was about to do so, the door flew open.

"You got to go! Patrollers comin'!" Sam hissed the words.

Sukey left through the open door as though shot from a gun. Sam rushed in and pushed at my back. "Go! Go," he said. Suddenly, I was running, with only the jacket in hand. Through the rain I saw Sukey's form cutting across the open field, moving so fast that I had to push myself to catch up with her.

"Mr. Burton! Mr. Burton!" The call for me came through the rain. Hearing Pan's anguish, I turned back to see his small figure coming at a run. "Don't leave me! I'm coming with you! Wait for me, Mr. Burton!" he cried.

Sukey was a distance ahead, but she, too, heard Pan's cry and stopped. I took hold of Pan's shoulders and shook him. "Go back! Mr. Spencer will get you out tomorrow in the wagon. It'll be safer for you that way. Go now!" I tried to turn him around.

"No!" the boy pleaded, grabbing hold of my wet shirtsleeves. "Take me with you. I don't want to be alone! Don't leave me here. Please, Mr. Burton!"

Sukey came running toward us, uttering frantic guttural sounds. Seeing her desperation, I grabbed Pan's hand, and we sprinted after her when she lit out once again.

We stayed low to the ground, racing through the storm that crashed around us. By the time I realized we were heading toward Southwood, I didn't know what to do but follow, hoping that Sukey had a plan.

She didn't stop to rest when we reached the safety of the bushes that defined the two farms but picked up her pace as she ran down what appeared to be a deer path. We followed, Pan clinging to my hand, all three of us panting for air, until we reached the backside of the South-wood quarters. There, a Negro man waited in the shadows.

Sukey and I both sank onto a fallen log, while Pan dropped to the ground. I had scarcely caught my breath when I realized I had left the gun behind. I was furious with myself, but it was too late to go back. The man rubbed Pan's bare feet with some strong-smelling grease, then had me remove my boots and replace them with some odorous deerskin slippers.

"Indians make these. It the bear grease that stink. Throws the dogs off." He knelt and slipped a pair over Sukey's bare feet, and as he did so, she arched her back. With a shock, I saw her advanced pregnancy. How had she run like that? Surely she couldn't hope to escape in that condition.

The two of them exchanged a private look as he helped her to her feet. "You gon' be all right?" he asked her. She nodded. "Keep usin' this," he said, handing her a package of bear grease. He took her face in his hands. "You 'members where to go?" he asked, looking deep into her eyes. "First get to that big barn with that weather vane on top. The man there get you goin' the right way." She gave another nod, and after she grunted something unintelligible, he kissed both sides of her full face before gently pushing her away. "Go on, then, we got everythin' in place here to throw 'em off. We make sure you get a good start."

We moved quickly, this time along a tight path through brush and brambles. When Sukey began to slow, I thought she might have lost her way, but after she found the trail that ran alongside the river, her speed picked up again. We moved faster still at the sound of dogs in the distance. I almost barreled into Pan when Sukey stopped suddenly and pointed down toward the water. Pan clutched my arm. "I can't swim!" he whispered.

"Neither can I," I said. "Sukey!" I whispered as loud as I dared, but she was already gone, sliding down the embankment to the river's edge. We dared not lose her and slid down the hill to find Sukey alongside the river, tossing away branches to uncover a small wooden raft. The barking of the dogs grew closer as we pushed the raft to the water's edge. Sukey waved for the two of us to get on the craft, then shoved us off before she heaved herself up. Pan, terrified, clung to the raft as Sukey and I each grabbed a pole. My arms shook from the strain of the strong undertow, but we were close to the opposite riverbank when a lone hound shot out of the woods and began a wild bark. The answering howls from the pack were distant but bone-chilling.

I jumped off the raft into thigh-high water and reached for Pan, catching him by the waist of his pants. Sukey, too, leaped off, then pushed the craft back out for the current to take hold of it. As it swiftly swept away, we slogged over to the riverbank and pulled ourselves up onto the land and into the dense undergrowth. We lay there, winded, scanning the other side of the river, where the lone dog continued to yowl.

Sukey grunted softly as she turned to her side, readjusting the pressure on her swollen stomach. I, too, felt pressure on my stomach and realized it was my old jacket. In the fray, I had stuffed it into the waist of my trousers. Though the answering call of the other dogs was receding, when Sukey again rose to her feet, Pan and I followed close behind.

We traveled due north. Though the land was flat, it dipped and rolled to accommodate the numerous small streams we crossed on foot. When in water, Pan clung to the waist of my trousers, but when we traveled the dry land, he made a point to walk on his own, keeping pace with me and glancing up often, I suppose to gauge my mood. We rested only after a particularly difficult water crossing and it was almost daybreak when we came upon what appeared to be a small forest. There, Sukey kept us to the periphery of the dark woods. As the sky began to lighten, we could see the outline of some outbuildings and a white clapboard house. Sukey pointed to a large barn topped by a weather vane—a large arrow encircled in metal and showing up dark black against the sky.

"Quakers," she scratched into my palm, then motioned for us to follow her. For the first time since our departure, I felt something akin to relief.

"What she say?" Pan whispered.

"Quakers," I answered. He asked for no further explanation, and I didn't offer one.

Naturally, I was familiar with Quakers and their anti-slavery views, but in my Philadelphia social circle, they were criticized for so plainly expressing their opinions. Now I could only hope that what I had heard of them was true.

We slipped into the largest of the three barns and sank down behind a stall. It seemed we had only just settled when a woman came into the building. Her face was protected from the early-morning sun by a wide-brimmed bonnet, while her brown dress and dark green apron were cut full enough to accommodate her pregnant abdomen.

She went directly to a bin and scooped out some grain, separated it into two troughs, then went to a large barn door that opened to a pasture. Calling her cows by name, she encouraged them to enter and patted their rumps in greeting as they lumbered toward their stalls. After the Quaker woman settled herself to do the milking, Sukey stood. Startled by the abrupt appearance of Sukey's face over the partition, the woman gave a sharp cry of alarm, then covered her mouth with her hand.

Sukey looked down at me helplessly, apparently out of ideas on how to continue. I saw no way out and slowly, so as not to scare the woman further, rose to stand beside Sukey. The woman gaped wordlessly.

"I apologize, madam," I said. "We did not wish to frighten you, but we need your help."

Still she stared.

"We are being pursued as runaway slaves," I said, even now sickened at associating myself with the word.

When Pan peeked over to see the Quaker woman, she lost her hesitation. "Come," she said, and we followed her at a run into the house.

She took us down a wide hallway and into a whitewashed parlor, smaller than another we had passed but still substantial enough to hold a large fireplace, a tall-case clock, and a good number of plain chairs suspended from wall pegs while looking up, Sukey tripped on the gray braided rug, and I caught her just before she fell onto the spinning wheel and the numerous baskets of unspun wool and cotton surrounding it.

Bright light streamed in through the large uncovered window. Now I saw what Sukey had been staring at on the ceiling. Above us hung an enormous quilt suspended by ropes and attached to a huge quilting frame.

The Quaker woman moved quickly and, from a basket, withdrew a large metal ring that she secured into one of the wide floor planks. After grabbing hold of rope and attaching it to the floor ring, she worked a pulley until two wide floorboards creaked and lifted. When she urged us into the dark hole, I dropped down almost three feet, then reached for Pan as Sukey awkwardly slid down on her own. A faraway voice called out, and the three of us sank to the dirt floor as the boards were quickly lowered.

The voice grew louder. "Lillian?"

"Mother?" our hostess called out.

"Yes," came the reply.

"There are guests."

"But Joel is not here!" the mother objected.

"They have need," the daughter replied. "And the patrollers are sure to come."

"Then a quilting party?" Their conversation was as efficient as their surroundings.

"Yes," Lillian agreed, and their footsteps receded.

It was dark in our dugout, but there was enough light from gaps in the floorboards to see that the space was wide enough to hold at least four adults. How many had made their way to freedom by hiding out here, and why would Quakers risk their lives like this, I wondered.

It wasn't long before the floorboards were raised again. We were relieved to see Lillian with some milk and bread as well as three pallets and a chamber pot. They would hide us, she said, until her husband felt it safe for us to leave. Cautioning us to silence, she quickly closed us in again.

We ate wordlessly and rolled out our pallets. Soon both Pan and Sukey fell into a deep sleep. I lay back as well, but sleep would not come. My mind raced, and the space closed in on me. I worked to regulate my breathing in an effort to fight panic. How had I come to this? And how would I find my way out?

I looked at Pan. Asleep, he looked more helpless than ever. As sickly as he was, I wondered if he could survive this journey. Why hadn't he stayed back? He would have had a better chance that way. I was furious with myself for not refusing him. What if he were to die and this was all for naught? Bitterly, I thought of burying Henry, and of the promise that had brought me to these circumstances.

I glanced at Sukey. When was her baby due? She was the one who knew the route, but her swollen abdomen suggested an imminent birth. What would happen to us then? Surely a newborn would put an end to our flight.

I shut my eyes. Each fear raised another, but what overrode all of them was my most immediate concern. Where was Rankin? Was he already with the patrollers? I knew what would happen if I was found. I would be tried as a Negro for murdering a white man, and my fate would be sealed. I would be hanged.

After hours of torment, it almost felt a relief when a shuffling commotion began above us.

CHAPTER THIRTY-NINE

1830

James

THE PATROLLERS' HEAVY feet woke Pan and Sukey. We three held our breath as the gathered quilting party above us stitched on the lowered quilt while they greeted the intruders. Their friendly greetings were not returned. When the patrollers shushed everyone and stood to listen, the silence grew almost unbearable. Then a child cried and was joined by another. Soon after, the disgruntled patrollers left, though the women stayed on to stitch while their children settled to play at their feet.

Hours later, all was silent, but that evening, after the clock bonged for the tenth hour, we were brought up from the underbelly of the house. We needed a stool to help Sukey out, and while the husband frowned uncertainly at her pregnancy, there seemed no choice but to lead us away.

The tall Quaker man strode forward, sure and direct on a path that he knew well. Both Pan and Sukey stayed strong, and we traveled wordlessly for much of the night. Just before daybreak, the man stopped to leave us in the shelter of dense woods. He spoke low, going over our directions as he handed us a packet of bread and hard cheese. "Stay to the north." He pointed. "And stay alert," he needlessly added before bidding us good luck and farewell.

We found our way through the woods, which opened to an orange sky and fields of cotton that stretched endlessly before us. We all gratefully sank to the ground; within minutes, Pan was asleep beside me. Sukey lay down, and though she was restless, to my relief she did not try to communicate. Finally, by midafternoon, after no sign of human life, I could no longer take the wait. Though we had been advised to stay hidden and to travel only at night, I had seen no one about through the day and thus decided it was safe to leave before nightfall. When Sukey realized my plan, she shook her head in disagreement, but after Pan and I stepped out together, Sukey reluctantly followed.

The sun beat down as we moved through the cotton fields, crouching low to bypass the small farms set back on sloping hills. On occasion we heard the bark of a dog; at the sound, we froze and dropped to the ground, only to rise and move again when reassured that no one was about. Pan was silent, but his energy remained high, while Sukey's face glistened from the heat. Once or twice she stumbled, but I kept on, relentlessly moving us forward, mindful only of reaching safety.

Our destination was north, where lay the Great Dismal Swamp. Once there, traveling the outskirts, we would come to a cross-canal that cut east, a waterway we would follow inland for ten miles, where it connected to the main canal. Along that canal, we had directions for a safe house where lived a friend of Doc McDougal.

Even as the sun set, it was insufferably hot. I missed my hat, which, along with the gun, I had regrettably left back at the house. What I clung to was my old jacket—counting on the jewels, if necessary, to buy our way to Norfolk.

We pushed on, resting in small patches of trees long enough to catch our breath, and by nightfall we had reached a dense pocket of green forest. I wavered, uneasy at the spongy feel of the soil.

Uncertain, I looked to Sukey. "Are we in the swamp?" I asked, but she shook her head. Seeing my hesitation, she pushed past me to take the lead, fighting through the vines and briars until she found a stream. There she dropped to her knees to drink, and after Pan and I did the same, Sukey broke off chunks of bread and cheese and we all ate hungrily.

"These bugs gettin' to me," Pan whispered. All three of us scratched mercilessly at the chiggers that had embedded themselves under our skin. As the mosquitoes and biting flies bore down, Sukey withdrew the animal bladder filled with thick bear grease.

"Whew! This got some smell to it!" Pan whispered when she dipped the yellow grease out and silently showed him how to rub it on his face and exposed skin. At another time, the smell alone would have prevented me from using it, but when she offered some to me, I, too, used it liberally. When our faces and limbs shone from the thick ointment, Sukey grunted and rose heavily, motioning for us to follow her across the shallow stream.

Again we fought through dense underbrush that tore at our clothing and at our skin until we made our way through to an opening on the other side. There, lit by the night, lay open fields of corn. Sukey pointed into the distance, then firmly grasped my hand. "Swamp," she scratched into my palm.

"What she say?" Pan asked.

"She said that up ahead is the swamp," I said, squinting to better see the dark outline of tall trees.

"Are we almost home when we get to the swamp?" Pan asked.

"No," I said, and that silenced him again.

There were some night hours remaining, ideal for traveling, but relieved to be this close to the swamp, and with the cover that the corn stalks would provide, I sank to the ground and declared that we would take a short rest. I had not slept since leaving the Spencer home, and I felt overcome from exhaustion. Sukey, though, shook her head, and motioned for us to continue on. I disregarded her and scraped together a bed of leaves for a pillow, and when I lay down, Pan followed suit. Finally, Sukey, sighing heavily, did the same. Minutes later, all three of us were sound asleep.

I awoke with the early-morning sun in my face. I leaped up, startling the other two out of a sound sleep. "We slept too long," Pan noted, while Sukey and I stared at each other, disbelieving the hour. I longed for a drink from the stream, but that would have meant backtracking, so I promised myself we would have water as soon as we reached the swamp. By my estimation, we were under five miles away, a destination that could be reached easily before noon.

I looked out across the lonely cornfield. Seeing no humans about, I decided that we would take the same risk and travel during daylight. Again Sukey objected but followed when I scooped up my jacket and moved out.

WE HAD BEEN moving swiftly for a good long while and had almost reached the outskirts of the swamp when a gunshot burst through the still air. Startled crows cawed and flew up as Sukey and I flung ourselves to the ground, parallel to each other, between the rows of corn. Pan, confused, stayed standing until I yanked him down behind me. When a crashing noise came toward us, Sukey rose to her hands and knees, then lifted up her skirt and clamped it in her teeth as she began to crawl forward. I crawled, too, with Pan close behind, until the gun blasted again. We all hit the ground just as a huge black bear crashed by in front of us, trailing blood. Though still a distance away, the sound of men's excited voices grew closer. We dared not move. Unexpectedly, the bear circled back toward the hunters. With whoops of surprise and a rifle report, their shouts receded, and we rose again to our hands and knees.

We scrambled until we reached the safety of the swamp and there had to push through tangles of thick vines and briars before we were in far enough to hunker down. The ground we sat on was damp and spongelike; the forest around us was so dense that it appeared black, but we had reached the great swamp. Gasping for air, we sat staring at one another, disbelieving that we had reached safety.

We had only just caught our breath when we heard shouts, followed by more shots from a rifle. Now came the barking of dogs. As one, we scrambled to our feet to push farther in.

With the sound of dogs sharp in the air, we tore our way through, deep into the tangled overgrowth and darkness, until the sound of men and dogs began to fade. We dared not rest. I hated the way the soft boggy land gave under my feet, but I hated even more stepping into the tea-colored water to weave our way, knee-deep, through the maze of jutting cedar roots that buckled up as twisted barriers. From above, thick, corded vines, netted with Spanish moss, draped down to ensnare us. With each vine I pushed away, I thought of the cottonmouth moccasins, the copperheads, and the rattlesnakes known to inhabit the place.

We struggled on, Pan surprisingly agile in water that was at times waist-deep. Sukey suddenly grunted and pointed ahead to what appeared to be a small green island. Exhausted, we slogged toward it and finally onto the dry piece of land where, in the midst of towering white oak and green pine, there lay a massive overturned oak.

The enormous root ball rose at least six feet into the air. After Sukey cautiously pulled back the thick overgrowth of moss and vines covering it, she waved us over to show us a cavelike hideaway. We were peering into the dark interior when, from behind, something massive came barreling through the water. As one, we dove into the shelter, letting the heavy vines swing down behind us.

The interior was dark, low, deep, and wide, and as the crashing sounds grew dim, I whispered in relief that it must have been the bear escaping the hunters. When Sukey nodded agreement, she tapped my arm and I gave her my palm. "Rest," she scratched, and then encircled her abdomen with her hands.

"What she say?" Pan asked, tightly clutching my arm. "She say something 'bout her baby comin'?"

"No, she wants to rest," I said.

"Good," he said. "I'm sure glad to hear there's no baby comin' now."

I was on edge with the nearby hunters and would have pushed on through the swamp, but Sukey lay back with a sigh. Pan did the same. I stayed sitting up, too uneasy to rest. I looked about the dark cave and worried what would come next. We had the patrollers pursuing us, and though it was not likely they would come this deep into the swamp, there was the danger of escaped slaves—men desperate enough to live in this ungodly habitat who did not welcome intruders.

Finally, I lay back to close my eyes, but moments later, I was swatting frantically at a gigantic spider that had crawled onto my face. I sat up, shuddering, squinting in the dark to see where it had gone. Pan and Sukey were resting, but I was overcome with the hopelessness of what lay ahead.

Lost in this overgrown quagmire, we had to find the cross-ditch that would eventually lead us over to the main canal. Assuming we could find it, we had to follow that cross-ditch on foot, traveling the ten miles of rough towpath only at night, since barges would be coming through by day, no doubt some with patrollers eager for the large bounty.

Then there was the danger of the animals. This huge swamp was known to shelter not only bear, of which we had evidence, but also other predatory animals such as wolves, panthers, and bobcats. Alligators lived here as well, but it was the snakes I feared the most.

I had not yet told Sukey that on our crawl for the swamp, I had lost our supply of bread and cheese. What, I wondered, would we do for food? Fortunately, the tea-colored water surrounding us was drinkable, and though we all had an earlier fill of it, I now slipped out for more.

A wide shaft of light traveled down the incredible height of the trees. I might have seen a certain beauty in it had I not been so anxious. I went to the water's edge and knelt on a mass of ferns, there to cup my hands and slurp up the brown water. Then, as I splashed my face, Sukey quietly joined me. She hunched down to drink, but when she leaned over, she gave a startled yelp. I sprang up, thinking she had seen something I had not.

She avoided looking at me as she awkwardly rose to her feet and I went cold when her hands gripped her swollen abdomen. Was it possible that she was ready to give birth?

Pan suddenly emerged from the cave. "Hey, Mr. Burton! You give me a scare," he said, rushing to my side. "I woke up and thought you went without me!"

His eyes followed Sukey walking heavily back toward the cave. She stopped at a nearby tree and broke off a small branch—about a foot long and one to two inches in diameter—and took it with her as she crawled into the cave.

Why did she want that stick? Did she mean to kill the child? I had heard of Negroes doing things like that. Bile rose in me. What kind of mother would do that? I must leave now! Without her! I sat arguing with myself while Pan squatted beside me, studying my face. "You think she gonna have that baby?" he asked. "Mr. Burton! What we gonna do with a baby?"

I shook my head in response while trying to think clearly. From inside the cave came a sharp cry of pain. "Stay here," I said to Pan, then went back into the cave. Sukey met me with a loud moan.

"Quiet! You must be quiet!" I stared at her as my eyes adjusted to the dark.

She clapped her hands over her mouth, but when she tried to shift again, a low animal sound escaped from under her hand. She looked at me in apology.

I looked away, but she waved me forward and then tapped at my clenched fist. Though dreading the message, I gave her access. "Baby coming," she wrote.

I pulled back my hand and rubbed the palm with my thumb as though to erase the message. This was impossible! We couldn't journey out with a newborn. We both knew it.

Without warning, her body stiffened. Dear God! I thought. She is having the child! I rubbed my face with my hands. What to do! I must leave before they hear her and find us! Yes—yes! I would take Pan and leave!

As though she read my thoughts, Sukey grabbed at my hand, and her torn fingernails scratched into my palm, "Take baby." I stared at her hand as she wrote it again. "Take baby."

What did she mean? Take Pan? But no, she had said "baby." Did she actually expect me, a man who knew nothing about childbirth, to somehow deliver a child and then flee with it? The idea was insane. I wouldn't sacrifice my life like this! I scuttled to the opening and glanced back at her beseeching eyes.

When Sukey stiffened again and gave a muffled cry, I leaped from the cave.

CHAPTER FORTY

1830

Sukey

T HE CHILD'S BEEN coming since early today, and sure enough, just like I was afraid, Jamie goes running off without me. From the start, I see he don't want nothing to do with me, 'cause I see him as colored and he knows, being with me, he's pegged for a nigra.

When Jamie goes, it's easy to decide. Without him, I got no hope. Before the animals get us, I gon' let the baby die. I won't look at it. I won't help it breathe. The reason for me to run was to get this one free. But I can't make it out of this place by myself.

My stomach turns hard again and the pains burn. Push, push . . . I try hard not to make a sound. Don't want no animals showing up. I feel around me for the stick. I put it in my mouth and bite down. I'll get this child out, and then we both can die in peace. I seen worse ways to die.

All a sudden the boy shows up. "I'm here, Sukey. I can help." He grabs hold a my hand and gives me his palm. "Tell me what to do," Pan says.

"Get outta here," I write, then slap at him to get him movin'. I hear him cryin' when he goes out, but now I can get my business done.

I bite down. Push, push. Don't make no noise! Pain, push, pain, push. Huuuh! I feel it come. It plops out. Lil arms, feet, pushing out. I feel it moving!

My head throws itself back and forth. I'm fighting with myself, not letting my hands reach for it. But then it cries.

I grab down, bring it up, and push it against me to stop it from breathing. The little mouth is working for air. I push in harder. I grunt and bite down hard on the stick, but this time the stick snaps, and that's when the mama in me takes over. She spits out the wood pieces, grabs at the bloody cord, bites through it, frees the child, then gives it my breast. When the child latches on, I look down and see it's a girl, and all that's left of me howls for mercy.

"Don't cry, Sukey! Don't cry!" The boy is back. "I'm gonna help you out!" he says, and I reach to kiss his sweet hand.

CHAPTER FORTY-ONE

1830

James

PANIC LIT A fire in me. When I passed Pan, I grasped his arm and shouted for him to run. When he fought me, I struggled to keep hold of him.

"We've got to go!" I called out, holding tight. "We've got to get out of here!"

"What about Sukey?" he cried, pulling away. "She's by herself, having a baby."

"We can't stay!" I looked around wildly, sure I heard our pursuers. "Come! We've got to go!" It did not occur to me that the heavy panting I heard was my own breath. Believing that we were to be killed, I began to shout in terror. "Come! Come!" I pulled roughly at his arm, but he freed himself and backed away.

"Mr. Burton!" Pan called out. "You not thinking right!"

I left him then and ran. Pan's call long faded and still I ran, the sound of my own rasping breath fueling me. My terror had broken free, and escape was all I knew. Perspiration dripped into my good eye, and near blind, I was in the water, stumbling over cypress roots, then back on dry land, tearing through thickets of juniper and green briar.

It was the appearance of the bear that brought me back to my senses. The black bear that had been wounded earlier in the day emerged from the green and roared his protest as I struggled onto his small dry island.

On first sight, I addressed him as though he were human, but as my reason returned, I stopped my muttering and slowly backed into the water. Something long slithered around my leg, and I stood frozen, waiting for the snake to kill me first.

The bear moved forward, his hackles up. Slowly, he swayed toward me. Foam frothed and flew from his clacking teeth and when he charged, trapped in a tangle of cypress roots, I waited for death. Then, unbelievably, not twenty feet from me, he splashed down. My legs gave way and I slid into the brown water as death tremors shook the bear's body. When my strength returned, I crawled back up onto the island to sit, stunned. I was alive! Somehow I had survived.

I looked about, disbelieving. What had I done? I had abandoned Pan, but worse, I had left Sukey while she was birthing a child. What kind of man was I? When I thought of them alone, and of the animals that might approach the cave, I got to my feet. I must go back.

Still dazed, I set off, but night was falling and I soon found myself lost. My only hope was to wait until morning, so I found a dry spot where I waited out the night.

I awoke with the morning's light. My head felt clear, and after I had drunk my fill of the tannic water, I set out once again. I remained lost, circling for hours, until I remembered a technique that Henry had taught me to find my way back to his shelter. I set up triangles of long sticks on the edges of dry land, and by late morning, I had found my way back to the small island.

Pan sat alone outside the cave under a pine, and a more forlorn-looking child I had never seen. When he noticed me, his eyes lit up, first in relief and then in fury.

"Did she have the baby?" I asked.

He looked away, refusing to give an answer.

I went to the cave and held my breath as I pulled back the entrance covering. "Sukey," I whispered, and a small mewling noise answered me. Sukey raised her head, then with a sigh, let it fall back again. An overpowering stench filled the cave, but I was drawn in, first by remorse and then by astonishment when I saw something suckling at

Sukey's breast. "Forgive me—" I began, but Sukey's hot hand grasped my palm. "Water," she scratched, and when she scratched it again, I realized the urgency. I couldn't think of what to use for a receptacle until I remembered my leather slippers. Though wet and worn, they were largely intact.

Pan looked up as I exited the cave. "She needs water," I said.

"I've been trying, but it don't stay in my fingers. All night I was looking for something to put the water in." He leaned his head on his knees and began to cry.

"I'm going to try to use my shoe," I said. He didn't follow me down to the water, but watched from his sitting position as I rinsed out my slipper as well as I could and then hurried back while cradling water in the awkward container.

When I lifted her head, Sukey's skin felt hot and dry. Though a good deal of the water spilled down her neck, she drank thirstily, and I went back for more. When she was sated, I attempted to take the baby from her, but she shook her head and clung to it tightly.

I left her then, needing to escape the oppressive odor. Pan was still seated under the pine, but when I sat next to him, he turned his back to me. "Pan?"

"I don't like you no more," he said. "When I get outta this mess, I'm going to live with my daddy. He don't have much, and he's gonna whoop me for goin' to the docks, but he don't never leave me like that the way you done."

"I'm sorry, Pan," I said. "I don't know what happened. I guess fear just got the better of me." I shook my head in disbelief, remembering the overriding panic.

"You don't know what happened? What happened is you run away, leaving Sukey and me here to die."

"But I came back," I said.

"Why?" he asked.

"Because I care about you."

"Phhh! I got a daddy who care about me! All I got to do is get back to find him."

The truth came out. "Pan," I said, "your daddy came with me to find you."

He turned enough to give me a skeptical look. "He come with you? Then where is he?"

"He got sick up in Norfolk. I called in a doctor, twice, but he couldn't help."

He swung toward me in fury. "You saying he's laying sick someplace? You run off and leave him, too?"

"No," I said, realizing that I should have waited to tell him.

"Then where is he?" he demanded.

"I'm afraid that he died."

Pan got to his feet and took a few steps away before he turned back. His dark eyes narrowed. "Why you saying that?" he asked.

"I'm sorry, Pan," I said. "Maybe I shouldn't have told you this now."

"You saying my daddy come down here to slave country and he die? You telling me the truth?"

"Yes, Pan," I said. "I'm afraid I am."

His chin trembled as he fought for control. "You sure the slave catcher don't get him?"

"No, Pan. He had a cough, and then he got very ill. I was with him when he passed away."

"You was with him?"

"I was, and I was there when he was buried. When we get out of here, I can take you to see his grave."

"I don't want to see no grave!" he said. Slowly, he walked to the water's edge, where he slumped to his knees. There he leaned in to himself and began a desperate call for his father.

I followed. "Pan, I'm sorry."

"Go away," he shouted, and struck out at me, and I knew then to let him be.

At a loss, I decided to see to Sukey and forced myself into the sickening smell of the cave to face the task of cleaning her up. Her torn petticoat lay beside her and she closed her glazed eyes after I tore loose a large piece and told her of my intentions.

I had not expected to see such a fresh amount of blood, and while my stomach heaved, I cleaned her as thoroughly as I was able. Off to the side, I found the umbilical cord attached to a small piece of what I guessed to be afterbirth. Though uncertain, I suspected there ought to be more.

I don't know how many trips I made out to the water to rinse the rag, but only later, as I gathered moss to pack between Sukey's legs in an attempt to stanch the blood flow, did I see Pan take notice.

During my ministrations, the baby gave an occasional soft mewl, but I didn't touch it. It was impossibly tiny, and I was sure it could not survive for long. Finally satisfied that I had done all I could, I returned outdoors and went to sit beside Pan, who remained at the water's edge.

"If she is to get well, I'll need your help, Pan," I said.

Pan sounded drained when he spoke. "That lil one so small, it can't even cry. Those the kind that die. I saw it when I was helping Sukey in her sickhouse."

"I agree that it looks weak, but we must do our best for Sukey. Can I count on you to help me out?"

"Wasn't me who go running off," he said bluntly.

"I won't do that again, Pan," I said.

"We'll see," he mumbled.

"Pan, I'm sorry," I said. "I'm sorry about your father, but always remember that he was a good man."

He kept his eyes away from me. "He was so good, then why did he always go running off and leave me and my mama?"

"He was scared, Pan. He was scared of getting caught."

"I don't hold with him leaving my mama to die like that," he said.

"I know it doesn't seem right, but I guess his fear of getting caught was bigger than anything else. I suppose I did the same thing last night. My fear just took over."

He sniffed loudly before he turned to me. "And what was you so afraid of?" he asked.

I picked up a nearby twig and used it to poke at the mossy ground. "Pan, the truth is, I've been scared and running for most of my life."

"What was you running from?" His voice was hard.

I took a deep breath. "To start with, when I was a young boy, I thought I was white. When I was just around your age, I found out that my mother was a Negro. Since then I've been trying to pass as a white man. It's a secret that I've been hiding all of my life."

"You saying your mama was colored like me?" he asked, his curiosity sparked in spite of himself.

"That is what I am saying," I said, digging deep into the moss while he stared at me. "And we can't return to Philadelphia because of it," I added.

Pan's thin shoulders sagged. "It don't matter, Mr. Burton. We all gonna die out here anyway."

His hopelessness startled me. I forced a confidence that I did not feel. "Pan! We're not going to die! We will come through this, and someday you will be the man your father always knew you would be. We'll get through this. I promise!"

"We'll see," he said, unconvinced, then clutched at his stomach as it growled audibly.

"This morning I ate some huckleberries," I said, pointing to the abundant blue fruit. "They went right through me, so we can't eat many."

"I ate them, too," he admitted. "But they make my stomach hurt."

"If we're going to be here until Sukey recovers, we're going to have to eat something more substantial," I said. "But I don't dare try to get a fire going."

"When my daddy got nothing else to eat, he eat grubs. Say they give you some get-up-and-go."

"Let's go find some," I said, and though the idea was less than appealing, I knew their nutritional value.

The earth on this island teemed with oversize black beetles, and where there were bugs, there were grubs. We didn't have to look far for decaying logs, and when I turned the first one over, there squirmed the large white larvae. Pan watched as I picked one up.

"You gonna try it?" he said, grimacing as I held it up.

I did not allow myself to think before I tossed one in my mouth and began to chew. Biting down into the soft body, I began to retch but quickly ate some huckleberries and forced myself to swallow. "Ahh," I said. "Not bad!"

"Then why you look like you about to bring it back up?" he asked.

"I'm just getting used to the fine flavor," I teased, and was rewarded with a flicker of a smile. "Come on." I handed him one, taking another for myself. "If your daddy ate these to survive, so can we."

The next one went down more easily. Though the taste was bitter and the texture appalling, I forced down a few more of the large globs. Pan ate two. When we knelt to drink water, a sizable grasshopper landed between us, and Pan snatched it up. "He ate hoppers, too, but the legs got spikes and got to come off first." He plucked off first the head and then the legs. "Here," he said. I was unsure if the offer was a token or a challenge, but I knew it was edible and accepted it. It crunched as I chewed and I swallowed plenty of water to get it down.

"Not bad," I said. "Now let's find one for you."

"Maybe later," Pan said, and again gave me a ghost of a smile.

Our stomachs rumbled, but we retained the food, so we gathered some grubs and huckleberries for Sukey. She chewed and swallowed some berries but refused a second grub. As though the effort had taken all of her energy, she closed her eyes and let the babe slip down beside her, where it lay mewling. Finally, I took it from the cave.

Pan followed me to the water's edge and watched over my shoulder as I lay the bundle down to unravel the soiled petticoat. A ray of sun broke through the green canopy to cast golden light on an infant so minuscule that I might have held her in my one hand. Her wrinkled body squirmed as she squinted against the sun, while the sparse downy hair on her head stood out like that of a newly hatched bird. Unexpectedly, my heart twisted with tenderness.

Her umbilical cord had been tied off with a strip of fabric. Again I marveled at Sukey's determination to save her child's life. The cloth around the baby's bottom was crusted to her. "You got to get her washed off," Pan said, testing the water with his hand, "but you got to do it quick."

"Get ready," I said, lifting her up and dipping her in to soak while Pan rubbed her clean. Her little breaths came in surprised puffs while her extremities reached out in an odd quivering stretch. "Best get her out now," Pan said.

On impulse, I slipped her shivering body inside my torn shirt to warm her against my own skin. Pan fetched another piece of clean petticoat, then lined it with soft moss, fashioning a clout before we swaddled her into a bigger piece of cloth. Through it all, the tiny bit of life made soft mewling sounds.

Sukey slept on. We kept the babe with us and sat under the pine to study the now fresh-smelling bundle. As she looked out, I was astounded to see curiosity in her large dark eyes. When she mewled, Pan reached over to pat down her hair. "You sound like a kitty," he said. "Let's call her Kitty."

"Don't get too attached," I warned. "I doubt she will live." She gave a huge yawn, and when I gently tapped her tiny chin, her fingers quivered up and grasped mine. In spite of my own warning, I felt my heart give over.

THE AIR DURING the day was hot and often humid, but it did not rain, and the days passed swiftly as I sought to care for the four of us. I gave to Pan and the baby what was left of the bear grease and fought to keep from scratching at the oozing raised red rash that covered my legs and arms. While my unshorn facial hair served as a barrier against the biting flies and hoards of mosquitoes, my torn and tattered clothing did not. As Sukey weakened, the baby increasingly became my focus. Each day she survived felt like a victory.

In spite of my best efforts, by the third day Sukey was no longer lucid. Pan had found an old turtle shell, and though she drank water from it readily, she always turned her face away from the grubs. The morning I found three duck eggs, I rushed in with one for Sukey, but was disheartened when she turned her head in refusal. I later cracked open all three, and Pan and I gratefully swallowed the rich nutrients, a welcome change from the usual grubs, grasshoppers, and huckleberries.

By the fifth day, Sukey refused even the berries. Thinking it was the effort to chew that stopped her, I chewed the food myself before pushing it into her mouth. That almost ended in disaster, for the paste dropped back in her throat and choked her. Though I was able to have her cough it up, the episode left her drained. When I cleaned her that evening, fresh blood, a great deal more than usual, soaked through the packed moss.

The following morning Sukey was no longer responding, though she still swallowed water when I put it in her mouth.

Kitty suckled vigorously when I held her to Sukey's breast. I wondered if she was getting enough nourishment, and as her mother's life ebbed away, I argued with myself about what to do. Should we just leave and try to save Kitty? How many hours could a baby survive without milk? Yet I could not abandon Sukey while she was still alive; at night there were too many carnivores about. Finally, on the sixth day, Sukey provided the solution.

Around noon, while Pan gathered grubs, I took Kitty for another feeding and there discovered that Sukey had died. I had sensed her death coming, but the reality of it shook me. Clutching Kitty, I scrambled from the cave and called for Pan.

He came at a run. "She's dead," I said abruptly. "We have to leave."

He hung his head for a moment, then lifted it again. "We got to bury her," he said.

"We can't. We have no tools. And you know she would want us to take care of Kitty first. We need to find some milk for her as soon as possible."

"How we gonna do that?" he asked.

I handed Kit to him as I reached for the primitive basket that I had fashioned from the plentiful reeds in preparation of our departure. "I don't know, but we don't have a lot of time," I said. I lined the basket with plenty of moss and then added what was left of Sukey's petticoat. Settling Kitty in the basket and tucking my jacket into the waist of my tattered trousers, I announced that I was ready to leave.

Pan looked lost and walked back to the entrance of the cave. "At least you got to say something," he said.

"You're right," I said, joining him. I tried to think of some words, but when I lowered my head, nothing came. The baby squirmed, and while I readjusted her, Pan grew impatient. "You can say something nice about Sukey, and then I suppose you can ask my mama for some help, but she don't seem to be around since I got took."

"How about your daddy?" I asked, feeling more comfortable invoking Henry.

Pan shrugged.

"Sukey was a good woman—" I began.

"But now we need some help," Pan interrupted. "Daddy, if you see us out here, you got to get us some help." His voice choked at the mention of his father, and my own eyes blurred. I looked up and took in the beauty of the long green swags and red flowering vines that draped across the cathedral-sized trees. Under this protective canopy, an unexpected peace washed over me and gave me newfound strength. Through Pan's sobs, I spoke out in a strong voice. "Henry and Sukey," I said, "you were both brave and good, and because of it, we know you are with the Lord. Please ask Him to help us out."

I was rewarded for my effort when Pan rubbed his face dry and looked up at me. "You did that good, Mr. Burton," he said. "Now we best get going!"

I DECIDED WE would go north to the cross-canal, but there, instead of going east to the large canal, as instructed, we would turn west, where I had been told civilization was close by. I didn't know what story I would tell, but our only hope to save Kit lay in that direction.

As we traveled, I felt that we were being watched. The night before, wolves had sounded particularly close, and I worried that they were stalking us now. I didn't allow myself to think of what might happen to Sukey's body back in the cave.

As before, we fought the endless vegetation, and while Pan kept up the pace, he traveled silently. Alone, I might have despaired, but saving both Kit and Pan gave me purpose, so I plunged ahead, using the moss-covered trees and bits of sunlight for direction. A few hours into our trek, we came to a dry spot where I decided to check on a silent Kitty. I held my breath when I lifted her still body from the basket. "Kit, Kit," I called, tapping her satin face until she gave a weak cry.

Pan grabbed hold of my arm so abruptly that I almost dropped Kit. "Mr. Burton!" he whispered as a short Negro man stepped out from the trees. "He got a knife!" Pan pointed to the long curved weapon the man carried.

"Don' mean no harm!" the aged man said, quickly sheathing his weapon and attaching it to the cord that held up what was left of his pants. "I's Willie," he said. "Been watchin' you. What you doin' with that baby?"

"She needs milk!" I said.

"Come, we get some," he said, and motioned us forward.

"Let's go," I said to Pan.

The old man turned southeast and moved so quickly that had we not been so determined to keep up, we might have lost him. Within a half hour, we arrived at a large island. There, back in the woods set three small huts, similar to those of the quarters on a plantation, but these were built up on stilts. Under the shacks, chickens pecked in the dirt, and a staked goat bleated out a greeting to Willie. An old woman, seated in the doorway of the largest hut, gave me a startled look.

"Peg! Come!" Willie waved her over. The old woman hesitated until she saw Pan. Then she set aside the basket she was weaving and came forward.

"Please! She needs milk," I said, holding Kitty out. My heart sank when the baby's little arms flopped down.

"Do you have some milk?" Pan pleaded. The woman leaned forward for a better look, then abruptly went for a bucket that hung from the side of the hut. In a few minutes, Kitty was slurping warm goat's milk through a small piece of swamp reed.

"Can't she have more?" I asked when the feeding stopped.

"Fir's we got to see if she can hold it down," Willie said to me.

"Like he know what he talkin' bout," Peg mumbled to herself. "Give me that chil'." She snatched Kitty from my arms. "Give the boy somethin' to eat," she directed Willie, her deep, gravelly voice all the more surprising because of her tiny frame.

"Can Mr. Burton have something to eat, too?" Pan asked, and the woman gave me a dark look before she walked away.

I was concerned for Kitty, but Willie waved me forward. "She take care a that baby. She jus' don' like to see no white man here. Come." He led us over to a fire pit. From a large black pot, he ladled out simmering stew into bowl-sized turtle shells, then handed us each a rough wooden spoon. Pan looked as though he might weep at the sight of the nourishing stew, and we both ate with relish while Willie disappeared into the hut. When Pan went into the woods to relieve himself, I sat back against a tree and closed my eyes in momentary contentment.

Suddenly, I was thrown to the ground. Though it was futile, I fought a ferocious-looking Negro, one who was twice my size. When he flipped me around to face him, his long tangled hair fell forward into his unshaven face but didn't conceal the hatred in his dark eyes. Willie and Peg, with Kitty in her arms, rushed from the house. "Pete!" Willie called. "Let him go!"

"What this white man doin' here, Willie?" the large man shouted.

"He lost, but he got two little niggas with him," Willie said.

"Oh, he gon' be lost, all right," Pete replied with a harsh laugh.

I groaned when his knee dug into my stomach. A knife pricked my neck, and I closed my eyes. Let it happen fast, I prayed.

"Let him go!" Pan flew out from the trees to strike at the large man's back. Pete caught Pan with his elbow and sent the boy flying while he twisted what was left of my shirt and pulled me to my feet.

"What you doin' out here?" he asked, pinning me against a tree.

I spat dirt from my mouth. "I'm trying to get up north! We came from a place south of here. There are patrollers after us."

"South a here? You talkin' 'bout Southwood?" Pete asked, and I nodded. "You hear that, Willie? He say he comin' up from Southwood!" I had long since lost my eye patch, and Pete studied my useless clouded eye. "So you that one-eyed man they sayin' is black! There men all over the canal lookin' for you. They give big money for you. Where's the gal you was runnin' with? Name a Sukey?"

"She died," I said.

Pan pointed to Kitty in Peg's arms. "That's her baby."

"And who's you?" Pete asked.

"I got took for a slave," Pan said, "and Mr. Burton is taking me home."

Pete turned back to me. "You say Sukey, the one who run that sickhouse, she die, and that's her baby?"

"Yes," I said, unexpectedly hopeful. "There's a man who lived somewhere close to this swamp who went by the name of Doc McDougal."

"Ol' Doc. Yeah, we know a him, don't we, Willie?"

Willie nodded.

"He has a friend, Mr. Spencer," I added. "If you can get word to Mr. Spencer of our whereabouts, I'm sure he could help us out."

"How you think anybody gonna get you outta here? They huntin' you like a dog," Pete said.

"Look," I said, pleading now, "I came down here to find the boy. He was stolen from Philadelphia."

Pete grunted, then he and Willie exchanged a furtive glance.

"Please," I begged, "I need your help."

"We'll see" was Pete's answer.

CHAPTER FORTY-TWO

1830

James

DURING THAT FIRST week, as Kitty adjusted to the goat's milk, Pan and I grew stronger from the hearty stews cooked by Peg. The woman liked no one and especially disliked me, but Pan trailed her as a boy might a mother. Soon she was favoring him and even taught him to milk her beloved pet goat, the only living creature she seemed to care about.

Willie usually left early in the morning to hunt or forage for food. Though Pete left each day as well, he was more secretive about his doings.

One evening, after we had all eaten our fill of a roasted wild pig, Peg divided the remainder of the meat into two wooden buckets before Pete and Willie carried them out into the night. "There's others needin' food" was Peg's explanation to Pan, and later that night Pan told me more: "She say there's others who live out here. They was all slaves, just like Peg and Willie, and they all been here for a long time. She say this is their home now."

Toward the end of the week, Pete came back with news that there were patrollers along the canal route searching for us. "Everybody want that money," he said, and worried that he and Willie were not immune to the same temptation, I began to press for a departure date.

"We got to wait," he said, then indicated with a nod for me to continue chopping wood.

I was so anxious to leave that, foolhardy as it would have been, I might have taken Pan and Kitty and struck out on my own. However, through Willie, I learned that this island had been chosen for their home because it was protected—surrounded by alligator and snake-infested waters. As dangerous were the numerous still ponds around the island, covered by a greasy surface sheen that camouflaged thick sucking mud. "Man don't know where he goin', he step in that, don' never see him again," Willie said.

ONE EVENING TOWARD the end of the second week, as Willie, Pan, and I sat at the fireside and watched while Peg tested the readiness of a roasting possum, Pete burst through the trees.

"We set for tonight! 'Fore sunup, we got to get you to the cross-ditch. Barge comin' up, gon' take you to a wagon that get you to No'folk."

My chest began to thump. Weren't the patrollers still out there? I had been waiting for this, but now I was afraid to leave. Daily I had reviewed each fear and obstacle we might face. The most concerning had to do with Kitty. "What about Kitty?" I asked. "What will we do for milk?"

The question hung in the air as I looked from one to the other.

"Best you ask Peg if she give you her goat," Willie finally said.

Peg shot him a sharp look.

"But . . ." Pan protested, knowing what the animal meant to Peg.

I looked to the old woman, certain of her denial. She clutched her hands together as she gazed at her prized goat, then turned back to Willie and gave a quick nod. I was disbelieving, yet I looked to Pete. "How can we take a goat?"

"You think that the biggest thing we ever carry out?" Pete asked, then went silent as though he had said too much.

Peg went over to the fire and removed the possum from the spit, then pulled the sweet potatoes from the coals. No one needed further encouragement to eat, but as we did, Peg went off to her hut. I leaned over to Willie and asked if she was coming back out to join us. He shook his head. "Let her be. She gettin' used to the idea of losin' her goat—and the boy," he added, nodding to Pan.

It had grown late, but as we prepared to leave, Peg returned to insist that we give Kitty a last feeding. Pan, as excited as I had ever seen him, went to Peg as she fed Kitty. "Do you want me to write to you and tell you how we got through?"

"You know I can't do no readin'," she said.

"I can draw some pictures. How 'bout that?"

"You good at it?" she asked.

"Not as good as Mr. Burton," he said.

"I want 'em from you," she said.

Pan looked around as though he'd suddenly remembered our whereabouts. "Where should I send them?"

"Send them to that Mr. Spencer. He'll get them to me," she said, solidifying a connection I had guessed at.

Pan watched as she changed the baby's clout and then settled Kitty into a new moss-lined basket. "You gonna miss Kitty, Miss Peg?" Pan asked.

"She too much work," Peg said, handing Pan a small leather bag that held clout-sized pieces of cloth, a small turtle shell, and fresh reeds for Kit's feedings.

"Thank you, Miss Peg," Pan said, and Peg's eyes glistened before she turned back toward her hut.

I followed. "Miss Peg," I called, addressing her with the formality that Pan always used.

"What you wantin' now?" she asked, turning back to face me.

"I want to thank you. I can never replace your goat, nor can I ever repay your kindness, but please take this." I reached for her hand and pressed my grandmother's large garnet and diamond brooch into her palm. "Get that to Mr. Spencer and he will get more goats for you, if you like," I said.

She closed her hand around the jewel, then turned and walked away.

When I picked up Kitty's basket, Willie stole a last peek. "You raise her up good," he said. "You tell her 'bout us out here. How Peg do for her."

PETE MOVED SWIFTLY, leading the muzzled goat through the impossibly thick vegetation. Each time something large slithered into the watery underbrush, the goat panicked and pulled back, until Pete, frustrated with her resistance, picked her up and slung her around his thick neck.

Even with Pete burdened, Pan and I had to work hard to keep up as he navigated first the boggy land and then the gnarled and slippery tree roots. Though now familiar with the night sounds, I was often startled by disturbed wildlife as it flew up or rustled past us in the undergrowth.

Kitty seldom fussed, and Pan remained close to my side, but it was such a difficult hike that I had little time to worry about what lay ahead. My most immediate fear was that I would lose my balance and take Kit into the water, so I gripped tight the walking cane Willie had thrust into my hand on our departure.

We trekked deep into the night, and even Pete appeared winded by the time we caught sight of the towpath. The night view of the winding canal was deceptively peaceful; overhead trees leaned in to one another, their branches folded together across the water as though in prayer. Down a distance, a long stretch of the canal was open to the sky, where the black shadow of a nighthawk glided across the still water.

A lone owl hooted and wolves howled as though in answer. I grew increasingly anxious as I watched Pete pace the bank. Suddenly, he rushed back to where we waited in the underbrush. "Somethin' comin'!" he whispered, and through the shadows, as though moving through molasses, a small barge pulled into view. As it moved closer, I could make out a Negro man and a smaller boy moving toward us on the towpath. Each had hold of a long pole secured to the craft and with these they pushed the boat forward.

"Come on, come on!" Pete waved us forward as the barge hit the bank. "Quick, climb up," he urged as he reached for Kitty.

I hesitated. What if, once I was on the barge, he meant to keep her?

"Jus' do what I say!" he said, grabbing for Kitty's basket.

"No!" I argued, until a woman on the barge reached down.

"Gib me the chil'," she whispered.

I handed Kitty up, and in short order, Pan and I found ourselves on board and standing next to piles of cut wood, melons, and sacks of grain.

"Come, quick, get in here," the barge man said, standing at the back and tossing away a stack of wood to expose a small trapdoor. He opened it and pointed. "Quick, get in," he said. Pan leaned on his haunches for a look inside. "Both of us is supposed to fit in there?" Pan asked in a whisper, and the man nodded. The small barge, not more than a large raft, was built so low and loaded so heavily that it was impossible to believe any space could exist underfoot. Yet there it was.

I hesitated, dreading the idea of that small space. I turned and saw Kitty in the woman's arms, then saw Pete sling up the objecting goat.

"Go on." The woman waved at me. "Go on. Get in. I got the chil'."

To my later regret, I did not thank Pete, thinking only how I didn't want to wedge myself into that narrow dark enclosure. But there was little time as the barge man urged me in. I forced myself to my knees and slid in, then encouraged Pan to wedge himself in beside me. We lay flat on our stomachs in the narrow damp space. "You got to stay quiet!" the barge man warned as he closed the door behind us. Wood clunked as it was tossed to cover over our hideout. Within minutes the raft bumped away from the canal banks and we slid off silently, but for the sound of the canal water rippling under us.

CHAPTER FORTY-THREE

1830

Pan

WHEN WE GO from Willie and Miss Peg's house, I'm not scared no more because I know my mama's watching out again.

Miss Peg give us her goat because she's a good woman, but she don't like Mr. Burton for being a white man, even after I tell her that his mama was colored. "You sure she colored?" Miss Peg asked.

"I'm not sure of nothing no more," I say.

"Why not?"

"'Cause after my mama die, she say she was gonna look out for me. Then I got took for a slave. Where was she then?"

"How'd you get took?" Miss Peg asked.

"I snuck down to the docks, where I wasn't supposed to go."

"Huh! How you expec' your mama to look out for you when you act the fool?" she asked.

I never look at it that way before, so that night, when Mr. Burton's sleeping, I talk with my mama. "You take care of Kitty and me and Mr. Burton, and I don't ever act the fool again." Then I go to sleep, 'cause now I know she's looking out for me.

MR. BURTON AND me is squished tight in the bottom of this boat. I see Mr. Burton's scared and that he don't like this no better than me, but I'm glad I'm not on my own like I was under that wagon seat. I'm just hopin' Mr. Burton keeps hisself settled. I never seen nothing like it when Kitty was comin' and he took off runnin'. I always thought Mr. Burton was something like God—that big a man. But then he goes off, leavin' Sukey and me. I'd of expected something like that from my daddy, but I was wrong about that, too. Turns out, afraid as my daddy was for getting took again, he come down into slave country looking for me. I'd never guessed he'd a done that. He musta cared for me that much. Makes my throat hurt to think about it.

My daddy was right. There's nothing worse than being a slave. I can't stop wonderin' what's going to happen to other boys like me now that Sukey is gone. Who's gonna help them get outta there?

Feels like this boat is movin' through the water at a fast clip. All I can think is that I don't know how to swim if it gets a leak. I can't talk to Mr. Burton 'cause we was told to stay quiet, so I close my eyes and try to think of something else. I don't want to remember Southwood and what it's like to be a slave there, so I think about Miss Peg and how I told her that I would draw her some pictures. She told me that she and Willie help out other runners all the time, but always Negroes. She don't take to Mr. Burton. "He act too white for me," she said.

But I say to her, "If I was white like him, I'd be actin' white, too."

"Why?" she said.

"For one thing, they don't take no white boys and sell them for slaves," I said. She give me one of her looks but don't say nothing.

"For another, white people don't have to be scared, like my daddy always was, always looking over his shoulder."

"I guess you's right, but no white man ever done me no good," she said.

I told her about Mr. Spencer and how he helped me out. "He was white," I said. "What about him?"

"I s'pose everybody got a little good in 'em," she said.

"Mr. Spencer got a lot a good in him, and so does Mr. Burton. You just don't want to see it," I say, and she shoots me a look that shuts me up.

Truth is, I don't know what to think of Mr. Burton no more. After he runs off and leaves me alone with Sukey, I got no use for him, but then he comes back and I see how good he takes care of Sukey and Kitty. I never would've pegged Mr. Burton to be a daddy, but with Kitty, it's like she's his own. He claims when we make it out of here, he's going to raise her free. I figure it'll fall on me to raise Kitty up, because Robert don't know nothing 'bout babies and if Mr. Burton is still gonna be white, Kitty will be down in the kitchen with Robert and me.

I wonder what kinda kitchen that'll be. Mr. Burton said we can't live in Philadelphia no more, so where we end up at, I don't know. I sure hope Mr. Burton means to stand by me and keeps me with him like he said he would, but you never know with a man who runs like that.

Even though I keep thinking that Philadelphia is where my mama and daddy live, in some ways I'm glad that we're leaving. That way, slave catchers come looking for me, I'm gone. Wonder how long they keep looking for their slaves that run? Daddy said they never stop.

CHAPTER FORTY-FOUR

1830

James

W E WERE DRAWN through the water for what seemed an eternity. I tried not to panic at being trapped in the small enclosure, but as the long hours passed, I grew increasingly distressed. My one relief was Pan beside me, who was silent but as brave as any man.

It was difficult to gauge time. We must have traveled for hours and had gone through at least two tolls before I sensed that our direction had changed and that we were traveling north. I was proved right when the man above, as though speaking to the woman, announced loudly, "We on the big canal now. Won't be long before we get to the landing."

Soon, amid sounds of horns and chugging, our small barge lifted and sank in the water as larger boats went by. Where were we headed? Surely a small craft such as this would not travel up as far as Suffolk or Norfolk!

It felt a lifetime had passed before the barge began to bump and thud in docking. Greetings were shouted, and through them I learned that I was on Joe's boat. He was well known and heartily greeted, as was his son, but his wife, Miss Lou, was noted with surprise. "See you brought the missus" was heard more than once.

"Joe, you got yerself a new lil one?" a voice called out.

"No," he called back, "Miss Lou been keepin' the baby for her sista till she get her health back."

"Hey, Joe, you sellin' that fine goat?"

"Nope, 'fraid not. I got to keep her for the baby. Chil' nothin' but trouble! All she can take is that darn ol' goat's milk."

"Joe, you got yerself some mighty fine melons there."

"I cain't sell them here. I'm takin' them up to the hotel. I promise las' time out I'd be back with 'em."

"You mean to tell me you still goin' up there today? You never gon' make it."

"No, it okay with you we bank up here for the night, leave first thing in the mornin'? What you fellas charge me for that?"

"How 'bout you give us some a those melons and we call it even."

Joe laughed, as did the others. "That sound good 'nough," he agreed.

And so we anchored for the night. Joe and his family stayed on the raft while visitors came by. They brought food, and Pan and I suffered when we caught scent of roasted chicken.

As they ate, the small group above us spoke like old friends, catching up on the latest gossip. One man stayed behind after the others left. Joe brought him to the back of the barge, where they sat down together and their conversation was easily overheard.

"Patrollers been through a couple times these pas' weeks. Ain't seen this kinda fuss in a long while. They got their eye out for a one-eyed black man who they say look white as them. He's with a nigga boy and a slave woman carryin' a chil'. I hear there a lotta money ridin' on them."

"Sound like those patrollers a rough bunch," said Joe.

"They's rough, but nothing like the one that come through on his own. Seen him before. Name's Rankin. Claims to know the man who runnin'. He set to find him."

"He must be wantin' that money real bad," said Joe.

"S'pose so. All I know is he sure do mean to find him. Say, you got your free papers on you?"

"You know I don' go up this water without 'em," Joe said.

"Jus' keep your eye out. Don' moor up if you see them patrollers."

"Times like this," Joe said, "I sure do wish I had me a gun."

The other man gave a deep-throated laugh. "You an' me both, Joe. 'Magine us two niggas with guns. Whooee, can you see it now! We do ourselves some huntin'!" His voice grew low. "See here, I'm slidin a knife under this pile a wood, 'case you got need of it. Traded with a Injun for it jus' the other day. I'm not needin' it right now, an' there ain't no harm in it sittin' here."

"I sure do thank you," said Joe. "I got me a small one, but one that size—"

"This one do the job, is what it do."

"I s'pect so," said Joe, and their conversation ended when the two parted.

Trapped as we were, on hearing Rankin's name, all I wanted was escape. I used all I had in me to fight the instinct to call out to Joe for release.

As the night deepened, everything above us grew silent and time lost meaning. Pan slept, his head turned away, and as I listened to his shallow breathing, the concern I felt toward him was akin to what I felt for Kitty. There had been a dramatic change in Pan since his abduction and it angered me to think of how the past months had affected him.

I wanted to join Pan in sleep, but I passed the night fighting a terrible thirst that grew with each lap of water against the raft. My need became so strong that I was tempted to lick at the damp floor, though I restrained myself, knowing the folly. Twice I heard Kitty cry, but each time I was relieved to hear shuffling and noises from the goat, and then she became quiet again.

I must have slept, for I was startled awake when our barge began to move out. My head ached from the cramped position I was in and when I turned my stiff neck, it was to see Pan's eyes staring into mine.

"Mr. Burton! I peed on myself!" Pan whispered softly.

"Me, too," I whispered back, and we exchanged a grimacing smile.

As we traveled up the canal, my anxiety grew. Where were we going? Who would be helping us? Had arrangements been made for Kit? How could I transport the goat? Where was Rankin?

When we docked again, I guessed it to be late afternoon. As everyone left the barge, it felt like we were being abandoned, yet we dared not speak. Later that evening, Pan clutched my arm as footsteps approached; then came relief on hearing Joe's low voice, who came with his wife and another man. Within minutes they had shifted the cargo, and the trapdoor was finally opened. They took Pan out first, but there was a whispered argument when he did not want to leave without me.

"Look, boy, you got to stay quiet and listen. We tryin' to help you. Now come with me," the woman said, then whisked him away. When Joe encouraged me to back out, my legs were too numb to move, so he and his accomplice grabbed hold of my feet and dragged me out. I clung to them as they half carried me off the barge and up onto dry land, where they set me down. Where was I? I looked around as I stretched my limbs and saw our small craft tied in a secluded inlet. Up ahead, more sizable boats were anchored at a large dock lit by the welcoming lamps of what appeared to be a hotel.

Again the men helped me to my feet. My strength was returning, and we soon made our way into one of the large barns. We hurried past the horses, quietly munching hay in their stalls, to a small feed room at the back. There, bags of feed were piled high, but to the side was a small opening where the two men silently pushed me through. No sooner was I in than they began to seal up the entry.

"Where's the boy?" I whispered.

"We bring him to you later," I heard.

"How long will I be in here?" I asked, dreading another enclosure.

"I don' know, but there's some water and somethin' in there to eat," Joe said.

Before the last bag was put in place, I poked my head out. "Wait! Where are we?" I asked.

"We at the hotel that sit at the border 'tween Carolina an' Virginny," said Joe. "You got a ride comin'."

"A ride?" I asked in disbelief. "What kind of ride?" I remembered Kitty. "Where's the baby?" I asked.

"I brings her and the boy to you when the time right, not befo'," Joe whispered, slinging the last bag into place and blocking further communication.

Though the small space was dark, when I slumped to the floor, I felt the supplies that had been left for me. My hands shook as I tipped up the small bucket of water and drank from it. Then I fell to wolfing down all of the bread and dried meat. I drained the bucket of water and then lay back.

I woke with my stomach cramping, and though I fought for control, I heaved up my meal as I lost control of my bowels. When I recovered, I sat back to consider my miserable state. My clothes, already in shreds, were impossibly soiled. My hair had not been cut, nor had I been shaved in many weeks, and a stench rose from me that reminded me of the afternoon when the slave coffle passed by. I remembered well my disgust when their ripe scent lingered. Now I was left to contemplate the privileged position from which I had made a judgment.

Too weary and sick to think further, I laid my head down again and fell asleep. I was unsure how long I slept, but I awoke suddenly, startled by Joe's voice. He was hurriedly dismantling my protective barrier, and when the bags were lifted away, he urged me out.

It was dark in the room, but as my eyes adjusted, I saw Joe first, and then another dark face came into view. I stumbled back in disbelief. Nothing could have prepared me for the sight of Robert!

CHAPTER FORTY-FIVE

1830

James

W HAT ROBERT'S INITIAL feelings were at seeing me in my terrible state, he did not say, but after a few slow moments, he greeted me with a nod. "Good evening, Mr. Burton."

"Robert!" was all I managed to say before he turned to Joe.

"We will need fresh water and plenty of it," Robert said.

I had already peeled away my soiled clothing when Joe returned with a bucket of water and as I washed myself down, Robert told me about a waiting carriage. Then, to my amazement, he produced some of the clothes that I had left back at the Spencers'.

"How did you get these?" I asked as I gratefully slipped into clean drawers, a fresh white shirt, and my worn but clean riding clothes.

"I will explain all of that later," he said, handing over my riding boots.

"I have Pan with me," I said, struggling to pull the tall boots over my torn and swollen feet.

"I know. They just put him in the carriage," Robert said, and I could have wept in relief.

"Do you have the baby as well?" I asked.

He straightened to look at me. "The baby?" he asked.

"Yes." I turned to Joe. "Where's Kitty?" I asked.

"I go for her now," he said.

"A baby?" Robert asked again.

"Yes," I said. "She is only a few weeks old. What size is the carriage?"

"It's yours—the one I brought from Philadelphia."

"Good! Then we'll have room for the goat."

"The goat!" Robert said.

"I need it for the milk," I said.

Robert looked at me in dismay. "The carriage is already filled to capacity. There are two women along for the journey."

"In the carriage?"

"We have no choice in the matter. They've come to assist us," he said.

"Well, we need to make room for the goat," I said.

He stared at me. "A goat!" he repeated.

Why, in all of this, was he fixated on the goat? I wondered. "The goat has to come!" I insisted.

"As you wish," he said. I buttoned my waistcoat, and Robert handed over a pair of spectacles instead of the expected eye patch. "These are meant to change your look," he explained.

"Are we ready to leave?" I asked, fitting them to my face.

"The carriage is ready, sir, but first we must drive over and pick up the women where they are staying at the hotel. Then we will leave."

"You take the carriage up to the hotel and gather the women. Then come back here for me."

"Leave you here? Are you quite certain?" Robert asked.

"Yes," I answered. "Go ahead! I'll be waiting for you with the baby."

Robert left but twice turned back to see if I had changed my mind.

"Go on," I encouraged him.

Kitty was asleep when Joe arrived with her. When I took her in my arms, I was so relieved to see her that I kissed her satin face. When I looked up, Joe had left.

I paced with Kitty as I waited for his return, wondering why it was taking him so long. I remembered the offers of money that Joe had for the goat. Was it possible that he did not mean to return? Kitty could not survive without the milk.

Carefully, I cradled the sleeping baby between two bags of grain, then hurriedly slipped out of the feed room into the barn. From there I ran out. It was farther to the water than I remembered, but when I got to the barge, I found Joe struggling with the frightened goat.

"I tryin' to tie up her mouth," he grunted. Together we quickly finished the job. "Here, take this," Joe said, and reached under the pile of wood. "Careful with it." He handed me a long sheathed knife. "It got some cut to it."

"I'll get it back to you!" I said gratefully, while Joe scooped up the goat and left at a trot.

"Look! There is the carriage!" I said in a loud whisper, pointing to where it stood in the shadow of the barn. "You take the goat to the carriage. I'll get Kitty," I said, and sprinted ahead.

I might have rushed in, but there was light from a lantern back in the feed room, and I doubted Robert would have brought it. I heard a threatening voice and dropped down to edge my way forward.

"I'm askin' you one more time, where's James Pyke at?"

A cold chill covered my body. I could not mistake Rankin's voice.

"I do not know a James Pyke," said Robert.

Where was Kitty? I moved closer but stopped when a floorboard creaked.

"You don't know him? Somebody at Southwood say you was down there looking for him."

"I've come to the Carolinas to take a young lady back to Philadelphia to attend her school," Robert said, his voice high and afraid.

I inched forward again.

"No white girl's gonna travel with no nigra!"

"She has her maid in attendance, sir."

"'Sir'! 'Attendance'! Listen to this nigra talk like he think he somethin'!"

Kitty gave a sudden cry.

"What's that you got back behind you?" Rankin asked in surprise. "Give it here!"

"No!" Robert argued.

I crept forward, unsheathing the knife and gripping tight the bone handle. Kitty cried out again.

"It's just a nigra baby! She yours?" the man asked.

"Don't hold her like that! Give her back to me!" Robert exclaimed as Kitty screamed.

"I'll snap her neck like a chicken, you don't tell me where Pyke is." He dangled Kitty by the arm.

"No!" Robert begged.

I was almost close enough to lunge when I tripped on a floorboard. Rankin swung around and dropped Kitty with a thunk. She shrieked, but with his pistol pointed at me, I dared not reach for her. "Well, now, Jamie Pyke!" he said. "I've been waiting on you! Can't see much a your nigga mama in you, but you sure do look jus' like your daddy."

I froze. The man's hair was white now, but he was as ugly as I remembered. I spat out the words: "I have no father!"

"Oh, you got a daddy, all right." He laughed. "I was there holding your mama down for him when Marshall got on her. You shoulda heard her screamin'. Nothin' like a nigra woman who puts up a good fight!"

His gun was leveled at my chest. Powerless, I felt like a small child again. "Why would you do that to her?" I asked. "Why would you do that?"

"That nigra Belle always did think too high on herself, not wanting somebody like me!" he said, sneering. "Even said no to your daddy when he got on her, and he was the masta!"

"She had a right to say no!" I shouted.

"She was a nigra!" he growled. "And then she had you. Thought her yella baby was somethin' special, so I fixed her good! Took you away! Oh, the hootin' and hollerin' that woman did when I got hold a you."

I dared not look Robert's way as he eased a pitchfork from the wall. Though Kitty screamed, I knew I had to keep Rankin's focus on me.

"So you took me?" I asked. "It was you who took me away from her?"

"Boy oh boy, you sure did make a fuss leavin' that mammy a yours." He laughed. "You two sure did raise a stink!"

Robert grunted as he thrust the sharp tines of the pitchfork into Rankin's back. The gun flew, and Rankin yowled, twisting in pain. As he turned back for Robert, I used the knife to end Rankin's life.

Robert scooped Kitty up from the floor, then swayed and sank onto a sack of grain, but my strength grew to that of two men. I slung bags of feed aside and pushed Rankin's body into the soiled hiding spot that I knew well, then quickly stuffed it up again before I rushed us out to the waiting carriage.

The carriage door was flung open and we were not yet seated when the horses pulled out. Robert pushed past the frantic goat and dropped onto a seat, while I, clinging to Kitty, was saved from being thrown forward when someone clutched my jacket and pulled me back. "I got you, Mr. Burton," Pan said, and I felt a swell of relief to know he was safe as I sank down beside him. The goat bleated, Kitty wailed, and our carriage raced ahead.

"Are you all right?" I asked Pan.

"I was scared for you and Kitty," he said.

"We're safe now," I said in an effort to comfort him.

"And thank heavens for that! What a relief to find you safe!"

I looked about in surprise. "Adelaide Spencer!" I said, recognizing her voice even in the dark. "Is that you?"

Before she had time to reply, another woman across from me reached out her arms. Her dark face looked out from under her traveling bonnet. "Mr. Burton, give me the chil'." It was Hester!

"Be careful with her," I said, my arms suddenly feeling lifeless as I handed her over. "I don't think she's been hurt, but she's been badly frightened."

The carriage swayed and creaked, and the dark swamp flew by. The goat fought for footing and bleated mercilessly until she finally dropped onto the floor amid the feet and baggage. "Where are we?" I asked.

"By now we should be safely in Virginia," Robert said, "but we will keep the pace for a good number of miles."

"We picked you up at that hotel because it was at the border," Addy broke in.

"Should a crime be committed by you in North Carolina, you cannot be arrested for it in Virginia," Robert said pointedly. "Patrollers from North Carolina have no say in Virginia."

"And where are we headed?" I asked.

"We're on our way to a tavern just past Suffolk, where we will rest and change out our horses. From there we will travel to a ferry that will take us across the James to Williamsburg."

"Excellent!" I said, and sat back, trying to take in this turn of events. Was it possible that we had made it to safety?

"Shhh, shhh," Hester crooned to Kitty. We all grew silent, soothed by her voice and the repetitive grinding and clanking of the carriage wheels. After the baby quieted, Hester spoke low. "Mr. Burton?"

"Yes, Hester?"

"Where Sukey?"

Pan, wedged next to me, stiffened.

"Hester, she's gone," I said.

Hester turned and looked out into the night.

"But you are holding her daughter," I offered.

"We go back a long way," Hester said.

"She was a brave woman, Hester. She saved our lives."

"She help a lot of others, too, but all she ever want is for her babies to go free."

"Kitty will be raised free. I will see to it that she has every opportunity," I promised.

"Who gon' care for her?" Hester asked.

"I will see to it," I repeated. I leaned my head back and closed my eyes, meaning to quiet Hester. I needed some time to think. Now that I had reached safety, new worries began to bombard me. What awaited me in Williamsburg? And where was I to go from there? Without a home, I could provide nothing for Kitty and Pan, never mind my daughter. Images of my home in Philadelphia kept coming to me, and I felt sick with longing.

When Hester placed a sleeping Kitty in her basket, then settled herself for a rest, Pan did the same. Addy surprisingly took to the idea of sleep, bundling her green shawl to use as a pillow. Silence descended as we traveled on.

Only Robert and I remained awake. He stared out the dark window, and though I wanted to converse with him, I found myself at a loss for words. I was trying to formulate a plan for my future, and I wanted to make the right decisions for all concerned—not only the children but Robert as well. I had no home to offer Robert, and especially after the trauma of the last few months, I felt that the kindest thing I could do for this good man was to give him a substantial stipend and relieve him of his service to me. But right now I could not face that.

I leaned forward. "Robert," I said softly.

"Sir?"

"Thank you. I don't know that I would have survived today without you. I'm sorry for the position I put you in."

"We both knew the danger, and we need never speak of it again."

"Thank you for coming for me, but was it wise to leave Williamsburg? Are you certain my daughter is well cared for?"

"Fear not." He gave a quiet laugh. "As necessary as it was to come to your assistance, I would not have left if I hadn't been sure of her well-being. Your young Miss Caroline has quite stolen everyone's heart."

"What does she look like, Robert?"

"My description would not do her justice. Her eyes are as blue as the sky."

"Is her temperament that of her mother? Is she gentle?"

In the night light, I saw his smile. "You will not be disappointed," he reassured me.

"And Williamsburg?" I asked. "What awaits me there? What is the mood?"

His smile left.

"Robert?" I asked again.

"It is welcoming enough, sir."

"Yet?" I asked, hearing his hesitation.

"Yet I would prepare you for some controversy with regard to the guardianship of Miss Caroline."

"Controversy? With whom?" I asked. "Have the grandparents . . ."

"No, no! It is the two women. Miss Meg and Miss Eleanor have both fallen under Miss Caroline's spell."

"But they know that she is mine?"

"Well. Yes. However, I believe they've decided that she would be better raised with them, feeling they are more qualified to shelter and raise a young girl."

"And they are prepared to voice this to me?"

"Yes, sir, I do believe so."

"We shall see," I said. "Surely they have other interests."

"Indeed. They are taken up with their school."

"And they seem equally invested in this venture?"

"They are, though I'm afraid their livelihood is in jeopardy."

"In what way?"

"It seems they offered some evening classes to Negro children, and because of it, the school's enrollment has dropped off dramatically."

"I see," I said, understanding too well the full implication of their problem. "So it is not a town that would take to the likes of someone . . . like me."

"No, sir, I do not think it would serve you well."

Exhausted, I sat back and rubbed my face with my hands. I hadn't expected to make Williamsburg my home, but I had hoped that it might serve as a resting place for a few months. Again I thought of the comfortable home that the Burtons had gifted me, and my heart ached. "Oh, Robert," I said, "what I wouldn't give to go home to Philadelphia!"

Robert nodded sympathetically, and we fell silent once again.

IT WAS DAYBREAK when we drew up to the small tavern where we were to change out our horses. We disembarked with great relief. During the last miles, Kitty had squalled from hunger while the goat bleated out her own distress.

Inside the tavern, after fresh milk was supplied for Kitty, the women were shown a room, while Robert as my valet and Pan as my servant accompanied me to a room of our own. There, Pan slept while I, in preparation for Williamsburg, was provided with the luxury of a hot bath. Later, as Robert shaved me, I asked how it was that he had known to come for me.

"I received a note from Mr. Spencer advising me that you and Pan were in jeopardy. I needed nothing more to arrange for a carriage."

"So you traveled directly to the Spencers'?"

"Yes, and I waited there until Mr. Spencer and the others could plan your safe passage."

"And what of Miss Adelaide? How was it that her father allowed her to accompany you?" I asked.

He shook his head with the memory. "Sir, I have never seen the likes of it. It is not in my place to judge the decision of a father, but Mr. Spencer did not appear to have a choice. On the day I was to leave, there she was, dressed and toting bags packed for travel. In spite of Mr. Spencer's objections, Miss Adelaide stepped into the carriage and refused to come out. As time was swiftly passing and your safety was tied up in it, her father was forced to include Hester before he would allow his daughter to leave. On our arrival in Williamsburg, they are to return home immediately with a male cousin."

"Why did she insist on coming?" I asked.

"She was certain that she could ensure your safe passage by naming you as her tutor."

I couldn't help but chuckle and shake my head, but Robert was not amused.

Refreshed after a few hours' rest, I sent word to the driver to prepare for travel and then arranged for us to have a meal. When our small party convened in the lobby, Kitty, Hester, Pan, and Robert were taken to a back room where the Negroes ate, while Addy and I were shown into the dining area.

Though I had little appetite and was anxious to be on our way, Adelaide was no sooner seated than she removed her purple gloves and helped herself to a biscuit, one so hot and fresh that steam escaped when she tore it open. She slathered it with salted butter, topped it with a hearty slice of ham, added two thick slices of pickle, set it together, and passed it over to me. To please her, I took a bite, and she smiled as she prepared another for herself. As she ate, she gave a few soft moans of pleasure but said nothing else until she finished the loaded biscuit and drained an oversize mug of heavily sugared and creamed coffee.

"And now, Mr. Burton, I am pleased to say that I feel more myself," she said, sitting back with a satisfied sigh. "Were you . . ." Her words faded as my thoughts traveled ahead to what awaited me in Williamsburg.

"Mr. Burton!" Her agitated voice broke through.

"Pardon me?" I said.

"I asked if you were not surprised to see me?" She sniffed.

"Oh! I was," I said. "Indeed!"

"Well, if Father had his way, I would not have come. I don't know what he will have to say on my return," she said.

"Then why did you insist on coming?" I asked.

"How could I not? They were saying such vile things about you! I decided you had need of my protection."

"Your protection!"

"Father said that he could not leave Patricia and me alone again, so he could not come with Robert to vouch for you. Of course, the solution was quite simple. I would come along and pose as your student. If any authorities had questions, I would tell them you were my tutor. After all, that is the truth." She smiled.

"And why would you do that for me?"

"A man who is willing to risk his life for the cause has nothing but my admiration." She buttered another biscuit and drizzled honey over it before she handed it to me. "You'd best eat another," she said.

I took the warm bread from her, wondering at her fire. "The truth is, Miss Adelaide, you know little about me."

"Mr. Burton, I assure you, I know everything that is important. You are an admirable man who came to release that poor young boy from slavery. You upset that miserable man Bill Thomas, and he set out to destroy your good name, accusing you of heaven knows what. When he did not find you at our home, he hired others to bring you back so he might press charges against you for theft of his property. Because of it, your life was in danger."

I shook my head. "I don't understand how your father could have allowed you to leave under such dangerous conditions." I said it more to myself than to her.

"Father has no idea what to do with me. I believe you suggested that yourself."

"But at your young age?" I said.

"I will be sixteen in two week's time," she said.

I laughed. "Exactly! You are still a child!"

Her eyes flashed. "I am not a child," she said. "I may be young, and my cousins accuse me of being naive, but I was willing to sacrifice my life for you and your young Pan!"

"Miss Adelaide," I said with true remorse. "How could I be so thoughtless? Of course you are not a child. You are a young woman, and a most brave one at that. I shall never forget how you saved Pan's life."

"And I came prepared to act as your protector as well!" she said.

"My dear, I assume that you planned to use your beauty as your weapon?" I asked, trying for levity.

"No, I planned to use this!" she said, opening and tipping forward her leather reticule to reveal a small pistol.

"Adelaide!" I said. "Where—"

"It was Mother's!" she said defensively. "Don't be so concerned. I am quite capable of using it. Goodness, I've known how to use a gun for years!"

I sat back from the table to stare at this willful girl.

She met my gaze. "Life is meant to be lived," she said, "and I mean to live it!"

I laughed aloud, causing the few others dining to look in our direction. "Miss Spencer," I said, leaning forward, "what a pleasure it is to know you."

"Now, that, Mr. Burton," she said, adjusting her lavender and green traveling bonnet, "is more to my liking."

WHEN WE ALL crammed back in the carriage, to everyone's joy, we left behind the goat and carried instead a hamper filled not only with a fine lunch but also with two cold bottles of goat milk, more than enough to see Kitty through the last of our journey. We were certain to make it to Williamsburg by evening, and though my relief was great, my heart dreaded the arrival, for then I would be forced into decisions that I did not want to make.

CHAPTER FORTY-SIX

1830

James

I T WAS EVENING when we rolled up to our destination. Yellow candles flickered in the many windows that fronted the street of the Madden home.

According to Robert, Mr. Madden had died ten years previous during an influenza epidemic, but the elder Mrs. Madden, my grandmother's sister, still lived in their home, though she was now something of an invalid. Miss Meg, her daughter, and Miss Eleanor, Lavinia's daughter and my half sister, both resided with her. It was thanks to Miss Meg, who had retained the integrity of the property with vigilant maintenance, that the house presented such a pretty picture.

It wasn't as large a dwelling as many I had seen, but it was sizable enough that a number of servants would have been required. The two-story home was painted white with black shutters and had low wings that rambled off on either side. Gardens in the front were surrounded by white fencing, while brick paths wound back to whitewashed outbuildings.

Two women rushed out the door as our driver pulled the horses to a stop. I was the first one out. The older woman, who came forward carrying a lantern, was short and rather round. Her hair was knotted at the back of her head, with gray and brown strands frizzing out from the security of hairpins. If I had been pressed, I would have guessed her to be in her early forties. She had a lopsided gait, and because of a cane, she was more slow-moving than the redheaded younger woman who sprinted in front of her.

Lavinia! I stopped myself from calling out her name, for of course it couldn't have been her. Yet here was her replica, though this woman was no more than in her mid-twenties. In the end, the eyes made all the difference. Where Lavinia's amber eyes had been demure and shy, Miss Eleanor's were blue, bright, and bold, and they did not hesitate in their examination of me.

"Brother?" she asked, coming forward and offering her hand.

I took it and leaned forward in a bow. "I apologize for my appearance," I said, infinitely grateful for the haircut and shave Robert had given me back at the inn.

She continued her unblinking gaze. "I see no similarity in our appearance," she announced.

"Yes, well . . ." Startled by her forthright remarks, I had no answer. Just then, Hester emerged from the carriage with a squalling Kitty. Relieved at the distraction, I moved to take the babe while Hester lifted her skirts to step down.

If either Miss Meg or Miss Eleanor was surprised to see a Negro baby thus placed into my arms they hadn't time to absorb their astonishment before Robert and Pan stepped out. Then Addy, the last of our lot, made her appearance. Her lavender traveling dress was heavily wrinkled, and a lengthy tear down the side exposed her petticoat. She had long since abandoned her bonnet, and with a flourish, she swung back her thick black hair. Pausing on the top step, she looked around at the astonished faces that stared up at her, then waved her bonnet in a full sweep as she exclaimed to all, "We have finally arrived!"

From the little I knew of our hostesses, they defied ordinary convention and lived, if not on, then close to the fringe. They recognized in Adelaide another like themselves, and their acceptance of her was immediate.

AFTER PAN, HESTER, and the baby were taken to their quarters in one of the outbuildings, Caroline was brought to me. She was everything Robert had said she was. A beautiful baby, indeed, with sky-blue eyes and such fair skin that I wondered how she would handle the sun. On first sight of me, she wrinkled her full round face and began to howl. Everyone laughed as I tried to soothe her, but she continued to object to me so vehemently that Miss Meg scooped her away.

"She does not know you. You must give her time," each of the women said reassuringly. I was not so certain.

I WAS GIVEN a large comfortable room in the main house, with Robert made available to me in a small room adjoining mine. Though I was exhausted, sleep would not come after we retired.

In the last few months, since I'd lost Caroline, danger had been a constant. I had been on the run until my deadly encounter with Rankin. Now, in this peaceful room, back in orderly civilization, I felt disoriented.

I expected to feel more at home in these surroundings. I, too, had searched Miss Eleanor's face, expecting to see some family resemblance, but had found none. The fact that she so looked like Lavinia, yet held such an opposite disposition, further bewildered me. The worst of it was when I recalled Rankin's words about my mother. Unable to rid myself of the thoughts of her abuse by Marshall and Rankin, I could not rest.

Until now I had not known that I was conceived in violence. I had judged Belle harshly for having given herself to Marshall. Understanding now that she had been molested, I wondered how she could have tolerated her pregnancy. Surely she could not have loved me. Yet Rankin had said that my removal from her had been an act of vengeance. It could have been that only if Belle had cared for me.

From old habit I began to pace; when the floorboards creaked, afraid of disturbing others, I seated myself next to the open window. The road below was worn smooth and the gardens groomed. All about lay order and serenity. I struggled with questions late into the night. Should I try to make a home here in Williamsburg? Robert did not think this place would welcome me. Where, then, did I belong? Was my birth an accident of fate, or was my life intended to have some purpose?

CHAPTER FORTY-SEVEN

1830

James

I N THE MORNING I was invited into the dining room for a morning meal, and there to meet the elderly Mrs. Madden, who had been asleep on our arrival. I had met her as a child, for she was my grandmother's sister, and though I was young, I knew that she strongly disapproved of my grandmother's attachment to me. Yet Mrs. Madden was my great-aunt, and I felt hopeful of a warm reception. However, when Miss Eleanor presented me, I soon learned otherwise.

After the introduction and before we sat to eat, I asked if Hester was available, as I wanted to know how Kitty had fared through the night. Mrs. Madden requested that I wait with my business dealings until after we ate, and manners dictated that I oblige.

After Miss Meg, Miss Eleanor, and Miss Addy had all been seated, I took the position indicated for me at the foot of the beautifully set table. This signaled for Mrs. Madden, who sat at the head, to ring the hand bell for the kitchen staff to bring in the food.

It had never been my habit to eat a large morning meal, so when heaping platters of bacon, sausages, and eggs arrived, I held back my surprise. Both of the Negro servants left, but one soon returned with a platter of waffles. Behind her followed Pan, carrying a crystal decanter of warm maple syrup. A clean white shirt and oversize trousers hung from his slender frame. How thin he looked! His hair had grown back enough to partially cover the scar on his head, but his ears poked out as endearingly as ever. He made an effort to act the servant, but his smile for me was so genuine that I broke protocol and greeted him enthusiastically. "Pan!" I said. "How are you feeling today?"

Mrs. Madden looked at me quizzically.

"I am good, Mr. Burton," he said. "I'm helping out in the kitchen."

"Place the syrup on the table, and then you may leave," Mrs. Madden said to Pan. He looked to me for direction.

"Here." I patted a spot on the table. "Put it down here and I will see you later." I smiled and nodded him toward the door.

"Do you allow that kind of familiarity with all of your servants?" Mrs. Madden asked as he left.

"I do," I said, causing her lips to purse.

Silence fell over the table until Adelaide spoke up. "You should see how well he treats Kitty."

"And who is Kitty?" asked Mrs. Madden.

"Yes, well," I stumbled, "she is a child I have taken responsibility for. She is the daughter of . . . a friend."

"And where is this Kitty?"

As one, all of the women stared at me.

"Indeed," I said, looking to Miss Meg.

"Hester cared for her during the night," she said.

"Hester?" asked Mrs. Madden.

"She is my family's servant," said Addy. "She is traveling with me."

"This is all too much for me," said Mrs. Madden. "I like my home to have order."

"I appreciate your position, Mrs. Madden, and I assure you of my gratitude for the hospitality you have shown all of us," I said, doing my best to offer genuine appreciation for the shelter she had provided baby Caroline and Robert in my absence.

"I don't see that I had a choice," she replied.

"Mother!" said Miss Meg.

"It is true. After the two of you"—she nodded toward Miss Meg and Miss Eleanor—"offered your help in spite of my opinion, what choice was I given? Both of you are too headstrong for your own good. Is it any wonder that neither of you are married?"

After Miss Meg and Miss Eleanor exchanged a quick look, Miss Eleanor took a bite of waffle to hide her smile.

"Mr. Burton is our guest, Mother," said Miss Meg.

"How long will we have the pleasure of your company?" Mrs. Madden asked me pointedly.

"If I could have another day or two," I said.

"You may have as much time as you require," said Miss Meg. "Mother and I are happy to accommodate you and your household as long as you have need."

"Thank you," I said. I looked at Mrs. Madden when I spoke. "I'm sure that Grandmother would be happy to know that you have included me as family."

Mrs. Madden met my gaze and glared. She opened her mouth and I braced for her response, but she clearly thought better of it and returned to her food. I, too, turned to my plate, and amid the clinking of cutlery and china, I ate as a man starved.

AFTER THE MEAL, on Miss Meg's request, I followed her to the back parlor. At first glance, the room looked comfortably furnished, but after Miss Meg sat, she began to pick at a loose thread on the arm of the settee, and I noticed the wear on the rest of the furniture.

"I must apologize for Mother," she said.

"I understand her position," I said. "I'm afraid she will always see me in a way that does not conform to her standards."

"How nicely you put that."

We looked at each other, neither holding back in our examination. I felt strangely comforted to be with someone who actually knew me.

"To look at you, no one would ever know that your mother was a Negro," she said bluntly.

"So I understand," I replied.

"It should not make a difference," she said, "but I'm afraid that for people such as Mother and many like her, it does."

I said nothing.

"I will not inquire of your past difficulties, but perhaps you would tell me where it is you plan to travel from here. Your Robert indicated that you have permanently left Philadelphia and are looking to relocate? I would love to welcome you to Williamsburg, but we are not immune to gossip, and I'm afraid you would never be accepted into society in this small town," she said openly.

Though I did not feel that it was her aim to hurt me, the truth of her comment stung. I took a long deep breath before I leaned forward. "Miss Meg, I appreciate your being so forthright. Let me assure you that I have no intention of residing here. However, the debt that I owe both you and Miss Eleanor is one I doubt I can ever repay."

"There is no need to repay us. It was our pleasure to help out a family member in a time of need."

There was a quiet knock on the door before Miss Elly entered. "May I join you?" she asked.

"Come." Miss Meg patted a space on the settee beside her.

"Your mother is settled in her room," Miss Elly said to Miss Meg, then to me, "but she was in a fine temper, admonishing me for referring to you as my kin."

I was surprised at the openness of both these women. Taking a cue from their honesty, I directed a question to Miss Eleanor. "Have you had recent word on your mother or . . . mine?"

"As a matter of fact, I have. Belle is doing very well. As usual, she is at my mother's side and has no patience with what she calls my interference."

"Your interference?" I asked.

"If you can believe this, Mother is actually considering marriage. Imagine!"

"She is?" I asked. "Have you met the gentleman?"

"Yes, many times. He is a neighbor of ours and has been ever since I can remember. He has four boys, all under the age of twenty. When I was younger, before I came to Aunt Meg's school, I shared a tutor with the two oldest. Those two Stephens boys were impossible! Can you imagine my quiet mother with a houseful of boys, one more rowdy than the other?"

I smiled. "That does present quite a picture."

"I'm afraid she's going ahead with it and is planning a wedding. Can you imagine? A wedding! At her age!"

Miss Meg laughed. "Please don't belabor the point, Elly. She is not that old. Don't forget that your mother and I are of a similar age."

"No one should marry in their forties!" Miss Elly shivered at the thought.

Miss Meg laughed and patted her younger niece's hand. "We will attend the wedding in October and then must only let your mother know how pleased we are for her happiness."

"Oh, Aunt Meg, sometimes you sound just like her!"

Miss Meg turned to me with a concerned look. "Are we truly so uncivilized that we would discuss our small family drama when you are having such a struggle with your own? Forgive us. Please."

"On the contrary," I said. "I would like to know more about you. I understand that you have a school?"

The two women glanced at each other, then grimaced. "We do," said Miss Meg, "but we've met with some difficulty. Because of our liberal views, we are never certain the doors will stay open."

"Your liberal views?" I asked.

"Last year we began to hold classes in the evening for Negro children," said Miss Eleanor. "Some of the townspeople objected and withdrew their daughters from the day school."

"Do you still hold the evening classes?" I asked.

"We do," said Miss Meg, "but our enrollment for the day students is not what it once was."

"So you require funding?" I asked.

"Always," Miss Meg agreed. "Yet somehow we make it through each season."

"Perhaps I can help," I said.

"In what way?"

I looked down at my trousers. Although Robert had done his best, my clothes were travel-worn. "Though I may not give the appearance, I am a man of some means," I said. "I would be happy to contribute."

The two women exchanged a happy look, then smiled at me.

"We would be delighted to accept any assistance," said Miss Meg.

"How wonderful!" agreed Miss Eleanor. "But—" She looked to her aunt. Miss Meg, acknowledging her niece's stare, inhaled deeply, as though for courage.

"Mr. Burton. In light of your kind offer," she said, "we would like to present an offer of our own."

"Yes," I said, leaning back in my chair and crossing my arms while steeling myself for the question.

"We would like to keep young Caroline," Miss Eleanor burst in. "Please say we may! These past months she has become the center of our lives. We are both in love with her, and we would like to raise her as our own."

"It is true, she already feels like our own," Miss Meg added.

I leaned forward. "But she is my daughter. She has my blood, you understand."

"We do," said Miss Elly, "and that is why we thought you might agree. She need never know!"

Though Robert had prepared me for this, a sickening note lay behind their offer. They were not disguising their intent; they were openly saying that my daughter would never know me as her father. Were they right? Was this, then, the best solution?

"I need time to think this through," I said.

The women graciously assured me that they understood. We adjourned after I asked to be excused from the upcoming afternoon meal.

"Would you join us for a late super?" Miss Meg asked, then smiled. "We will be alone. Mother does not enjoy the evening meal with us."

"I will be there," I said, forcing a return smile.

I found Robert waiting in the hall and requested that he have Hester bring Kitty to my room. However, it was not Hester but another Negro woman who came with Kitty. Robert introduced her to me as the one who had come from Philadelphia to be Caroline's wet nurse.

I took Kitty and placed her on the bed to better examine her. Uncovered, she pumped her arms and legs joyfully. When she cooed up at me, my heart twisted. Quickly, I bundled her up and gave her back to the nurse. The time had come to make decisions that could not be made with a tender heart.

"Where is Hester?" I asked Robert.

"She left a short while ago with Miss Adelaide. You were with Miss Madden and Miss Meg when Miss Adelaide's relatives came for her. Miss Adelaide did not want to go without seeing you first, and I apologize, sir, but she extracted a promise from me that you would come to see her later in the day. She sat in a chair and refused to leave. I'm afraid there was no way around it." Robert could not keep the annoyance from his voice. I would have smiled under different circumstances.

I turned my attention to Caroline's wet nurse. The young Negro woman appeared downcast and, when questioned, was quick to say that she wanted only to return to her home in Philadelphia. How well I understood. I assured the woman that we would soon see to her return, and she smiled with delight. Taking advantage of her response, I asked if she, in the next few days, was willing and able to provide sustenance for Kitty as well as for Caroline.

"I's doin' so already. This lil one don' need much," she said.

After she left with Kitty, Robert stood back. I sat on the edge of the bed, unsure of how to disclose my decisions to Robert. "Walk with me," I said, and after he fetched my hat, we left for the outdoors. I didn't speak until we had walked out a good distance on the country road.

"I would prefer to be staying at an inn," I said, "but I don't want to be turned away, should rumors already be afloat. We must leave here as soon as possible. By tomorrow, if we are able."

"Yes, sir," was Robert's eager response.

"I do not know where I am bound," I said.

"Yes, sir," he said again.

"You have no obligation to me, Robert." I dreaded what I needed to say, but I forced myself to follow through. "I know that you consider Philadelphia your home; as you know, I can no longer consider it mine. That limitation is from my own doing, but you should not be penalized for my mistakes. I will give you a substantial purse, and I shall be pleased to give you excellent references."

"Mr. Burton! Are you saying that you no longer need my services?" Robert's voice betrayed his shock.

"I will always need a loyal friend," I said, unable to supply another answer.

"And you are dismissing me because I have done something wrong, something inappropriate?"

"Quite the contrary, Robert. You have provided everything and more, but I must release you. I have no idea what I will do or where I am going. I don't know where I belong, Robert. I need to free myself of all encumbrances. I need time to—"

"And what of Miss Caroline? What of Pan? And Kitty? Will you release them as well?"

"Miss Madden has offered to take Miss Caroline on as her own, and you must see the wisdom in that," I said. "As for Kitty, I will pay the nurse a generous stipend to take her back to Philadelphia if she will agree to care for her in her home. Perhaps in time . . ."

"And what of Pan?" Robert's voice rose in anger.

"I will find a school and provide for him in that way. Perhaps Miss Madden has a suggestion. One up north, of course."

I was surprised how easily the plans fell into place, for I had formulated them only in the last few hours.

I walked on, lost in my thoughts, before I realized that Robert was no longer at my side. I turned back and saw him standing in the middle of the road, staring at me in astonishment. I waited for him to walk up to me, but when he remained where he was, I retraced my steps.

"Mr. Burton," he said, his voice quavering, "forgive me for what I am about to say."

"Speak freely, Robert." Determined not be swayed, I looked away as I prepared to allow him his opinion. That much I owed the man.

"Mr. Burton, I will leave if you wish, but my choice would be to stay in your service as long as you will have me. I am willing to make my home wherever you choose to settle. But I would also ask that you reconsider what you have in mind for your three young charges. I ask—no, I plead that you not leave them behind."

"I must, Robert," I said. "I cannot assume all of that responsibility. I will continue to present myself as a white man, for that is the way I view myself. Given the facts, society does not accept me as such, and thus I must keep my past hidden. This lack of truth-telling is a difficult way to live and not one that supports family life. If I were to raise these children and my lies were uncovered, how would they view me then? No! It cannot be. If I provide financially for them and see to their proper placement, surely you agree that I am meeting my obligations."

"No, Mr. Burton, I do not agree! How necessary is it for you to live as a white man? Yes, there will be consequences, but slowly, society is advancing. Miss Caroline has already lost her mother. Would you abandon her as well? And when she is older, won't she have the same issues to face? Who better than you to guide her through? Pan admires you above anyone else, and after the loss of his father, he needs your guidance. As for Kitty, you've provided her freedom, but you would send her off without the benefit of your care?"

Anger overrode my guilt. He, of anyone, should understand my decision. "Robert, please! I've made up my mind. I cannot do it!" I began to walk toward town.

"You would discard all of us so readily?" he called after me, and when his voice broke, I didn't need to see his face to know that he was shedding tears. I increased my pace. I couldn't afford his sentimentality. I had made the best decision for everyone. Robert would see that in time.

As I got closer to town, I thought again of my conversation with Meg and Elly, wherein they had made it clear that though they were ready to take my child, I was not welcome. I had to look no further than Mrs. Madden to understand their position, though I had hoped that in Elly, I might find a sense of family. I had not, and apparently, neither had she.

I reviewed my decision to release Robert and place the children, and I still saw it as the best solution. However, an overwhelming loneliness descended over me as I walked toward the Madden house. I felt as lost and lonely as if I were thirteen again.

On my return, I left for the bank with the express purpose of setting up an account according to the need of each child.

With the bank manager's enthusiastic reception, I wondered if he had not yet heard of my questionable status in Williamsburg society, or if he was willing to overlook it because of the size of my account. He took me back to his office, and as we settled across a desk from each other, he began with superficial conversation. I soon had enough, but when I interrupted him to explain the reason for my visit, he raised his hand to stop me. "Excuse me," he said, "but before we go any further, I should give you this." He unlocked his desk drawer to pull forth a letter.

"I would have brought this to you, had I realized you were in town," he said, handing it over. "This came through a few weeks ago from your lawyer in Philadelphia. I have reason to believe that the contents are sensitive, as his cover letter asked that I present it to you in person. Perhaps you would like to read it before we proceed?"

He busied himself as I broke open the red wax seal of the thick cream-colored envelope.

Dear Mr. Burton,

I write to you with terrible news. Last week my husband, Mr. Cardon, was felled from a weak heart and it has left him quite incapacitated. Since then, he expressed his deep regret at sending Caroline's child from our home. After some consideration I decided to tell him of my part in placing her with you. Mr. Cardon received the news not with anger, as I had expected, but with joy, and now his only wish is to see her again before he departs this world.

I implore you to find it in your heart to bring our grandchild to visit with Mr. Cardon before it is too late. I give you my word that you will be received as a welcome guest in our home. As for your return, your secret was never revealed, and should you again decide to reside in Philadelphia, my complete support would be yours.

Most humbly,
Cristina Cardon

Disbelief coursed through my body. I stared at the letter, my heart thudding as I read it again. It had been dated three weeks previous. What had happened in the interim? Was Mr. Cardon still alive?

A thousand questions bombarded me. Might this be a ruse so they could take Caroline from me? Or could it mean that I might safely return to Philadelphia and once again take up residence? I must tell Robert! At the thought, I leaped to my feet, my mind racing with the options open to me. The startled bank manager stared at me, and I called on all of my reserves to sit back down and see to the business at hand.

In the end, I drew up papers to provide a substantial yearly sum for the support of Miss Meg and Miss Elly's school. With that completed, I discussed the business of transferring my monies to Philadelphia. Then I left in haste to make my way back to the Madden household.

CHAPTER FORTY-EIGHT

1830

James

I FOUND ROBERT IN his room. His eyes were red-rimmed when he opened his door, and though surprised that I wanted to enter, he gave me ready access. I didn't wait for him to speak but instead thrust the letter into his hands.

"Robert, read this," I said. "Tell me what you think!"

He scanned it, then backed up to sit on the edge of the bed while he read it again. I perched on a chair as I watched his face, unable to keep a grin from my own. He looked over at me. "What does this mean?" he asked.

"Assuming the letter is genuine, it means that we can go home!"

"And who might return with you?" he asked with a surprisingly imperious look.

"Why, Robert, you, of course!"

"And Miss Caroline?" he asked.

"Yes! She would come with us," I said.

His gaze was unflinching. "And what about Pan and Kitty? Are they still banned from your care?"

I sighed and looked about the small room that Robert was soon to vacate. It was a quarter the size of mine, yet he had arranged it well to suit his needs. Across from the single bed, a clean shirt and a brushed pair of pants hung neatly from pegs on the wall, while under a small washstand set a shining pair of black shoes next to a shoe-polishing kit. I realized I had never been in a room of his and I resolved that in the future, he would have every comfort he might want.

"Robert," I said, "forgive me. I was wrong. You were right. Whatever comes, we will take the children. All three of them. They are my responsibility. But I will need your help. Can I count on you for that?"

He stood. "Mr. Burton, I did not give you my resignation. I am still at your service as long as you require my help."

Though it clearly made him uncomfortable, I grasped his hand in both of mine. "Thank you, Robert! For . . . for everything you have done for me," I said, and this time it was my voice that quavered.

MY DECISION TO leave as quickly as possible was motivated not only by my need to escape Mrs. Madden's company but also my desire to return home. I had Robert locate and hire two drivers for our carriage that same day. When I went for supper with the women, Robert made the necessary preparations for our small party to leave in the morning.

As we enjoyed our evening meal, I told the two women of my donation to the school and of how they could count on my continued support. Naturally, they expressed deep gratitude, but then I took a deep breath. "I will not go into unnecessary detail, but I am pleased to say that there has been a change in circumstance and I am now free to return to my home in Philadelphia."

Miss Elly gasped aloud when I announced my decision to take my daughter with me. Unable to contain her tears, she left the room at a run.

"She will see the wisdom in time. After all, you are Caroline's father," Miss Meg said. Though her eyes had filled, too, she retained her composure.

"I am so grateful for everything you have done," I said, "but might I ask one more favor of you?"

"Certainly," she said.

"I have a package that I need delivered to Belle, and I do not trust it to the post," I said. "When you travel down for the wedding, would you give it to her?"

She graciously agreed, and I went quickly to my room and returned with the parcel.

"This has great monetary as well as sentimental value," I said.

"Then it will not leave my side until it is in Belle's hands," she promised. I didn't explain that the package contained a boy's jacket with jewelry sewn into the seams. Neither did I tell Miss Meg that the contents included a letter I had written that afternoon.

Dear Belle,

I have only recently discovered the circumstances of my conception. To know that you cared for me in spite of the cruelty you suffered argues that the goodness in humanity can survive through the most difficult challenges.

Only recently have I come to acknowledge that I have been living a life of fear. I was driven by hatred for those of the colored race, instilled in me from a grandmother I loved and a society that supports her beliefs.

I once considered the Negro unfeeling and mindless, closer to an animal than a human being. I have since come to know the true Negro; I have seen the bravery and superior intelligence that it takes for one of color to survive under the cruelest of conditions. Though I still puzzle at my place in all of this, I hope that I have inherited the kindness and strength of your good spirit.

I do not know for certain what my future holds, but I believe that I will continue to live as a white man. Certainly it is the easiest path, though I now have two Negro children in my charge. I plan to raise and care for them as I would my own. How that will play out remains to be seen.

There is a third child, my biological daughter and your granddaughter. She is blond and blue-eyed, and though she has been known as Caroline, from today forward, she will be called Belle.

We both know why I will not travel to see you, but if you would consider a visit, or if you wish to come for a permanent stay, you have but to tell me and I will arrange the accommodations.

Lastly, I am enclosing the jacket with the jewels that you gave me on my departure. Two of the items are missing, but the use of each was invaluable to me. Thank you for this generous gift. Be assured that I no longer have need of it.

I do not look at the jacket without remembering the moment you handed it to me. You stood back and waited for some expression of my caring. I apologize for my inability to thank you as you should have been thanked. You gave me life, Mother, and there is no greater gift. I thank you now.

> *Your son,*
> *James*

I AWOKE JUST as the sun was rising and went to the window to look out on what promised to be a clear day. Below my window, a young boy was seated on the front mounting stone; from his jutting ears, I recognized Pan. Beside him was a small brown bundle that must have included his few possessions, and next to him was a birdcage that was almost the size of the boy. With a jolt of joy, I realized that Robert had somehow kept Malcolm with us.

Because we had an early-morning meal, I was able to escape another encounter with Mrs. Madden, although both Miss Meg and Miss Elly were present. I tried to ease Caroline's departure by telling them that I would expect, at a minimum, a yearly visit from them.

When we waved goodbye, our vehicle was again filled to capacity, and the din inside was deafening, with both babies crying and Malcolm screeching his discontent. Pan raised his hands to his ears. I had him cover Malcolm's cage, and thankfully, the upset bird, after some final squawks, was silenced. I lifted Kitty from the basket and asked that she be fed; the nurse, holding Caroline, said she must be attended to first. I immediately decided that as soon we reached Philadelphia, Kitty would have her own wet nurse.

We traveled on, and after Caroline was fed, I reached for her. Again she took one look at me and began to howl.

"Here, sir, give her to me," Robert said, holding his arms out. "Now, now, sweet child, your Robert is here," he soothed. On recognizing his adoring face, she settled and soon smiled, as did I to see Robert so smitten.

WE HAD BEEN traveling under an hour and but for the creaking of the wagon, all was finally quiet. On leaving Williamsburg, we had passed a surprising amount of incoming traffic, yet now we were quite alone. I was not surprised that Pan was dozing after I learned he had been seated at the curbside since daybreak.

I watched him sleep, his head resting against Malcolm's covered cage. What might have happened to him had Sukey not intervened? I thought again of how she had saved my life, then remembered those in the swamp who had saved us. I was thinking again of Peg and how she had sacrificed her goat, when our horses began to slow and one of the drivers shouted down, "Somethin' fast comin' up from behind!"

Robert and I exchanged a look of concern. "Pick up the pace!" I called to the driver, and we surged ahead.

I had seen to it that both drivers were armed, so we weren't as vulnerable as we had been a few days previous, but we were still in a slave state. Was it possible that I was yet being pursued?

We were traveling so quickly that when our large carriage hit a pothole, it tilted and swayed dangerously. Intending to instruct the driver to slow down, I removed my hat and stretched my head out the window. Before I called up to the driver, I glanced back to see what I could. Through the thick dust stirred up from our wheels, I saw a small open gig gaining on us. But it was the driver's black hair fanning out and the purple and green bonnet she waved that gave me recognition.

"Stop the carriage!" I called, then turned to Robert while laughing aloud in disbelief. "It's Adelaide Spencer!"

Robert's scowl did not hide his feelings.

We were rolling to a stop when I hopped out to greet Adelaide as she reined in her lathered horse. "Mr. Burton! How could you have forgotten about me?" she cried. "You didn't even come to say goodbye!"

She winced when I lifted her down from atop her gig, even as I saw another rider approaching in the distance.

"Did I hurt you?" I asked. Concerned, I lightly touched her injured arm.

"It is healed," she said, jerking back.

"Forgive me, Miss Adelaide," I said. "I meant to come see you before I left, but unexpected circumstances called me away. I was going to write you a letter."

She tilted her head away, insulted. "A letter!" she exclaimed in disgust.

More drastic measures were called for. I took her hand and spoke earnestly. "Forgive me, Miss Spencer. You must know that I am forever in your debt."

She raised her eyebrows. "Indeed?"

"Most certainly!"

"Surely, then, a final visit was in order."

I glanced off to see the other rider fast approaching.

She noted it as well and sighed. "It is my uncle. It's a wonder he didn't kill himself on that horse. And his death would have been on you, Mr. Burton, for having forgotten me!"

"Miss Adelaide, I assure you that I did not forget you. Unfortunately, an emergency has presented itself and I am rushing back to Philadelphia. My child's grandfather is quite ill."

"He is dying?" she asked.

"I'm afraid that might be the case."

"But you were going to write a letter?" she asked.

"A very long one."

"And you still intend to do so?" she asked.

"Adelaide Spencer!" the rider called out on his approach. "Your father will hear about this!"

Adelaide pushed back her tangled hair and tied on her hat as the obese man tried to gain control of his frothing horse. I went to him and held the reins so he might dismount.

Panting heavily, he slid from his horse. Adelaide ran a few steps toward him to scoop his hand up in hers. "Uncle, dear, I am so sorry! I didn't mean for you to follow. Yet how fortunate! You now have the opportunity to meet the famous artist Mr. James Burton."

"Young lady!" he began.

"Don't be angry," she stated. She touched her pink cheek to his gloved hand. "I had some final words for Mr. Burton, and you know what I am like. When my mind is made up, there is no turning back. It can't be helped, Uncle! Surely you understand? I am so like you. It is our nature."

As was wont to happen in Adelaide's presence, the man was left speechless, and she turned back to me. "We will meet again, Mr. Burton? Promise me!"

I gave her a quick bow and smiled. "We will meet again, Miss Spencer. I am sure of it."

Cries were beginning to seep from the carriage, and with that as my excuse, I said my goodbyes before I vaulted back into the fray.

Our ride lurched forward, and as I settled back and studied our small group, I realized that I was surrounded by those who most mattered to me. Was caring for them, then, to be my purpose?

With Robert and the nurse each tending a baby, I looked to Pan staring quietly out the window. He was far removed from the effervescent boy I once knew and his silence troubled me. "Pan?" I said. "Aren't you happy to be returning home?"

Tears filled his eyes before he turned and leaned his forehead against Malcolm's cage.

"What is it?" I asked as I touched the boy's thin shoulder.

"I keep thinking about my daddy," he cried.

"Of course you do," I said, patting his shoulder. He straightened up to dry his face with his jacket sleeve, then sniffed so thoroughly that Robert handed him a handkerchief. Pan blew noisily, then passed the cloth back to Robert.

"You may keep that one," Robert said, not unkindly. "Tuck it in your pants, and when we get home, we will get you set up with some of your own." Pan did as he was told before he rested his head back against the seat. Still he looked pensive.

"Is something else troubling you?" I asked.

His large dark eyes met mine, but they were afraid. His chin wobbled as he held back tears. "What if they come looking for me? What if they take me again?" he whispered, as though afraid the words might give substance to his fear.

I was jolted by his words. Over the years he had won me over with his open and loving nature, but until this moment I had felt our lives had little in common. Now I recognized his terror and thought of how mine had wrongly affected so many of my choices. I would not let that happen to Pan. He would know security and love, regardless of the opinions of society.

I took some time to think it through before I spoke. "Pan," I said, "I have a question for you."

He took a deep quivering breath before he looked at me. "What, Mr. Burton?"

"I know that your father was unable to give you a last name because he did not have one of his own," I said.

"That's 'cause he was a slave," he said defensively.

"I know, Pan. But I was wondering, if I were to adopt you, would you consider taking mine?"

"What do you mean?" he asked.

"When you were stolen, I had no legal rights to you, but if I adopt you, no one can ever take you again. Your name would be Pan Burton."

Pan was silent for a long while before he responded. "You mean you would take me for your own boy?"

"Yes, that is what I mean."

"But I have a daddy."

"And Henry will always be your father. He was a brave and good man, and my hope would be that one day you will be just like him."

"But you are living white. How can you have a black chil'?"

I looked over to Robert for help. "I don't know yet, but we'll manage," I said.

"How you gonna do that?" Pan asked.

"By overcoming one obstacle at a time," Robert offered.

"What is a obstacle?" Pan asked.

"A difficulty—like a rock on a path that one must step around or over," Robert interpreted.

"How about lifting it out of the way?" Pan asked.

Robert smiled when he nodded in agreement. "That, too, Pan. That, too."

Pan glanced at Kitty resting peacefully in the arms of the nurse. "What about Kitty? Can she have your name, too, so they can never take her away?"

"What do you think, Robert?" I asked. "Can we do it? It will be quite a task to manage a household with three children."

"It will be a happy home," Robert said.

That thought silenced us, and we all sat back in quiet contemplation, each no doubt mulling over his own concerns, until Pan spoke again. "Mr. Burton?"

"Yes, Pan?"

"I can't stop thinking about what's gonna happen to any others who get took, like Randall and me. What about the runners who come through and got to get away? If Sukey isn't there, who's going to help them get out?"

This time I had no answer. Until now, consumed by my own troubles, I had given little thought but to my own circumstances. As I considered Pan's words, I thought again of what might have happened to the two of us if so many others had not risked their own lives. I remembered everyone: Sukey and her man at Southwood, then the Spencers and the Quaker family, and finally, Willie and Peg and all those who helped us through the canal. Surely, given my release and fortunate circumstances, I might take some responsibility.

"Pan," I said. "Do you know who can help?"

He shook his head.

"I will," I said.

"What can you do?" he asked.

"I don't know yet. This is new to me. But to begin with, as soon as we get home, I will write to Mr. Spencer to ask how I might be of assistance."

"You're not just sayin' that?"

"No, Pan. You have my word." When I met his eyes, I saw what appeared to be a glimmer of his former self.

"Can I help, too?"

"First, Pan, you must get an education. And Robert and I will need your help in raising the girls. But when you are grown, if you still choose, we might work on this together." He studied me with such fervor that I laughed. "Come here," I said to him, and dismissing all my usual inhibitions, I pulled him under my arm. How good it felt to embrace this brave boy.

"Mr. Burton," came Pan's muffled voice.

"Yes, Pan?"

"I'm glad we're going home."

I held him closer still. "So am I, Pan," I said. "So am I!"

AUTHOR'S NOTE

THOUGH THIS is a work of fiction, for readers familiar with the history of Philadelphia, I am aware that over this time period the Peale Museum made a transition to Baltimore. However, in the interest of this story, I kept it in Philadelphia.

ACKNOWLEDGMENTS

Rebecca Gradinger—I cannot express how grateful I am for all of your tireless efforts. Your belief in my work inspired me to my best self.

My gratitude extends as well to everyone at Fletcher and Company, in particular to Melissa Chinchillo, Grainne Fox, and Rachel Crawford for their many successful efforts on my behalf.

Trish Todd, your insight is, as it was before, a benediction. Beth Thomas, how fortunate I am to have you with me a second time.

I thank my faithful first readers who didn't stop at the first go-round: Charles Grissom, Eleanor Dolan, Diane Eckert, Carlene Baime, Bob Baime, Judy Chisholm, Ann Kwan, Leah Weiss, Teresa Morrow, and Reginald Brown. Your careful consideration and suggestions were exactly what I needed.

While I was researching the Great Dismal Swamp, two wonderful people came forward to help. Penny Leary, retired director of the Dismal Swamp Welcome Center, and George Ramsey, Southeast Representative for the Virginia Canals and Navigation Society, both provided, again and again, the detailed information that I sought. As well, they arranged a boat tour with Robert Peek, lock keeper and bridge tender, and the day we spent exploring the mysteries and waterways of the forbidding but fiercely spectacular Great Dismal Swamp is one I shall not forget. For those interested, Robert Peek offers boat tours to the public; you will find him at www.greatdismaladventures.com.

Pin-feather painting might be a lost art, but for Colin Woolf. To learn more about his amazing work, go to www.wildart.co.uk.

My research took me from libraries in Philadelphia to historical sites in Louisiana, and though they are too numerous to list here, I am indebted to all.

There were times when, in the writing of this story, I questioned my ability, but the doubt did not live long, for I was graced with the support of my lifelong friend Carlene and my dear daughter, Erin. Though they both know what they are to me, I thank them again.

Finally, I remember Lisbeth Walker, a dear friend who recently went before me. Her final message was one of gratitude, and it is in her memory that I list these many blessings.

ABOUT THE AUTHOR

Kathleen is happily rooted in Southside, Virginia, where she continues to write.

Glory over Everything

FOR DISCUSSION

1. "I had met Henry twenty years earlier, when, at the age of thirteen, I arrived in Philadelphia, ill and terrified and fleeing for my life." How does James's flight from Tall Oaks mark his life going forward? Why does Henry come to James's aid, and what does he represent to James? What details from their early interactions complicate their relationship as adults?

2. "I had never and would never consider myself a Negro. In fact, the idea disgusted me." How does James reconcile his biracial identity with his own racist attitudes? To what extent does his denial of his ethnicity serve as a means of self-preservation in the racist society he inhabits?

3. Why does Pan's unexplained disappearance distress James? Compare and contrast the dangers from slave catchers that Pan and James face. Why do you think Kathleen Grissom chose to alternate these characters' narratives at key points in the novel?

4. Why does James conceal his biracial status from Caroline Preston, the married daughter of socially prominent Philadelphia aristocrats? How does her pregnancy threaten James's entire existence? How might Caroline's discovery of his biracial status have altered the trajectory of the novel? Why do you think Kathleen Grissom chose not to pursue that story line?

5. "'I can provide [room and board] for you in my home, where you will be downstairs with our household help.'" As a newly minted apprentice at Burton's Silversmith, why does James feel insulted to live belowstairs with the black servants? How do Delia, Ed, and Robert react to having a white person living with them?

6. Describe James's relationship with Mrs. Burton. What role does the bird Malcolm play in their bond? How is their connection strengthened by the tragedies they have experienced? How does James's discovery of the Burtons' views on slavery affect him?

7. From the reactions of his white and black acquaintances, how convincing are James's efforts to pass as a white silversmith in Philadelphia? What does Delia's theft of James's letter in the aftermath of his adoption by the Burtons suggest about her intentions? What reasons might Delia have for outing James?

8. "I had loved [Mrs. Burton] as a mother . . . a difference existed after she learned the truth from Delia. Yet I did not hold her responsible; how could I blame her for an inability to love the part of me that I, too, loathed." How does Delia's revelation of James's race affect his relationship with Mrs. Burton? What does her dismissal of Delia imply about her acceptance of James?

9. James refers to his attraction to Caroline Preston as an "uncomfortable fascination." How does Caroline characterize her feelings for James? Given their differences in age and social class, what explains their connection? To what extent is Caroline's mother, Cristina Cardon, an enabler of their illicit affair?

10. Discuss the remarkable events that converge to liberate Pan from the Southwood plantation. What does the collaboration of Sukey and the Spencer family in the daring rescue suggest about the racially progressive views of many white Americans during this era? Given the unique dangers James faces in his efforts to re-

trieve Pan from the plantation's overseer, Bill Thomas, why does he persist?

11. "From above, thick, corded vines, netted with Spanish moss, draped down to ensnare us. With each vine I pushed away, I thought of the cottonmouth moccasins, the copperheads, and the rattlesnakes known to inhabit the place." What does the Great Dismal Swamp represent to runaway slaves and their pursuers? Why do the runaways seek refuge there, despite the many dangers? Why does the Spencer family, along with many others, fear it?

12. Why does Sukey's delivery of her baby in a cave in the Great Dismal Swamp cause James to panic and flee? How does Pan respond to James's act of cowardice? To what extent does James redeem himself in Pan's eyes through his treatment of Sukey's infant daughter, Kitty?

13. "Where, then, did I belong? Was my birth an accident of fate, or was my life intended to have some purpose?" How do the circumstances of James's birth and upbringing shape his sense of self at the beginning of the novel? By the end, what events have enabled his new understanding and acceptance of himself?

14. How does Kathleen Grissom's use of multiple narrators deepen your appreciation of the work? If the author had chosen to include other characters' perspectives, whose would you have been especially interested to read, and why?

15. In James's last letter to his mother, Belle, he reveals his decision to change his daughter's name from Caroline to Belle. What role does his servant Robert play in the radical transformation of James's feelings for his mother? Discuss how the conclusion of the novel brings the arc of James's character full circle.

A CONVERSATION WITH KATHLEEN GRISSOM

Can you reflect on how your phenomenal success as a first-time novelist has affected your life?

Over these past few years, what to me has the most meaning are the exchanges that I have had with so many wonderful book clubs. That the readers connected so deeply to the characters in *The Kitchen House* gave me a sense that I had done my job. From the beginning, I wanted others to experience the story as vividly as I had.

You have related the unusual origins of *The Kitchen House*: how a historic map of a house you were renovating in Virginia included a detail about slaves that began to obsess you and kindle your creativity. How would you compare that experience to the series of events that led to your writing *Glory over Everything*?

In many ways the experience was very similar. Once again, in *Glory over Everything*, the characters appeared spontaneously and insisted that I write their story. After finishing *The Kitchen House*, I had every intention of writing about Crow Mary, a Native American woman who led a fascinating life. I went out to the Crow reservation in Montana to study her culture and to search out more documentation. Yet, while researching Crow Mary, though I felt her spirit, something was stopping me from absorbing her culture in the way I knew I must. In fact, it began to feel as though a veil had come down and Jamie, Belle's son from *The Kitchen House*, was standing in front of Crow Mary to let me know that I was to tell his story first. So, with some initial reluctance, that is what I did.

The success of *The Kitchen House* was due in part to its adoption by book clubs around the country. Why do you think *The Kitchen House* lends itself so well to group discussion and interpretation?

Though some might expect *The Kitchen House* to be a story of race, most come to see it as a story of humans, all caught in the trap of slavery. *The Kitchen House* is a story of complicated characters and nontraditional relationships. Through discussion, these are looked at closely and, as is often the case, new insight brings clarity and even compassion.

In *Glory over Everything*, you revisit many members of the Pyke family that you portrayed in *The Kitchen House*, but you shift the focus of your narrative to Belle's son James. Can you compare your experiences in narrating books from both a woman's and a man's perspective?

The gender actually made little difference. In *Glory over Everything*, I heard Jamie's voice as clearly as I'd heard Lavinia's and Belle's from *The Kitchen House*. The difference was that both Lavinia and Belle were open to me and very forthcoming; whereas Jamie, a man with a secret, was guarded and kept me at a distance when I first met him. For that reason, I found Jamie both frustrating and intriguing. Fortunately, other characters, such as Pan, were quite verbal and gave me deeper insight into Jamie, until gradually he became less cautious and was ready to reveal himself.

The Kitchen House* relates the intimate details of the lives of the slaves of Tall Oaks, as told from the perspective of a young white girl. *Glory over Everything* examines the lives of black and white characters mainly from the perspective of a biracial male narrator who is passing as white. How challenging is it for you to get yourself inside the heads of the fictional characters you create? Please describe the kinds of research you do before you begin writing.

The best way for me to describe the way this process works is to say that I don't get into their heads, but they get into mine. They come fully formed and are complete characters. I don't always see them, but I feel who they are in the deepest sense. Jamie was not particularly likable when I first met him. Eventually I came to understand his deep fear, and as my compassion and understanding for him grew, he opened up to me.

For my research I visit the places I feel my characters inhabited. There I walk and absorb whatever comes to me. There are times when I come upon something, such as a torture device, that I feel such pain and despair that I want to fall to my knees. Often I cry over it after I uncover the details of how it might have been used. When I see something that gets me happily excited—perhaps an artifact at a historical site—I research it with joy. I've learned that when I have this type of strong reaction, one of my characters wants me to have the information so they can use it to better tell their story.

How did you decide to set *Glory over Everything* in Philadelphia? What plot opportunities does an urban setting provide that a more confined or rural setting, such as a plantation, does not?

I don't decide on the setting. My characters do.

I always saw Jamie in Philadelphia. I've been there a number of times and happen to love the city, but curiously, when I began my research, I found the city to be overwhelming, just as it initially was for Jamie. It wasn't until Jamie left for the rural South that both he and I felt less constraint.

Glory over Everything **is narrated by James Pyke, Pan, and Caroline Preston. How did you decide to tell the novel from these three characters' perspectives?**

Actually there is a fourth voice—that of Sukey. In fact, hers, I believe, is the soul of the story.

Interestingly, I don't choose who will be the characters to speak. They present themselves to me as though in a movie. They arrive fully formed and each speaks in his or her own distinctive voice. I can't say that I decide on who will speak—instead, as the characters appear, I go with the ones who take center stage.

You have mentioned that the troubling aspects of slavery were extremely challenging for you to write about in *The Kitchen House*. To what extent was that the case in *Glory over Everything*?

Writing about slavery, I'm sure, would be challenging for anyone. However, Sukey's narrative was so painful that I cried my way through her story. Each time she spoke, I dreaded what was to come. Yet I loved her so that I couldn't wait to hear what she had to say.

As well, I loved young Pan, and to see his innocence taken away was heartbreaking.

In writing *The Kitchen House*, many times I considered stopping because of the violence. This time I better understood the process, and realized that, though there were times I was in tears, I needed to write what I saw. I feel that my job is to tell the story so the reader can see and feel what I see and feel.

In many respects, the Great Dismal Swamp seems almost like a character in *Glory over Everything*. Can you describe your acquaintance with it, and how it became such an essential part of the novel?

Once I knew that some of my characters were headed in the direction of the Great Dismal Swamp, I began to visit and research the area. In time I learned about the Maroon societies that had once lived there. These communities were formed by escaped slaves who not only found refuge in this swamp but made a home for themselves in what many consider a hostile land.

As the name suggests, the Great Dismal Swamp can appear forbidding, but after visiting it a number of times I found incredible beauty there as well. For those interested in learning more about the Maroon communities, Daniel Sayers, an anthropologist who studied the Great Dismal Swamp, wrote a book titled *A Desolate Place for a Defiant Peo-*

ple. As well, some of the artifacts that he uncovered are displayed at the Smithsonian National Museum of African American History and Culture.

You have said that "DNA isn't what family is about. . . . I believe family is about love, and love is color-blind." To what extent does the denouement of *Glory over Everything* bear out that conviction?

Once again, in *Glory over Everything*, need and love create a family unrelated by DNA. I might add, with this mention of DNA, that I always found it unusual that family is most often defined as those who share the same blood. Doesn't every family begin with partners who don't share the same DNA?

Do you know if you will return to these characters in a future novel? What kinds of considerations factor into your decision making about your future writing projects?

As soon as *Glory over Everything* is published, I am heading out to Montana to once again begin my research on Crow Mary. Her call to me becomes stronger every day.

I do have a niggling feeling that others from *Glory over Everything* might want their stories told, but this time I have already done some bargaining. First Crow Mary, and then . . . we shall see.

ENHANCE YOUR BOOK CLUB

1. Ask members of your club to consider the social and political causes that are most important to them. How willing would they be to risk their lives to improve the lives of total strangers? Consider what leading a double life as a secret member of the Underground Railroad would have been like in nineteenth-century America.

2. *Glory over Everything* confronts many serious questions of race and prejudice. Compare the state of race relations in the nineteenth century with those of the present day. To what extent does racial prejudice persist in our country? How does James's anxiety as a biracial person passing as white compare to the concerns of a person of mixed race in America today? Consider the case of Rachel Dolezal, a white woman who claimed to be and passed as African-American.

3. Toward the end of *Glory over Everything,* James undergoes an epiphany in his thoughts about race, himself, and his role in the world. Ask members of your group whether they have ever experienced epiphanies relating to their personal identities, faith, careers, or relationships. If they have, discuss what spurred these realizations. How did these epiphanies enable them to change or refocus their lives?

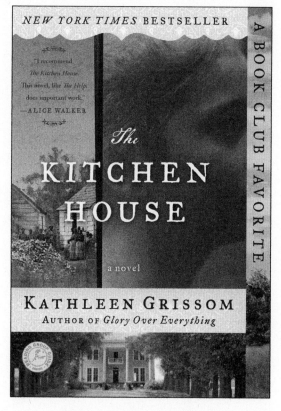